A *GLOBE AND MAIL*
"BEST READS OF THE SUMMER" PICK

ONE OF THE *JEWISH NEWS* "BOOKS THAT ARE A
MUST-READ THIS SUMMER"

A *FORBES* "BEST HISTORICAL NOVELS
FOR SUMMER 2019"

"Epic...Barenbaum carves a fresh story from some of the period's
most evocative and disturbing details."
—*New York Times*

"A thrilling adventure."
—NPR

"A rousing debut...Fans of Kristin Hannah will enjoy Barenbaum's
exhilarating tale."
—*Publishers Weekly*

"Heart-pounding historical drama."
—B&N Reads, Best Books of 2019 So Far

"*A Bend in the Stars* is a vivid and wrenching debut, full not only
with the darkness of history but also with hope—a literary saga
for fans of *The Invisible Bridge* and *All The Light We Cannot See*.
Love and war and relativity weave together seamlessly, and we're
left understanding that there's more than one way for the
universe to bend."
—Rebecca Makkai, author of the National Book Award Finalist
The Great Believers

A BEND
IN THE STARS

Rachel Barenbaum

GRAND CENTRAL
PUBLISHING

NEW YORK   BOSTON

Grand Central Publishing
Hachette Book Group
1290 Avenue of the Americas, New York, NY 10104
grandcentralpublishing.com
twitter.com/grandcentralpub

Originally published in hardcover and ebook in May 2019
First trade paperback edition: May 2020

Grand Central Publishing is a division of Hachette Book Group, Inc. The Grand Central Publishing name and logo is a trademark of Hachette Book Group, Inc.

The publisher is not responsible for websites (or their content) that are not owned by the publisher.

The Hachette Speakers Bureau provides a wide range of authors for speaking events. To find out more, go to www.hachettespeakersbureau.com or call (866) 376-6591.

Library of Congress Cataloging-in-Publication Data

Names: Barenbaum, Rachel, author.
Title: A bend in the stars : a novel / Rachel Barenbaum.
Description: New York : Grand Central Publishing, [2019]
Identifiers: LCCN 2018046461 | ISBN 9781538746264 (hardcover) | ISBN
9781549175718 (audio download) | ISBN 9781538746271 (ebook)
Subjects: | GSAFD: Love stories.
Classification: LCC PS3602.A775343 B46 2019 | DDC 813/.6--dc23
LC record available at https://lccn.loc.gov/2018046461

ISBNs: 978-1-5387-4628-8 (trade paperback), 978-1-5387-4627-1 (ebook)

Printed in the United States of America

LSC-C

10 9 8 7 6 5 4 3 2 1

For Adam
And for Ezra, Lily, and Jonah

In physical reality one cause does not produce a given effect, but a multitude of distinct causes contribute to produce it, without our having any means of discriminating the part of each of them.

—Henri Poincaré,
"The Measure of Time," 1898

2000: Philadelphia, United States

Ethel Zane stood next to her granddaughter, Lena, in the museum's rotunda and tried to catch her breath by pretending to examine the painting in front of them. The oversize canvas once served as the backdrop for a ballet, a Russian *Romeo and Juliet*, and Ethel had studied it so many times she didn't need to look to see its brilliance. A sun and a moon hung together in a sky ignited by shades of orange.

"Are you ready, Bubbie?" Lena asked. Her curls were dripping, and the dress she'd spent so much time choosing was splotched with rain. "They're waiting for us."

"After all this time, another minute won't hurt." If only she could smoke inside.

Lena threaded her fingers through Ethel's. "I've always loved the romance in this."

"It's not romance. This painting is about an eclipse." Ethel pulled her granddaughter close. "See, the sun and the moon are converging. There's the eclipse. And from that you're sensing passion. You have it, Lenaleh. Passion like that eclipse, like the painting, the kind that makes a woman want to jump into the bath with a man after a sweaty day."

Her granddaughter threw her head back and laughed. Another woman might have been embarrassed, but not her Lena. Ethel was proud of that. "I suppose with the right man, anyone would like that bath," Lena said.

They took the stairs, slowly. At the top, a bar glittered with champagne. A florist leaned over a vase heavy with the lilacs Ethel could smell from across the room. On the landing stood the great-grandson of Uncle Vanya's old friend, Dima. The young man was tall, taller even than Lena. He had deep-set eyes and a thick frame as if there was a sailor's bearing in his bones, like his great-grandfather. He took Ethel's other hand. "Thank you for coming to celebrate my uncle Vanya," she said. "None of this would have been possible without Dima. He was a great man. I just wish I'd had a chance to meet him myself."

"If only he'd told me more about what happened in Russia before he died, about their adventures during the war and the competition with Einstein."

Ethel frowned. "That's the problem. Life doesn't travel in a straight line. Knowing the end doesn't mean you can follow it back to the beginning." She paused. "And I'm not sure they would have called their time together adventures. There was the need to survive, no?"

They turned the corner and Ethel saw the exhibit's title: *The Race to Prove Relativity*. Then came the shock: a photograph of her mother, Miriam Abramov, hung on the wall. It was one Ethel hadn't seen before, one the curator must have found at the last minute. The image was part of a constellation of other new prints, each in their own frame, capturing pieces of life in 1914: the Bern clock tower, a Russian port, the czar's troops boarding a train, but none of them were important. For Ethel, her mother was all that mattered, and she hurried closer to get a better look. The picture had been taken before Ethel was born, back in Russia. Her mother looked so young as she stood in front of a slice of a shtetl and stared down the camera. Her doctor's coat was smeared dark, and her face was lined with dirt. She must have been working herself to the bone, but still there was an energy to her. It was conviction. Ethel knew it as a quality she saw in herself and in her granddaughter, a quality passed through the blood. How did Mama stand so tall while the world around her was shattering into war? And who was the man next to her? He wore a military greatcoat and a cap with the visor pulled down so low Ethel couldn't see his face. Instead of looking into the camera, the soldier looked at her mother. He was inclined toward her, drawn by gravity.

Lena squeezed Ethel's hand and pointed to the opposite wall. Across from the image of Miriam hung a collection of more photographs, academics posed in front of telescopes. One had a scale model of the solar system suspended behind him. These were all physicists arrayed in orbit around Albert Einstein.

"Where's my uncle Vanya's photograph?" Ethel asked. He should have had pride of place above Einstein—Vanya was the whole reason they were there.

"I thought they'd found the journals, that this was about Uncle Vanya's work. Don't they know what he did?" Lena asked.

"They do now." Ethel reached for Einstein's photograph and plucked it off the wall. It was easier to do than she'd imagined. An alarm blared. The curator and his assistants came running. "History needs a narrator," Ethel said. "Perhaps this museum chose the wrong one."

Tammuz

The Hebrew calendar is based on three astronomical phenomena: the rotation of the earth on its axis, the revolution of the moon around the earth, and the movement of the earth around the sun.

The fourth month in the Jewish calendar is Tammuz, from the Aramaic, meaning *heat, fire*, or *sun*. It is said that during Tammuz, in the midst of battle, Joshua ordered the sun to stand still. God heard his pleas and the day stopped. Only the moon continued, sliding in front of the sun.

I

1914: Kovno, Russia

On the eighteenth of Tammuz, Miri Abramov sat at the window in her room watching the slip of a moon emerge behind the mottled rooftops of Kovno. Her shoulders were slumped forward, and curls escaped from the braid running down her back. She was exhausted from tending to dozens of patients and couldn't stop thinking about one in particular—the fishmonger. She lit a cigarette, watched smoke finger the polished glass in front of her. He had been beaten so severely Miri didn't recognize him, and his was a face she knew. He brought her family his catch every Monday. The word *Jew* had been scrawled on his chest with so much hate that the charcoal used to write it cut his skin. The letters oozed red. His ribs were cracked and Miri was sure his spleen was pierced. She needed to operate to save his life, but she wasn't a surgeon. She was still training, couldn't do anything without permission, and all the surgeons above her—men—disagreed with her diagnosis. They said he was only bruised. But she'd watched his condition deteriorate. She'd recorded his pulse rising, his blood pressure dropping, along with his increasing confusion—all signs he was bleeding internally. Would he make it through the night?

The grandfather clock downstairs struck the hour. It was time for supper. Miri stubbed her cigarette in a pile of ash on a cold saucer and made her way into the hall. Standing on thick, woven carpet, Miri took a deep breath and arranged her face. Making an appearance downstairs in the crowded sitting room where she'd find her grandmother always made Miri feel as if she were onstage. The house, the paintings, the silks and velvets were props in Babushka's exquisite theater. Her grandmother was Kovno's most illustrious matchmaker, and she was paid in gifts. Everything her family had was chosen for them. The house was given by the owner of the brick factory on the night of his wedding. Beds were delivered by a carpenter once he held his first child. Baba's clients furnished one room and then another. All of her needs were provided for in this way. Babushka found wives for tailors who sent clothing, and fishmongers, like Miri's patient, who delivered food. The only thing Baba refused was help. She didn't want a cook or a maid. She was the keeper of secrets, she explained with a wink—one clients never questioned. And Miri knew they were lucky to live so well, especially when so many Jews scavenged for food and heat. She was grateful for it, but none of it felt like a home.

Baba was her home and had been since her parents left for America fifteen years earlier when Miri was six and her brother, Vanya, was twelve. The plan had been for the three of them to join Mama and Papa after they were settled, but their parents' boat sank during a storm. The loss spun Miri into a darkness that left her limp. Every night after Babushka kissed them and thought they were in bed, Vanya rocked Miri until her silent tears stopped, and whispered stories their mother used to tell. Stories about brave girls and boys who fought Baba Yaga. Stories about fearless children who dared travel across Russia in search of treasure. Miri's favorite was "Levi's Monster." Levi refused to follow the rabbis and throw his sins into the river every year at Rosh Hashanah. Instead he let them pile up until they grew into a powerful ogre that Levi had to defeat to save his wife and children. Like Levi, Vanya pushed Miri to fight, and she did. She learned to tuck the darkness away. Sometimes, though, it iced its way back, and she felt it then as she stood outside her room worrying about the fishmonger. But she had to go on, Vanya would say. And she knew he was right. She straightened her back and started down the stairs.

In the front hall, Miri found the usual line of mothers and grand-mothers spilling out from the sitting room. The few that spotted her nodded a greeting, but she knew they didn't dare stand or move to kiss her for fear they might lose their place. All were waiting their turn for an audience with Babushka, for a chance to plead for help in matching their children. Miri leaned against the polished wooden doorframe. It wouldn't be long before Baba spotted her and realized how late it was. Then she'd finish for the night and Miri would help her usher the women out so they could sit down to eat together.

Baba sat on her perch, dressed in aquamarine with her thick silver braid resting over her shoulder. She was as wide as she was tall, and she had a chair on stilts, with a footrest to match, so she could sit at eye level with her visitors. She held the hands of the seam-stress, Katinka, who was afflicted with a curved spine that kept her half-bent. She was there for her son who had a business delivering vegetables. "He's a good boy," Katinka said. Miri knew that since Baba held Katinka's hands, they were just beginning and the seam-stress would be cut short.

"Does he drink too much?" Baba asked.

"Sometimes." Every woman knew to be honest.

"Does he fight? Use his fists?"

"Never."

"Good," Baba said. "What else?"

"He tells me stories about love, about the future."

"He understands better days will come. Perhaps not this year but they will come." Baba paused and looked up, sensing Miri's arrival. She nodded at her granddaughter, then leaned toward Katinka. "You'll unwrap his story for me in the morning." Katinka exhaled, showing she understood this meant Babushka would consider his case, and her chest crumpled as if she'd been holding her breath.

"Thank you. Thank you," the seamstress said.

Babushka squeezed Katinka's hands. "More tomorrow. All of you, more tomorrow," she said as she turned to face the rest of the room. The women grumbled. Some must have waited for hours and still hadn't been heard. And while the rabbi stayed as late as he was needed, Babushka did not. Her clients knew she required sleep to clear her head, to make better matches, and so no one argued. They all wanted to remain on Babushka's better side.

Just before Miri stepped into the room to help urge the women along, Yuri walked in through the front door. She heard him even before she saw him. One of his legs was shorter than the other, and the shim he used to compensate creaked when he walked. His gold watch swayed like a pendulum from his vest, and he was still in his white surgeon's coat. "Yuri Chaimovich!" Miri said, excited and alarmed because they'd already said their good-nights at the hospital. His being there meant something was wrong. She hurried to him. Before he'd even had time to hang his hat, she asked, "What's happened? Why have you come?"

"It's agreed. Finally." Out of breath, he put his bag down and took her hands. They stood eye to eye. "You left early. For the first time." He gulped for air. "The fishmonger, if he survives the night...The other surgeons, they've agreed you're correct. His spleen must be removed. And they've agreed *you* will do it. *You* will operate—alone." She must have stepped forward. They were closer now. He kissed her cheek. "You're being elevated to surgeon."

"He'll be saved?"

"Yes. By your hand."

"It would be better now. We need to operate now." Hearing the news also had Miri out of breath. Her words came quickly. "He'll lose less blood. Have a better chance. To live."

"You know the operating theaters are shuttered at night. We can't see well enough." He pushed so close his legs pressed on her skirts. "Did you hear me? You're being promoted."

"Surely we can compensate with candles. Gas lamps."

"We can't." He cleared his throat. "Miriam. You're a surgeon now."

The house behind them was loud with women's voices, but as the news took hold it all seemed far away from where Miri stood. "Surgeon?" she said. "You're certain?" So many mocked her ambitions because she was a woman. Enough told her to give up the dream that she'd begun to hear them, to accept she would never be promoted no matter how great her skills. But oh, how she wanted it. The title would allow her to act without seeking permission, which meant she'd save so many more. She reached for a bench to steady herself.

"I wouldn't say it if I wasn't certain. You'll save him. Tomorrow. On your own." Yuri smiled. He rarely showed emotion. To gain a patient's trust, he taught, a doctor must appear impartial, neutral to all news. But when he broke his rule for her, she loved it. She thought he looked lighter, younger. "I'll be there, if you need me. But you will operate on your own."

"How did you convince them?"

"Dr. Rozen, can't you hear me?" Babushka called. From the front door, there was a clear view of her on her perch, half teasing, half scolding. How many times had she addressed Yuri? "Dr. Rozen, I asked if you'd care to greet the other women in the house?"

Yuri turned to face her. "Yes. My apologies." He removed his coat and hat and started toward her. Baba's clients made room for him to pass. A few tucked their heads together, likely to gossip about Yuri, or Miri, or both. Their engagement was recent and still had most of them reeling. When Yuri first arrived in Kovno, many of the women had tried to steer him toward their own daughters. He was handsome, respected, and well-off, a bachelor with enviable manners. You want a nice girl, they'd said, a quiet girl to make you a home.

What he wanted was Miri.

Yuri was the only surgeon in Kovno willing to train a woman to reach his rank. The only one brave enough to stand against those who tried to shame him for it. In time, he and Miri had become so close they were rarely seen apart. Still, the women staring now had never gotten past their surprise when the doctors paired themselves. Everyone had assumed no man would have Miri, a headstrong girl, they'd said, who had the gall to think she could work alongside men. But Babushka knew. The day Miri accepted Yuri, a weight came off her and she whispered to Miri that it was *bashert*, meant to be. And she was quick to dispel rumors that she'd had anything to do with the match because, she knew, Miri didn't want her to interfere—never had, not there.

By appearances, Miri and Yuri were a natural couple. They were both educated and accomplished, devoted to their patients. She was darker and flushed where he was pale, but there was no doubt they fit well together. Yuri was a gentleman. He was faithful and kind. There was a softness to him, a layer he kept hidden, one that Miri adored. In private, Vanya insisted to Miri it wasn't a softness, it was something broken, but Miri expected nothing less from Vanya. He was her big brother. He had always been overprotective, and he worried too much because he loved her. He didn't know Yuri, not like Miri did.

"Good evening, Mrs. Abramov," Yuri said. He leaned in to kiss Babushka once, twice, three times before they spoke. Miri couldn't hear what passed between them and so she watched. At a glance, Yuri looked more Russian than Jewish. He was impeccably dressed and sturdy where so many were tattered and gaunt. He had blond hair that had begun to lose its color and blue eyes that other women admired for their appearance but that Miri treasured because they never missed a detail. Even when patients swore they'd described every ailment, Yuri saw more. Just that week he'd treated a rash that might have been confused with smallpox, but Yuri knew it to be varicella. And while women sometimes remarked that his face was attractive save for his ears, Miri thought those ears that stuck out too far were perfect because they detected the slightest rattle in a child's chest when early diagnosis was the only hope for a cure.

When Yuri made his way back to Miri, she pulled him into the shadows under the stairs, where they'd have privacy. "Tell me more about Sukovich, the fishmonger. What happened after I left?"

"I've told you what matters."

"You're keeping something back. How did you persuade them?"

"I brought your notes to the other surgeons, told them how you'd watched your patient decline throughout the day. It was your persistence that made them reexamine him. Now they agree with your diagnosis." He paused. "Perhaps it was also the crime itself. The brutality. Does it matter?"

It didn't. All that mattered was saving Sukovich. "Let's go back to the hospital. Prepare for the surgery. I can't make a mistake. He'll be even weaker tomorrow."

"No." Yuri held her arms in his soft hands. "You're ready, more than ready. Trust yourself." He brushed a black curl from her face, tucked it behind her ear, and smiled. "Tell me." His voice dropped lower. "Weddings. They're in every nook of this house. But never ours. Will you marry me now that you're a surgeon?"

"You can't ask me that now, Yuri." She looked over her shoulder to see if anyone was watching them. "I have my first surgery tomorrow. And—and think of all the women we lose in childbirth."

"I love you, Mirele. I'll take care of you. See you through it."

"What about my training? I have more to learn. And I have to take care of Vanya and Baba."

He pulled her to him. "I'll take care of them. You can continue at the hospital after we're married. You know that."

"Can't these intimate moments wait until the wedding?" Vanya said. Miri hadn't heard him coming. He slid between them so Yuri had to step back. Silhouetted in light spilling from the kitchen down the hall, Vanya's thin frame looked feeble compared to Yuri's, his clothing threadbare in contrast to the doctor's tailored suit. In better light, it would have been even more clear that they were opposites. Vanya was green eyes and wild black curls, while Yuri was bleached and straight. Vanya put a possessive arm around his sister's shoulders. In his other hand he held a plate with cheese and bread—his dinner. Miri knew he'd go back to his room and eat there while he worked on equations for relativity until he fell asleep at his desk.

Yuri, always nervous around Miri's brother, fumbled and then held out his hand to shake Vanya's. "Good evening, Ivan Davydovich."

"Relax." Vanya raised his eyebrows and offered a smile without any warmth. "You think I don't know you've kissed your fiancée?"

"Be nice," Miri said. She nudged Vanya. "Yuri, he's only teasing you."

"Of course. You do have a lighter side, don't you? What brings you to the house?"

"Sukovich," Miri said. "He's my patient. You heard about the beating?"

Vanya pressed his lips together and nodded. "Our fishmonger. It's been getting worse since Beilis." Mendel Beilis was a Jew living in Kiev. When a local teenage boy was found stabbed fourteen times, a lamplighter swore he'd seen Beilis kidnap the boy. Beilis was jailed for blood libel regardless of the fact that a half dozen Jewish witnesses saw him at work when the murder occurred. The lamplighter was a police pawn, a petty thief, beaten into making his statement, and because he wasn't a Jew his words held weight. It took two years for that truth to come out—two years during which Beilis rotted in a cell and Russians freely attacked Jews on the street in the name of revenge. Once the lamplighter recanted, Beilis's name was cleared but the shadow of the ordeal lingered. Newspapers reported on retributions still being extracted from Jews caught in the wrong place at the wrong time—Jews like Sukovich, whose only transgression had been catching more fish that morning than his non-Jewish competitors. "I read Russians are blaming us for the war, too," Vanya said. "There isn't even a war yet. But they're blaming us."

"There will be war," Miri said. "Since the archduke's assassination, it's inevitable."

"In any case," Yuri said. He cleared his throat. "Miri treated Sukovich. She diagnosed internal bleeding. She'll remove his spleen in the morning. She's being elevated to surgeon."

"At last!" Vanya kissed his sister and kissed her again.

"Enough," she said. "We'll celebrate when Sukovich lives."

"No. I must congratulate you now. Can't you see? It's awful and wonderful. Awful for Sukovich. Wonderful for you. And for your other patients. Think of all the others you will save now," he said, beaming. "So long overdue. Mirele, come, I'll find vodka."

"Yuri will join us," she said.

Vanya paused only for a moment. "Of course, *brother*," he said, and went to the kitchen.

II

Miri couldn't sleep. She was too terrified the fishmonger wouldn't make it through the night, too ashamed she hadn't done more to convince the surgeons to operate sooner. And so she lay awake envisioning the surgery, thinking about poor Sukovich and his family. How would they eat if he died? The hate unleashed on him was reprehensible, made worse by the fact that no one intervened. What if it were Vanya or Yuri who had been beaten?

Night ticked forward, and it occurred to Miri that the surgeons only agreed to the operation after the surgical theaters were closed. That meant if Sukovich pulled through to sunrise, he'd be so weak that no matter how perfectly she dissected and sutured, his chances would be minimal. Had they agreed because they knew she'd fail? No. No matter how much they might resent a woman in their ranks, no surgeon would put Miri's demise above the life of a patient. Would they? She climbed out of bed, added a log to the fire, told herself all that mattered was that Sukovich had a chance and that she'd be able to save more lives going forward. But, after all the condescension she'd faced, after the indignities Yuri himself had suffered for taking her on, what could Yuri have said not only to convince them to listen to her, but to promote her?

She'd met him when she was just seventeen. Yes, she was young, but she'd been pushed by Baba's unusual belief that education brought opportunity even for girls. Since her first day of school, she'd thrown herself into her studies and outpaced everyone around her, like Vanya. She passed all the basic levels permitting females by the time she was thirteen. After that, instead of calling Miri home to marry, Babushka encouraged her to study to become a midwife. "I know you, child. Your heart isn't full unless you are helping others, and a midwife helps more than most understand," Baba had said. It was a violent, bloody business, and Miri wasn't scared by any of the gore she saw. Rather, she excelled. Soon, Baba encouraged her to sit for university entrance exams, where Miri could earn a degree as a lower-level physician. Vanya helped press her case. Miri was accepted and, again, exceeded all expectations. And while nearly a dozen Russian women had earned medical degrees in France and Switzerland and then returned home to practice, Miri was the first to achieve her rank from within her own country. And once she started, she realized how much more she could do for patients as a surgeon. She'd spent every day since searching for someone to train her— someone like Yuri.

"Have you ever met a female surgeon before?" Yuri asked when they met at her interview. They were standing in the door to his office. The space was small, crammed with a desk, two chairs, and filing cabinets, yet every book, paper, and pen seemed to have its place. His window looked out on the brick factory below, and the room smelled sharp and hot like a furnace. Men's voices seeped through a cracked window. The foreman had them working at a furious pace.

"No, I haven't," she admitted.

"I've worked with one. In Zhytomyr, where I studied." Did he hold Miri's hand for too long or did she imagine that? "Please." He bowed, asking her to come inside, gesturing toward the seat across from his desk. As she settled, Miri managed to knock over an inkwell somehow. It was large and heavy and had been perched on the edge of the desk closest to her. The black liquid splattered on her skirts and on the floor. At home, she would have hurried to stanch the mess, but there in Dr. Rozen's office, on the most important day of her life, she froze. To her surprise, he also seemed stuck. Ink ran over the sloped floorboards and made it halfway to the window before either of them reacted.

She was certain he'd hold it against her, that he'd stalled because he was about to dismiss her. Surgeons couldn't blunder. "I'm so sorry," she said, twisting her fingers in her lap, waiting for him to ask her to leave. Instead, Yuri came around the desk and reached for a broom in the corner. He started sweeping and quickly had a pile of dust he used to absorb the liquid. Soon she'd learn this grit was from the brick factory. Their kilns' soot-filled smoke infected every crevice in the hospital, no matter how hard anyone tried to scrub it away. And Yuri, who valued privacy, rarely let anyone try. "I'll see to the rest later," he said, returning the broom.

She'd prepared for anything but kindness like that, and her surprise at his reaction, combined with the fear that he might not accept her now, brought on anger and the tug of tears. But she couldn't let herself cry, not there. How many times had she been told emotions were what held her sex back? "Confront what scares you," Baba always said, and so Miri took a deep breath and asked, "Should I go?"

"Not if you want to become a surgeon." He paused. "I know what it is to be a stranger in this hospital. I told you, I haven't been here long."

"Why?" She meant, Why do you want me to stay? He misunderstood.

"I left home, came here, because it was time. Isn't that why we all leave, at some point?" He paused. "Dr. Abramov, let us begin again." He went to his seat behind the desk. His face was neutral somehow, as if nothing had passed between them. "Tell me about your studies." She followed his lead and fell into the material she'd prepared. She talked about her classes. He quizzed her on anatomy. She knew she was speaking too quickly, but she was nervous. And she sounded rehearsed because she was. "What do you prescribe for a patient with insomnia?"

"Nothing until I've examined him. Presenting symptoms can be misleading." She regretted what she'd said as soon as it came out of her mouth. He narrowed his eyes and she hurried to fill the silence with what she knew he expected. "Chloral hydrate, opium, perhaps morphine."

She wanted to explain, but Yuri interrupted. "Some people are born to be surgeons. I can see that in you." How? How could he see anything in such a short period of time? And the comment, it was too personal. That made it unnerving, but also gave her courage.

"Does that mean you're willing to take me as your student?"

"Doesn't Russia deserve every surgeon she can muster?" He smiled. "You know the czar, his men, they don't believe women should even be physicians. Certainly not Jewish women. It could be dangerous, if you're ever brought in for questioning."

"Why would I be brought in for questioning?"

"I can't say. No one can, in Russia."

"All I want is to help."

"I understand. But keep in mind you're not choosing an easy path. You and I would both have to make sacrifices. Are you prepared for that?"

Sacrifices? Miri climbed back into bed and pulled the blankets around her. Who, or what, was being sacrificed by the decision to allow Miri to operate on Sukovich in the morning?

III

Miri came down to the kitchen before dawn and found her grandmother already there, lighting the fire. Breakfast was Babushka's one demand, the time Miri and Vanya were required to join her, together, no matter how early that meant they had to eat. As the women set to preparing the meal, Miri worked in silence, thinking about the fishmonger, picturing the surgery to come as she arranged silverware, cheese, and bread on the massive table. The wooden surface was scarred from chopping. Nothing sat straight. Babushka took one of the pots down from the wall to boil water for eggs and tea. The steam released the smell of lavender from the dried plants hanging around the room, meant to cover the lingering smell of onions.

A quiet knock on the back door announced the arrival of the baker's son. The boy, no more than ten years old, held up an envelope. A few years earlier, the Okhrana, the czar's secret police, had started reading the Abramovs' mail and reporting what they found to Vanya's superior, Kir, at the university. In response, Vanya started giving his correspondents their neighbor's address because he thought so long as there was bread, no one cared what a baker said or did. Miri was amazed the ruse worked, continued to work after all this time, that the seal on this letter was tight. It came from America. From that professor again, the scientist who'd promised to work with Vanya on relativity and to find him, Miri, and Baba a way out of Russia. For all the lofty dreams the American had spun for Vanya, he had yet to come through. But this envelope was thicker than most—perhaps thicker than any. Had something changed? Were they equations? Miri paid the boy with a sweet, kissed his cheek, and sent him home. After she closed the door behind him, she held the envelope up to the light to see if she could read any of it, but the paper was too thick. She grinned, thinking no one had any idea what Vanya was up to with the American.

"Well?" Baba asked.

"We'll have to wait," Miri said, still smiling, now shaking her head. She placed the letter on Vanya's plate and went back to preparing the meal.

As Miri and Baba worked, the sound of Vanya pacing above was between them. His footsteps were steady like a metronome in time with the beat of calculations. If that professor did find a way to bring them to America, she'd make Vanya go without her. She'd told him she wouldn't leave Kovno. That Yuri wouldn't go, either. But if Vanya had the chance, he had to take it. Brilliant, sweet Vanya would never survive a war. He'd be too caught up in his equations to dodge bullets if they ever came close. And if he were shot away from home, he'd be left for dead until another Jew found him—which is what happened to the fishmonger.

Sukovich. What if Miri made a mistake while operating? Surely any of her seniors would be quick to criticize Kovno's first female surgeon, especially one they resisted promoting in the first place. No slip would be excused. But how many would even bother to come and watch? She fumbled the bread knife in her hand, stabbed the black loaf she'd been cutting.

"Believe in yourself, child," Baba said.

"But the other surgeons, they could change their mind. They could decide not to elevate me. And if I do anything wrong, Sukovich could die."

"He could also die if you do everything right." Baba spooned strawberry preserves into each of their mugs. "Stay strong. It's all you can do. And eat. We're lucky for the food."

"Are you ready?" Vanya asked. Miri hadn't heard him coming. She startled and he took up the knife, set to slicing the rest of the bread. "You'll save him. I know it," Vanya said as he slid a thick piece onto Baba's plate, then one onto Miri's before serving himself.

"Is your lecture ready, Vanya?" Baba asked.

"I'm not teaching. I told you last night. I'm going to the hospital, with Miri. To watch."

"No," Baba said. "Positions for Jewish professors are few and far between, and Kir will be looking for anything to hold against you. You can't afford to go to the hospital."

"Kir would never cut me loose. Today is for my sister." He paused. "But I'll bring notes. And I won't cancel yet, just in case I can still make it in time."

"It's better you don't cancel at all. Going today could hurt your sister's chances. And the fishmonger's."

"How?"

"By turning this all into a spectacle."

"Isn't it already a spectacle?" He reached for the envelope. "When did this come?"

"Ten minutes ago," Baba answered. "Did you hear me tell you to go to the university?" Miri stopped listening while Baba and Vanya went back and forth. Instead, she tried to imagine the surgeon's scalpel in her hand, each step she'd take. After she'd pictured the final suture, she pushed her chair back and headed for the door. Vanya scrambled behind her, stuffing the letter from America and a page of half-made lecture notes into his pocket.

"I have a good feeling, Mirele," he said as they walked outside.

On a normal day, Yuri picked Miri up in a horse-drawn taxi. He'd stop in front of Baba's house, step down in a starched suit, with his creaking shoe, and offer his hand to help her climb inside. But last night she told him she'd rather walk. The fresh air would help clear her mind. And so she took a deep breath and started down the street with her brother. The sun had just broken out over the city and glinted off rooftops and windows, making her squint. The smell of sewage and waste wafted from the gutters.

Baba's home was situated in the center of Kovno, on a hill that was uniformly drab, carpeted in gray stones that formed the sidewalks, streets, and squares. Faded row houses wove together in jagged lines and severed at haphazard intervals. But if Miri looked up, beyond the gray, there was a sweeping view of the city's borders that stood in gorgeous contrast. Two rivers converged in Kovno, and their waters nurtured the forest, framing the city in shades of emerald. Kovno was Russia's gateway to Europe, a cosmopolitan melting pot. It was said that Czar Nicholas, and his father before him, believed that if Kovno fell, they'd lose their empire, and so they spared no expense on battlements. Protruding from the lush outskirts, on one side, past the factories, were massive forts, the railways that supplied them, and quarters for the soldiers that manned them. On the other side was the suburb of Slobodka, where most of Kovno's Jews lived. Its wooden hovels were angled into the overgrown forest and looked as if they were drowning in mud, a sinking reminder of the life the Abramovs had been lucky to escape.

When Baba moved to Kovno, from Odessa, she was young and a fierce believer that Jews could live in modernity, in peace, next to Russian neighbors—and she wasn't afraid to share that view. Her eloquence attracted attention and helped her gain favor in the Jewish community, especially among those who believed the same. Her ability to make anyone comfortable, to pry secrets, and to keep them to herself helped her rise. A steady stream of mothers and grandmothers flocked to her. She never judged. She never gossiped about babies being born less than nine months after a wedding, or broken hearts that needed to mend. She accepted people for who they were and was rewarded for that with the house and presents that kept her far from the slums she had been so eager to escape.

There's nothing wrong with enjoying luxury, she warned her grand-children, so long as you remember it can all disappear faster than it arrived.

Miri and Vanya passed soldiers on patrol on every block. "Let's walk faster," Miri said.

"Speed won't help us escape them," Vanya said, nodding toward a pair with guns slung over their shoulders. "The overarching fact is war is coming. That means we don't have a future here in Russia. It's too dangerous for Jews."

"Even if I wanted to leave, I can't. None of us can. We don't have papers."

"I'm working on that."

"With your American?" Miri shook her head. "He's been promising for too long for me to believe anything. Besides, I've told you. My patients need me."

"Mirele, if this war comes, life will be worse for us Jews than it will be for Russians."

"Vanya, please."

"You're scared. I understand. Mama and Papa died going to America. That doesn't mean we will. We must take that chance. It's what they wanted."

Miri pointed to Vanya's pocket, to the envelope she'd seen him stash before they left. "What does he want? You usually tear into his letters right away."

"I haven't had a chance to read it. I—I wanted to wait."

"For what?" The tram clacked. Its metal wheels groaned. Vanya said nothing as he and Miri slid into an alley where it was darker but not crowded, a shortcut to the hospital.

IV

Two nurses met Miri and Vanya the moment they set foot inside the dark hospital. By the way they pounced on his sister, Vanya deduced they'd been waiting for some time and were as anxious about the surgery, about Sukovich, as Miri. The fishmonger was the fourth Jew beaten that month because of his religion. He was injured far more severely than the others, but surely the nurses suspected, like Vanya, that with war on the horizon, more would come. They took his sister by the arm and led her through the maze of corridors while Vanya trailed behind. Like the rest of Kovno, the Jewish hospital was made of gray stone, with heavy walls no amount of plaster could seal. Cold air seeped through cracks. But whereas other buildings were decorated with cornices and pillars, this hospital was plain. No benefactors wanted to waste money on design. Every kopeck went toward function and care, and so the building was constructed as a square with identical squares nested inside, creating wards and hallways all cut at ninety-degree angles. There wasn't a soft curve in the building.

The nurses ushered Miri into the small kitchen off the women's ward, Miri's office, leaving Vanya to wait in the hall while she changed. As soon as he was alone, he pulled out the envelope from America, from Professor Eliot of Harvard University. They'd been corresponding for two years, since Vanya's publication in which he'd challenged the German-Swiss physicist, Albert Einstein.

Einstein, a Jew himself, had been a young patent clerk about Vanya's age when he first published a string of papers outlining

brilliant new ideas about the laws of physics and the speed of light—
and how they affected time. Soon, a critic, Alfred Bucherer, began
to refer to Einstein's work as "*the* theory of relativity," and the title
stuck.

Back then, nearly a decade ago, Vanya was a teenager, and he
devoured Einstein's work not only because his ideas were a leap
forward from the foundations set by Galileo and Newton but also
because they surpassed the work of his closer contemporaries,
Michelson, Poincaré, and Lorentz. At first, most of the so-called
experts dismissed Einstein. After all, the patent clerk wasn't even
able to secure a job as a professor, but those who took a closer look,
like Vanya, understood Einstein's principles were revolutionary, and
he couldn't keep himself away. Day and night he studied Einstein's
work.

Then in 1909, as Vanya sat at the window in his room watching
a storm savage Kovno, he realized something that would change
his life. Wind rattled the shutters. Thunder rumbled up through
the floors, and lightning struck two trees in the forest near the city.
According to Einstein's favorite demonstration of relativity, a person
watching lightning strike a moving train from a platform, centered
at the midpoint, might see two bolts hit the train at the same time,
while someone sitting inside the moving train might observe the
strike in the rear a split second later than the bolt hitting the front.
Meaning, the same event that was simultaneous for one observer was
not for the other. Vanya thought about this as he watched one of the
struck trees fall, watched a wagon on the road speed up to get out
of the way, only barely escaping the path of the trunk in time. Any
slower, Vanya thought, and that poor man and his horse would be
dead.

That was when Vanya made the crucial connection. He jumped
up, knocking books and papers everywhere. Of course! Einstein's
theory was based on objects moving at constant speeds—but that

wasn't an accurate representation of the universe. Some objects, like the wagon, were accelerating. Einstein's theory wasn't complete.

A monstrous clap of thunder rattled the windows. Vanya bent to retrieve his notebook, and as he did, he realized something else. "Gravity," he said, looking at the papers that had fluttered to the ground. Acceleration and gravity were both missing from Einstein's work. He had only accounted for special situations—not for realities like the accelerating wagon—which meant Einstein hadn't finished. Even more, it meant Vanya could work to complete the theory, a broader general theory that would be just as groundbreaking as the one Einstein had already proposed.

Vanya plunged himself into the problem and soon discovered he wasn't alone. Just three months later, Einstein published a paper in which he also declared his original theory was lacking, and by 1910, Vanya was spending every waking moment working through the details and implications of a general theory. Without realizing, he missed meals. And sleep. Baba and Miri prodded him to take better care of himself, but he couldn't concentrate on his health— only on this idea that felt more powerful than any that had come before. An idea that changed the way the universe was understood because, Vanya discovered, it meant space wasn't a flat plane. Space curved around the objects in it. That meant light didn't travel in a straight line, rather it traced the divots created by the sun, the moon, and other matter.

Light bends.

How could Vanya prove it? He needed equations to describe it, to predict by how much it bent. And he needed physical evidence— like Einstein's example of the train being struck by lightning—only it was more difficult to capture light bending. The only time to witness it was during a total solar eclipse. When the moon blocked the sun, its closest stars would be visible, and through a photograph he could capture it happening, measure it, and share it as his proof. The math would take time, but the photograph could be taken at the next solar eclipse, due in 1914. And while it could have fallen anywhere in the world, luck was with Vanya—it was due over Russia.

Vanya worked tirelessly to garner support for an expedition, for funding and equipment to photograph the eclipse, but wasn't able to raise a single kopeck. Vanya tried to console himself by arguing that math was his specialty, not photography, and so he filled notebook after notebook with his attempt at equations, but his math wasn't working. Nor was Einstein's. The patent clerk, now finally a professor, published a series of field equations he said calculated distortions in space according to general relativity. Many in the scientific community seemed to accept them—but Vanya felt Einstein's math wasn't much better than what they already had from Newton. And both Newton and Einstein failed when it came to calculating Mercury's changing orbit, the ultimate test. Yes, Einstein was off by only minuscule amounts, but correct equations, ones that captured the truth, wouldn't be off by any measure.

Vanya published an article laying out his case that Einstein's math was mistaken. Reactions were mixed. Those who'd already tried to discredit Einstein because of his religion, or because of what they thought was skewed scientific reasoning, continued to declare the entire theory of relativity worthless. Others called Vanya's ideas desperate and self-aggrandizing, but Einstein himself published an article agreeing with Vanya. Even more, Einstein challenged Vanya and every other physicist in the world to a race. He wanted to see who could come up with the correct field equations the fastest— along with a photograph of light bending at a solar eclipse to check those equations.

Not long after that, Vanya received his first letter from Professor Eliot. It was transcribed in careful Russian, by a translator. Eliot praised Vanya for his math and arguments, declared that he, too, was working to correct Einstein's field equations, only he was getting nowhere. Perhaps they could share notes, work together? They started a correspondence, and by his third letter, Eliot announced the math was beyond him but he believed in Vanya. "Only two men in the world are capable of this," Eliot had written. "You, dear Abramov, and Einstein." Furthermore, since Eliot couldn't help with the figures, he'd gone ahead to help with what he called the "easy part," mounting an expedition to Russia, an expedition to witness and photograph the eclipse. They would be a team in which Vanya solved equations and Eliot provided photographs. He expected Vanya to meet him in Minsk for the eclipse and to join him at Harvard afterward. Harvard's president had already approved a position for Vanya—so long as he came with the prestige of correct field equations and photographs. Vanya was elated. So was Baba. Russia was becoming increasingly unsafe for Jews, and she wanted to leave before Kovno turned into another Odessa. Back then, he had had sixteen months to refine his work. The eclipse was coming on August 21, 1914, and he knew he could solve the math by then and take them all to America.

While Vanya toiled over the equations, dozens of other universities also announced expeditions to Russia for the eclipse—all set on beating Einstein. And while they all mustered equipment, none came close to the equations. Then came the rumble of cannons in the Balkans—war. One expedition was canceled after another. Eliot was the last holdout. It wasn't until May that Vanya received the devastating letter announcing his Harvard funding had been frozen. After that letter, after Vanya recovered from the shock, he'd written to Eliot to ask if he was able to produce the field equations, would the offer to come to America, to Harvard, still stand. He hadn't received a reply. Not yet. Not until this morning. And he hadn't dared tell Baba he was worried because by now, she was set on leaving, convinced their lives depended on it. She and Miri fought about it often. Miri believed they still had a future in Kovno, a reason and an obligation to remain in their home—but Vanya sided with his grandmother. With war coming, with more Jews being beaten like the fishmonger, it was time to leave. Expecting bad news, he couldn't bring himself to read the letter in front of her, didn't want to admit he might have lost their way to safety. But now that he was alone, he tore the seal and ripped the envelope. The message was short.

Dear Professor Abramov,

I write with good news concerning our efforts. A professor from Chicago, Russell Clay, has vowed to use his own personal funds to secure equipment and mount an expedition to Russia. Riga is his target city. Bullets will not keep him away, Clay wrote in his announcement. He also shared that he hasn't solved the equations. He's focused solely on photographing the event. Even in the face of war...

Vanya felt a jolt. It was incredible. Fantastic news. He only knew his hands were shaking because the paper fluttered. There were thirty-nine days remaining until the eclipse. Could he still have a chance to photograph it? Surely, Eliot wouldn't send such a letter if it weren't true, but why hadn't Vanya heard anything about this Professor Clay? Could the American even put together the equipment and a team in such a short time? Vanya wanted to keep reading, there was more to the letter, and a long article included, but he heard Yuri coming from around the corner. If Yuri saw it, they'd argue about America again. Like Miri, Yuri didn't want to leave, and Vanya didn't want to get into it. Not today.

He fumbled to put the letter back into his pocket as he heard Yuri approaching, his shoe creaking. To Vanya, Yuri had always seemed cold, but Miri said it wasn't so. He gave affection when he meant it, not because it was expected as a part of good manners, she said. But Vanya thought his sister misunderstood. Yuri wasn't restrained. He just wasn't passionate the way she was—the way she deserved. Vanya was about to step forward from the shadows and greet Yuri when the letter slipped from between his fingers and fell. As he reached for it, he heard another older man approach. Another surgeon. "Dr. Rozen," the man said. His voice was low and something in his tone told Vanya to stay back. Vanya watched from around the corner. The surgeon hobbled toward Yuri. Under his white coat, his suit was too large for his frame. He appeared to be shrinking inside the fabric. His eyes burrowed under so many wrinkles it was hard to tell if they were open or closed. Yuri himself was a vision in white, draped in a smock, with a mask loose around his neck.

"Good morning, Doctor," Yuri said.

"Yes, yes. I want you to know, it's a fine thing you've done." The elder surgeon clapped Yuri on the shoulder. "You're an upstanding man. You'll make a fine officer."

"Shh," Yuri whispered. Vanya froze, still in the shadows.

"Why hide, Doctor? It's an honorable thing you've done. None of your peers—not one of the other men in this hospital—was going to stand up to volunteer. We would have had to draw lots if not for you. An interesting condition, though, your request," he chortled. "I know you're in love, but tell me, truly, how can you think a woman would be up to the job?"

"I've watched her work for years. She's more than capable."

"Still, she's a medusa who's snared you. She may be well trained, but emotion will always cloud her judgment. She can never be as reliable as a man," the elder doctor said. "Son, all gentlemen are ridiculous when it comes to women."

"Please keep your voice down," Yuri said, sounding nervous.

"You're truly not going to tell her? You haven't learned yet, but she'll find out what you've done. Women have a way." The elder surgeon continued, "Your sacrifice is admirable so long as she feels the same. With her ambition, who's to say? At least the czar won't send surgeons to the front. Only medics."

Vanya's hands were cold with shock. He could barely believe what he'd heard. Yuri had traded himself for Miri's promotion. His sister would never want that. She'd think Yuri didn't believe in her; she'd want to earn her own way—and would never dream of putting Yuri in danger. She loved him more than her career. Surely, if Yuri knew his sister at all, he must have understood that. Still, it surprised Vanya that Yuri had done this for Miri. He hadn't expected such bravery.

Vanya could hear Yuri still trying to silence the elder surgeon, but he continued bumbling, "Of course, you, Dr. Rozen, you're likely the only one among us who knows how to use a gun, who might survive if it comes to it."

"I can't believe it." Vanya didn't mean to say it out loud, but he did.

"Believe what?" Miri asked. She'd sneaked up behind him. He jumped and tried to force a smile. She'd changed into the same white uniform as Yuri, only she wore skirts.

Vanya kissed her hand. "It's not important now."

"Dr. Abramov," Yuri called. His voice was relaxed as if nothing had passed between him and the elder surgeon. "I hear you. You're ready? Sukovich can't wait much longer," he said as he turned the corner. "Ivan Davydovich?" Yuri stopped, held out his hand. "I didn't know you were coming."

"I wouldn't miss it," Vanya said. "I don't miss anything, in fact."

Yuri blinked at him, startled. Before he could say another word, Miri strode away. "We need to go. Now," she called over her shoulder.

V

Vanya stood in the gallery of benches that lined the balcony above the operating theater and watched his sister below as she marched into the room, emanating confidence. He was filled with pride because, regardless of what Yuri had done, Vanya knew she'd earned this day, this position. She'd worked toward it ever since she saved their cousin all those years earlier. Yuri followed her with a smile as if he'd done nothing wrong. And Vanya found that as much as he wanted to be angry with Yuri for his lies, it wasn't that simple. Yuri had given Miri the greatest gift anyone could give. It was a supreme act of generosity.

The men around Vanya, students and surgeons, were crammed together shoulder to shoulder with no room to spare. Vanya was sure his sister hadn't expected so many people to watch, but word must have spread that Dr. Rozen's woman would be operating for the first time on her own and they'd all come to witness the spectacle. The space filled with the smell of stale clothing and carbolic.

"She'll kill him. Mark my words," a man next to Vanya said.

"Of course she will. Why would they trust a woman with a man's life?" agreed another.

But what about Sukovich himself? None of them discussed the crime or the hatred that could kill them all. Vanya kept his mouth shut and his hand in his pocket, fingering the letter from Eliot. He spotted the elder surgeon from the hallway in the front row.

Miri looked up to address the gallery, and the room went silent save for a moan from the fishmonger. Vanya knew Miri didn't want to waste time talking, but she had to follow protocol. She introduced herself as Dr. Abramov, the lead surgeon, Yuri as her assistant, and then presented her patient, his condition, and her plans for the operation. When she turned to begin, a nurse fastened her mask for her, and the men in the balcony all leaned forward, up on tiptoes.

"I've heard she's as skilled as Olevovich was at that age," one murmured, comparing Miri to the chief of surgery.

"That's a lie," another disagreed. "Leave women to tend to their own."

Vanya was tempted to challenge them, but he held his tongue, letting their criticism boil with the heat that crept into the gallery and left the voyeurs dripping. As Miri worked, Yuri stood over her and pointed to the patient, to implements. Behind his mask, Vanya was sure Yuri was whispering instructions. And he was also sure Miri wasn't listening. Vanya knew the look in his sister's eyes. It was pure concentration. She was doing the work on her own. Dissecting the spleen from surrounding tissues. A complicated, blood-filled procedure she was handling perfectly, it seemed.

And then, suddenly, Vanya heard the man next to him hiss, "Too much blood!" He leaned even further forward. The comment was followed by other murmurs around them.

"She's enlarged the tear."

And: "She's killing him."

Quickly, Yuri took the instrument from Miri and she stepped back. A nurse began using sponge after sponge in the fishmonger's chest. Had Miri made a mistake? Or, as she'd predicted, had they operated so late that his body had given way?

"Hold this," Vanya heard Yuri say in a voice louder than it needed to be. "I'll tie it off." More blood and sponges. Miri eased down to Sukovich's side and stroked his palm just as Vanya used to stroke hers when they were children and she was scared. Finally, Yuri made a show of handing Miri a curved needle, asking her to close the incision. At that, Miri let go of Sukovich. She leaned in and narrowed her eyes. The look, the posture, Vanya knew. She was doing all she could to hold back the darkness, and tears. She was angry and ashamed. Couldn't Yuri see that crack in her? Why didn't he say anything to defend her, to tell the room it was Miri who'd made the correct diagnosis, that she'd started perfectly?

"What we expected," the man next to Vanya said. Was he smiling?

After the last stitch was tied, the men around Vanya surged toward the exits, but Vanya stayed. Baba had raised them to respect pain, to fight through it, but that didn't mean Miri needed to feel it on her own. Vanya wanted to comfort her, but she'd never forgive him if he did that in front of her peers. And so he waited in case the room cleared and she looked for him. But she didn't. She disappeared through the side door without even glancing up at the gallery. "Damn Yuri," Vanya muttered. He could have helped more.

Vanya checked his watch and realized he still had time to run to the university for his lecture. As much as he didn't want to go, he knew he should. Baba was right; Kir didn't need more ammunition. It was lucky he hadn't canceled after all. Vanya hurried through the hushed hospital, past people waiting in line to be seen, and through the heavy front doors. Outside the street was loud—a main thoroughfare—packed with the frenzy of Kovno's workers. Vanya bobbed past carts piled with vegetables, fish, and coal, past wagons loaded with soldiers and cannons. On the corner closest to the edge of the square, he waited for the tram. A woman across from him was selling blankets. They hung from lines on display like laundry. A small girl played in them, pressing her hands into their wool while her sister batted at her profile. The tram choked to a stop. Vanya elbowed his way on.

As the noisy tram slinked through the city, Vanya reached into his pocket and ran his fingers over Eliot's letter. An expedition. Coming to Russia. Even now. Incredible. He burned to read the rest, but he couldn't manage it on that crowded tram. If only he could solve the math before the eclipse. He tried to push past what had happened to Miri and concentrate on his equations for relativity. At least that was something he could fix.

He asked, again, the question he'd been asking himself every day for five years. How to account for acceleration? And gravity? How he wished he could ask his Papa. Baba had been mother and father to them both, more than any child could hope for, but Vanya longed for those afternoons he'd spent in his father's workshop as a child. "Look around," Papa used to say. His father had sold watches and clocks. When he could, he'd taken in repairs and taught Vanya about the gears and mechanisms. "No clock can ever be perfect." The first time Papa had said that, Vanya was nine years old. He was bent over a workbench, clutching a screwdriver and a loupe. The smell of grease was thick between them along with the remnants of smoke from Papa's pipe.

"I don't understand," Vanya said.

"You see all these clocks on the walls? Not one tells the same time as another. Even if their hands point to the same hour and minute, their second hands aren't in sync."

"We could fix that."

"Perhaps we could make it look precise to the human eye, but to make it truly exact is impossible. It is beyond any human ability. No clock can precisely match another." Papa smiled through his thick beard. "You're fighting nature. Think about it, my boy. If time existed naturally, every clock in this room would read the same."

Vanya had never considered it before but nodded as the idea worked through him. "You're right. The moon doesn't tell time."

"Of course not! Our watches can't mark the rising or setting of the sun or the moon—those change every night. What's it matter to the moon or to the stars what any clock says? Still, time is important to us. For trains. For anything with a schedule." The idea was radical.

Vanya knew it even then and he loved his father for it. Later, after he'd lost his parents, when he discovered that the great scientists of the day were focused on the problem of synchronizing clocks, he couldn't turn back. Especially not when he discovered Einstein's work at the patent office was dedicated to reviewing inventions for aligning clocks, inventions such as pneumatic tubes and blasts of air. His father was right: time was a human invention. Like Einstein, Vanya came to believe time was relative. And defining a second or an hour was arbitrary—but sequence was absolute. A tree falls. It cannot rise up and become whole again, just as an egg breaks and its shell cannot be reassembled, regardless of how anyone defines the time it takes for these events to happen. How did that fit into field equations?

He closed his eyes to picture the problem, but then the tram stopped hard and sent Vanya into the window. Looking out, he realized he'd missed his stop. Not by much. He hurried for the door and ran down the cobbled streets toward the university.

VI

Vanya ran into the auditorium where he was scheduled to speak and found every seat was already taken. Still, he hoped he could slink down the aisles to the stage unnoticed, avoid the need to return false smiles and handshakes. Quickly, quickly he hurried with his head down and his hands in his pockets. It helped, he knew, that most of the audience expected this behavior from him. Since Vanya had applied to the university eight years earlier, he'd been the center of attention and held apart, much to his dismay. He wrote his entrance exam in twenty minutes, scoring perfectly, while others toiled for more than six hours and still didn't derive every answer. Once he started classes, he didn't have to attend lectures that explained proofs and methods because he came to solutions on his own. Instead he spent hours in the library digging into Minkowski, Einstein, and others. Students and professors alike watched him from afar. He heard them whisper, calling him "that odd Jew." He learned to be grateful that he was left alone. It gave him time to work.

It was Kir Romanovitch, the chair of the new Theoretical Physics Department, who was the first to breach the barrier and come near Vanya. Kir approached him in the library one night when he was working late. Vanya was sitting under a smattering of light that rendered Kir a towering shadow. His dark suit and hair made him hard to see in that setting, but the smell of his cigars was as distinct as any line. Without smiling or extending his hand, Kir put a copy of a recent math journal in front of Vanya. "Mr. Abramov, you know this Henri Poincaré?" Kir said, pointing to an article. "You've studied his gravitational waves?" Vanya was so stunned that such a powerful man was paying him any attention that all he could manage was a nod. "Good. I don't care that you're a Jew. You'll lecture on Poincaré next week."

Vanya was thrilled. He practiced with Miri, writing and rewriting that lecture. Only a few professors attended, but word spread that the Jew's work was astounding, and others began to approach him, asking for his advice or help. Vanya was happy to work with anyone he judged serious by their commitment to math. Those who wouldn't sleep until they had a solution, or a hint of a solution, were those he gladly spent long hours with in the library, working through equations. He loved going over problems with them, much as he loved talking through his own ideas with Miri at home in Baba's kitchen. Though Vanya didn't bother with compliments when answers were correct, his colleagues were drawn to him, to his passion. Of course there were plenty who persisted in resenting him, but they didn't concern him as long as they stayed out of his way.

After he was awarded his degree, he was elevated to professor, a position that made him formally "useful" and gave him the freedom that came with that status: higher pay, the chance for advancement, and the ability to travel anywhere in the empire. *Useful* Jews were part of the czar's plans for Russification. To unify his empire, to assimilate its outliers, Nicholas needed modern, educated Jews, and the promotion meant the czar's men gave not only him a wider berth, but Miri and Baba, too. It was how Vanya had helped Miri get her training to become a doctor and how they were able to remain in a house in the section of the city where they lived—where only *useful* Jews were now permitted. Every year, more students came to learn from him. And every time he gave a lecture, the auditorium was full. That day he walked in after Sukovich's surgery was no exception. There wasn't a free seat in the room. It was good he came, after all: his absence would have been noticed.

Vanya took hold of the chalk and put the folded piece of paper with his spare notes on the lectern. He decided since he wanted to work through the question of acceleration anyway, he might as well do so here. Perhaps if he could explain it to his colleagues, he'd figure out how to use it for himself.

The solution he needed for relativity held two sides, linked by an equal sign. On one side sat the distribution of matter and energy in space—the stars. On the other sat the geometry of space—the stage. The two were linked, not separate. He compared this relationship to apples bobbing in water. Every time the apples moved, the water also moved, putting the equation back into balance. One always affected the other—in different ways at different times. How could he express that? In his mind, Vanya ran through his notebook, ticking through pages and pages. He needed a framework, what mathematicians called a tensor, to represent all four dimensions. He focused on the Italian mathematician Gregorio Ricci-Curbastro because Ricci's tensor accounted for acceleration. It was so new, Vanya figured no one in the audience had even heard of it.

He turned to the board and started working at a furious pace, sensing rather than calculating the curves and height of space as they changed under his chalky fingers. When he came up short, he knew it because he could feel it. Each time he erased his work and started again. A cloud of dust sent him into a coughing fit and he didn't pause to recover. Nor did he take questions.

"Another way to understand this problem," he said, rolling a clean board out from the corner. "Imagine you've put a blanket on a laundry line." He thought about the tram stop earlier. "A child stands behind the blanket and sticks her hand into it so you see her fingers' profile on the opposite side. That sheet is equivalent to space. That hand is equal to a star, or even a galaxy. The correct tensor, and equation, will define both and include time—marking when the hand and the blanket were in that position. And when she moves her hand, imagine it's fused to the fabric. Just as a star can't simply leave space, her hand can't lose contact with the wool. It doesn't matter how it changes, or accelerates, or when. The correct equations will still hold true." That's what he was after. That's where Einstein had failed. "Watch," he said when one person asked for clarification. It wasn't until fifteen minutes past the hour that he noticed he'd run late. "Sorry," he said, stopping abruptly, knowing he was no closer to a solution. He'd been so focused on the math that he was surprised when he turned to face the audience and found rows and rows of men working to keep pace, copying every notation he'd made—not seeming to care that he'd gotten nowhere.

Vanya took a bow, as was expected of him. Before he stood, he was swarmed. "Professor," they all seemed to yell at once. "Why gravity? Why are you focused on gravity and acceleration?"

"To understand spacetime, we must understand gravity," Vanya said. "It slows time."

"Isn't that what the German is saying?" one student asked.

"Professor Einstein?" Vanya asked. "He's Swiss now."

"He has German blood. How can we trust that?"

"He's a worthless Jew," another said. And the room went silent.

Vanya cleared his throat and tamped down his anger, steadied his voice even as his face turned red. "The country Einstein calls home doesn't matter. Nor does his religion. Ideas matter. Science above politics," Vanya said, knowing it was more of a wish than reality. The truth was that, like Einstein, everyone in that auditorium thought of Vanya as a Jew before they thought of him as a scientist. Even Vanya himself thought that way. That was likely what fueled his obsession with him, the fact that Vanya had more in common with Einstein than with any man in his field. Both were outcasts from the day they were born. This bond kept Vanya fascinated. Since he'd first read about the theory of relativity, he'd tried to dig as deeply as he could into Einstein's life. All he found, all that was available in Russia, were tidbits he could learn from journals and newspapers. Back in those early days, most established professors around the world dismissed Einstein as a radical at best and a fool at worst.

Vanya taught himself to read German so he could master Einstein's publications. He saw Einstein adopted a patent examiner's approach to writing scientific papers—he didn't cite foundational sources. And Vanya began to do the same. He was chastised for it but he refused to change. Why did it matter who inspired him or came before him? His work was replacing that entire foundation anyway.

Vanya once paid double the value of a journal just so he could own a photograph of Albert Einstein. He propped the picture up on his desk at home. In the photo, Albert stood in front of the Bern clock tower near his patent office. He had a thick mustache and curls. His eyes looked sleepy. His jacket was too large. His tie wasn't straight, and his collar, was it crooked? Vanya was a fatherless eighteen-year-old when he found that photo, and afterward he tried growing his own mustache—unsuccessfully. He also stopped making sure his suits were well tailored and his own ties were straight. Baba hated it, said that, as a Jew, Vanya couldn't afford to look the way he did, but he fought back, countered that what mattered was math not religion. He could be sloppy in appearance but not in work. Since he continued to progress, there was little she could do to stop him. But when he tried to convince Miri to do the same, to stop worrying about the tightness of her braids and the starch in her collars, Baba scolded him. His sister, Baba said fiercely, was a woman fighting for respect. She couldn't afford to be sloppy anywhere.

Vanya answered every question the students and professors asked after his lecture. One by one, the crowd thinned until Vanya was left alone. He stayed at the blackboard and continued. He was close. He could feel it. But was Ricci the right tensor?

"Maybe I can help?" The voice came from a shadow in the back of the auditorium. Vanya startled. The chalk snapped.

"Kir?"

"I said I might be able to help," Kir said, smiling. He was halfway down the stairs in the auditorium, coming straight for Vanya. He wore his signature black suit. *Strong like a Russian bull* is the phrase that came to Vanya when he looked at Kir, because of his build and his self-assured arrogance. It was that demeanor, his ability to intimidate, not his work, that had earned Kir his title as department chair. He was a proficient mathematician at best, Vanya had come to learn.

"I'm fine, sir," Vanya said, forcing a smile of his own. "I don't need help."

"Yes, but it's all so interesting," Kir continued. They were the same words he'd used at Vanya's very first lecture on Poincaré. Back then, Vanya was so flattered his face had flushed. Kir had patted his back. His palm spanned the entire width of Vanya's left side. "You're certain what you've presented is correct?" Kir had asked Vanya's twenty-year-old self.

"Of course."

"Good, good. Then you won't mind if I check your notes?" Kir was already reaching for the stack of papers in Vanya's hands. "See if I can make sure you haven't missed anything?" Vanya couldn't object. Nor did he want to, not then. Kir was the center of his academic universe, the chair of his department. There could be no higher compliment. Vanya had handed over everything he had, expecting to hear back soon. But he didn't.

It took six months for Vanya to realize what had happened. Vanya's lecture on gravitational waves was published and credited to Kir and Kir alone. When Vanya confronted him, Kir smiled. "You know this is my work. You merely made suggestions."

"But...," Vanya tried.

"Did you write a single word that appeared in that article?" No.

Vanya hadn't. His work was confined to numbers and equations. Kir's grin grew. "Don't forget, I was the one who gave you that article. Do you think you would have come up with anything if it hadn't been for my guidance? You must learn there's an order to things."

"B-but," Vanya stuttered, feeling the first shock of shame. "The others who attended the lecture, surely they know?"

Kir leaned closer and whispered, "Remember, you're a Jew." That was when Vanya understood that no one would defend him. No one would risk their career and family for him.

Vanya's work brought Kir fame—and power. Scientists across Russia elevated him to the top of the academy, and that only made Kir bolder and more aggressive. "Tell me what you're working on so I can help," Kir would say when he tracked Vanya in the halls or waited for him in Vanya's office under the guise of giving him another article to study. "You should be grateful I'm looking out for you. Protecting you."

Vanya tried to cloister himself away while digging deeper into Albert Einstein. Still, Kir found his ways. He waited at the tram stop, lurked in the halls outside the classroom and in the stacks at the library. He even hovered over Vanya when he helped his peers. Eventually, Kir told Vanya that to retain his position, he'd need to present a lecture every month. Before the lecture, he had to submit his notes to Kir. Vanya had no choice but to agree. He couldn't lose his professorship—he needed it for Baba and Miri as much as for himself. They'd be thrown from their house, even from Kovno, if he was demoted and declared no longer *useful*. What did it matter if Kir saw his notes, he said to himself the first time he handed them over. Then Kir returned them, the exact same equations, only rewritten in Kir's hand. "I've added ideas," Kir said with a smile. "And I've already circulated these to the department." Which meant he'd told the other professors the work was his, not Vanya's. Surely they knew the lie, but still no one said a thing. It was a wonder Vanya had published that single article in which he declared Einstein's math mistaken. He'd only managed it because Kir thought the business of Jew arguing against Jew was below him.

"This lecture today, it was about your fight with Einstein, no?" Kir said now, standing in front of Vanya in the auditorium. The sound of voices and footsteps slid from under the door. For a second, Vanya thought about running, but didn't. His hands went cold. Sweat slid down his back. Kir continued. "You forgot to give me your notes for today."

"I—I wasn't prepared ahead of time. I'm sorry."

Kir frowned. "You know I can get you anything you need to solve this."

"You couldn't get me funding. For the eclipse."

"No." Kir dropped his chin, and something like disappointment flashed across his face. It was the first time Vanya had ever seen him flinch. "No. The czar is staring down war. Using his coffers for bullets, not photographs. Besides, pictures are nothing. It's math that matters." Kir cleared his throat. "Let me look at what you have." When Vanya hesitated, Kir continued, "A family like yours needs help. These are tough times. With war on the horizon, I can keep you safe." Kir held out his enormous hands, pointing toward Vanya's notes, and Vanya handed over what he had—the piece of paper he'd stashed in his pocket before he'd left with Miri. Kir raised an eyebrow but didn't comment. As he looked over the paper, he murmured, "Tell me. Your sister. Did she save that Jewish wretch this morning?"

Shocked, Vanya spoke without thinking. "My sister has nothing to do with this."

Kir didn't take his eyes off the paper between them. He added, "Did you hear about my promotion? I run the university now. Appointed by the czar himself."

"Congratulations. On your new position," Vanya mumbled. Then he hurried to the side door. He tripped. Fell into the first row of seats and righted himself. He'd banged his shin, badly. He tried to walk without limping, felt his face burning red with pain and anger.

"Good day, Vanya Abramov," Kir called after him. "My regards to your family."

VII

I almost killed him," Miri said. She and Yuri stood in a corner at the end of the women's ward. It was late and all the other doctors had gone home. Miri's arms and legs had never felt so heavy, and her head ached. She'd seen dozens and dozens of patients after the fishmonger's surgery, but he was still all she could think about.

"You saved him. The diagnosis, that was the hardest, most important part," Yuri said.

"Don't say that. Not to me. He would have died if you weren't there."

"Every surgeon makes a mistake their first time."

"Not like that. I don't deserve it."

"Surgeon? The title?"

"And your comfort. You should be chastising me."

"Never. Let me play for you. Please? You're a surgeon now, and I promised I'd play when you became a surgeon."

He was so secretive about the piano. She only discovered by accident that he played, late one night when the hospital was deserted. Miri had just begun her apprenticeship with him three months earlier. She'd stayed to watch over a lonely old woman who surely wouldn't make it through the night. Miri knew the nurses could tend to her patient in her absence, but she was fond of the woman and wanted to stay with her until the end.

Near midnight the woman took her last breath. Miri pulled the sheet over her patient's face, then stood and walked toward her office. Miri meant to fetch her things and go home, but she was stopped by music. Gorgeous, tragic music. It came from the piano in the basement—the only space the hospital had had for the instrument when it was donated. The notes were quiet and slow. Melancholic. She tiptoed around the hard, squared edges of the stone stairwell leading down to the basement, needing to see who could play so beautifully.

She tried not to make any noise. She didn't want to interrupt, assumed it was a patient's brother when she saw a man at the keyboard. And she didn't want to be seen. Baba had warned her against being alone with strange men enough for her to know better. As she slid closer, she heard more fury in the notes. Then a finger that dragged instead of struck. Miri wedged herself against a crate of bandages stacked along the wall. The smell of damp mixed with the earthy scent of the underground.

The pianist played by the light of a single candle that lit the keyboard, not his face. He didn't have music in front of him; he played as if the instrument were an extension of himself, his fingers dancing at an impossible pace. And then a pause. Miri held her breath until he sank back into the keys, this time at a softer, slower rhythm. How long did she listen? She couldn't say. When he finished, he bent forward in exhaustion. Miri felt she was intruding on a moment more intimate than any man would want a stranger to see, but in that silence she was trapped.

Eventually, the man let out a mournful sigh and pushed back from the piano. When he turned, she saw his face. She must have made a noise at her surprise. "Who's there?" he asked.

"Miriam Davydovna." He looked as startled as she felt, staring into the dark, searching for her. "I'm sorry. I didn't mean to intrude." She wanted to say more, to explain she'd been moved by the music, that it was the most gorgeous she'd ever heard, but she didn't dare. Not with him looking for her like that.

"Do not apologize." His lips turned up. It wasn't quite a smile but it was close, and it helped her step forward. "Music is meant to be shared. How long were you there?"

"Not long." She hated lying. "Awhile. You play beautifully."

"It's an awful hobby."

"How can you call it awful?"

"What doctor's down here in the basement instead of up with his patients?"

"A human one," Miri said.

They walked back up the stairwell together. She said she should be getting home, but he invited her to stay and have tea. Before she'd seen him as a mentor, as a brilliant surgeon focused on medicine, but now she wanted to know why a musician with so much talent hid in the basement playing for no one. Why wasn't he at home, with his family? She'd been working with him for months, she realized, and yet she knew nothing about him.

She set a tray of biscuits on the table. The chair scraped the floor as he pulled it out for her. Babushka taught her grandchildren to be aware of their surroundings at all times, to look for clues that could reveal a person's true story, what lay beneath their veneer. It was crucial to know who would risk their life to save yours, but before, Miri had never dared to try to scrape beneath Yuri's surface. Now she took in his buttoned-up vest and jacket, his stiff doctor's coat. Appearance was important to him, that was clear. How had she missed that scar just above his lip? The skin had been stitched back together. It was a cut she'd treated on many children, the result of a fall, but Yuri's scar wasn't that old. It was still tinged pink, not white. Didn't he say he'd left Zhytomyr recently? "You never told me why you left home," she said.

He kept his eyes on the steam coming off the tea between them. "Please, don't ask me about home, or about the piano."

"Why not?"

"It's my only request."

"Will you play for me again?"

The biscuit in his hand snapped. "When I secure your promotion."

She was certain he'd forgotten that promise made years ago. But now he took her hand as they stood, again, in the dark hospital, with Sukovich recovering near them. He guided her down the squared marble staircase and back into the basement, invited her to share the piano bench. She sat so close their legs pressed together. She could feel he was nervous.

"This is Schubert. A sonata. His saddest and most gorgeous," Yuri said.

"That's why you like it? Because it's sad?"

"No. And yes." He shook his head. "I think it sits where it should."

He played even more beautifully than she remembered, and just as the music had carried her away before, it did so again. She felt his love and loss. The sadness he'd never wanted to share with words poured out, tangling with her own anguish over Sukovich and her mistake that could have cost him his life. Yuri's hands moved so quickly there was a dark rage to them, and then they stopped, paused before sneaking back into the light. By the time he finished, they'd both been transported beyond themselves, and as the keys still vibrated, he turned and kissed her with a passion she'd never felt from him before. She wrapped herself around him, broke into goose bumps at the electric thrill of his hands, his fingers reaching up her skirt. He'd never touched her like that, and she found herself lost and open to him. But just as he trailed the top of her stockings, he pulled away.

VIII

After his confrontation with Kir, Vanya didn't bother taking the tram back to the house. He ran with an abandon he hadn't felt since their summers in Birshtan, where he and Miri used to spend the hottest months of the year with Baba at their dacha. The summer cabin was tucked in the hills, near a river and sulfur springs. It was small, with two rooms and a loft where they slept, tucked in by flowers, trees, and Baba's vegetable gardens. They'd stopped going when Vanya was made a professor, but before that they spent every summer under their grandmother's eye, training in self-defense the way she herself had once been trained after she escaped Odessa and was saved by the Romani in their camp in the woods. "Enjoy what we have but always prepare for it to disappear," she'd said. Though Baba meant the warning to be taken seriously, those summers were idyllic. The only time they'd been able to truly relax and laugh since their parents died. Vanya and Miri spent half the summer floating in the water, stuffing themselves with berries and vegetables so fresh the soil on them was still moist. The other half they spent skinning what they'd killed. Or, to be precise, Vanya spent watching Miri skin what she'd killed because he could never bring himself to do either. And when she was done, they would run, play games, and race, pretending an enemy was behind them. Which was how Vanya ran now, only none of what he ran from was a dream. Kir hovered as real as Baba had warned.

Vanya stormed through the back door, ran up the stairs, and went straight to his room. He hurried past stacks of books on the floor, over piles of notebooks, and stumbled into the chair at his desk. His hands shook. It took three tries before he could strike the flint and start a cigarette. Then he leaned back and looked around at the papers covering the walls. Every sheet was filled with notations and calculations—his work on relativity. Vanya closed his eyes. If Kir took credit for Vanya's work on relativity, he'd never be able to secure his post at Harvard. And there was no doubt Kir meant to threaten Miri. How had Vanya gotten his family into such a mess? He bowed his head so his curls fell on his face, and he pinched the skin on the bridge of his nose, trying to balance himself. Numbers and equations were the order he understood, not university politics.

As he leaned back, the envelope from Professor Eliot fell from his pocket. It was crinkled and covered in chalk. Vanya scrambled to pick it up, pulling the paper with so much force that he ripped it and the folded article alongside the letter landed on the bare floorboards. He started, again, from where he'd left off.

By the time you read this, Clay is likely to be well on his way. Perhaps he will have already arrived. I'm enclosing the announcement in English. It includes the equipment he's bringing in case that might be helpful. I've elected to send this quickly rather than delay for a translation.

I'm hoping you'll find your way to Professor Clay. I don't know him personally and can't provide an introduction, but from what I can deduce he's well respected in Chicago. Both his equipment and intentions appear to be top notch.

We at Harvard are still eager to have you and your family join us in Cambridge according to our original terms. We wish you luck.

Original terms. That meant they'd only help Vanya and his family if he had both the equations and the photographs. And the news that this professor Clay was coming meant Vanya still had a chance at both. The room around him fell away as he pictured what he had to do to get his family out of Russia. Riga wasn't far. Just a few days by train. And he had thirty-nine days to make his way there. He could use his savings to bribe the right officials for papers and a train ticket. And if he had the equations, there was no question Clay would invite him to join the expedition and allow him to use one of his photographs to prove his math. Vanya would even pay for the privilege if he had to. He reached for his Russian-English dictionary. He'd taught himself to read enough English that he could translate the article himself tonight and as he cracked the spine to get started, he grinned. He could still save his family. And he could still beat Einstein.

IX

The next morning, earlier than usual, Miri sat in the kitchen. She hadn't slept and wanted to get to the hospital early to check on Sukovich. If he was awake, she wanted to be the one to tell him what happened, to check his sutures and to change his bandages. When Vanya made his way downstairs, he looked exhausted. His eyes were nested in dark circles, his hands stained with ink. Somehow he looked taller and thinner, as if he were receding into himself. He leaned down and kissed her cheek. He didn't say anything to try to alleviate her guilt and shame over the operation. He knew better. Instead, he refilled her cup with tea and added one spoonful of jam, just as she liked it.

"Vanya, is that you?" Baba called from the pantry, where she was measuring flour.

"Yes. Good morning, Babushka."

"You were up working on equations?" Miri asked.

Vanya shook his head. "Did you talk to Yuri?"

"About what?"

Just then someone knocked on their rear door; sharp, hard staccatos shook the wood. Miri stilled the spoon in her glass. The tea continued to swirl but the fruit sank. No one came to the house at this hour except the baker's boy, and he never knocked like that.

"Who's there?" Babushka asked.

"Ilya Dragunovitch." The police officer they secretly bribed to keep them safe, who warned them when tax collectors were trolling, when the Okhrana took an interest in them or their friends. Baba hurried him inside and then leaned into the alley to see if he'd been followed. There was no one. She shut the door quickly behind him. Ilya was short with pitted skin and downcast eyes as large as prunes. His jacket was damp. Even though it was early, Vanya poured him vodka.

"Say what you must," Babushka ordered. "You shouldn't be here near daylight when someone could see you." Her green eyes were narrow, and her gnarled fingers twisted together. Miri moved to stand at her grandmother's side.

"I had to come," Ilya said. "Terrible news. You've heard about the archduke. Assassinated in Sarajevo."

"That was more than two weeks ago. What's happened?"

"Conscription. For the Jews. War is coming quickly." He kept his eyes down and drank the vodka in one swallow. "The Jews leave soon for the south. They'll be first in the line of fire. Ivan Davydovich…Vanya, professors won't be spared. You're not *useful* in war." *Useful.* The word was like a slap. Miri reached out to squeeze her brother's shoulder. Ilya continued, "No Jewish man or boy will be spared. Not doctors. Not anyone."

"Surgeons?" Vanya asked. "Surgeons will be sent to the front?"

"*Jewish* surgeons will go to the front," Ilya said. His visor slipped from his hands. It thudded against the floor. The medallions on his chest clinked as he bent to retrieve it. He looked toward the door before he continued. "Stragglers will be executed. I'm sorry. I am."

"Don't be, child. You've done well to warn us," Babushka said.

He looked again at the door, more anxious this time. "I must go. I can't be late."

"Of course," Baba said. Miri was taken by how calm Baba sounded, how she could remain in control even now. Baba slipped money into Ilya's pocket. "Thank you. Truly."

When he was gone, Baba turned to face her grandchildren. Vanya was crumpled in his chair as if he'd been injured. "What is it?" she asked him.

"He said *Jewish* surgeons will be sent to the front."

"You're worried for Yuri?" Miri asked.

"It's not what you think," Vanya said.

"We'll pay whatever bribes are necessary to keep you both out of the war," Miri said.

"What do you mean, Vanya?" Baba asked over Miri. "Not what we think? How?"

"It's too late," Vanya said.

"Nonsense," Baba said. "We have time to flee before we witness another Odessa."

"There won't be another Odessa," Miri said. "Russia has changed since then."

"Oh, Mirele," Baba sighed. "Death will come again. They'll blame us Jews. For war. For starvation. Cold. Haven't I taught you? Hasn't the past been loud enough?"

"Even if you're right," Miri said, "we've been through this. I have patients who need me. I can't leave them. And we don't even know if it's true, about the conscription."

"It's true. Ilya's never failed us," Baba said. She was right. If the odd little Russian officer said Jews were being conscripted, they were being conscripted. Both Yuri and Vanya would be taken. Baba continued, "Do you want your brother or fiancé to die serving the czar?"

"Neither of you heard me," Vanya said, his voice rising. "It's already too late to run."

The kettle on the stove hissed. Miri's stomach tightened. "Why?" she asked, her voice quiet.

"Yuri," Vanya breathed.

Baba came closer, slid her curled fingers over Vanya's. "What has Yuri done?"

Miri's mouth was dry. The air felt like sand on her tongue. Vanya looked at her and didn't blink. "He's volunteered for the army."

"How do you know?" Baba asked.

"I heard him talking to a senior surgeon. While Mirele was getting changed. Yesterday."

"He wouldn't do that," Miri said.

"I'm sorry, Mirele. I should have told you right away."

"But it doesn't even make sense," Miri continued. "Volunteered? Why?"

"Tell us exactly what you heard," Baba said.

"He traded himself. For Mirele. In exchange for her promotion. The hospital was asked to provide one surgeon. They were going to draw lots. But Yuri…"

"He'd never do that," Miri said, her voice so rough she didn't recognize it. Baba reached for her, wrapped her hand through her granddaughter's so her fingers entwined in both of her grandchildren's. "He wouldn't," Miri said.

"Perhaps he didn't weigh the consequences," Baba said. "Men can be rash."

Even as Miri opened her mouth to protest, she knew Baba was right. Of course, this explained everything. Many feelings came at once. Sadness. Fear. Anger. Guilt. Disappointment. More than anything, didn't Yuri realize she wasn't willing to risk losing him—ever? "I have to find him," she said. "Talk to him."

"Not yet, Mirele," Vanya said. "There's something else." He pulled an envelope out from his pocket. Miri recognized it. The letter that was delivered the day before. Vanya moved to open it but Baba stopped him.

"Not here," she said. "The neighbors will be up soon. We can't risk them hearing all our secrets. Come to the cellar."

"No. I have to find Yuri," Miri said.

"Not yet," Baba said.

X

Vanya opened the hatch hidden in the kitchen floor, and Babushka hurried down the secret stairs as if she were strengthened by the news of their danger. In contrast, Vanya slumped and Miri felt her own shoulders stoop as they trailed behind. How could Yuri do this? she asked herself as she looked for a match and began lighting candles. He would never survive a war.

The cellar space around them was large, spanning the kitchen. Moisture made the room smell like mold. There was a fireplace stacked below the one in the kitchen so it shared a chimney and could burn without being detected, keep them warm even in the coldest winter. Shelves lined the walls with what should have been canned fruits and vegetables, but instead were piles of books—Miri's medical texts.

The cellar had started as a shelter when Miri was a child, but as she'd grown, it became her office. Babushka wouldn't let her use any other space in the house, because if the Okhrana ever came and found so many books in Miri's room, Baba said, they'd suspect they were harboring a spy, or worse. They'd never believe a woman—a Jewish woman—was a doctor. Especially when their own officers couldn't even read. By the time anyone bothered to check on her story, it could be too late. And so the underground had become Miri's retreat. She'd covered the dirt floor with rugs. She'd installed sconces that held dozens of candles. She'd brought down a desk and kept jars of specimens in formaldehyde. Like Vanya, she pinned her work in front of her, but instead of equations she displayed diagrams of the body and anatomy, attached them to the front of every shelf so they hung down as a curtain over the books. Just two nights before, she'd mounted specifics for the dissection of a spleen.

Babushka allowed it all so long as the space under the stairs was clear, the space where they sat now, on cots facing one another. Vanya wound the phonograph, a gift from a politician on his daughter's wedding night, which they used as an extra layer of sound protection. Notes from a violin concerto rang in a high trill as Baba pulled Miri and Vanya so close their curls mingled. Without fresh air the room's smell turned to must and heat, making Miri feel even heavier.

"In the blink of an eye, life changes," Babushka said. "Mirele, are you listening?"

"I'm trying. It's just—" She bunched her hands into fists. "Yuri." She hit her thigh.

"You must put your anger aside."

"But…"

Baba cut her off by holding up her hand. "Our escape is all that matters." Since surviving the pogroms, Baba had made an escape route for every house she'd occupied and journey she'd taken. She'd mapped out passages through the mountains and along rivers. She'd checked train and boat schedules and always knew when and where to find a way out. And she'd shared it all with her grandchildren, made sure they could do the same. And do it quietly, because the key to escape is secrecy. Even friends must know nothing. "Miriam?"

"Yes. I'm listening."

"Good. We follow the first path we planned. North by land, west by sea. We leave for America. Today."

"Baba, we don't have papers. And Yuri…," Miri said.

"That's what I'm trying to tell you," Vanya interrupted. He held out the letter from Eliot. It was dusted in chalk and wrinkled as if it had been read a thousand times. "We don't need another word from Yuri. He did what he did. Now we focus on this." He shook the letter. "Our way to America runs through Riga. I'm heading to Riga."

"Riga?" Miri asked.

"Yes. For the eclipse."

Miri shook her head. "How can you even think about the eclipse when Yuri's about to be sent to the front? When you'll likely be forced there as well?"

"That's just it. I need to leave for Riga before my orders come in. While I still have room to go," Vanya said. "There's a new expedition. Eliot told me about it. An American scientist named Russell Clay is planning to photograph the eclipse from Riga. In thirty-eight days. He's due to arrive any moment. If I can get there and show him the math, he'll share the photos. Then Eliot and Harvard will have us."

"This Russell Clay, he's already agreed?" Baba asked.

"No. But I can convince him."

"You can't be serious," Miri said. She let go of Baba and walked across the room, started ripping down her diagrams of the spleen. The sound of paper tearing made Vanya flinch, but she didn't stop. "You don't have equations yet. And why Riga?" Vanya had talked enough about the eclipse that she knew all the other expeditions, before they were canceled, were headed inland where the ground was flat and open. Riga was a bustling port. It would be hard to find a vista wide enough for a clear view.

"I'll have the math in time. I know it. And Riga, it's still in the path of totality, still along the centerline." Vanya took a deep breath. The violin unfurled into staccatos off the phonograph. "Clay based his decision on something called the cloudiness factor. He's taken the historical average of weather patterns, decided his best chance for clear skies lies in Riga."

"You trust a man who uses the past to predict the future?" Baba asked.

"I don't trust him. I don't even know him, but he's all I've got. There's nothing I can do but accept it and find him. Convince him to take me. And he will. Once I have the equations. I know it. I can't miss this chance. For science. For us. There's no other way."

"That's absurd," Miri said. She threw the destroyed diagrams into the hearth and turned to face him. "Riga's outside the Pale." Surely Vanya knew. Even *useful* Jews needed papers to travel outside the Pale, and those took time to obtain. "The eclipse can't be your priority. Not now. Besides, you could be wrong about relativity."

"I'm not. This idea, this theory." He stopped. "Gravity bends space and light. The eclipse will prove it. And that proof, it will change everything." Vanya lit a cigarette and handed it to his sister, then lit another for himself. The tobacco worked its way into Miri's bloodstream. She felt the prickle in her chest, the rush in her head. Yuri and her brother, neither of them were thinking straight. How could these men be so brilliant and so naive at the same time?

"You can't go," Miri said. "Neither can Yuri. Baba's right. We need to get you both out of Russia before the czar's army devours you. We'll leave today."

"You know we'll never make it anywhere without papers," Vanya said.

"Nonsense. I have a plan," Baba said.

"Yes, but the czar's army has swelled in Kovno. If we run, we'll be caught," Vanya said. "Professor Eliot. Did you hear me? His offer stands. A legal way to America. Besides, proving relativity is about more than war. It's about progress," Vanya continued. "War will come. I have no doubt. It will end, too. And then, in time, another war will erupt. Isn't it possible that if we know our place in this universe, we'll have less to fight over? More to work toward?"

"Wait for a better time," Miri said.

"There won't be a better time," Vanya said. "I'll go to Riga. You and Baba will meet me at Aunt Klara's in Saint Petersburg. For Rosh Hashanah. That should be enough time for us all to travel. And there will be fewer soldiers there. Then we'll go north, then west to America. Together."

"Your American at Harvard will support us? You're certain?" Baba asked.

"If I have the equations and photographs, I'm certain."

"A tall order."

"All of us. Including Yuri?" Miri asked.

"You still want him? Yuri?"

"His intentions were pure even if his actions were misguided," Baba said. And Miri couldn't object. Even as angry as she was.

"Baba's right," Miri agreed. Her voice sounded furious. Still, there was no question in her mind. "I love him. He did it for me."

Babushka continued, "Vanya, I don't like that your plan requires us to be apart. Nor do I like that it keeps us in Russia longer, but if Eliot supports us, you make a good argument that our passage would be safer. I can't dispute that."

"Then it's decided," Vanya said.

"No. It's not," Miri said. "It's a terrible plan. If Vanya goes to Riga, he'll be dodging the conscription order. Riga is west, not south where the Jews are headed. Which means he'll be called a deserter. Vanya, they won't show mercy if you're caught deserting."

"They won't catch me."

"Your sister has a point," Baba said. "Imagine the torture they'll inflict on you for running to Riga. If they call it desertion and kill you, that'll be the best of it. You know what they do to families. A death sentence is never singular."

"Please. The Okhrana are after the Bolsheviks. Not scientists."

"You're wrong. Think of the Sokolovs." Jewish Kovno would never forget the Sokolovs. The child was twelve when his mother refused to send him to the army, and they couldn't afford the exemption tax. A day later the Okhrana hung the entire family on the same post, left the bodies to rot for a week. "Perhaps there is another way.

The czar won't want a cripple. Miri, you can take a few fingers."
Baba used her hand to snip the air. Vanya flinched back on the cot.

"No, no," he said.

"You won't be able to shoot. But this way, you can go to Riga
without worry."

"Baba, please," Vanya said, paler now. "I'll leave for Riga before
the orders come through so I can say in good conscience I'm not
deserting. If the Okhrana come for me, I'll hide. Just as you've
taught. Trust I can do that."

The music from the phonograph caught a crescendo that bit
through the cellar, climbing, climbing. And then the needle slid from
the record. Babushka took a deep breath.

"No," Miri said.

"What do you mean, no?" Vanya asked.

"I mean no. You can't do it. You can't run to Riga alone. It's too
dangerous."

"Mirele, do you think you can stop him?" Baba asked.

"I have to."

"I'll find you. After the eclipse," he said.

"That's what Mama and Papa said, too. We'd be together again."

"This is different."

"Yes. This is war." Miri began to shake. She crossed her arms over
her chest to hide her trembling. It wasn't just that she was terrified
of losing Vanya and Yuri. It was that she felt like a spectator in her
own life, watching it crash, and there was nothing she could do to
stop it. Vanya would go. She saw that. But she had an idea, or the
beginning of one. Maybe Miri could help keep him safe—at least a
little longer. "Do you have a way to Riga?" Miri asked.

"Not yet."

"Delay. Please. Give me an hour," Miri said. Before he could
respond, she ran up the steps.

XI

Miri stood in the street just outside the house, still trembling, flooded with anger and fear. Horses clopped past, covering the stink of rot with manure and overpowering birdsong as their shoes ground against stone. Miri took a deep breath to get a hold of herself, then balanced on tiptoe, searching for Yuri's usual black taxi driven by the hunched man with a great white beard. She didn't see him yet, but she expected he was on his way to pick her up so they could go to the hospital together, going through the motions as if this were a normal day because he didn't know about the conscription order. Nor did he know she knew what he'd done.

Furious as she was, she had to focus on a plan because what mattered was the future—keeping her brother and fiancé safe. Baba was right; Yuri's intentions had been pure.

When she didn't see him coming, she ran down the street, searching. If only Yuri would listen, perhaps she could keep them both safe. She grabbed the handle of a carriage she was sure held her fiancé. The man inside was too surprised to say anything before she slammed the door, sputtered back.

Where was he? She craned her neck, stared through windows. *There.* Miri was certain this time. "Yuri," she said. Before she could manage another word, he pulled her inside.

"What's happened?" he asked.

"Please. Stop the horses," she said between gasps. She didn't realize how fast she'd been running. The wheels came to a halt.

"Tell me. What is it? Your grandmother?"

"Vanya heard you," Miri said. "With Rubenstein, I assume. Vanya heard you. The deal you made. For my promotion." Yuri still held her, but he turned away. "You traded yourself. How could you?" She was crying now.

"Should I continue, sir?" the driver called.

"No. Not yet," Yuri said in a rasp Miri had only ever heard from patients in pain.

"How could you?" Miri asked again. "How could you do it?"

"I did it for you."

"The others will hate you for it. And me. Even if it saves them, they'll hate that you've forced their hand. You could lose your position, your standing."

"What do I care?" Yuri said. "You and your grandmother talk about real friendships, about people who can be trusted. Are any of them true friends?"

"They're Jews."

"So what? You're all I care about." He held her tighter. "You have your brother and grandmother. You can't understand." He stopped, and she could feel him willing himself to stay in control. "I have no one else left."

"What do you mean?" He'd never said anything like that.

"Now's not the time."

He was right. She took a deep breath and tried to stop her tears. "You've volunteered. It means you have a say in your posting? Not like conscripts. For the right price?"

"Why?"

"I need you to go to Riga. With Vanya. There's a new expedition meeting there."

"For the eclipse? He's still talking about that?"

"Of course. And I want you to take him." Yuri grimaced and Miri realized her voice had stopped shaking. "Hear me out. You tell me that in some situations there's never a good choice, or a right choice." She explained about Ilya's visit, the conscription order, and the expedition to Riga. If Vanya succeeded, he could take them all to America.

Yuri didn't respond, not at first. Instead he stared through the window. The streets were swelling with men and women, bicycles, carriages, and cars. "You want me to secure a post in Riga and take Vanya with me?" She nodded. "I'd have to make him my medic."

"Use my baba's rubies." Gems from a necklace they'd started taking apart a year earlier. They still had a dozen left. "Whatever you need for bribes. Just do it."

"No."

"No? After what you did, after you volunteered without even discussing it with me, you won't consider it?"

"I'm sorry I didn't tell you. I'll say that a million times, but I don't regret it. And I can't take your brother to Riga. Even if I agreed, he wouldn't. He's never approved of me."

"He's my brother. He'll never think any man is worthy. You know that."

"What if he dies under my watch?"

"It won't be your fault."

"In your heart, you'll blame me."

"That's not true. I'll know together you were stronger. No one survives without help. Please. You owe me this."

"Owe you?" He stopped and looked at her. "I've never heard you speak like that."

"Only thirty-eight days. We can escape afterward. Professor Eliot will bring us to America."

"All of us? Including me? You're certain?"

"Yes."

"We will be deserters. If we leave for the eclipse, and to meet you afterward, they will try to hunt us down."

"Yes, that can't be avoided. For Vanya there's no other way." She spoke quickly and her arguments sounded only half formed because they were. But since that was all she had, she kept pushing. "Vanya won't leave Russia without witnessing this eclipse, can't secure our way to America without it. This is his life's work. And there aren't as many troops in Riga. Perhaps by then they won't even be able to spare soldiers to track you down. Besides, even if you stayed, neither of you would survive a war. Vanya, he'd rather calculate trajectories than return fire. And you, you wouldn't fare much better. You're too gentle. And being cloistered in a hospital won't keep you safe." They looked at one another. "Please, Yuri. We'll meet in Peter. From there, to Finland. To Sweden. And now we have a way to America." She took his hand. "You and Vanya. If you must serve, if Vanya must see his eclipse, can't you do both, together?"

"We'll marry in America?"

"Yes. We'll meet at Rosh Hashanah, marry in America."

"Mirele. I'll take Vanya with me to Riga."

XII

O nce Vanya and Yuri both agreed to Miri's plan, time ran too fast. In less than an hour, they'd packed their bags and marched together to headquarters, where Vanya volunteered before the conscription order was made public, and together he and Yuri requested a placement in Riga. That was the only way, Yuri said, because volunteers had some choice in their placement, with the right bribe. Conscripts had none. And once they were gone, as much as Miri wanted to grieve, she willed herself to believe it would work as planned, that they'd reunite in Saint Petersburg soon. There was nothing else she could do. At least Vanya had taken a few of Baba's rubies to pay for the photographs, for bribes—or for both, if necessary.

They had only barely moved swiftly enough. Before nightfall, the czar's army swooped down. No Jewish house was spared. No Jewish child over the age of eight was safe. When Babushka heard the first glass shatter, a window next door, she grabbed Miri. "We must hide," she said. "Looting will be the best of it." Tzvi, the boy who lived across the street, yelled for his mother. Miri wanted to rush to him, to hide him with her and Baba, but before she could move, she saw him heaved into the back of a wagon. That poor child.

Baba took Miri's arm. "Hide," she hissed. All the kindness in her voice was gone, replaced by an urgency Miri had never heard. "Survive."

But before they could move, a soldier burst through the kitchen door. An ogre caked in mud. His eyes were narrow and cold. Baba was the first to confront him. He brushed her aside as if she were an insect, and she hit the wall. The pots overhead rattled. One fell. It landed with a thud that left it lopsided. Miri screamed. "I'm fine, child," Baba mumbled, but Miri saw her gaze was unfocused.

Miri heard the soldier coming toward her. She didn't have time to bend for the dagger in her boot, the one Babushka insisted she take everywhere, so she grabbed the misshapen pot, whipped around meaning to defend them with it, but in that same instant, he took hold of her wrist and the two were locked together. The pot in her fist hung suspended over them. The soldier looked surprised by her strength, by the fact that she didn't let go or give in. But he was stronger and he seemed to like taunting her, not overpowering her as quickly as he could. She understood that once she stopped fighting, he'd be merciless.

"Maratovich, enough," Ilya Dragunovitch yelled. He shoved the soldier away. "Leave this Jewish whore. Go! Our orders are for men and boys only." Ilya shook a piece of paper between them to show Maratovich the supposed orders, but Miri saw that Ilya held the paper upside down, and Maratovich didn't object. They were both illiterate. The pot fell. The soldier skittered to the door, and Miri staggered back. Terrified and full of rage.

"Dr. Abramov," Ilya whispered once Maratovich was gone. "Are you okay?"

"Fine."

"I almost didn't recognize you. Did he hurt you?"

Could she recognize herself? She'd never fought anyone in her life, not really. Her dress was torn. Her hair was loose. She didn't see any cuts or blood, but still she felt injured.

Babushka was talking, waving for Miri to come close. "Stop muttering," Baba said.

"I wasn't." Was she?

"A ruby. Give Ilya a ruby." Yes, Baba was right. Miri reached into the secret pocket sewn into her grandmother's belt and took one. "Child, clear your head."

Miri caught Ilya at the door and slid the gem into his hand. He closed his fist around it. Then Miri went back to her grandmother. "We need to get into the cellar and hide," Baba said.

"Not yet. I'm going to the Yurkovs'." Their neighbors. The bakers. "I'll bring their boys. They can hide here. With us."

"Mirele, you're not thinking. Ilya can't protect you out there. You won't make it to the Yurkovs'. If they're smart, they'll be hiding, too. All we can do is try to stay alive until the morning. By then, maybe…" She didn't need to finish for Miri to understand. Baba was right.

Miri opened the hatch in the kitchen floor and helped her grandmother down the stairs. The cellar seemed darker than it had been. And the smell of mold was replaced by something metallic, something closer to blood. Baba slumped onto the cot where they'd sat just that morning, a lifetime ago. Miri pulled a blanket over her grandmother and climbed into bed with her, tried not to imagine what was happening to their neighbors even though their screams were piped through the chimney. When the terror hit a crescendo, it made Miri shake so violently her teeth chattered. Even with her eyes open she couldn't stop picturing little Tzvi being heaved into the wagon, hearing his mother's screams. She hated herself, hated that dozens of neighbors all around them were suffering and she couldn't, wouldn't move. That she wasn't helping.

"There's nothing we can do. This isn't Zhytomyr," Baba said as she stroked Miri's hair. Baba had told Miri and Vanya stories about the famous Jews of Zhytomyr at least a hundred times, and with each repetition the story started larger, more like a fairy tale—but better because it was true. Led by youth groups, the Jews of Zhytomyr stood to fight when a pogrom broke out. They turned the attacks into a bitter battle, killed as many as were killed. The czar's men won—but the Jews of Zhytomyr fought, and that was what mattered. They inspired others to do the same. But there in Kovno, there were no youth groups or trained Jewish fighters. If Miri tried to take a stand, she'd be slaughtered. "One day, Mirele, it will be different. Perhaps in America."

Miri nodded and realized they were alone. Truly alone. Everyone they loved was dead or far away. Had Mama and Papa felt this way when their boat sank? What if the Russians started burning houses the way they did in Odessa? Baba had been right. In the blink of an eye, Kovno had changed. But did they have to run as far as America to find safety? Life in the United States wouldn't be perfect, only better. The Okhrana wouldn't come in the middle of the night. Neighbors wouldn't disappear. They had family in a city called Philadelphia. Baba's cousins had written describing their lives there, saying their work left them bone weary but safe. Safe. Only now did Miri understand what that word meant, did she begin to understand what her grandmother must have seen as a girl.

When the screams died down, Babushka fell asleep and Miri lost herself thinking about her mother. She remembered her smell, the creams she used on her dry, cracked hands, her promises that they'd meet in America. Of course, now that would never happen. What else would she lose? Miri was scared to get on a boat, scared to stay, but she understood she had no choice. Not anymore. She kept her eyes wide and waited for morning.

XIII

Only two of the Abramovs' windows were smashed that night. Ilya had protected them, and so Miri rewarded him with another ruby in the morning when he sneaked into their house before dawn to tell them the conscription roundups, and looting, were over. The additional ruby was a rich payment, yes, but both Miri and Babushka were alive, and that was worth any jewel. And they needed him to continue protecting them. For now, he was their best hope.

Miri watched Ilya tiptoe off over shattered glass. Would Vanya and Yuri find a man as good as Ilya to help them, too? Then she turned back to the house and went into the kitchen. She didn't know what to do. She was used to Babushka taking charge, but she feared her grandmother was more shaken than she'd admit. She was up in her room, resting. Ilya had helped carry her up, and now Miri stood staring at the lopsided pot still on the kitchen floor while she heard women outside sweeping splintered wood and glass. The neighbors were scrubbing away the blood because once it was gone they would be free to imagine their children were safe. They could dream their sons were the lucky ones who'd make it back alive. Miri had seen too many women at the hospital who'd done the same in the past, and it broke her heart.

Miri thought about going to help them, but she couldn't bring herself to step outside. She was still shaking. Was still scared and ashamed of herself for it. And on top of it all was another layer. Anger. She was still enraged that Yuri had gone behind her back, enraged that Vanya put the eclipse above their safety. And, this was the heart of it, disappointed in herself for letting it happen, for pushing the two men she loved into the army, the very place she had hoped to protect them from at all costs. There hadn't been time to think. Had she acted too quickly?

Miri went to check on her grandmother. Baba's eyes were closed, but Miri knew from her breathing she was awake. "What do we do?" Miri asked.

"You go to the hospital." Baba's voice was weak. "Appearances are important."

"But we're leaving."

"Not until Rosh Hashanah. If we leave earlier, people will be suspicious. We don't want questions. The women will be here soon. We'll mourn together. Dream of our boys coming home."

"I don't know if I can go to the hospital."

"You must. Our neighbors look to us for strength, and we will provide it."

Miri knew Baba was right. Theirs was an odd position in Kovno. While on the surface the generosity of Baba's clients made it appear that Miri's family, the Abramov family, was integrated into the Jewish community, they weren't. Kovno's poorer Jews thought the Abramovs were above them, and the richer Jews believed they were below them, but both agreed Baba's position went beyond matchmaker— she was the anchor that held the community together. And they needed her and her sitting room where they could gather because, above it all, Kovno's Jews were united by ideas, by the belief they could assimilate and become *Russian* Jews, not just Jews. Nearly one quarter of Kovno's population was composed of Jews who shunned their ancestors' black hats and insular enclaves, who chose to dress and work in the mold of their cosmopolitan neighbors. Kovno was one of the few cities in Russia that permitted its Jews to make this choice, to join guilds, become politicians, and even live in the center of the city as long as they were *useful*. All for a price, of course. A double tax and an outrageous tariff on "Jewish meat," on butcher shops, grocers, and professions. This group believed their updated way of life was worth it, even worth the lingering violence against them. Or they had. Now what did they think? Baba was right; many would arrive soon to discuss and debate.

Miri helped her grandmother out of bed. She brushed her hair and braided it, her hands becoming steadier as she worked. By the time her grandmother was ready to receive clients, Miri was, too. Downstairs they found a dozen women collected outside their front door. Miri and Baba hurried them in, and then Miri excused herself and started toward the hospital—alone, painfully aware of Yuri's absence.

She walked over blood in the cracks between cobblestones and found a woman cowering at a wall. Her eye was injured. The woman had her hand over it, and blood had dried down the back of her arm even while it trickled through her knuckles. "I'll help you to the hospital," Miri said as she pulled the woman to her feet. In another block, an old man with a wagon saw them. Miri had set his son's broken leg a year earlier. The man offered to take them. "Thank you," Miri said, and helped the woman into the wagon. Along the way they stopped to pick up a girl with a broken arm, a woman left for dead but who rasped loud enough for Miri to hear, her skirts gone, and others. None beaten as badly as Sukovich. At least on the surface.

Dr. Kozlov, Yuri's replacement, met Miri at the door just as she was leading the injured inside. He told Miri she was permitted only in the women's ward, that she was prohibited from operating. Already, it seemed, with Yuri gone, the power of her promotion diminished. But didn't she deserve that, after she'd failed? Either way, she was too tired, too scared to object. And there was too much work to be done to worry about her own position now.

After twelve hours on her feet, stitching wounds, setting bones, and wiping tears, Miri was near collapse. She staggered to her office and sat down in the chair across from the sink. From that angle she stared into a mirror. She had her grandmother's green eyes and dark curls, the same ones Vanya inherited. Yuri called her beautiful, but that night she recognized the beginnings of the same circles she saw under Babushka's eyes, along with the same lines around her mouth. She felt far older than she should.

XIV

When Miri came home she expected to find her grandmother in their sitting room, surrounded by a crowd of mothers and grandmothers still consoling one another or debating how to move forward, how to save their sons, but from three blocks away, Miri saw the house was empty. The lights were on, but there were no women standing near the windows, no carriages parked in front. And it wasn't just their house. The neighborhood was deserted. Even the street cleaners who made rounds at this hour were missing. The conscription order had hit hard, yes, but it felt too quiet even for that. Something else had happened. Miri broke into a run. Her footfalls ricocheted off the gray stones, sounding louder than they should. "Babushka?" She must have yelled. A neighbor opened a window.

"Miriam Davydovna, do you need help?" Elena Levovna, the baker's wife, called.

"No. Thank you." Miri hurried inside. Just past the door she found Ilya.

"We've been waiting," Ilya said. His voice was harder than it had ever been. His eyes, though, were soft and apologetic. He raised a finger to his lips, asking her to keep quiet. She didn't understand, but already she knew something bad was coming. Her heart rattled.

"What are you talking about?" Miri whispered.

He gestured with his chin toward the sitting room and used the same hard voice. "Dr. Abramov, I presume? Your grandmother is waiting for you." Still not understanding, Miri dropped her bag and pushed past him. She found Baba in her chair with her fingers twisted together in her lap. Her skin was pale, translucent, and her shoulders were folded forward so she looked smaller. "Baba," Miri said, dropping to her knees next to her. "What?"

"Mirele, please, greet our guest." Baba inclined her head toward the shadow at the cold hearth, and Miri smelled the stranger before she saw him, the reek of stale cigars and sweat. He hovered in the corner. A tall, thick man dressed in black. He was wound with strength and his eyes were so dark they matched his suit. Although they'd never met, she knew him because he was exactly as Vanya said he'd be.

"Miriam Abramov," the man said. "It's a pleasure. I've heard so much about you. From your brother, of course." She knew that was a lie. One of Baba's first rules was to keep home at home. Miri calculated she could have the horn-handled dagger from her boot in a heartbeat.

"Kir," she said. Though she tried to keep her voice polite, it came out sounding like a hiss.

"Yes. Kir Romanovitch," Baba said. "The chair of Vanya's department." The one who stole her brother's work. Babushka must have known that was what Miri was thinking because she glared at her granddaughter, a warning.

"I've been your brother's mentor for all these years. Teaching him what I can. Did he mention I've been promoted? I'm now the head of the university." He gave a shallow bow. "I'm worried for Vanya. I do hope he wasn't caught up in that nasty business, the conscription. Ilya Dragunovitch, please." He signaled for the officer to come closer. "Light the fire. The women are freezing. Look at how they tremble." Kir turned back to Miri. "I came as soon as I could."

"You're too late," Baba said. "Vanya's gone. I told you."

"Yes. He should have come to me. I told him I could keep him safe."

"Maybe he didn't want your help," Miri said, even though she knew she shouldn't.

"My granddaughter means that Vanya is proud to serve Russia," Baba intervened.

Ilya stumbled into the room. He struck a match and it broke. He tried again, two, three times before the kindling under the grate caught. Flames slapped the bricks. Smoke spiraled. "I could have kept Vanya from the war. We're so close to an equation for relativity," Kir said.

"Of course," Baba said.

"I thought you were denied funding for it," Miri prodded.

"He was thrilled for your support," Baba said, her voice rising over Miri's.

Kir ignored them both and continued, "I was the one who pushed for his acceptance into the university, you know. Despite him being a Jew."

"Tell me, how can we help you?" Baba asked.

"I'm hoping to carry on," Kir said. He approached the fire, took the poker from Ilya, and stabbed a log. "I'm hoping he's left notes behind, some of what we were working on. I want to finish what we started." Liar, Miri thought. Kir looked at her as if he'd heard. "Imagine what it would mean for Russia, for the work on relativity to be finished by a Russian. Not that I expect either of you to fully understand. But you do know the czar's glory on the battlefield could be magnified by my—our—glory at the university."

Miri expected Baba to object, but instead she sighed. "Look through his things. Maybe you'll find what you need," she said. "Take it all."

"Baba?"

"His room is upstairs."

"Good. Ilya will show me. I understand he knows the way." Kir paused to let his words sink in. Miri tried not to let him see her cringe. No one was supposed to know about their relationship with the officer. Kir flashed a cruel smile. "Yes, Ilya Dragunovitch has become very close to your family. I know all about it. But after tonight he'll come with me. You'll need someone else to keep watch. I've already made the arrangements."

"You're putting us under guard?" Miri asked.

"After all that's happened, you need a guard to keep you safe. Don't you think? Surely Vanya would appreciate it," Kir said. "Miriam, you've seen what's happened without protection, the wounds your Jewish neighbors bore, that you stitched today? The watch will be around the clock. Someone will accompany you to the hospital. Another will stand outside your front and back doors. We will make sure you're never hurt again."

"I don't—" began Miri.

"Thank you for looking out for us," Baba interrupted.

"Of course. This way you'll be safe. And when Vanya comes home, or tries to contact you, I'll be able to help."

"Oh, now I understand perfectly," Miri said. She looked to Baba to say something but her grandmother only nodded. How could she keep her face so still? Her anger under control? It took all Miri had not to spit on Kir before he turned to go upstairs. Ilya went after him, but his toe caught the side of the divan and he tripped.

Baba leaned down and put a hand on his shoulder. "Is your family safe?" she whispered.

Ilya nodded. His eyes were wide and scared. He scrambled to his feet and up the stairs. Once both men were in Vanya's room, Baba pulled Miri close. "Our poor Ilya."

"Anyone can be cajoled into talking," Miri said.

"Yes, of course. It's what I've always said."

Miri got up off her knees and sat next to her grandmother. Above, she heard books hit the ground, papers ruffle and tear while she watched the logs crumble in the hearth and disintegrate into ash.

Ilya came down five times carrying bundles of journals and notes. Miri assumed Kir would try to reconstruct Vanya's equations, but he'd never succeed. She knew her brother well enough to know he'd taken the notebooks that truly mattered. It was why Baba was so willing to let Kir take whatever he wanted; still, Miri hated how easily she'd given in.

After Kir left, Baba turned to Miri. "We go upstairs now," she said. "And burn whatever remains." Miri nodded. Before following Baba, she peeked through the curtain. In the thin lamplight coming from the corner, she saw the new guard posted at their door.

XV

Before Miri left for the hospital the next morning, Baba leaned close and whispered, "Start keeping track of the guards. They'll have a schedule. When it's time for us to leave, we'll need to know them better than they know themselves. Which ones sleep. Which ones drink."

"You can't escape a cage until you know its shape and weakness," Miri said.

Baba smiled. "Good. Now go." Miri kissed her grandmother and left through the back door. She didn't recognize the officer stationed there. Still, she nodded a greeting just as Babushka had instructed. And she nodded to the other guard who appeared a block later and followed her to the hospital, keeping a distance of ten paces between them.

At work, Miri fell into her routines, making her way through the women's ward, checking on patients she'd seen before and tending to those who were new, but not performing surgeries. Dr. Kozlov didn't bother checking in. She was too rattled by the guard looming in the corner to care that he ignored her. At the end of the day, when the sun sank and three stars rose overhead, she walked home and fell into a fitful sleep in Vanya's room, curled under his sheets remembering the nights he used to read to her until she fell asleep, or whispered their favorite fairy tales. Like this, her days fell into a rhythm where she worked from dark to dark, never setting foot in the sunshine.

Soon the unseasonable cold was swept away, replaced by

unrelenting heat. Warm rain spread pollen over the city. There wasn't a crack that wasn't contaminated with green dust. News from the borders began to percolate and none of it was good. Soldiers trickled into the hospital with training injuries. Already they were losing eyes, ears, and limbs. Miri checked everyone to make sure they weren't Vanya or Yuri. She'd seen the damage that bullets and fire caused. Even her fiancé might go unrecognized in his own ward.

All the work and waiting exacted its toll. Miri was forced to take notes when before she could remember. At night she stared at the moon for hours from Vanya's bed, imagining she could see it waxing larger. She found comfort in the thought that Vanya and Yuri were looking at the same moon. Yuri had asked Miri to marry him under a full moon. Where were they now, Yuri and Vanya?

Then came the boy. It was late. The hospital was dark and quiet save for the occasional moan. He was no more than twelve years old, lying on a gurney in the hall just outside the women's ward, the only space available when he came in. Miri didn't know how he'd escaped conscription. Above the blanket his face was serene, beautiful—but too white. She asked the nurse, Tamara, the child's name. "Anatoly," she said.

Earlier that day, he'd been felling trees and the ax had slipped, or he'd missed. Either way, the blade had sliced his thigh. The old man paying him to do the work had fought in Japan and knew how to tie a tourniquet. As Anatoly lay in front of Miri, he was still alive, only barely. He'd lost so much blood that if she made even a small mistake, there was no question he'd die. She'd located the vein she thought was the main source of blood loss and tied it off, but she couldn't be sure that was it until she removed the tourniquet. After that, if there was another bleed, she might not be able to save him. There just wasn't time. "Doctor." Tamara was looking at her with concern.

Miri blinked away her memory of the fishmonger, focused instead on the anatomy of the thigh. Then she asked, "You looked for Dr. Kozlov?"

"He's gone."

"And the others?"

"It's late," Tamara said, and Miri understood not a single other surgeon was still there. But she knew that without asking. She was only stalling. She also knew that even if she sent for a surgeon now, none would come. Not at this hour. Not for a child from the slums. Tamara ran a hand over the boy's forehead and pushed his hair back the way a mother would. Her dark skin was soft with wrinkles. She had a speech impediment, and while most assumed she was slow, Miri knew better. "He's lucky you're here," Tamara said.

Miri pretended there was something in her eye so the nurse wouldn't see her tears starting. Yuri told Miri that every surgeon makes a mistake the first time they operate on their own, but with Sukovich he'd been by her side. Now, Miri was alone.

She took a deep breath and double-, triple-checked to make sure she had the right clamps and sutures. Then she nodded to Tamara and counted down from ten. At zero, she untied the tourniquet. Blood came instantly, and Miri knew her worst fear was real. She searched for the artery, but it had retracted, which meant it was the source. She dug into Anatoly's leg, searched for the end so she could clamp it shut. She hoped since he was so young his body would be pliable but it wasn't. It was stiff, as if he was fighting her. His muscles flexed and his joints went rigid. She couldn't see. There was too much blood. She pushed deeper, knowing she was causing more damage than she should, but at least he might live. Finally, she could see enough to parse muscle from vein, and it was then she realized the blood had stopped. Anatoly was dead.

"No. No," Miri said. Tamara had her arm over Miri's shoulders.

"Shhh," the nurse whispered. Was Miri yelling? Tamara held her with a force that made her quiet but not calm. Her panic expanded so the room went darker and a high-pitched ring strangled her ears. Until a few weeks ago, she had never made mistakes like this. Yuri—any other surgeon—would have saved him, she thought as she dropped to her knees next to the table. She rocked back and forth. He had been so young. Too young. Why wasn't Yuri here? Tears dripped off her chin and marbled into Anatoly's blood on the floor.

Tamara was next to Miri now. "No one could have done better," she said.

"He was only a child."

"Yes. But think of the little girl this morning. You sewed her finger, saving it. You perform wonders."

"Not enough."

"Doctor," Tamara said gently. "When will it be enough?" She helped Miri to her feet and down the hall. "Let's get you cleaned up." Miri gave her one hand to scrub and then the other. The nurse peeled away Miri's surgical gown while Miri felt the black shroud of guilt tighten around her. "Anatoly is no longer in pain. He is at peace. But you are here," Tamara said. "We need you here." She bustled into another room for a clean towel.

"Do you?" Miri asked the empty room. It was the one question that terrified her the most.

When Tamara returned, Miri sat slumped in the same chair she'd sat in the night she made tea for her and Yuri after she discovered him at the piano. She was certain now the other surgeons were right in doubting her. "I need to find his mother," Miri said. She likely didn't even know her son had been injured.

"I will tell her," Tamara said. "Tomorrow. She lives in the slums by the river."

"No. I have to find her. Tonight. She should know tonight."

"I'll go with you, then," Tamara said. "Your guard will keep us safe."

"No. I can't take him there. He would terrify the neighborhood."

No Jew wanted to see an officer lurking, especially at night. "Tell me where they live. I'll go without him."

"How?" Tamara asked.

That was the only easy answer Miri had. Every summer in Birshtan they practiced evasion because Baba insisted the day would come when they'd need to know how to escape. "I'll wear your nurse's hat. You'll take my coat. We'll fix our hair the same way and slip through the back door. You'll go first. Walk to my house. I'll leave ten minutes after you and walk to Anatoly's. The guard, Igor, will follow you. He won't know better. If you walk in the right direction, in my coat, it'll be enough." Miri was certain it would work. "Walk slowly to give me as much time as you can."

"But, Doctor, he's there for your protection. Not mine."

"I don't need it."

"What happens if he finds I've tricked him? What do I do when I arrive at your house?"

"If he stops you, tell the truth. That he's confused us." Better to make it Igor's mistake than Tamara's treachery. "And if you get to my house without being stopped, you can slip through the alley to the main street and walk home from there. Now tell me, where do they live?"

Tamara hesitated but only for a second to check on Igor. He wasn't even looking at them. He was focused on a woman feeding her new baby. Tamara leaned in and described Anatoly's neighborhood, told Miri how to wind through the streets to find his house on the darker side of Kovno. "It could be dangerous," Tamara warned.

"I'll be fine," Miri said. "I'll take my doctor's bag, just in case." Soon, Miri was outside turning down Vilnius Street while Tamara walked in the opposite direction with Igor ten steps behind. Miri knew she should have been scared or elated that she was finally free of her guard, but all she felt was black sadness for Anatoly, and for his mother, whose life was about to be destroyed.

Miri hurried. Without the sun, the air was tinged with the smell of damp and the limestone buildings that framed the road looked darker than they should. As she descended into the slums, streetlights cast shadows that magnified the laddered appearance of the tiled rooftops. She tucked Tamara's hat into her bag and tried to think about how she'd break the news to Anatoly's mother. She thought she was following Tamara's careful directions, but she didn't know this section of the city, and in four turns she was lost. She tried to retrace her steps, but when she came out at the river, she knew she was even farther from where she wanted to be, deep in the city's underbelly of mills and factories. She looked around, tried to plan her route home. The triangular roof on the tower of Kovno Castle loomed in the distance. The bulk of the train station rose nearby, and the Great Bridge hung overhead. She'd always seen it from above where the stanchions were polished and the road sparkled with lamps, but from this new perspective she saw it was decrepit. And the riverbank that appeared pristine was in fact a wasteland of gravel littered with rags and fish heads coated in pollen.

At least she knew the way back from here. As Miri turned toward the path leading uphill, a train shot over the bridge. The wheels pummeled the rails with a force that made the shore vibrate. Cattle car after cattle car barreled across. When the engine's roar was gone, Miri heard a new sound. Splashing and kicking at a desperate, fevered pace. Someone had fallen from the train and was swimming toward her.

Miri crouched in the shadow under the Great Bridge and watched the swimmer. There was no wind, no moon, only the reflection of streetlights on the river. The swimmer was a man. His kick was fierce but he pulled with only one arm. The water rippled in strange patterns under his desperate stroke. He must have been injured. And the river's temperature would only make his swim harder; its water flowed down from ice in the mountains so that even in summer it was frigid. Still, he fought. She wondered who he was—a Bolshevik? A criminal? She couldn't bring herself to leave until she was certain he'd made it safely ashore. Miri narrowed her eyes, as if squinting could help her see him better, but instead she heard footsteps nearby. On the other side of a hodgepodge of weeds and brush she saw the silhouettes of two men making their way up the river, walking in her direction.

The men stumbled. Drunk. Were they coming for the swimmer? Miri realized she was hidden from view and trapped. If she moved, they'd see her. If they came for her, no one was there to help. She braced herself against a damp slab of stone.

"Tili Bom," the men sang. "Close your eyes…the night hides everything. The night birds are chirping." Their words were slurred. They plopped down on a fallen tree with a thud that cracked the trunk. They spilled over the side, laughing, and then climbed back up, set to starting a fire. Miri waited for the drunks to look at the swimmer. He was at the shore now, but they kept their backs to him. They were consumed by vodka, nothing else.

The swimmer swayed in a reflected pool of light from the lamps on the bridge. Water vapor melted up from his skin and clothes, the contrast of hot to cold blurring his outline. Still, Miri could see he was tall. His hair was black and it hung down, ragged. He examined the beach as if searching for danger. When his glance reached the bridge, Miri knew he couldn't see her but she felt he looked straight at her. She expected to see a fierceness in his gaze. For him to survive that fall, and that swim, he had to be ferocious, but in his face she saw he was terrified. He dragged a huge piece of cloth, maybe a coat, twisted around his foot and took four steps into the shadows, where he was hidden from the drunks by the brush. His teeth chattered as he fell on one knee.

She guessed he was near Vanya's age. He wore a uniform and when the buttons on his tunic caught the light, they glinted at uneven intervals. Mismatched buttons meant he didn't have access to proper supplies. Jews and Gypsies were denied those basics but they were supposed to be posted in the south, far from Kovno by now. Could the swimmer be either?

Miri looked again to the drunks. They were blind to what was happening behind them. Best to run, she decided. She stood and a single branch snapped under her weight.

"Who's there? How many of you?" the swimmer asked, looking straight at her.

"Four of us," Miri said in the deepest voice she could muster. Before she could turn to run, he had her. One hand around her arm. The other over her mouth. She hadn't thought he was well enough to move that quickly. She shoved him, pushing hard where she saw blood between his shoulder and neck, and he grimaced, releasing his hold. He bent forward with his hand on his wound but didn't come back at her.

"Please. I won't. Hurt you," he said between gasps. "I just want you. To be quiet. So the drunks. Don't hear." He looked up. "Can you help me. Find a doctor?"

"Doctor?" Miri asked. He dropped back to his knees. Landed with a thud that sent up a spray of gravel. "Why would I help you?"

"You haven't run yet. I'm hoping that means you might have a reason."

"If you could make that swim, you're not dying," she said. "You likely only need stitches. The cold will keep down the swelling. You'll lose less blood. There's a hospital in the city."

"You're a nurse, then?"

"No. I am a *doctor*," she answered and then cringed. She shouldn't be telling him this much. Nor did she feel she had the right to the title, not after Anatoly. The drunks bellowed another round of "Tili, Tili, Bom."

"Doctor? Will you help me?" She stood in silence. "If I wanted to hurt you, wouldn't I have done it already?" This was true, though he might have only been waiting for his strength to return, to get from her what he needed. But there was a gentleness under his desperation.

"You don't want my help. I killed a boy today," Miri said.

"I don't believe you."

"I'll take you to the hospital. That's all."

"No. No hospital. Can't you stitch me together in an alley?"

"Why would you trust me?"

"I see your bag. If you're not a doctor, you know enough to speak like one." He took his hand from his wound and looked at his palm, saw the blood, and reached back for his shoulder. "Kovno's Jewish hospital is famous. Modern. Not like any Russian hospital. I believe they'd appoint women. That's your hospital?"

She knew better than to admit she was a Jew. "My sex doesn't bother you?"

"No. I need a doctor. And I like women." A small grin slid across his face. And while she hesitated, she took a closer look at the swimmer in front of her. When people are in unbearable pain, they often lash out, but even at his lowest this man was kind. There was a weight to him, something she couldn't define but that she could trust. She took a step closer, placed one foot on the object he'd dragged from the river. It was a military greatcoat. The lapel faced up, and in a sliver of light she read the name *Grekov* embroidered on the pocket. It was strange to see a winter coat in summer, a greatcoat with a name on it. Stranger still to think he'd dragged it while he swam, but she didn't have time to ask questions. The drunks could notice them at any time. And while she took this in, he also seemed to be considering her. He eyed her dress, her hair, perhaps deciding if she really was a doctor. He was near enough now to touch.

"I would need to examine the wound," she said. "I mean, I need to see the skin, to help." He nodded to tell her it was okay and stayed still as she peeled back enough of his tunic to see thick blood oozing just where he'd held his hand. The cut was as long as her thumb, and deep. "A knife?" she asked. He nodded again. She ran her hands over his chest, pressed his ribs to make sure they weren't broken. She felt for a swollen abdomen. Nothing. He had no other injuries. He wouldn't die from blood loss, but it would weaken him. "I'll bandage the wound so you can run and find someone else to stitch you back together."

"Thank you." The soldier looked back at the drunks and then stared out at the river while she unfastened the rest of his jumbled buttons. His top was part of a cavalry uniform. It didn't match his coat or pants. The movement it took to pull his tunic down must have caused enormous pain, but still he didn't cry or yell. He squeezed his eyes shut, curled his lips around his teeth, and bit down as if he were used to pain. She couldn't help but feel sorry for him, for that. She reached for her bag and wrapped a bandage over the wound, then around his chest and under his arm to secure it. She pulled as hard as she could. Pressure was the only way to slow the bleeding. He sucked in air as she tied the knot. Then she pulled his tunic closed and held out her hand to help him up. His calloused palm chafed against her own. "No one will ask questions if I bring you in to the hospital. They won't find out you've deserted."

"I'm not a deserter."

A glass bottle shattered. The sound was close. Miri's chest went tight. The drunks' singing had stopped. They were no longer perched on the tree trunk. She scanned the riverbank, frantic to find them, but didn't see them anywhere. "Can you run?" Miri asked.

"*Mir muzn. Nu, kum,*" the swimmer said. *We must. Come.* Yiddish. He knew she was a Jew; he trusted her to know that he was, too. And even though she was in more danger now with the drunks after them, there was relief in knowing that. Miri reached for her dagger. Could the swimmer fight with one arm? When she looked up to see, he was gone. In the next instant, a fat hand grabbed her wrist and squeezed so hard she was forced to drop the blade. She couldn't move.

Miri was alone.

"Shhhtop where you are!" the drunk who held Miri yelled after the swimmer. He wore a hat that flopped over his face and wielded a broken glass bottle as a weapon. Miri felt terror like she'd never felt before, pounding and visceral. And she felt a burst of strength but couldn't do anything with it—she was trapped. The only thought in her head was Baba yelling, "Escape." Miri kicked at the drunk's shins but he moved out of the way. "What's a lady like you doing out here with that deserter?" he asked.

"Let go." She tried to pull free but he held tight.

"Oh, she fights?" He sounded as surprised as he was amused. "Oleg, you see her knife?"

The second drunk stepped out of the shadows. His smell was rank. He was bald, missing two front teeth. "There's a ransom for deserters," he said. "Deserters like yours. Where's he?" She spit in his face. "Ah, he's deserted you, too?" The bald man threw his head back and laughed as he wiped the mess away. He wasn't nearly as drunk as the other. "Sergei," he continued, "you lazy rat! You see she's alone? Bring her to me. I'll show her the way a real Russian man acts."

As the one with the hat, Sergei, yanked Miri forward, he stumbled. Miri took the opportunity. She kicked, and this time she landed her heel on his shinbone. He howled and fell, dropped the broken bottle. Just as he tried to push himself upright, Miri kicked his knee out from under him. He slipped and landed facedown with a thud. Something under him crunched. He moaned and she pulled her hand back to strike him, but the bald man grabbed her arm and yanked her off his friend. He'd pulled her so hard she thought her shoulder might come clean out of its socket. He drew her close. Her back was against his chest. He smelled like rotten fish. "I like that you're feisty," he said. He moved and she heard his belt buckle clatter.

"No." Panic. All she felt was panic. "No," she yelled as loud as she could.

"Oh, yes."

She stomped his toe. He loosened his grip enough that she wrenched free. The bald drunk lunged after Miri, and at that same moment the soldier that Miri had helped flew out of the dark and caught the drunk by the waist. Whatever blood loss had frozen him before, he ignored, tackling the drunk so they rolled toward the river, grinding against rocks.

The drunk with the hat moaned again. But this time his lungs rattled. Miri heaved him onto his back and skittered away when she saw the broken bottle now lodged in his chest. Blood poured from his mouth. The shards had pierced his lungs. He was drowning in his own blood.

She looked back at the two men fighting, rolling on the ground. The soldier landed a blow to the drunk's ribs, at his kidneys. The drunk reeled and tried to slink away, but the soldier used his legs like scissors to catch him and pin him down. Then in one swift motion the soldier landed a vicious strike, his fist to the drunk's jaw. Even from twenty paces away, Miri heard the bone crack. The drunk went limp and collapsed.

In the next instant, the soldier was in front of Miri. "We must go," he said.

She didn't move. She couldn't. All she could do was stare at the dead drunk. Sergei. The second person she'd killed that day. Yet she could still hear the echo of the belt buckle, still feel the terror it brought. "I said we need to go," the swimmer said. His voice sounded far away even though he was in front of her. "Can you hear me? Doctor?" The soldier leaned down to hoist her over his shoulder.

She jumped to the side where he couldn't reach her. "Why would I go with you?" she asked, shaking her head.

"I didn't mean to leave without you. I thought you were behind me."

"Why did you come back?"

"I repay my debts."

A train rumbled over the bridge. The light on its pilot swept across the beach, catching the bottle jutting from the drunk's chest. "He's dead," Miri said, still stunned.

"Self-defense." The soldier's voice was calm. "He would have killed you. Or worse. Please. Come, we must leave before someone finds us."

"We want someone to find us. That other man needs help."

The soldier leaned down toward Miri and somehow forced her to focus on him. "If someone finds us here, we'll both be thrown in prison. Probably killed. I'm a Jew. I believe you are, too. That dead man is Russian. No one will bother to hear our story or even ask why."

"You're wrong. I'll tell the truth. That I was defending myself."

"Has the truth ever helped in our country?" He winced and grabbed his shoulder. "Please, let me see you home, make sure you're safe. Deliver you to your family. You saved my life."

"I didn't save your life. I bandaged your shoulder."

"After I'd fallen from a train and was left to die. I'm not sure I would have gotten up if not for you. Come."

"I don't know you."

He dropped his chin to his chest and raked his hand through his hair. Further downriver, there were voices coming toward them. Men were hurrying to the camp where the drunks had made their fire. What had they seen or heard? The soldier looked over his shoulder one more time and bowed. "My name is Aleksandr Grigorevich Petrov. Call me Sasha. I am a private in the Russian Imperial Army, or I was until an hour ago."

"That odd coat you're carrying says Grekov."

"It's not mine. I can explain. But not now. There's no time."

"What happened to Grekov?"

"He thinks he killed me. He threw me from the train."

"Why?"

"Please. I can explain everything but right now we must run."
The swimmer was as tender with her now as he'd been vicious in the
fight only moments earlier. He slung the greatcoat over his shoulder
and pointed to a path that led up toward the castle. "This trail?"

He was right; they needed to run. But Miri was trained to trust
no one. To go her own way. And yet—he'd come back for her. Had
fought for her. And now they were wound in a murder together.
"This way is better," Miri said. She kneeled down for her dagger in
the dirt, then started walking in the opposite direction. The soldier
followed.

XVI

D octor, which way?" Sasha asked. They stood at the edge of the trail above the river. The men below were shouting. They must have found the drunks, one dead and one with a broken jaw. It wasn't likely the drunk who survived could speak, but if he could, had he gotten a good enough look at Miri or the soldier to describe them and report them? Had he seen her doctor's bag? Miri hurried into an alley with the soldier on her heels. He was right, she thought, nothing good would come of being found down there. She'd killed a Russian. If she were caught, she'd be hanged. She directed them around a corner. "No." Miri doubled back. She wasn't thinking straight. She needed to calm down. "I meant this way."

They walked along a dirt trail that ran behind low-slung wooden homes. Here the bookbinders and the blacksmiths, the barbers and the millers clustered together and kept their distance from the beggars. Each had a yard, some with a garden. Miri was aware she was making too much noise, her feet heavy, but she couldn't help it. How was the soldier so quiet? And why was he wearing that greatcoat?

He was right about avoiding the hospital, too. There, people would ask questions: Who is this man? Where did you find him? The guard, Igor, once he found her, could report the soldier to Kir, and they'd both be whisked off to the Okhrana for an interview where she was sure they'd find a way to make her talk. They always did. She'd admit she knew the soldier was a deserter, that she'd helped him and that she was a murderer—and they'd both be killed. She couldn't let that happen. She'd take him home. Babushka would know what to do. And Miri would stitch him together. She'd have to. And she'd have to help him get away somehow because Miri's fate was now tied to his. If he was caught, he'd talk and lead them straight to her. Oh, if only she could get a hold of herself.

The farther they walked, the larger the image of the dead drunk loomed in Miri's head. Was there blood on her dress? On her hands? Was it from Anatoly or the drunk? She washed in a rain bucket. Scrubbed as long as she dared. The closer they got to the center of Kovno, the more she looked over her shoulder.

Miri directed Sasha behind butcher shops and cafés. It was dark so they couldn't avoid the heaps of slops piled for feral cats. They walked straight through the detritus, close now to Miri's house. Her neighborhood acted as a border, a no-man's-land. Below lived the families who worked for a wage. Beyond lived the families who paid those wages. Half a block from home, Miri stopped and signaled for Sasha to do the same. She couldn't risk one of Kir's guards seeing him. Even they wouldn't believe Sasha was one of Baba's clients, not as he stood now dressed in rags, spattered in mud and blood. She peered around the corner, staying hidden in the shadows. Not a single candle burned in the windows above. The Khalskis' dog was quiet. The Rusnaks' baby wasn't crying. But there was the smell of bread coming from the Yurkovs' bakery. And in the dim light of the guard's single candle, she saw his face. "Good," she breathed. "It's Arkady Vladovich tonight." They were lucky.

"Your house is guarded?" Sasha asked. "Who are you?"

"I'll explain later."

"Your head is muddled. We can't go near an officer. Not now."

"We'll be safe once we're inside. Where else can we go?"

"An alley? The forest? Anywhere."

"This is our best option. I need to stitch your wound."

"You'll do it, then?"

"Yes," she whispered. "And then you'll rest. The last place anyone would look for a deserter and a murderer would be inside a guarded house." She handed Sasha a key and told him to wait where he was. "There's another key hidden under a cobblestone. I'll pretend I need Arkady's help to get it. While he's bent over, hurry behind me and go inside." She saw Sasha hesitate, was certain he was thinking he should run. "You have no choice. And he's drunk. My grandmother will have known something happened when I didn't come home. I'm certain she's given him vodka—I just hope she hasn't slipped out herself to look for me." She saw him hesitate still. "What else can you do?"

"Hide somewhere else."

"Maybe tomorrow, but not tonight. You still need my help, don't you?" He leaned against the stones. "Please, trust me," she said. "We're both Jews. We'll both die if we're caught. I won't let that happen."

"Jews turn on one another. Where did you learn to fight?"

"My grandmother. She fled Odessa. During the pogroms. Gypsies took her and her sister in, taught her to fight, and she taught me. Listen, do you have a better choice?"

"No," he admitted, and nodded slowly. Something tugged at her, told her once she left she might not see him again, but there was no other way to sneak him into the house. Miri started walking. This time she made noise on purpose. "Arkady Vladovich, nice to see you," she called.

"Where've you been?" he grunted. "Igor's been looking for you for hours."

"I stayed late at the hospital." She tried to sound confident. "I didn't see him when I left. Where was he?"

"He followed a nurse. That idiot."

She stood in front of him now. "Did my grandmother give you that vodka?"

"Course." He winked and held up the bottle. It was half-empty.

"You know these are dangerous times, since the conscription order. We've been locking our doors and I'm not used to it. I've forgotten my key again. Would you help? We keep a spare under here." She pointed to the spot and he tripped toward it. He was too drunk to notice she stood on the stone while he hunched over and tried to dig his fingers under it. Miri signaled for Sasha to hurry, and he started walking so quietly it was as if he floated toward the house. Just as the door closed behind him, Miri removed her foot. Arkady flew backward. Miri thought he was crying, but he wasn't. He was laughing. She grabbed the key and thanked him, went inside before Arkady managed to make it back to his feet. It wasn't until she stood in the kitchen that she realized she was out of breath, that her heart was pounding. Sasha was across the room from her, waiting. She held her finger to her lips and stood still, listening.

"What is it?" Sasha asked.

"My grandmother might have gone to look for me. Or she might be here. If she's home, she might not be alone. She has visitors sometimes at night. She's a matchmaker. I wouldn't want them to see you." Her clients came at all hours, especially the ones with secrets they needed to bury, but not tonight. Her grandmother's snore came from the sitting room. The only other sound in the house was the ticktock of the grandfather clock.

Standing there, she realized Sasha was as tall as Vanya. The tang of wet wool hovered around him along with the scent of pine, the smell from a campfire. She closed all the curtains and lit a candle. He looked around as if cataloging the space. He seemed to take in the scarred table, the pitcher that held wooden spoons next to the stove, and the dried lavender. Miri reached to help him take off the greatcoat. It was covered in pollen and still damp, heavier than she expected. His face crinkled in pain as she eased his arms out. And in the light, she saw his lips were blue, shivering. She hesitated only for a moment before letting him into the family's secret. "Our cellar.

You'll hide there," she said as she heaved the hatch open. "I'll boil water. Wait for me downstairs. There's a cot and blankets."

"And no way out."

"I've told you, you can trust me."

"You never even told me your name."

His comment caught her off guard. So much had passed between them already, and yet he was right, they were strangers. Miri had never before understood when Baba said that blood is a tie that binds stronger than any other—blood spilled together or blood made together.

She bowed, imitating the gesture Sasha had performed at the river. "Miriam Davydovna Abramov. Miri," she said. His expression didn't change. His eyes were still narrow, his face still wary. She could feel him calculating. She was sure he'd leave. Wouldn't she? Rather than go down into a stranger's cellar? But then he bowed back and made his way down the stairs, clutching his bad shoulder.

As soon as she saw him reach the bottom step safely, Miri turned and stepped—straight into Babushka, who stood in the doorway that separated the kitchen from the hall. She was a vision in white, clad in her dressing gown and crowned in curls that fell down her back. Her ruby ring glinted in the candlelight. "Did Arkady see you bring that soldier inside?" Baba asked.

"Of course not. I thought I'd heard you snoring. How long have you been there?"

"Long enough." Baba came closer. She touched Miri's skirts, her cheek. "I knew to get Arkady drunk when you didn't come home. Where have you been? You're filthy. And that man, who is he?"

"A Jew. A soldier who helped me. I lost a patient. A boy. I tried to find his mother in the slums, to tell her what happened, and I got lost. Came out under the Great Bridge." Miri stopped. She was speaking quickly, but Baba was keeping pace, of course. "I killed a man. There. On the riverbank. He came for me and I killed him. That man downstairs, he fought to protect me."

"You killed a Russian?" Her eyes were searching her grand-daughter's face. Miri didn't have to answer for her grandmother to know. Baba dropped into a chair.

"I only meant to defend myself."

"And the soldier in our cellar?"

"He beat the other Russian. Broke his jaw. There were two drunks. And I helped him, too. It's how it started." Miri tried to arrange the pieces. "I found him at the river. When I was lost. He was injured. I was bandaging the wound. The drunks came after us. They wanted—" She pulled her skirt, unable to speak for a moment. "The soldier was only helping me."

"Mirele, he's not Vanya or Yuri. Or the boy you lost today. Even if he saved you, harboring him means death. Already, Russians are looking for reasons to kill us. He can't stay."

"He's a witness."

"Which is why we need to get him out of Kovno, not keep him here." She looked over her shoulder, didn't speak until she heard Arkady whistling. "Tell me. Why did you trust this soldier enough to help him?"

Was it instinct? A feeling? Miri couldn't think of a logical explanation, and yet she knew she was right. She also knew that wasn't good enough for Baba. Like Vanya, their grandmother required proof. "What's done is done. Where else can he go?" Miri said.

"Oh, child. You don't deserve this." Baba took a deep breath. "It's better you killed that drunk than let him have his way." She took another breath. "And I have no doubt you did all you could for the boy you lost at the hospital. Yuri himself couldn't have done more."

"He might have."

"Maybe. Maybe not. Doing right doesn't always feel good." Baba reached for Miri, wrapped her in her arms, and held her so tight that Miri felt her skin contouring around her grandmother's, shaping to fit into her soft curves. "We need to think," Baba said. "Sit and think and plan. If only we had more time." She ran her nail over Miri's scar, the one between her thumb and pointer finger, the scar she'd carried since the day Babushka taught Miri and Vanya to sharpen their horn-handled daggers. "This Jewish soldier, he helped you at the river? He fought for you?" Miri nodded. "Then he can stay for the night. Only one night. I will come up with a plan for him."

XVII

Miri headed down to the cellar with a pot of boiled bandages and her doctor's bag. "Your babushka. She wants me to leave," Sasha said. He'd managed to light the candles in one of the sconces and sat under a blanket on the cot. His tunic hung from a nail on one of the posts.

"Not yet. She said you can stay while I help you. Stay the night."

"It wasn't your fault, you know," Sasha said.

"I could still hang for it." She paused. "And I feel the guilt." The guilt for killing the drunk. And Anatoly.

"You must move forward." It was something Babushka would say. Look to tomorrow. Always tomorrow. Miri lit a taper for the other candles and the hearth. As she bent down to arrange kindling, she flinched at the sight of the torn diagrams of the spleen.

Fire caught in the grate. The wood was dry, and as it burned it released a sweet smell. Miri walked around the room lighting candles, all the while keeping her eyes on the soldier. In the growing flames, she saw him for the first time clearly. He was ragged and filthy. His eyes were so dark they were as black as his hair, but they were bright. A scar ran from his nose to his ear, cutting through thick stubble. One of his cheeks dimpled when he pressed his lips together.

She pulled a bench over to the hearth and asked Sasha to come and sit next to her. He tried to get up but his knees buckled from either exhaustion or blood loss, or both. She reached an arm under his, and as she put her hand on his waist, her fingers wrapped over his bare skin, too late for her to pull the blanket between them. She startled at the touch.

"What is it? Am I too heavy?" he asked.

"No." The soldier groaned as she helped him to the bench. Slowly, tentatively, she slipped the blanket off his shoulders. Dried streaks of blood pointed down his arm and reminded her of Anatoly's leg. Had that only been a few hours earlier? She started to unravel the bandage she'd tied at the river. It was blood soaked and stiff. He bristled with pain as she slipped the knot out. "I only have a small dose of morphine. Would you like it?"

"No. The pain will keep me awake. I can check your work." He tried to smile.

She didn't return the grin as she picked up the tweezers. Stitches were simple enough, she told herself. She'd made thousands before. There was no reason to be scared that she'd kill him, too. But she was. She reached for a boiled bandage and began wiping away the dirt and blood smeared around the wound, picking out gravel stuck below the surface. Sasha clenched his teeth. "I need to see your entire shoulder," she said. With Yuri there, she wouldn't have hesitated to pull the blanket down further, but here, alone, it was different. She cleared her throat. "The blanket. I need you to remove the blanket."

Sasha eased it down until his chest was bare. He shivered. His skin was smooth, but bruised. He'd been kicked in the ribs. He bore a tapestry of scars only a fighter could have earned. The largest one ran across his chest. It had come from a shallow cut. Under the stink of river water, Miri caught the same smell of sweat, of him, she'd caught earlier. She touched him with her fingertips and he flinched. "I'm sorry," she said.

"Just never had a woman ask me to take such a close look before." It was a hint of flirtation, a jab at humor, and it made Miri relax just a bit.

"I don't believe that." She smiled and felt him relax, too. She set to cleaning the wound. As she worked, memories from the river, Anatoly, and even Yuri fell away. All she saw was her patient, someone who needed her care. Pushing deeper under his skin, she found sand and realized she needed to keep him distracted from the coming pain. "Tell me about the scar on your chest."

"It's a knife wound. Fighting is a good way to earn extra kopecks." She nodded.

"The pain's about to get worse." Out of carbolic, she dipped the bandage in vodka. "How did you get into the river?"

"When did universities begin allowing women?" Miri squeezed a soaked bandage over the wound so alcohol spilled into the gash. Bubbles gurgled up. Ash fell from the log in the fire.

"One woman a year joins the Kovno Medical Academy. I was the first Jewish woman."

"Good. It's competitive. I'm in the best hands."

Miri smiled. "Tell me about the name on your coat. Grekov."

"I lied to you." At his words, Miri jerked her hands to the side, jabbing the tweezers at a painful angle. "Aye," Sasha yelped.

"You lied?"

His explanation came in bursts between pauses he took to manage the pain. "I wasn't thrown into the river. I jumped. I was wrestling. With Grekov. He's my captain. A Russian." Still wary, Miri went back to work. Sasha squeezed his eyes shut. "Grekov. The famous fool. That's why he was given a Jewish unit. It was a wager. Grekov challenged the great General Radkievich to Durak. You know it?"

"Of course. The loser's left with all the cards."

"Right. There was no way to win. Victory meant death. Loss gave him Jews. Command of us Jews. Ah!"

Miri held up a blood-soaked pebble in her tweezers. She threw it into the fire. "Why do you have his coat?"

"We were on the train. Cattle cars. Jewish transport. We wrestle, to pass time. Never with Grekov. Tonight was different. 'Fight me or die,' he said. Drunk. Aye, that hurts!"

Miri paused. His face was paler than when she'd started. "Do you want the morphine?"

"No." He pointed to the bottle of vodka Miri was using to sterilize the tweezers. She nodded and he took a long drink. "I let Grekov win. But he challenged me again and again. Told me to fight harder. Drunker Grekov got, worse he wrestled." Sasha took another swig from the bottle. "Then, I won. Grekov stood. 'Bullet or beating?' he asked.

"He whipped his gun across my face." Sasha pointed to a spot below his chin. Under his dark stubble Miri made out the beginnings of a purple bloom. The icy river must have held back the swelling. Miri threaded her needle and without warning eased it under his skin. It always hurt more when patients knew it was coming. Sasha jumped.

"Go on," she said, waiting for him to be still again. "Grekov?"

"Toe-to-toe. We stood toe-to-toe," Sasha said. "Same height but he's thin, no strength. The coat. It was hanging on the side. Next to the door."

Sasha stopped. He looked spent but Miri wasn't done. She needed him to keep talking, to keep him from focusing on the stitches. "How did you fall from the train?" she asked.

"I didn't fall. He punched me under the ribs. I pretended it hurt. He yelled, 'Open the door.' He poked his gun at my chest." Sasha put a hand in the middle of his sternum. Small, springy hairs went flat under his palm. "We were crossing a field and he wanted me to jump. But I'd die there. No cushion. Then I saw the river." Sasha stopped. He seemed to be organizing his thoughts while Miri tied off another stitch. "The river. I might survive the river. I held a strap hung from the side and taunted him. To buy time. 'You think you could push me out of this train?' Grekov landed a punch. Harder than I thought. He used his gun. See." He pointed to the bruise on his ribs. "I got up when the train was close to the water. Grekov yelled, pulled out his knife." Sasha forgot about his wound. He tried to lift his arms, to gesture with the story, but then grabbed his shoulder. "Ouf!"

"Try not to move," Miri said. She began winding a bandage across the wound.

"I ducked. But his blade hit." He pointed to the wound.

"Not a good strike."

"No. He can't fight. I didn't even feel it, not at first. I lost my grip on that strap. Reached for it, but this coat came away instead. I lost my balance. Had no choice but to push off. Jump toward the river." He closed his eyes. Tears tangled down his cheek. "I knew I had to hit the water with my feet in order to survive. Maybe the coat helped slow my fall. I don't know. And then I swam. You found me." He took her hand and looked up into her face. "Thank you."

"You will heal."

"Perhaps. But that boy, the one who died? He *was* lucky to have you, too. Maybe you underestimate yourself, Miriam Davydovna Abramov." How long did they sit there with the soldier holding her hand?

Eventually, Baba knocked on the floor above, breaking the moment. "I'm going to bed," she said.

"Good night." Miri's startled reply came quicker than it should, and she could hear Baba hesitating. "We're fine," Miri tried again, steadying her voice. Then the floorboards creaked as Baba made her way toward the stairs.

Embarrassed, Miri reached for her doctor's bag. She missed, knocked it to the floor. All her supplies spilled. Sasha got down on his knees to help gather what he could with one hand. "I'm engaged," she said. The words came before she thought about what she was saying or why.

"Of course." He smiled calmly, held out a rolled bandage and her stethoscope. Miri piled them back into her bag. "Tell me about your fiancé."

"He's kind. A doctor." Sasha looked at the hearth. The logs were embers now. "You should rest," Miri said.

"Tell me about the medical books. The ripped papers you put in the grate. Why is your work here?"

"You can read?"

"You think because I'm dressed in rags that I have no education?"

"No," Miri lied, ashamed. Didn't her own brother prove appearances didn't represent ability? She was about to apologize, when Sasha smiled.

"I'm sorry," he said. "I'd come to the same conclusion if I found me washed up on a beach. But I can read. My father taught me." Sasha groaned and stood. He pointed himself toward the cot. Miri put an arm around his waist to keep him from falling. This time she made sure the blanket was between her hand and his skin. He was even slower now than he'd been when they started. His steps were heavier.

"My brother loves to read, too," Miri said.

"Where is he? Was he conscripted?"

She shook her head. "He volunteered. So he could choose his post."

"What's his name?"

"Ivan Davydovich Abramov. Vanya. Have you met him?" It wasn't likely. But still.

"No. I can't think of any Vanya Abramov."

"He's run to Riga."

"For love?"

"Love?" Miri almost laughed as she eased Sasha onto the cot. "I guess in a sense. Vanya went to Riga for his love of science. To observe an eclipse."

"An eclipse? What is there to see in the dark?"

"A bend in the stars," Miri said.

There was a long pause between them. "He's missing?"

"Not yet."

"But you're worried. I can see that." He bit his lip, looked to be working through a stab of pain as he tried to settle. "I can find him. Help him come home to you. It would be a way to repay you for all you've done."

"You've already paid your debt. Coming back for that drunk was enough."

"No, I never should have left without being sure you were safe. And now you're risking your life, and your grandmother's, by hiding me. Did your fiancé offer to find him? Is he gone, too?"

"He left with my brother. They're together. Serving in Riga."

"I see. It's good they have each other. They're lucky."

"Yes," Miri said, hoping Vanya saw it that way. She added a log to the fire and settled on the bench to make a sling for her patient. By the time she'd finished, Sasha was in as deep a sleep as she'd seen. She crept upstairs, and for the first time since Vanya left, she didn't go to her brother's room. She went to her own room and slept.

XVIII

M irele, sweet child. It's time to wake up and go to the hospital," Babushka said. Miri opened her eyes and Baba kissed her forehead. Miri's first thought went to Vanya, and then to Yuri. Where were they waking up? Or had they been up all night? Were they getting enough food? Were they safe in Riga? She blinked and thought about Anatoly, about Sukovich. The soldier at the river. The drunk and the glint of glass in his chest. Babushka must have seen Miri's face change. "Mirele, it's done. Yesterday has passed," Baba said. "Don't linger on any of it."

"But the soldier, he's still here."

"Yes. And still in a deep sleep. I have a plan." She kissed Miri again. "We'll send for Ilya. I think we can still trust him to help with this because it has nothing to do with Kir or Vanya. When he comes, we'll pay him to say he caught the soldier stealing bread. The man is thin enough for anyone to believe he's starving. Ilya will be able to make the guards look the other way. Then instead of taking him to prison, Ilya will take him to the woods so he can run. Either way, the soldier will be gone. And you, you will remind yourself again and again. It wasn't your fault. None of this was your fault. Guilt will get you caught and killed. Now get dressed and come eat. Tell me more about the man you dragged in from the river."

In the kitchen, Babushka had heaped a thick layer of strawberry preserves onto two slabs of bread. The fruit smelled delicious, like candy. Miri had never seen her grandmother be so generous with it before and with a pang she realized the reason for it. They were leaving soon. There was no longer any need to ration berries or sweets for the winter. Miri slid into her chair across from her grandmother. The circles under Baba's eyes were deeper than they'd been last night. "You're worried that hiding the soldier will get us killed," Miri said. "Or are you worried that he might be dangerous?"

"Tell me, what did you find out about him?"

"His commander tried to kill him. He jumped into the river because it was his only hope."

"He knows Vanya or Yuri? You asked?" Babushka pressed. "Have they crossed paths?"

"He doesn't know them. But since I helped him, he says to repay that debt he'll find Vanya. Bring him to us."

"Vanya's not missing."

"We both have a bad feeling, Babushka. We never should have let him go."

"But Vanya has Yuri."

"And Yuri will need as much help as Vanya."

"The soldier knows about Yuri. That you're engaged." It wasn't a question, but a command.

"Of course."

Babushka spread strawberries on another slice of bread. Her knife chafed the crust. "I've never seen you let someone in so quickly."

"It's—it's that I've seen him at his worst, and he's only been kind."

"Do you think he's a spy?"

"No! Sasha's not a spy."

"Sasha, already? That's his name? Not Aleksandr? Oh, Mirele. He must leave."

"We should let him stay another day. He needs rest, time to heal. What does another day matter? His commander assumes he's dead. No one is looking for him. No one sees what they're not looking for. Isn't that what you always say?" Babushka shook her finger toward her granddaughter. The bracelets on her arms rang like bells, and she opened her mouth to reply but changed her mind. "He's a good person, Baba. I know it."

"We thought the Germans were good people. He could be a German spy."

"I'm not a German," Sasha said in Yiddish, standing at the top of the cellar stairs. He was so quiet even Babushka had missed him opening the trap door. In the daylight, he looked younger. And while he was dressed like any other bedraggled Jewish soldier with long, uneven hair and a uniform that made him look like a beggar, he held their stare. "Nor am I a spy. I'll swear to that. You can trust me. I owe your Miriam my life."

"Sit next to me," Baba said, making a show of using her dagger to slice the bread in exaggerated swipes. "Debt means nothing in war."

"To some, perhaps. But I mean what I say."

"Tell me, how do we know you're not a spy? A commander tossing his own man into the river? I've never heard something so ridiculous."

"I jumped. If I were a spy, I would be a merchant or working on the barges. I wouldn't be hiding in your cellar."

Babushka nodded. Sasha's eyes were wide and his shoulders were tight. He was right to be afraid of Babushka. As sharp in her old age as she'd been in her twenties, she might be slow to walk but was as fast with a blade as she'd ever been. "Can you leave today?"

"I'll leave as soon as you ask me to leave."

"Good, then eat and leave as soon as Ilya comes."

"Baba, he's lost too much blood."

Babushka ran her eyes over Sasha slowly. Miri knew she took in every fold and plane, wrinkle and line. "My Miri says you're true to your word. What do you say?"

"I say I am. And that I am your guest."

"One day under my roof. And then you're gone."

XIX

At the hospital, Miri was greeted by Tamara, who told her she'd already heard Miri never made it to see Anatoly's mother. "I got lost," Miri explained, shaking her head.

"Thank God you're safe. It's all that matters," Tamara said. "Two Russians were murdered at the river last night, near the boy's house. And to think you went without a guard." She pointed to an empty bed nearby. "The woman who was there last night, with the new baby, she knows his mother. She left already, to see to her other children, said she'd break the news to the family."

After that, Miri tended to patient after patient and couldn't bring herself to do much more than stitching and cleaning wounds. Weighed down by her guilt over Anatoly's death and her terror that she'd somehow be traced to the drunks' murders, she couldn't get her head straight all day. She referred anyone requiring a doctor or surgeon to Dr. Kozlov. Still, she worked until past sundown, wondering if Sasha would be gone before she returned, hoping he was already safe in the woods.

When she finally dragged herself home with a new, vigilant guard in tow, she found Baba presiding in the sitting room, as always, surrounded by women. There were no smiles or giggles as there had been before conscription. Instead, now they were ashen and still. The house smelled delicious, but strange. The chicken and onions simmering on the stove had a new spice added to them, one Miri didn't recognize. Baba waved Miri forward. "My cousin's son, Sasha. He's made dinner for us, Mirele. That's what you smell. Who knew a man could cook so well?"

"Ah, Cousin Sasha," Miri coughed in surprise. Someone must have caught sight of him. But why hadn't Ilya already taken him away?

"Lucky the bullet missed his bone. He'll stay awhile so he can rest. I already introduced him to the guards. Poor Arkady was so embarrassed to have been asleep last night when he arrived. I am going to find Sasha a good wife." Baba chattered away as she guided Miri into the kitchen and closed the door behind them. Then she took glasses out, clattering them on the counter to cover her lowered voice. "He's downstairs. Refused to take Vanya's room. While the kitchen door is closed, sneak into the cellar and check on him. I understand why you trust him."

"Why? What's happened? What about Ilya taking him to the woods?"

"Katinka saw him before we sent for Ilya."

"She knows his name?"

"Yes. Sasha Petrov, it's common enough. You know that. Besides, I couldn't find Ilya to help us." She shook her head. "Sasha told me how brave you were. And strong. And that he's sorry he hadn't realized sooner you weren't behind him when he ran. He thinks it's all his fault, all of it."

"That's ridiculous."

"Either way. I trust him." She filled the kettle and went still. "Kir came."

Miri stepped back, knocked one of the cups from the counter. The glass splintered across the room. "Why?"

"He's after Vanya. He knows he didn't go south, that he went to Riga. He wanted to know what your brother has planned."

"What did you say?"

"I said I don't know anything. You know Kir's new position. He's powerful. It was easy for him to find Vanya."

"But not powerful enough to fund an expedition."

"Enough with that. He has more power than us. That's all we need to know." She looked at Miri. "He's put Ilya on it. Ilya's going to Riga to bring Vanya home. It's why I couldn't find him, why we haven't seen him."

"Ilya?" Miri stepped back, felt glass crunch under her boots. "We need to warn them."

"We'll talk about this later. Now go. Check on our soldier. He'll want to see you."

"Our soldier?"

"Yes. He has offered again to help find our Vanya and Yuri so we can go to America. Maybe we need him now. So much has changed since they left. We'll have to see." Miri moved toward the cellar, and Baba stopped her. "Mirele, why didn't you tell him you're a surgeon?"

"I...couldn't."

"Sometimes even our best isn't good enough. But, Mirele—that doesn't change who we are." Baba kissed Miri on both cheeks. Then she took the kettle from the stove and made her way out of the kitchen.

Miri took a deep breath and eased down the cellar stairs, found Sasha asleep under a heap of blankets. The smell of fresh soap mixed with Vanya's cologne. For a second her heart leapt at the thought that Vanya had come home, until she realized Sasha had simply washed using Vanya's things.

The lines of pain and worry were gone in the soldier's face, but he was pale and the bruise on his cheek had flowered purple. She didn't want to wake him. Still, she needed to check for fever. She reached down to ease the blanket away. In the next instant, he shot out of bed and had a knife at her throat. She reeled back into the bookshelves. He followed, on instinct, the way an animal tracks prey. Texts fell at their feet. "I won't hurt you," she gasped. She grabbed his arm, wrapped her hands around the fist holding the blade. "It's me," she said. "Miriam. I won't hurt you."

Both stood holding their breath, staring, and then he dropped the knife. "I'm sorry."

"I came to…" She couldn't remember. A small slip and she would have been dead. He looked from her to the knife in horror.

"You just wanted to check on me, didn't you? I'm sorry."

"Yes. Yes. That's right." She remembered. "To see if you have a fever." She didn't dare reach to feel his forehead now. "How—how do you feel?"

"I don't know. Could you leave me?"

Miri backed up the stairs slowly.

XX

Thirty days to the eclipse. Seven hundred twenty hours. Forty-three thousand two hundred minutes. Time was running too quickly, Vanya thought, perched on a hill overlooking Riga's port. At least he would be able to see the eclipse here. And he and Yuri were safe, far from the front. But where was Russell Clay?

"Any sign of his ship?" Yuri asked. He sat on a stump next to Vanya, near the edge of the woods high on a stone ridge where they could look down at ships and across at the sprawling, glittering rise of the city. Every few seconds Yuri swatted at the mosquitoes. He leaned as far forward as he could, peering through a pair of binoculars down at the motley collection of boats. His uniform was pressed and clean, his hair slicked back under his cap. Why bother so much with appearance, anyway? Vanya might look rumpled in comparison, but he didn't care. If anything, he was proud that his priorities were with science, not appearance.

"It took us too long to get here," Vanya said. He kicked the brown bag at his foot, the one he carried as Yuri's medic. At least they'd made it.

In his mind, Vanya partitioned the port into a grid with twenty squares and scanned each section. The docks were rank with soot, covered in a layer of coal grime, but no matter. Under all that dirt, he saw only gold; in this city, thirty days from today, he and Clay would make history.

Clay's ship would be a three-funnel monstrosity, impossible to miss. "They're all too small, damn it," Vanya said.

"Then we should go."

"Go where?" Vanya asked. "Back to our unit? We have leave for another few hours. Besides, I've already been in trouble too many times." Punished for a sloppy uniform, for being late. He'd lost meals and his cot. "I'm done."

"You can't say that. Being a medic is keeping you alive," Yuri said.

"Nonsense. Being a medic, it got me here. That's all I needed. Now I have to focus on my work."

"That's too dangerous. You of all people know that. We must stick to our plan, not take any risks until we've found Clay, or we'll regret it." Just that morning, a young recruit named Evgeny had been lashed after being caught outside of camp. He said he was looking for food, that he was simply hungry, but their commander assumed he'd been trying to desert. Vanya didn't know which was the truth. They certainly weren't getting enough food. Either way, the beating Evgeny took was brutal. He'd likely live, Yuri said, but he'd lost a huge amount of blood, and no matter what he'd be disfigured.

"Evgeny got caught. I won't," Vanya said. His voice wobbled and he hoped Yuri didn't notice. "I won't let Clay slip past."

Yuri put the binoculars back into their case and tucked them into his bag. "You're sure, absolutely certain, Clay is due here, in Riga?"

Vanya reached into his pocket. He pulled out a frayed piece of paper. It was the translation he'd cobbled together of Clay's announcement, the one Eliot sent him. "Cloudiness factor," Vanya laughed to himself. Miri was right to call the measure, the number, absurd. But it brought Clay to Riga. That's all that mattered. Vanya read a passage out loud. "'Albert Einstein's hypothesis on relativity puts scientists into two sections: one opposed to breakthrough and one favoring. Come hell or floods, I plan to be in Riga on August 21, 1914, to photograph eclipse and settle matter once and for all days.'"

"You never told me it was a picture you were after, aside from math," Yuri said.

"What else would I need?"

"Measurements."

"Measurements that can only be taken from a photograph. The eclipse will happen too quickly for me to record what I need in the moment." Vanya sighed. "And other scientists will want to see the pictures to check and verify my work."

"What will you measure exactly?"

"The position of the Zeus star cluster. We can observe it at night and know its actual position, but what happens when it passes closest to the sun? According to relativity, that's when we can observe Zeus's light bending to gravity. To observe that, I need something to block the sun's light, so we can see past it—that's the eclipse. I'll measure Zeus's apparent position, compare that to its actual position. The right equations will have been able to predict exactly how much gravity shifts light."

"But didn't you say Clay's been chasing eclipses, recording them for years?" Vanya nodded. "Then surely if it's photographs you need, he has them."

"The images he has are all muddled. He didn't have the technology we have today."

"Brother, we have nothing. No cameras. No instruments."

"No, but Clay does." Vanya shook the translation. "Clay listed the instruments he's bringing, and he wouldn't come this far without them. Once he has a photograph, understands my work, I'm hoping he'll share it with me. Maybe he'll even let me help him. I don't know. If not, I will buy a copy from him. Take it with me to America."

Yuri shook his head. "If you're right, that he's coming to Riga, then he's late. Didn't you say he was due here last week?"

"Yes, but the date was an estimate. Given expected weather and the distance he wasn't exactly sure when he'd land. Besides, boats are often late." Vanya reached for his cigarette case, the one etched with equations. He'd spent hours, months, carving each line and symbol. Every time a new theorem was published, he studied the proof, and whenever he found something undisputedly new, he engraved the math in the silver. He offered a cigarette to Yuri. They smoked together, listening to the sound of ships creaking against the docks and men calling out orders below. The cigarettes tasted like sawdust. Vanya missed the sharp tobacco from Kovno. He missed smoking with Miri. She'd have an explanation for Clay's delay. Something that made sense.

"I miss her, too," Yuri said.

"How'd you know I was thinking about Miri?"

Yuri smiled at Vanya's surprise. "You lit my cigarette for me. You only do that for her."

"I never knew you were watching my family so closely." A foghorn blared. A narrow ship eased out of port. Its progress could only be tracked in relation to other ships. If he were on a boat below, Vanya thought, its speed would appear faster than it did from above.

"Vanya, come. We can't be tardy. Not after Evgeny."

Vanya stubbed out his cigarette. "You're right. Clay is overdue. Or we missed him. And we're too close to the eclipse to sit here day after day." Yuri nodded and offered Vanya his hand, to help him stand. But instead of clasping the outstretched palm, Vanya scrambled to his feet and took off down the hill at a run. He yelled over his shoulder, "Waiting won't produce answers."

"Vanya! This is ridiculous," Yuri called after him. "And dangerous. Please, come back."

Vanya went faster, ignoring Yuri's frustration. He wasn't going to miss Russell Clay. Eventually he heard Yuri's creaking shoe behind him, following all the way down to the ships. The closer they got, the louder the port became. Thick smoke from engines made it hard for Vanya to fill his lungs. He picked out men yelling in Russian, but the rest of the languages were a blur. The boats that had looked so small from above turned into massive beasts below. Wood moaned. Sails rattled. How much force did a ship have? Now there was a question with an answer, thanks to Newton. A problem easier to solve than finding Clay.

Yuri caught up to Vanya and grabbed his arm. "We must go back, brother," Yuri managed. He was out of breath. "These sailors, they're watching you. No good will come of it." Vanya ripped his arm away, but Yuri pointed to a group of men standing over a coil of rope. They'd stopped and indeed were staring. The czar had threatened to seize ships for his war, and if he did, these sailors would be forced to serve in the navy. Vanya couldn't blame them for hating Vanya and Yuri's uniforms, for despising them as servants of a ruler who cared nothing for his people.

Vanya pushed past Yuri, tried to walk among the sailors as someone who expected to be obeyed. The men he passed had darkened skin. Their clothes were patched. Their belts were strands of rope. They'd sailed the globe. They'd seen liars and cheats the world over. And they had to know he was a fake, but he tried not to let that worry him. He needed to find Clay.

A group of four men dressed in clothing that looked a little less gray than what others were wearing blocked the plank leading to their ship, the tallest and grandest in port. Their shoes were clean and they spoke Russian. Vanya focused on the oldest man in the group, the one who looked to be in charge. He had a black beard that grew right up to his eyes and poked out of his chin like spikes. He wore a vest and had forearms as thick as Vanya's thighs. "Would anyone like a cigarette?" Vanya asked. He held one out to the man with the spiked beard.

"Army rations?" the sailor grunted.

"Yes."

"Sawdust." The lines in his face cut deep as he laughed. "We have cigarettes ten times better from the Spaniards."

Dismissed, Vanya turned back to Yuri, but the sailor dropped a hand like a claw on Vanya's shoulder before he could move. "State your purpose," the sailor said. Yuri was right. They should have gone back to camp, but now it was too late. He couldn't run. Baba would have known to plan an escape before coming down the hill.

Vanya took a deep breath. "I'm looking for a steamer from America."

"No steamers come here from America."

"This one is called the *New York*. I know it's coming here."

"I don't care what it's called. You're wrong. Look around. This is a trade port. No passengers. No parasols."

"I'm looking for an American. Russell Clay. He'd arrive with dozens of crates."

"Scurry home," the sailor said. He shoved Vanya back toward Yuri.

"Try Libau," another man called. He was short with a razor-thin nose that was crooked in two places. "Americans go to Libau."

"Libau?" Vanya said. The name of the city had a recoil like a gun. Libau was south, too far from the centerline to make sense.

"Libau's the only place you'll find anyone fool enough to sail across the ocean in the middle of a war," the sailor with the crooked nose said.

"There's no war," Vanya said.

"Is that what they're telling the soldiers?" The sailors laughed. The man with the beard curled his lips. A wagon heavy with lumber heaved past, slowed by misshapen wheels.

Libau. What had Vanya missed? Could Clay have been diverted?

"Come," Yuri said. He tugged Vanya back toward the hill. "We'll return tomorrow, between exercises."

"No, I have another question." Vanya went back to the sailors. They stood in a tighter circle now, huddled around the man with the spiked beard. He was holding a polished box. Inside something gleamed. Vanya recognized the mark stamped on the silk lining.

"Won the Grand Prix Paris," the sailor said. "Says it right here. I traded for it. The man didn't know what he had. What it's used for. The idiot."

"She's a beauty. Even if she's German," the man with the crooked nose said.

"It's not German," Vanya said. Every sailor in the circle looked up at once. "Zenith is a Swiss manufacturer. It's a Swiss chronometer. And Grand Prix Paris, that's the model."

"How do you know?" the oldest sailor asked.

"I study time. May I? I'll show you something about this model." Vanya reached out to hold it. The sailor with the crooked nose shoved him back.

"What are you still doing here?" The sailor leered. He was so close Vanya saw skin peeling from sunburn on his nose.

"We mean no harm," Yuri said. He pulled Vanya toward the hill again.

"You thinking of stealing this watch? Or are you deserters?" the crooked-nosed sailor asked. He clenched his fists. "You look dumb enough to have a price on your head. I've seen it before, lice like you dragged back kicking and screaming. The reward's a tidy purse, isn't it?"

"We're not deserters," Yuri said.

"Then where's the rest of your soldiers?"

"We're here on orders."

"Orders? Soldiers never walk around alone like you two." The sailor smiled as he and his men formed a circle around Vanya and Yuri. All told, they were fifteen.

"We don't want trouble," Vanya said.

"Then why are you looking to steal the chronometer?"

Vanya cleared his throat and stood as tall as he could. "I wasn't about to do any such thing. I only wanted to show you how to use it, and to ask if any ships have arrived from Libau. Maybe the

American we're after, maybe he went to Libau first, then sailed here."

"It doesn't matter now," Yuri stepped in. "We're leaving."

"You are, now? As I see it, you're outmanned."

"And as I see it, if we don't report back soon, our captain will be more than happy to come down here and cut every one of your throats. Now, make way," Yuri said. He tried to push past but the sailors didn't budge. The wind kicked up and a metal clasp bounced against a flagpole. A seagull cawed. The sailor with the crooked nose crept closer to Yuri. He was shorter, twice as wide, and no doubt more than twice as strong.

When he swung for Yuri, hard, he missed but Yuri didn't strike back. Instead he dodged it, and another, before catching one to his ribs. One to his face. His cap flew off. The crowd cheered. Vanya tried to get closer but a fist clipped his chin. Vanya fell. His pants caught at the knee and ripped. The edge of his vision was black. He fought not to pass out. He was aware of men grunting. By the time he stood, the crowd was larger and louder. A man yelled for another to hold back Yuri's arms. "Let him go!" Vanya yelled as loud as he could. He might not have adored Yuri the way his sister did, but he was still family, or almost. Vanya tried to push past the sailors now hunched in a scrum. "I said let him go." Vanya kicked but no one seemed to notice.

"Enough!" someone yelled. A man Vanya couldn't see tossed a sailor to the side as if he weighed nothing. He shoved another and came to the center of the circle. "A soldier's not worth your skin." It was the older sailor with the spiked beard. He had a gold tooth Vanya hadn't noticed earlier. It glinted in the sun.

"We're fine here, Dima," the sailor with the crooked nose yelled. "Let us have our fun."

"Let the soldier go and I'll keep him away from you. Kolya, it's an order, not a question."

Kolya spat to the side and shoved Yuri forward, sent him to his knees. Yuri's nose was bloody. His shirt was stained. Vanya shoved his way through. "Just bruising," Yuri said when Vanya got to him. Blood trickled from his mouth. Vanya offered a handkerchief. It was white with blue stitches made by Babushka. The sailors loomed, still close.

"Help me to my feet," Yuri gasped. "I'll be fine." Vanya put his arm around his waist. Yuri limped. He was in pain, that was clear, and the men around them made way. Yuri reached behind a crate and picked up his bag, his binoculars. Vanya hadn't even seen him stash it there.

"You forgot something," Kolya called. He held up Vanya's medic's bag. Vanya didn't even know how he got it. Before he could step forward to take it, Kolya tossed it into the sea.

"Leave it," Yuri said and urged him toward the hill.

"Not a good idea to head in that direction," the sailor with the spikes called after them. "That hill's a stage. If you want to be out of sight, go the other way."

Vanya looked over his shoulder. "Leave us be."

"But you should know, I've seen your American. Or, I've seen an American," the sailor called. "He didn't come here by boat, but I saw him. Didn't catch his name."

"What?" Vanya turned.

"He came for a load of crates, like the ones you were talking about."

"Why didn't you say that before?"

"I'm saying it now." The sailor came closer. "Believe me or not, but I tell the truth." He kicked at the shard of a clamshell and handed Yuri his cap. "Call me Dima. What shall I call you?"

"Doctor," Yuri said.

"Doctor? Here?" Dima laughed. "You're in trouble, aren't you?" He hooked his thumbs in his belt and shook his head. "There was a ship came a few weeks past full of crates. That American, he must have come by train. He met the boat, had the crates loaded onto wagons."

"Where did he go?" Vanya asked.

"He's lying." Yuri pulled Vanya's arm.

"Straight to his hotel."

"How do you know?" Yuri asked.

"Who do you think unloaded all those crates?"

"Which hotel?" Vanya asked.

"Didn't say. But for a price, I can assist you in searching the premier establishments."

"Of course," Yuri said. "We have no reason to believe you."

"Tell me, what did you mean when you said you study time? How do you know Zenith?"

"First, tell me your price," Vanya said.

Dima laughed. "My price is higher than those cheap cigarettes you offered." He pointed to Vanya's feet. "I see your new boots. And I saw you had a pair of binoculars, up on that hill. Both will do."

"You were watching us?"

"I told you, that hill is a stage. Every day you come. Every day I watch."

"Then why not offer your help earlier?"

"I'm not offering anything but a trade. My guidance for those boots and binoculars. Do we have a deal? Or shall I feed you to the dogs, with Kolya in the lead?"

"We can still make it back to camp on time," Yuri whispered. "If we go now, there'll be no punishment." He was right. Vanya knew it, but Dima offered their first lead on Clay.

"If we don't go with this sailor, who else will help?" Vanya said.

"He could be lying."

"Or he could be telling the truth." Vanya looked over at the sailor. "You'll take us to every hotel until we find him, our American?"

"I'll give you the day," Dima said. "One day. If we don't find him by midnight, you owe me nothing. That's fair."

Vanya didn't even have to think it over. He took his arm from Yuri's waist and moved to shake the sailor's hand, but Yuri grabbed him. "There's more," Yuri said. "I always know when there's more. It's in their eyes. Tell us, sailor. What else?"

"Perhaps you're smarter than you look." The sailor stepped closer. "When I find this American for you, I have one more condition. A simple condition."

"What?" Vanya asked.

"If we find the American, you consider another business proposal."

"Consider? Or it's part of your price?" Yuri asked.

"I ask only that you listen. And consider. Perhaps you will accept. Now, we should start our search. Later, you can tell me what you know about chronometers."

XXI

Dima walked with a limp that made one shoulder dip with every other step. Still, he was fast, scurrying up and out of the port with Vanya and Yuri behind him. And while Vanya caught himself several times complaining about his sore chin, Yuri didn't say a word about the beating he'd taken, did everything he could to cover his own limp.

Soon, salty air gave way to the smell of coffee and perfume, and the piecemeal docks sank behind breathtaking architecture. Every facade was a sculpture. Flowering lintels held oversize, high-relief murals. Some depicted Roman myths, others Russian folktales. After a park, Dima stopped and leaned against a tree. At the port, he was well dressed compared to the other sailors. In the splendor of Riga, he was diminished to a figure in tatters. Even his skin looked sallow, the circles under his eyes deeper. And while Dima was less, Vanya and Yuri were more. They wore still-new uniforms, and soldiers and pedestrians nodded with respect as they passed, appeared not to notice the rip in Vanya's knee or the drops of blood on Yuri's collar.

"Start there," Dima said. He pointed across the street. "That hotel is the closest to the port. Very expensive. It used to host Americans, before the war."

"But there is no war."

"You still insist on saying that?" He pointed to the door. "I'll wait here."

Yuri and Vanya dodged a trolley. A troop of soldiers passed. Their pants were dusty. Their faces were unshaven. They must have just arrived. The influx of soldiers meant the czar was fortifying the port, that more and more units would join them.

"If we find nothing, we go back to camp," Yuri said to Vanya. "We still might be able to slip back in before we're missed."

"No. If Clay isn't here, we check the next hotel."

Yuri pinched the back of Vanya's arm and pulled him close. "Vanya, brother, you have no intention of returning at all, do you?"

"This is as close as we've ever come to Clay."

"How are we close? We have a sailor we can't trust saying he saw an American that may or may not have been Clay."

"It's more than we had yesterday. If you want to return without me, go."

"Miri would never forgive me."

"This can't be about my sister."

"How can you say that? Everything I'm doing is for your sister. And you, you don't know what you're walking into. You've never seen what the czar's men can do. What Russians do to each other— to Jews."

"And you have?" Vanya wrenched his arm away from Yuri. He reached for his own visor. He meant to pull it down, but his head was bare. When did he lose his cap?

"You don't know anything about me," Yuri said.

"If that's true, then we have a problem," Vanya replied.

"We'll search this hotel, and the next," Yuri said. "But then we're done. Do you understand?"

XXII

There were no Americans staying at the first hotel, nor had there been any in the past month. Yuri followed Vanya and Dima to the next hotel and then, after an argument that ended when they shoved each other and fell, to the next. Yuri never said he would stay, but he made no move to go, either. Instead, he walked slumped forward, sulking. They made their way through Riga in the shadows, terrified someone would stop and ask for their papers or why they were away from their unit. At first Yuri had whispered he was worried Dima might turn them in, but Dima seemed as keen to stay hidden as the two soldiers.

At one point late in the day, Dima took Vanya and Yuri down a narrow, older street lined with restaurants. It smelled like fried onions and boiled meat. "Americans used to congregate here," he said. But now it was empty.

"Stick to the hotels," Yuri said.

They tried four more locations and still found nothing. No American, or man named Russell Clay, had ever even written for a reservation. Near sunset, in front of a row of dark houses, Dima crouched behind a hobbled wagon, in a pile of straw. He gestured for Vanya and Yuri to also take cover. An army unit in formation was turning the corner, marching toward them. Their boots stamped in unison, trampling cobblestones. A woman in the house behind them closed her shutters. Then came a new sound. Steel wheels slammed against stone—a tank. Vanya had only seen one before. The wheels were constructed of metal plates that rolled over gears. The inventor of this Russian model, born and schooled in Riga, called them caterpillar wheels. The sides were reinforced with steel so thick it was impenetrable.

"Impressive," Dima whispered.

"Despicable," Vanya said. "Science should be for progress, not killing."

Dima, Vanya, and Yuri hurried forward to the next hotel, and the next. Vanya struggled not to lose hope. Near midnight, Dima's deadline, they stood in an alley to catch their breath. Seagulls cawed. Candles flickered through windows, and the smell of boiled potatoes was thick. Dima looked tired. His beard no longer spiked. "Why risk your lives for an American?" Dima asked. "Does he study time?"

"Do you intend to turn us in for the reward? Is Kolya reporting us now?" Yuri asked.

"Can't you see, he would have already turned us in if that was his aim," Vanya said. Yuri looked away, sucked on his cigarette. His cheeks turned concave as the tobacco singed.

"Doctor." Dima grinned. "Your brother has a point. If I turned you in, how would I get such nice boots and binoculars?" He paused. "Where'd you learn to fight?"

"I can't fight," Yuri said.

"That's a lie. I saw you at the docks. Kolya couldn't have hit you if you hadn't let him. Why? Where are you from?"

"Zhytomyr."

"Aha. That city has a reputation."

"You can't believe everything you hear," Yuri said.

"Then tell me this, why do you two stick together? I can't figure it out. All you do is disagree, and yet you fight for one another. I know you're not brothers by blood."

"He's engaged to my sister," Vanya said. "They work together at the hospital."

"A nurse and a doctor, a storybook tale," Dima said. "Now I see."

"My sister's not a nurse."

"She's a doctor, my student. She works under me at the hospital."

"All women are better under us, no?" Dima winked.

Yuri ignored him. "How do we know you won't turn us in?" he asked again.

"He wants his boots and—" Vanya started.

"I told you, I have a business proposal," Dima interrupted.

"Besides," Vanya said. "He's been seen with us. All day. If we're caught, the czar's men'll hang him for helping. You realize that, Dima?"

"I'm aware," Dima said. His gold tooth glistened as a truck hauling coal dragged past. "Come, to the next hotel."

XXIII

Inside the Hotel Neiburgs, Vanya and Yuri found the lobby empty. The grandfather clock in the center of the marble foyer was stopped. Vanya rang a silver bell at the front desk. A door opened and closed down the hall. Feet scurried and then a man in a red hotel uniform pulled back a curtain and appeared in front of them. "Can I help you, soldiers?" he asked. His eyes were wrinkled like raisins, and it seemed as if he had too many teeth for his mouth, all of them gray.

"We're looking for an American named Russell Clay. Is he your guest?" Vanya asked.

The man flinched, opened his mouth, and closed it just as fast. Then he peered over the desk and looked around the lobby. Vanya nearly smiled as the man's face cycled through every display of guilt Babushka had ever described. There was no question the man had seen the American professor. "I know nothing. God bless the czar."

"Liar." Vanya pounded the desk. He was not letting this lead slip away.

The manager shrank back. "I told you, I know nothing."

Out of patience, Yuri lunged over the desk and grabbed the man's hand, bent his wrist backward at an excruciating angle. "Yuri, stop," Vanya said.

"Not until this man tells us what he knows." He twisted the man's wrist harder. "I'm tired and we've risked too much. Now, tell us. Russell Clay. What do you know?"

The manager whimpered, "Better. To speak. In private."

Yuri shoved him backward. "Take us somewhere private and start talking."

They trailed the man down the hall. It was as empty as the lobby, and their footsteps echoed. They passed three offices, all closed and dark. Then they came to a fourth. Printed in gold on the frosted glass door was the manager's name: Vitaly Onegin. Onegin looked up and down the hall before letting them in. His space was cramped. It smelled stale and fit only a desk and a chair. He gestured for them to stand across from him.

"Why are you so scared?" Vanya asked.

"I honor the czar." He fell into his chair. The back collided with the wall where there was already a rut in the plaster. "It's dangerous to ask about foreigners."

"Tell us what you know and we'll leave," Yuri said.

"Yes, I can see you are a man...a soldier used to answers." Onegin pointed to Yuri's black eye. Then he produced three glasses and a bottle of vodka from his desk drawer. He was still shaking the way he had in the lobby. "A drink?" He paused to steady his hand but it was no use. He spilled as he poured. "Information costs money."

"We're not paying you a kopeck," Yuri said. But Vanya shoved his hands in his pockets and put most of what he had on the desk. All except the rubies, of course. The coins bounced. Onegin scrambled for them and began to talk.

XXIV

Outside the hotel, Dima stood at the head of an alley, waiting and smoking, watching the street. The ruckus of Riga, the clack of the tram, now interspersed with lorries carrying soldiers, set him on edge. God, how he missed the quiet of the sea. Even a storm with waves twice the size of his ship was preferable to a city. Riga in particular was vile, changing the way it was from a port to a military outpost. So much had happened in a few short weeks. All because the czar, who knew nothing about his people, his real people, wanted power. That's what war came down to—power. Show Dima a leader who cared when his people starved, and Dima would show you a fish that wasn't slippery.

What Dima hated most was the fact that there was nothing he could do about any of it. He had to keep his opinions to himself or risk being arrested—killed. You never knew who might report you. Friends turned on friends. He'd seen it. And already he knew this war would spare no one. It was only a matter of time before Dima's ship was seized and forced to haul supplies. The Russian navy had always been pathetic, scrambling for boats. Dima would never fight or sail for the czar, die making the rich richer. He spit on the ground, wiped his mouth with the back of his hand. No. He'd earn a little money from these two pathetic soldiers, and then he'd run. Maybe head south, out of Russia.

Dima was reaching for another cigarette when he heard footsteps coming in the otherwise deserted street. He peeked out from the alley. The man coming was short. His face was scarred, likely from pox, and his eyes were dark and large. Most important of all, he had a purse dangling from his belt. It was tucked inside his pants, but the outline was as clear as day. It was large and heavy. The fool.

The man came closer, looking from side to side. Dima could tell he was nervous by the way he kept peering behind him. No, not just nervous. Scared. Dima stepped out of the alley just as the man crossed in front of him. The man gave a yell. "Shut your mouth," Dima said. He caught him by the arm and hauled him into the alley, pushed him against the wall. The bricks were damp and covered in moss that made them slippery. The man stumbled. Dima held him tighter. "What are you looking for?" Dima asked. "With a purse like that, you'll get yourself killed if you're not careful."

The man grabbed for Dima's arms, tried to push him away, but Dima was stronger. Still, the man had a head on him. He struck out at Dima's throat, a fast punch that missed its mark but hit enough to make Dima stagger and lose his grip.

Dima grabbed the knife hidden at his waist. The man had already taken two steps, running back to the street. Dima dove, tackled him onto the scratched dirt and stones. The man went still when he felt the blade on his neck. They always did. And then Dima flipped him over so they were face-to-face. "Take the purse," the man said.

"What're you looking for out here? That purse is nothing but a trap."

"I'm looking for a sailor."

"This here's a port. There're sailors everywhere."

"I need one in particular. Let me live. I have more money. Not in the purse." This man wasn't a fighter but he wasn't a fool, either. Dima nodded for the man to continue. "A man at the docks told me to find a sailor named Dima, who could lead me to Professor Ivan Davydovich Abramov."

"Who's that?" Dima pushed the blade harder into the man's throat, nicked the skin.

"A man from Kovno." His voice was pitched higher now. Maybe he felt the blood.

"One man?"

"Two, but you knew that. Didn't you? You are Dima?" This man was smarter than he looked, Dima decided. Smarts could be as dangerous as strength. "Yes, I'm looking for two men together."

"Explain yourself."

"I'm Ilya Dragunovitch. A friend of Vanya's."

"You've come a long way for this *friend*."

"I've been sent for him. For his work. I went to his unit, but he wasn't there. I'm guessing he's deserted. He'll need protection, and I can protect him if he comes with me back to Kovno."

"He makes chronometers?"

Ilya blinked. "No. He's a professor. A powerful man, Kir Romanovitch, says Vanya has something he needs. They were working on science together. Vanya ran and took the work with him."

"You're saying Vanya is a thief?"

"Yes. I'm in Riga to tell him he's safe. If he'll come back to Kovno with the work, he'll be forgiven. His family, too. I have all the papers he needs to be released from his unit, so he can come with me."

"This Kir has Vanya's family?" Ilya looked down. "And you call Vanya a friend?"

"They're safe. In their house, going about their lives. Just a guard on them. And Vanya'll be forgiven if he cooperates. Kir said that." Ilya tried to take a breath, but with the blade at his neck he couldn't manage much. "Kir, he runs the university. You know what that means?"

"He has the Okhrana at his disposal." Dima looked back at the mouth of the alley. He thought he'd heard a footfall but there was no one. The street crackled with a tram. Dima dragged Ilya to his feet, kept the blade on his neck, and considered what he'd just learned—the accusation that Vanya had stolen something important. Dima had known criminals and could say with confidence that, whatever his other flaws, Vanya was no thief. "What kind of science is this Kir looking for?"

"I'm supposed to ask for something called equations. They're numbers."

"What kind of numbers are worth so much?"

"Kir only said they're powerful."

"Old magic?"

"No." And then: "I don't know."

"If they're working together, why can't Kir reproduce the numbers himself?"

Ilya shrugged and looked confused. But Dima wasn't confused. He was beginning to understand perfectly. "What's the other man have to do with this?"

"Dr. Rozen? Nothing. He's to marry Professor Abramov's sister. That's all." Ilya dared to lean back from the blade, and Dima pressed it tighter. The nick opened wider and blood trickled over Ilya's collar. An officer in the street blew a whistle to order a truck to stop. It was followed by a group of marching soldiers. They were preparing to enter the hotel where Vanya and Yuri were looking for their American.

"Are those men there with you?" Dima asked.

"No. I can't breathe."

"Why you, if you're a friend? Why would this powerful man ask you to chase after Vanya?" Dima didn't adjust the blade.

"Vanya trusts me. They're Jews. The grandmother's rich. She pays me to keep them safe. Has for years. I didn't know Kir knew. Can you help?"

"Help you find Vanya? A *friend* would ask me to help Vanya escape," Dima said, and then he shoved Ilya backward. This pathetic, groveling officer was after the young soldier to protect his own hide and, Dima was sure, to make money while he was at it. There was no heart in him.

"I don't think you understand," Ilya said.

"Oh. I understand perfectly. You're a lout." Still, Dima thought, Ilya had money to pay bribes. If Dima helped this pathetic bastard, he could be paid well, too. Vanya was a stranger to him, a man he'd known only a few hours. And it was risky to get involved with anyone connected to the Okhrana. Even more risky to help a Jew. On the other hand, this Vanya's grandmother was rich. If Dima played his cards right, he could get paid by both Ilya and Vanya.

"Pay me what you have now, all of it, and I'll help," Dima said. Ilya was already reaching for the purse. "Find me at the train station tomorrow morning. Bring more money and you'll have your professor."

XXV

Onegin, if you don't start telling us something useful, I'll slit your throat," Yuri said as he pulled a knife from his belt. Onegin's eyes went wide. Vanya couldn't believe what he'd just heard, but Onegin seemed more than convinced. Had Miri ever seen this side of her fiancé?

"You missed him by a week," Onegin said. "A week. His stay was brief, very brief. One night. He left a note for a friend, an Englishman who was supposed to meet him here. But he never came."

"Aloysius Barker?" Vanya asked. Barker was the photographer noted in the article Eliot had sent. "Hand me the note."

"I can't."

"Do it," Yuri said. He lunged forward, bringing the blade toward Onegin's chest, aimed straight at his heart. The manager held his hands up as if there were a gun pointed at his head.

"I burned it. Didn't want evidence. Besides, it was in English."

"Evidence of what?"

"Anything." He shook his head and blinked, hard. A tear slid from the corner of his eye. "Police came for Clay. I don't know why. Maybe just because he's American. They dragged him out of here like a criminal. Put him in a wagon bound for the port. He was yelling. Screaming. In English. I understood 'Brovary.' I guess he wanted to get to Brovary. There was something else he kept saying." He sniffled. Vanya slid forward onto the edge of the chair so the wood bit into his thighs. "Something about a line. A middle line. Yes, that was what he kept saying. Middle line."

"Centerline," Vanya whispered to himself. He recognized the word from translating Clay's article. The vocabulary was specific. Onegin couldn't have invented the story. "Did he board a boat? Clay, was he returned to America? And what about his friend?" Vanya asked.

Onegin made a tsk sound and rubbed his fingers against his thumb. "I heard he never made it to the port. He paid for his release. Bribed whoever needed to be bribed. Must have gone to Brovary. The friend, I told you, never came."

"Why wouldn't he stay in Riga?"

"His translator was a friend of mine. He works with the Americans when they stay here. Said Clay complained about the air. Too much soot. It would ruin photographs. But he wasn't a photographer so it never made sense for him to talk like that. That's all I know."

"His equipment?" Vanya asked. "Did he talk about his equipment?"

"He took care of a load of crates just before he was arrested. Translator told me. I have no idea what was in them or where they went."

Dima burst through the door. He was out of breath. His beard was back to spikes. "The army is taking the hotel. They're in the lobby," Dima panted, ignoring Onegin's startled protests. "Run."

With the door open, they could hear the click of soldiers' boots down the hall. If they found Vanya and Yuri, they'd ask for papers, papers they didn't have. And by now they'd been gone for so long, they wouldn't be lashed like Evgeny, they'd be hung for deserting outright. "Run!" Yuri said. He dragged Vanya from the chair.

The hall was a blur of tile and gilded woodwork. They turned and turned again. Skipped down stairs. They passed piles of onions and kitchen boys scrubbing and peeling. The back door was wide open. There were no footsteps behind them. Dima stopped so fast that Vanya barreled into him. "Take these," Dima ordered. He handed both Vanya and Yuri a crate of cabbage. "Look casual, like you're picking up food for your unit."

Dima opened the door and walked out first. There was enough light from the kitchen to see the alley was slim. Stone. Yuri followed with Vanya behind him. If they could just make it to the turn, thirty paces, there was a chance they could escape without ever being seen. It was too narrow to walk side by side. They moved in single file. Dima and even Yuri seemed to glide over the cobblestones while Vanya flopped and tripped. How did Yuri navigate so well while Vanya, who'd spent summers training with Baba, seemed to catch every uneven crack? There were voices behind Vanya, but the blood rushing in his ears was so loud he couldn't make out what they said. He just had to get to the corner, to the shadows.

"I ordered you to stop!" A hand landed on Vanya's shoulder. Vanya screamed. His heart banged so hard he was sure his ribs would crack. "Soldier, why are you carrying cabbage? Soldier!" Vanya dropped the crate. The heads rolled. "Your papers." The man holding Vanya was an officer. The medals on his chest were arrayed in perfect rows. His face was scarred by a line running from his forehead down over one eye. Vanya fumbled through his pockets, fingered his cigarette case. Would the silver be enough? If only he hadn't given so much to Vitaly. The officer snapped his fingers. Vanya showed empty palms.

"I could have guessed." The officer kicked a cabbage.

"I…" Vanya knew he had to be smart. A good idea was all that would save him, but he was good with numbers and folktales, not excuses. What could he say?

A whistle floated down the alley. Three notes. A signal. Dima? "Who's there?" the officer asked. "Popov!" He snapped his fingers. "Popov, see who's there."

Vanya hadn't noticed the soldier standing behind the officer. He was large, too large for the alley. He shoved Vanya to make way, and still his belly ground on Vanya's chest. A cat skittered, and the hulking soldier disappeared around the corner. There was a scuffle. A man grunted. The dull smack of flesh hitting flesh. Then the sound of a weight falling to the ground.

"Popov? Answer me!" the officer yelled. He squinted, trying for a better look, but didn't dare take a step forward. He shouted into the darkness behind him for backup. In that split second, Vanya twisted free and ran as fast as he could—until he turned the corner and fell on something. Popov. Yuri heaved Vanya back to his feet and they took off.

XXVI

Vanya and Yuri followed Dima through the twisted back labyrinth of Riga and turned onto a narrow street littered with restaurants for rougher locals. Men's voices mixed with accordions and spilled out through cracks in warped windows. How far had they run? Vanya couldn't judge. All he could think about was keeping pace and staying as far away as possible from any other soldiers. Suddenly, Dima swung himself inside a wooden door that looked like it had been repaired dozens of times. Vanya and Yuri followed.

The smell of salt water was the first thing that hit Vanya. Then came the stink of vomit and the cacophony of voices. Women, prostitutes, laughing. This was a sailors' public house. "Get away from the entrance, dumb bastards," a man called to them as he pushed through the crowd. He slammed the door shut and turned to face them, went still with the rest of the room. All eyes were on Vanya and Yuri—on their uniforms. "They with you?" the man who'd closed the door asked. Dima nodded and the man broke into a wide smile. He had blue eyes and only one arm. He wore an apron, and Vanya realized he was the barkeep. "Leave it to Dima to drag in stray soldiers. Step back from the window." Then he lowered his voice. "In here you're safe."

"Thanks to you, Pyotrovich." Dima nodded. He put a hand on Vanya's shoulder and led him and Yuri past men playing dice and cards, toward a table tucked under the stairs. The curtains over the windows were frayed. The candles on the walls gave off black smoke and the stink of lard but enough light for Vanya to see Yuri for the first time since they'd run from the Hotel Neiburgs. Yuri was winded and sweaty. His black eye looked worse, and dried blood ran from his nose to his lips. In the space of only a few hours, Yuri had transformed from the prim, respected doctor to a man who fit in among all the others in that bar, save for his uniform. Vanya pulled Yuri to the side so Dima wouldn't hear. "You fought Popov?"

Yuri rubbed his nose and winced. "I had no choice. I was protecting you."

"Why?"

"You're as close as I have to family. Dima helped. Popov was stronger than I anticipated."

"Dima fought for us?"

"I was just as surprised."

Their conversation was cut short when a sailor shoved them to the side so he could pass and wrap Dima in a bear hug. "Thank the lord you're safe," the man said in a booming voice. It took Vanya only a moment longer to recognize the crooked nose. Kolya.

"We should leave," Yuri said quietly. Vanya nodded and they shifted back against the wall while the two sailors clapped one another on the back.

Dima asked, "The czar's men didn't take our ship today?"

"No, not yet. There's always tomorrow." Kolya ticked his head toward Yuri and Vanya, who had made it only a few steps closer to the door. "What the hell are they doing here?"

"They're my guests." Dima gestured to them to come back, laughing. "Stop trying to leave. There's no place else that's safe. Pyotrovich, a bottle for the four of us. And dinner. Join us, Kolya." He grabbed Vanya's arm and took him back to the table. Kolya followed. As did Yuri, who kept his back up against the wall, his eyes on the sailors. Once the vodka came, Dima filled their thimbles and insisted they toast, and toast again. It didn't take long for the alcohol to ease some of the tension. Pyotrovich brought black bread and broth, balanced on a tray that he somehow managed to hold steady with his one good hand as he wove between tables. Toward the front of the room, two sailors were locked in an arm wrestling match. One was thick and broad, the other thin and twice as tall. Sailors around them cheered.

At their own table, Dima and Kolya talked about ships leaving, trying to dodge the czar's men, while Yuri and Vanya scraped at their bowls. It was Vanya who dared to address the sailors first. "Where's Brovary?" he asked.

"You found your man, then?" Dima asked. "I figured as much when I saw you in the manager's office. He's in Brovary?"

"What did you earn for it?" Kolya smiled, and slung an arm around Dima. "You slippery bastard."

"His boots and binoculars!"

"I lost my binoculars this morning."

"Fine, I'll take just your boots. That's enough," Dima said. "Brovary's outside of Kiev. A long way from here."

"We can't be sure Clay's there," Yuri added.

"He has to be. The manager said Brovary and used the word 'centerline.' It's a technical term for the darkest part of the eclipse," Vanya said. "He wouldn't have known it unless he'd heard it. And Brovary is in the centerline."

"An eclipse?" Dima raised an eyebrow. "That's what this is about?"

"Eclipse is the devil's work," Kolya said.

"I assumed you were looking for passage to America. That you wanted to track down an American to help you escape this hellhole," Dima said. "Does this have something to do with your university?"

"How'd you know Vanya has anything to do with a university?" Yuri asked.

"You mentioned it."

"We didn't."

"It doesn't matter," Vanya said. "We're going to the eclipse. The

American is going to help me with my work. Then we'll head to the United States."

"Vanya! Quiet," Yuri snapped. He was right. Vanya knew it the minute he'd said it. He never should have admitted they planned to desert for the eclipse, or to leave Russia. Babushka would have been embarrassed by the mistake. The Okhrana were always lurking, especially in a spot like this where men gossiped freely. And the memory of Evgeny, the lashes he'd taken, wasn't far. Nor was Sukovich or Beilis.

"Doesn't matter what they wanted. They found their man. Pay up," Kolya said. "I'll go for vodka. When I'm back, if you don't have your boots, I'll make sure you get them." Kolya pushed away from the table and stumbled through the crowd. More than one man slapped his back, threw an arm around his shoulders as he passed.

Vanya took a cigarette out and lit it on the lard candle, not risking his lighter being stolen. He felt as if every sailor in the pub was watching, even while they went about their business. The fat made the tobacco taste horrid, but still it was tobacco. A heavy man trudged up the steps. A cloud of dust fell over the table, into their bowls and thimbles. "What does your eclipse have to do with time? And the chronometer?" Dima asked.

"Math. It starts with math," Vanya said. "Tell me, how is your chronometer set?"

"Vanya, this is a waste. He's a sailor. Come, we should find a safe place to stay for the night," Yuri said. He leaned close to whisper, "Onegin could identify us. He saw Dima. Could lead them here." He made to stand but Dima held out a hand signaling for them to wait.

"The manager from the hotel?" Dima asked. "He's gone. Shot in the street." He shrugged. "After I left the alley I saw it, while you were still helping Vanya. Can't say why." And then: "If you leave, where will you stay? You're in uniform, in a sailors' neighborhood. You think you can make it without help?"

"Give him your boots and we'll go," Yuri said. "We'll risk it."

Vanya motioned for Yuri to give him a minute. "Please, Yuri. He's smart. Can't you see that?" Vanya turned to Dima. "Which clock do you use to set your device?"

"I never thought much about it. Any clock in the port."

"But what if that clock is wrong? You know a small difference here, spread over thirty days, can take you off course at sea."

"Aye, it's true. That's why I traded for the new chronometer. It's more precise."

"Only if you have the right time to start."

"Vanya, please," Yuri said.

"No, this is the heart of it. It's a problem for anyone who depends on a map or a schedule, and I have an answer." Vanya slapped the table to make his point. The thimbles rattled. "We use light. Light travels at a constant speed. That means we can use it to synchronize clocks. And the eclipse, it's part of my study of light. I use numbers, equations, studying light."

"You have so many answers," Dima said. There was a challenge in his voice.

"More questions than answers. But I'll figure it out. I'll get to the equations."

"So you don't have them, these *equations*?" Dima asked.

"No. But I will," Vanya said.

"Really?" Dima shook his head. Why was he smiling? He reached into his pocket for his own cigarette. He used a lighter instead of a candle, and immediately Vanya smelled the pure tobacco. An image of Miri sitting in his room, smoking, flashed in his mind. For the first time, he wondered if he'd see his little sister again. Dima leaned across the table. His barrel chest pushed the edge. "How will you get to Brovary?"

"We can figure it out," Yuri said.

"Are you certain? How would you have fared on the docks today without me? Or behind the hotel?" A cheer came up from the table on the far end of the room where the men had been arm wrestling. The thinner, taller man raised his arms in victory. "I can take you to Brovary."

"For another fee," Yuri said.

"I've worked coal depots. I know the trains and I can get you to Kiev."

"And what about your business proposal?" Yuri asked.

"My proposal?" Dima tipped his chair back. He circled one thumb around the other. The front door opened and carried a gust that sent the lamps flickering. "I'll let you keep your boots. And I'll take you to your man, in Brovary. I'll even help you secure passage on a ship out of Russia. Afterward..." He paused. "In exchange, you'll pay me the equivalent of my passage to America, as if you were taking me with you. That's my proposal."

"That's a fortune. Why would we agree to that?" Yuri scoffed.

"We don't have a kopeck," Vanya said.

"Nothing? Didn't you have to bribe the man at the hotel? Where'd you get boots like those? Binoculars? No, you're lying. You have money. Your family has a great deal of money."

"We left it all for this eclipse."

"Aye, then you are fools." Dima curled his lips around his teeth, went back to spinning one thumb around the other. Pyotrovich brought more vodka.

"What makes you think we need you?" Yuri asked.

"I speak English." Dima grinned. "I've sailed to England more times than I can count. I know the language. Do you think your American found a translator in Brovary? 'Cause the one he had is long gone. Mark my words, you'll need me."

Vanya fell back against the chair. In his frenzy, he hadn't considered the fact that if Russell Clay found his way to Brovary, he was likely there without a translator. How would Vanya communicate with him? Even more, how would Clay settle into Brovary, run an expedition off the backs of Russians, without a translator? Who knew if his English photographer had ever arrived. Vanya looked behind him to make sure Kolya was still at the bar and that no one else was listening. When he was sure it was clear, he looked back at Dima. "Prove it! Prove your English." He fumbled in his haversack and found Clay's article. "Translate this."

"I can speak, not read," Dima said. He pushed the paper away.

"Then I'll read in Russian, you speak the English."

"How will you be able to judge?"

"I've written my own translation. It's rough, but I did it."

Yes, there was a risk to Dima learning so much about their plans, but Vanya had no choice. If Dima truly spoke English, Vanya would need his help. Vanya read slowly in Russian. Dima responded easily in English—except when it came to technical terms and equipment. Vanya had never heard much English spoken out loud. The language sounded rough and weak at the same time, but so far as he could tell, Dima knew it.

"I still don't understand. Why risk traveling with us?" Yuri asked.

"Because you're here. Now. It could take me months to find another opportunity as lucrative, and I could be in the navy by then. Or dead." Dima reached for Vanya's thimble of vodka and drank it in one swig. "I'll have more proposals. You have to agree to listen."

"There's the trick," Yuri said. "I knew there was more."

"Doctor, no tricks. All I ask is that you listen. Spend the night upstairs. I'll get you a room. Think about it and tell me your answer at sunrise."

Vanya nodded toward the bar. "And Kolya? Your shipmates? Won't they miss you?"

"No one would blame me for leaving now."

XXVII

Vanya had to think clearly, but he wasn't sure he could. He'd been up all night, in the room above the pub, arguing with Yuri. Neither of them trusted the sailor, but Vanya was convinced they needed him as a guide and translator. Yuri disagreed. He thought the whole idea was ridiculous. They went back and forth, around and around. Near dawn, they settled into an uncomfortable silence; all that could be said was said. Twenty-nine days until the eclipse. There was no more time to waste.

A man kicked their door. "Time to go," Pyotrovich, the barkeep, called.

Vanya splashed water on his face and glanced at his reflection in the mirror. His skin was jagged with stubble, and his chin was swollen from the punch he took the day before. "Do you think Dima's told us his real business proposal?"

"No," Yuri said.

"Nor do I. But I also believe I don't have a choice. I need his help." He took a deep breath. "I'm going to Brovary. With Dima. What will you do?"

Yuri hunched over so he could look out the small window under the rafters. He took a deep breath. "I'll go to Brovary," he said. "With you. And then to Miri."

"Then we need to send a telegram. Brovary's far from Riga, in the opposite direction. And as deserters we'll have to be careful. Take back roads. Avoid trains. It will take much longer to get to Klara's from there than it would from Riga. Especially with winter coming, and I don't want them to worry. They need to know we won't be there for Rosh Hashanah."

"You can't tell them where we're headed. You know telegrams can be read by anyone."

"Kir?" Vanya rubbed his forehead with his fingertips as he thought it through. Yuri knew all about Vanya's situation at the university. As Yuri had become more and more part of the family, Miri had opened up to him about how Vanya's work had been stolen, how he'd been threatened. "You think Kir could be looking for me?"

"It wouldn't be a surprise. But now, also, the police. Our commander."

"Yuri, the way you suspect everyone. It's like Baba. Can't you see everyone needs friends?" Vanya looked up. "Still, you're right for now. I'll send a message only she can understand, telling her we're going to Kiev. It's close enough."

"Kir is a clever man."

"He won't figure it out. Even if he does, it will take time to search for us in Kiev—it's a large city, and he won't know to look for us with the American. My letters from Eliot, they went to the baker's house. Kir never read any of them."

"You don't think he's smart enough to figure it all out?"

"No." Vanya was about to open the door and head downstairs, but Yuri stopped him.

"Don't trust that sailor. He seems to know too much."

"What do you mean?" Vanya asked.

"We never told him you had anything to do with a university. I'm sure of it."

Av

The fifth month in the Hebrew calendar is known as Av. The first half of the month is marked as a period for mourning. It commemorates the destruction of the first and second Temples, and also the Jewish expulsion from England in 1290 and from Spain in 1492.

But no sorrow is all-consuming. Life is a cycle. The end of Av is said to be designated for finding one's *bashert*—one's soul mate. The Talmud tells that God declares whom a child will marry forty days before he is born, and the day on which these two souls find one another is considered to be one of the happiest days of the year.

I

K ir Romanovitch won't like it," Ilya said. "I'm supposed to bring the professor home. Already you've stalled. I was supposed to leave with him yesterday." He stood opposite Dima in the train yard amid the stench of burnt coal. The commotion of workers loading crates of ammunition was around them. All those bullets, Dima was certain, guaranteed this war would be a blood-bath. Ilya looked haggard and wrinkled, like he knew it, too. Pathetic. Turning on a man he called friend. Dima spit on the ground at Ilya's feet and Ilya flinched. He was afraid, yes, but worse, Ilya was off balance. Overwhelmed. This negotiation, Dima saw, was more than Ilya had anticipated.

"Kir wants numbers and this is his only way to get them," Dima said. "Vanya doesn't have them."

"Of course Vanya has them. Kir told me so himself."

"Kir lied. Vanya told me he doesn't have any equations. He's still working on it. I thought the extra day would help but he needs more time than that."

"Kir wouldn't tell me something that isn't true."

"You believe that?" Dima paused and let his words sink in. Then he pushed his finger into Ilya's chest and continued, "If Vanya ran, it was from Kir. This Romanovitch, he's powerful, no? He must have scared the Jew off."

"Maybe."

"No maybe. I know he did. Let's start again. Kir Romanovitch wants Vanya's numbers, but from what I see there are two problems.

First, Vanya doesn't want to give them to him. Second, Vanya doesn't have them. Not yet. That means if you take Vanya to Kir now, he'll never produce anything for your man. But if you leave Vanya with me, let him think he's free, he'll produce. And when he does, I'll get the numbers for you to give to Kir."

Ilya kicked a rock. It ricocheted off a rail with a ping. "But now that I found Vanya..."

"You're set! I'll stay with him while he works. I'll get you what Kir needs."

"I can't let him go like that."

"What choice do you have? What will happen if you return to Kir with Vanya, and Vanya doesn't have the numbers Kir expects? Even worse, what happens when he refuses to work?"

"Fine. Then I'll join Vanya. *I'll* travel with him."

"How would you explain how you got here? Found him? If Vanya's as smart as you say, he'll put it together. He'll see Kir's hand in it. Whether he trusts you or not—and he'd be a fool to trust you showing up here like this—he'll run. You'll never find him again." Ilya nodded, and Dima couldn't tell whether Ilya's cheeks burned because he was embarrassed or because he felt guilty. Either way, thanks to God he got the point. "All this is going to cost more than we agreed."

"I can't pay more."

"You have no choice." He stepped closer. "I'm going to have to stay with Vanya for weeks. While he works. And my time is expensive. You'll pay me what you have now. Then more, later. Did you bring the money?"

"Yes, but..."

"Enough with the stalling. If you're not going to pay me, then Vanya's right there." Dima pointed across the train yard, past crates of ammunition and the litter of seats and berths ripped from passenger cars to make way for supplies. It was risky, but Dima sensed he had the upper hand. "Take him if you want. But mark my words, Kir won't be happy." Ilya didn't move. Dima continued, "When we land, I'll send a telegram. Here. To Riga. I'll let you know where we are, and how close Vanya is to solving his math."

"No. I need to know where you're going. Now. So I can send a report."

"I don't know yet." The lie was easy. "They won't tell me. Just west. You need to trust I'll get what Kir wants."

"Why would I trust you?"

"Why wouldn't I get you what you want? I want my money." At least that much was true.

"And Vanya? Why does Vanya trust you?"

"I don't know if he trusts me. But he needs me. I speak English," Dima said with a smile that made him stand taller. "He'll need me when he finds his American."

"An American?" Ilya said and Dima realized his mistake at once. "I didn't know he was after an American. I'm guessing Kir didn't, either. Why?"

"Doesn't matter, does it? Do we have a deal?"

"I need to explain it all to Kir. Ask for more money."

"Then do it. I can stall for a few more days," Dima said. But he needed more than just money from this Ilya. He also needed assurances that Ilya wouldn't follow because if he did, he'd scare Vanya off. Or at least Yuri. And if Yuri fled, he'd take Vanya with him. Dima looked over his shoulder to be certain no one was watching. "Make sure you remind Kir how happy he'll be when he gets his numbers. The wait will be worth it. And tell him not to send anyone else. No other spies. I'll know if he's following us. And I'll make sure he never gets those numbers if he does." Dima took the purse from Ilya.

As he walked away, he realized he'd have to learn more about Vanya's work so he could be sure he was getting a fair price. What kind of numbers could be worth so much?

II

On August second, Baba sent a messenger to the hospital, asking Miri to come home. Baba had never done such a thing before, and Miri ran the entire distance. As she came in from the back alley, Baba met her at the threshold. "War's started." Germany had made its declaration against Russia. On the Jewish calendar the day was Tisha b'Av, the saddest day of the year. A day of fasting, the height of mourning. Dripping in sweat, numb from the news, Miri dropped to her knees and looked up at her grandmother. Baba's face was so pale Miri saw the web of veins under her skin. And her eyes were hollow, the bright green gone. "There's more."

"Vanya?" Miri asked.

Sasha closed the door and locked it. She hadn't even greeted him.

"War on Tisha b'Av is a terrible omen. It will be worse than we imagine," Baba said.

"I don't care about omens. Tell me what's happened," Miri said.

"Shhh." Baba held a crooked finger to her lips. She was right. Kir's guard was always close now. Baba hurried them both, again, to the cellar. "A telegram. Kir brought it," Baba said once she was on the cot and Miri had a record playing. She gave it to Miri.

The onionskin envelope was yellow with mud smeared across the front, and it was ripped. By the folded corners, it looked to have been opened dozens of times. Miri fingered the typed address for the baker's house. Kir had figured out their subterfuge. She ran her nail over the careful letters. Telegrams came during war only to announce death or injury, but this one was not official, not from the army. Yuri or Vanya? For a moment she imagined the news, whatever it was, wasn't real. Not until she opened it. Was it better that way, not knowing? Even with the music playing, the quiet was terrible. She tore into the paper.

Changing plans STOP Visiting Levi's Monster STOP Meet up in spring

"What is Levi's Monster?" Sasha asked.

"Not what. Where," Baba said. "Vanya's telling us where he's gone. Miri understands."

She did. After Mama and Papa died, Baba tried to hug and kiss her sadness away, but only Vanya could quiet her, with his stories. Her favorite was an old folktale about Levi. Levi was a busy man. A baker. At Rosh Hashanah, when the rabbi told him, and the rest of the congregation, that it was time to take a trip to the river so they could cast off their sins, Levi decided he had no time for it. Instead of whispering his wrongdoings into pieces of stale bread and tossing the tidbits into the water, he admitted his errors to scraps and threw them into his basement. Little sins don't go away when hidden like that, they turn into a larger monster, and in the old folktale, Levi had to face that monster. Often, Vanya changed a detail and made Levi a tailor, sometimes a farmer, but Levi's home was always in the same city—not Constantsa as the rabbis traditionally told the folktale, as anyone else would think. No. Vanya placed Levi in the city Miri dreamed of visiting one day. "Kiev," Miri said. Her mother's favorite place in Russia, where she'd gone with Papa on their honeymoon. "Vanya and Yuri have gone to Kiev."

She fingered the thin corner of the paper. It was dated nine days earlier. "Kir stormed into the house with it," Sasha said.

"Did he hurt you?" Miri asked, leaning closer to her grandmother.

"No. No. But he's smarter than Vanya ever gave him credit for.

He assumed it was a coded note from your brother. Found a rabbi to tell him the folktale. But I told Kir this wasn't about the old story. It was from a client; Levi is a common name. My client must have forgotten our address." Baba continued, "I told Kir my client's daughter was supposed to marry Levi's son, but he didn't show up for the wedding. The client is calling the ex-fiancé Levi's Monster and wants payment and a new match for his daughter in the spring."

"Kir believed you?" Miri asked.

"I doubt it," Sasha said. "But Levi goes to Constantsa, no? Let Kir go there."

"Either way, he's angry. Ilya must not have found them yet," Baba said.

Miri shook the telegram. "Maybe Ilya's missed them. They could have already left for Kiev." She stopped and pressed her lips together, dropped her hands into her lap as another thought came. "But Ilya will still be after them. And he might be able to track them, depending on the trail they left. Baba, we have to warn them. Vanya and Yuri need to know about Ilya, that he's there to bring them back to Kir. They can't trust him."

"How do you plan to write to them, Miri? There's no way to send a message."

"I don't know. Maybe I'll have to go find them myself. We need to save them before Ilya, or Kir, takes them."

"But I don't understand why they're going to Kiev, not staying in Riga," Baba said.

"I can only guess Vanya's found his American and followed him. From what I understand, the eclipse will be clearer in Kiev anyway. None of the other expeditions following the eclipse had planned on Riga." This American, he must have come around, decided he'd made a poor decision settling on that port. And even though their mother loved the city, Vanya would only go to Kiev to follow Russell Clay. It was far from home, far from Klara and their escape route.

He'd never been, didn't know a soul. And if he made it to Kiev, he was right to warn them. With war, and soon winter, travel could be difficult, especially as a deserter who'd have to hide somehow, in plain sight. He likely wouldn't make it to Klara's before snow set in.

"Maybe Vanya needs help?" Sasha suggested. "Maybe that's why he sent this."

"What kind of help?" Miri asked. The better question was what sort of help didn't he need? Vanya and Yuri were both accomplished in their fields, but neither paid attention to the world around them. Yuri would be no fiercer in a fight than Vanya. Neither had ever even taken a punch. Truly anything could have happened—or nothing. Miri paced to the hearth, where Sasha had hung the greatcoat to dry. It was stiff now with spots caked in mud. "It doesn't matter if he's asking for help. What matters is Vanya assumes he's safe. That we're all safe until spring. He doesn't know Ilya and Kir are after him. Nor does he know there are guards at our doors. And he's not thinking about what it will be like to be a deserter on the run."

Baba nodded. "You're right about that. He's not thinking clearly."

Miri continued, "The longer the Germans try to face Russia down, the harder it will be to travel, and the tighter the czar will make our borders. Vanya doesn't understand. We can escape to America now, but come spring our chances will be much lower."

"Mirele," Baba said. "You agree, then, that we must run to America?"

She took a deep breath. She'd seen the soldiers trickle into her hospital. She cringed every time she spoke to the guards outside their door. And Kir. He'd ruin Vanya. All of them. She loved Russia, but they had no future here. At least in America they'd have a chance at a new life. "I do agree. We have to leave. All of us have to leave," Miri said. "And I have to find them, bring them back. So we have a chance to make it out while we can."

"I'll go. To repay you," Sasha said. "With Grekov's coat, I can impersonate the captain, use it to navigate the trains to Kiev. I'll hurry them back."

"You can't go," Miri said. "You don't know my brother or Yuri."

"You can describe them. I'd be looking for a group of men working around a large telescope. An American. How hard could it be to find them?" He cleared his throat. "I can't stay here much longer anyway. Kir's guards, they asked me yesterday when I plan to leave."

"You didn't tell us that."

"I didn't want to worry you. You know the police have been investigating the drunks' deaths."

"If you're discovered as a deserter, you'll be shot." Baba paused. "So will we."

"I know." Sasha looked down at the floor. "And I don't want to bring you any more danger. I'm a dead man anyway. If I return, Grekov'll kill me for surviving. If I don't return, I'm a deserter and my sentence is also death. Until they catch me, I'll pretend I'm Grekov. As an officer, I can travel without papers. Secure your passage."

"Could you take us both with you?" Baba asked. She looked at him with her heavy eyes, and Miri thought she'd never seen her grandmother so tired, not even after the night they'd spent in the cellar. "If we travel together to Kiev, we can go straight to the border from there with Vanya and Yuri."

"Baba, you need to save your strength." Miri shook her head. "But even if we went together, what if we didn't make it to Kiev before the eclipse and we missed them? Vanya and Yuri will run to Klara's, and when we're not there—then what? We can't send word to Klara. That would be intercepted, too. And Kir? We need to keep Kir away from Kiev, lure him somewhere else." Miri could see her grandmother working through plans even as Miri spoke.

"Yes, that's right," Baba said. "We can't both go." She nodded. "It would be better for me to draw Kir away. I'll tell the women my sister is sick, that I need to see her. Then I'll slip out. Kir will track me to Klara's, but he'll leave me be. He'll want me as bait for Vanya."

Miri didn't like it, Baba sitting at Klara's as a lure without Miri, but there was no other way. They couldn't miss Vanya. And Baba couldn't make the journey to Kiev and then to America. It was too much for her. And Miri was certain that Kir wouldn't bother Baba any more than he already had. Not until Vanya was in his snare. "Sasha can secure *my* train," Miri said. "I'll find Vanya and Yuri and bring them to Peter. When we arrive, I'll get word to you so you can slip away from Klara's, meet us far from her apartment, far from any guards Kir has on you there. We'll leave before spring, while the borders still have holes."

"No." Baba shook her head. "You are a strong woman, but no young woman should travel alone. And Kiev's large. You'll need help."

"Miriam, I'll go with you," Sasha said. "I'll use the coat and we'll go together."

"I can't ask you to do that."

"I insist. Your grandmother's right. You can't go alone. It's not safe."

"I can't travel with a man who isn't family or my husband, not without a chaperone."

"Travel as cousins. Who knows the difference?" Baba asked. She took Miri's hands. Her blue veins twisted around gnarled joints. "Go with Sasha. I will wait for you at Klara's."

"And Kir's guards?" Miri asked. "How do we get past them?"

"You know Sasha's been digging in our basement?"

III

Eighteen days to the eclipse. Vanya could feel time passing quickly, too quickly, as he and Yuri hid in the shadows of the chapel in front of Riga's station, waiting for Dima. When Vanya and Yuri first met the sailor, Dima had been confident he could find them a way onto a train quickly, but he'd been wrong. And not for lack of trying. Every day for just over twelve days, Vanya and Yuri accompanied Dima from the public house where they'd been staying, to the station. They'd smeared their faces with dirt, wore rags they'd traded for their uniforms, and hid as crippled beggars at the chapel while the sailor scrounged for passage. The disguise made them invisible, and Vanya watched Dima bargain and hustle, but Dima reported all the trains were requisitioned for troops, for war. There was nothing for civilians. "I'll find a way," Dima said every day as they returned to the pub.

"A way to more money," Yuri whispered to Vanya in reply. But Vanya didn't care that payment was what motivated the sailor. All he cared about was getting to Kiev, and by now he was frustrated. They'd spent days watching the sailor, and Vanya couldn't afford to lose so much time. He needed to get to Brovary. Could he spare one ruby to pay for their passage? No. He couldn't touch them. He might need them for Clay.

"I think I could do better on my own," Vanya said.

"No. I think that sailor is our ticket. He's just stalling. He's up to something. I don't know what. Maybe he's waiting on payment for something else." Yuri leaned back against the stone wall. "When he's ready, he'll find us a way. Quickly."

"How can you say that? Or think that and still trust him?"

"I'm not the one who trusts him. You are."

"Then go." Vanya pointed to the street, and Yuri waved a hand to dismiss him. Vanya continued, "One more day. That's all I'll give him." Then he turned and huddled over his notebook as he had every morning they'd sat at the chapel.

He would have left on his own days ago but being away from Kir had put Vanya in a space where he was freer than he'd ever been, and those days he'd spent waiting were some of his most productive in years. He'd squared Ricci's tensor, and the expressions had begun to flow from there. Some of the more elusive numbers and symbols fell into place. But what about acceleration? He still hadn't figured that in properly. And he needed to, in order to convince Clay to take them. He pinched the skin on the bridge of his nose and leaned forward to think.

An hour passed. More. Yuri nudged Vanya and made him look at a plaque dedicating the station chapel that read "In memory of the miraculous survival of the Romanovs in the 1881 train crash, despite the insidious Polyakovs and their evil trains." Yuri said, "They're Jewish, you know. The Polyakovs."

"Of course they are."

Yuri pulled out a flask. "We missed Rosh Chodesh Av. We should have celebrated. Don't you and Miri always celebrate? Toast while you watch the thinnest moon rise and fall?"

"You know our custom?"

"I try to know everything about my fiancée. *L'chaim*." Both men took a long pull.

"Do you imagine she thinks about me?" Yuri asked, his voice softer than usual.

Probably, but Vanya didn't want to admit it. "Seems wrong, no? A celebration for Av? Even worse so close to Tisha b'Av. We should be crying, mourning, not drinking. Wait." Vanya leaned forward and squinted. "Is that...?" It was impossible. Or was it?

"Who? Did you see someone?"

"I thought I saw Ilya. The police officer." But Ilya couldn't be in Riga. He was posted in Kovno. Still, Vanya scrambled to his feet, felt his heart beating fast and hard. Did Baba send him to look for Vanya? Was something wrong at home?

"It's nothing," Yuri said. "A ghost from the imagination."

By the time Vanya had taken a few steps toward him, the man he thought was Ilya was out of sight. He'd lost him. "Yes." Vanya decided Yuri was right. Just a ghost. Neither Baba nor Miri would tell anyone where he'd gone. It was too dangerous. Even if something had happened.

"I see them, too. Miri's around every corner. And others," Yuri said.

"What others?"

Vanya was staring at Yuri, but before he could respond, someone whistled. Vanya recognized the light notes, the ones he'd heard in the alley outside the Hotel Neiburgs. It was Dima. The sailor stood forty paces away and waved for Yuri and Vanya to follow. Before going, Vanya looked back at where he thought he'd seen Ilya, but of course the man hadn't come back. Vanya and Yuri wound around to the back of the station, past crates of supplies destined for the front. How quickly war came, Vanya thought. Was Miri still denying they needed to leave? As they walked, Yuri spoke. "We should be going the other way."

"But you said that wasn't Ilya."

"No. I mean back to Miri." Yuri's voice shook. It was the first real anger Vanya had seen in him. "We're risking everything for your damn science during a war. Doesn't it strike you as absurd?" Yuri's voice rose. "I'm saying there are times when your family needs you. When you should be home to protect them."

"What are you so scared of?" Vanya shook his head. "My sister and my baba can protect themselves. Don't you know that? And it's not just about science. This eclipse, it's our way out."

"Doesn't it matter to you whether we live or die? Whether your family lives or dies?"

"That's precisely why we're doing this. To reach America—*all* of us." Vanya leaned closer to Yuri. "If you want to run, run. I never asked you to come. But if you stay, stop acting like a coward. It's enough."

"I'm staying," he said. "But for Miri, not for you."

"Then let's hurry." Vanya jogged the rest of the way toward Dima.

"We depart soon. Finally," Dima said when Vanya caught up to him, then he hurried Vanya and Yuri behind a cannon mounted on a handcar. "I've found us a job as cleaners. They call us engineers, but really, we're cleaning. Trees and branches block the lines. We'll clear the way, riding in front of that timber train." He pointed to a series of wagons so long that Vanya couldn't see the end. Each one was piled with one hundred pines. "The train goes across Russia, but we can get off in Kiev. Find our way to Brovary from there. As long as we find cleaners to replace us."

"I've never sawed a tree into pieces," Yuri said.

"You'll learn."

"What happened to the crew that was supposed to work this train?" Vanya asked.

"I bartered. Real cigarettes. Genuine tobacco."

"That's all?"

"All you need to know." They started walking. Rats scurried. Gravel crunched. Vanya felt he was closer to a graveyard than a train yard. "Five days on this train," Dima continued. "If we're lucky. Here we are."

They stood at the front of an engine that was already hot. A coal car was hitched behind, and a water wagon behind that. Trailing it all was a flatcar with pickaxes, railroad ties, and tools Vanya didn't recognize. They all looked heavy and coated in rust.

"Welcome aboard," a man said. He popped out from the first

car. "I'm Stanislavovich. Head engineer." His booming voice was pitched too high for his squat frame, and his lips were crooked. A mottled scar, a healed burn, left one side of his mouth higher than the other. "Pile those crates inside the engine room. They're our food, your seats. When you're done, we're off."

Up close, the compartment where they'd all sit was smaller than it looked from the outside. There was one proper seat perched next to the only window. Goggles hung from a hook. All around were a series of levers and valves. In the middle sat a coal chute thick with soot. Exhaust fumes sputtered into the space where they'd sit, which explained the half-built walls—a ventilation system. Dima started loading the supplies. Yuri and Vanya helped, careful to make seating alcoves for each of them. "Why only vodka?" Yuri asked over the roar of the engine.

"Bribes," Dima explained. "Food would go bad from the heat. We'll trade the vodka for food at coal depots."

"And the weapons?" Vanya pointed to two old-fashioned swords.

"The villagers out there, they're hungry. We could be a target, and that's all Stanislavovich could muster. It'll be enough."

Dima looked as if he had something else to say, but then the train jolted and he slipped—pitching backward toward the roaring coal fire.

Stanislavovich yelled, "Watch out!" Yuri spun to face Stanislavovich. He didn't see Dima fall, but Vanya did. Vanya lunged, shoving Dima to the side. The two men fell, breathless, against a stack of vodka. Vanya's hip throbbed. Dima moaned.

"You could have fallen with me," Dima said to Vanya, once he'd caught his breath.

Vanya stood, dusted himself off, and said nothing. Stanislavovich pulled the steam whistle, and the wheels rolled forward.

IV

Later that night, after they'd digested the telegram and made their plans, Babushka gave Arkady two bottles of vodka. He finished them, of course. Drunk. He passed out near dawn just as he always did. Still, they didn't want to risk walking past him. Instead, when Miri, Baba, and Sasha heard him snoring, they sneaked into the kitchen and eased down into the cellar, closing the hatch behind them. Next to Miri's desk, hidden by a carpet, lay the opening to a tunnel Sasha had dug into the Yurkovs' basement. It was just wide enough. Miri shimmied through, moved a barrel of potatoes Sasha used to hide the opening, and pulled herself into a dark cellar like theirs should have been, filled with preserved fruits and vegetables, and a proper stairwell leading to a door. Soon, Baba made her way through. Miri helped and Sasha scrambled behind her.

Then Miri eased up the stairs and into the Yurkovs' kitchen. They were already gone, across the street at their bakery. The house was dark and deserted. Still, she crept slowly toward a window on the far side of the room. The house was on a corner, and that end faced an alley Arkady couldn't see, even if he'd been awake. She slid the latch, lifted the frame without making a noise, and slipped through. Baba and Sasha followed. Outside, Miri hurried Baba into a wheelbarrow and covered her with a tarp. Then she pulled a scarf over her head like a woman from Slobodka. Sasha donned a yarmulke and picked up the handles on the wheelbarrow, and they started down the alley. Miri didn't dare turn to see if they were being followed, but she strained to hear something, anything, behind them. Beyond kitchen boys sweeping and rats scurrying, there was nothing. It wasn't until they were four turns away that she dared to look back. When she saw it was clear, they helped Baba out of the wheelbarrow and hurried to the train station.

It didn't take long for Sasha to secure their tickets and documents. As he'd predicted, using the greatcoat to impersonate Grekov worked beautifully. It helped that through a client, the week before, Baba had found him a proper uniform. He didn't have the right medals and medallions, but so long as he kept the greatcoat on, he looked right around the edges and no one would notice otherwise.

With the tickets, they made their way to the uncovered platform where they'd wait for Baba's train to Saint Petersburg. So far, they had been lucky, but that didn't mean their chances of making it onto any train were assured. The czar's forces could commandeer seats. Not even a captain could stand up to orders for an entire unit.

And so they waited, terrified. How long until one of the guards realized there was no one at home on Vilnius Street? Until they realized Miri hadn't left for the hospital? It was only a matter of hours before Kir's men came here looking for them. Miri kept expecting to see Arkady storming through the squat station, but no one came. Instead all she saw were faceless soldiers and countless layers of coal ash coating the stones. Underneath the soot, there were gleaming windows and golden cornices, but Kovno hadn't cleaned the facade in years and so the station was stained, tangled with a web of tracks and wires making it feel closer to death than it was to the lively European hub it used to be.

Miri held Babushka's hand so hard her grandmother had to ask her to loosen her grip. Sasha smoked cigarette after cigarette. Around, on all sides, were throngs of soldiers biting their nails, waiting for the same train.

The rails rumbled. A whistle blared and a train heaved into the station in a haze of pollen, exhaust, and steam. Miri held on tighter to Babushka. "Aunt Klara's," Miri said, fighting off tears.

"Don't come to the apartment. Send a message through the butcher when you arrive. He's a friend. Tell me where to find you, and I'll come."

Miri nodded and wiped her eyes. Every ounce of bravery she'd felt back in the cellar when they laid down their plans was gone. She couldn't remember a day in her life without either her parents or her grandmother, had never traveled without Vanya. "The word 'Jew' is not stamped on your forehead," Babushka whispered. She pulled her granddaughter so close there wasn't space between them.

The soldiers nearby started moving forward to board. Babushka tried to step toward the train but Miri wouldn't let go. "Mirele, it's time," Babushka said. She kissed her and slid her hands up to Miri's arms, loosening her granddaughter's grip. The train whistled, louder this time, sending pigeons scattering. "Go. The path ahead is never clear until it's the past," Baba said. Then she followed Sasha, who used his elbows to make way for her.

Miri thought about boarding the train. About going to Klara's. For a moment she pictured herself sitting with her aunt and Baba, the three of them waiting in silence on Klara's green sofa, in front of her dark drapes. But immediately after that came an image of her and Baba, stuck with Vanya at a closed border. Vanya being arrested, tortured. No, she had to go after her brother, bring him back as soon as she could. With Yuri. Through the train's window she saw her grandmother take her seat. Baba kissed her fingers and held them to the glass. The train's wheels turned.

Babushka was gone.

V

Miri couldn't move until the train's exhaust clouds faded to gray. She told herself there was an invisible thread connecting her to her grandmother, that the thread was stretching, not breaking. Finally, she turned to Sasha. He stood there with his good arm out to her, and even as she knew she shouldn't, she dropped her head on his chest and sobbed. He smelled like Vanya's shaving cream and Babushka's lavender. She expected him to urge her to hurry. He would have been right to do so—it was dangerous for him to show his face around so many soldiers, to wear Grekov's coat, and as much as she knew they should run to their own train, she couldn't. Not yet. Sasha gave her all the time she needed. And he didn't flinch at her being so close.

Another train pulled up to the platform. Not theirs. What if Vanya and Yuri were both already dead? "We can only try, child," her grandmother would say.

"We'll go day by day," Sasha whispered. Miri reached into her pocket for one of Babushka's embroidered handkerchiefs. She ran her fingernail over the tight, neat stitches. "When I left my family, I felt the same," Sasha continued.

"When did you leave?"

"Five years ago." He opened his mouth to say more but something caught his eye. He wrapped his hand around her arm and pulled. "We need to go."

"What is it?"

"Someone recognized the coat. I heard him say Grekov."

They walked back toward the station, the only way out, moving as fast as they could, dodging soldiers and marble columns. Under the massive, girded ceiling it was dark. Sparse light flecked with dust streamed through high windows. "Grekov! Captain Grekov!" a man called behind them. They walked faster but the man was gaining on them. There was no question he'd catch them. Miri's heart pounded so fast she didn't hear anything around her, only the blood in her ears. The soldiers. The supplies were a blur.

"Faster," she said. But they couldn't. With the crowd, they couldn't get away. How was that man gaining on them? Sasha pulled Miri behind a pile of burlap grain sacks likely destined for the front. They smelled like sawdust. He was bent over, out of breath like her. "Miriam, run," Sasha said. The scar across his cheek blazed red.

"Who was it? Who recognized you?"

"I don't know, but anyone who stops me is dangerous. Go."

"Grekov!" the same voice yelled. "Halt, I say!"

Sasha shoved Miri toward the door. She tripped and when she caught her balance, she saw him stepping out from behind the stacks of grain to meet their pursuer, a short, square-shaped soldier with rows and rows of medals pinned to his chest. His decorations jingled with every step. He had a mustache and pursed lips that made him look like a rodent.

"Grekov! The fool who challenged Radkievich," the man called. Sasha cupped his chin with his hand, a habit Miri had learned meant he was nervous. "Where are your Jewish dogs?" the officer laughed, a cackle that ricocheted off the marble. Sasha replied. Miri couldn't hear him but she saw his shoulders sag. Soldiers zigzagged around them ferrying crates toward the train. "Your coat should read Durak. Fool!"

Miri took a deep breath and stood as tall as she could. Stepped forward. She knew that the more ridiculous the lie, the more likely it is to be believed. She threaded her arm through Sasha's, felt him trembling. "Thank you for making my cousin slow down. I'd been begging him to let me rest," she said, tilting a hip to the side, trying to be as charming as she could.

The officer's dark eyes scurried from Miri to Sasha and back again. A grin broke over his face, and his thick eyebrows sprouted so far forward they looked like moving fur. "You devil," he said to Sasha. "I'm sure if Radkievich knew you had such a beautiful cousin, he'd never have sent you to the Jewish dogs. He'd have arranged a dinner." Sasha should have laughed but he was frozen, staring at Miri. At least the crowd of soldiers surrounding them meant they weren't standing in excruciating silence, but it was nearly as bad.

"She's been crying, your cousin?" the officer asked. "A broken heart?"

"What else makes a woman cry?" Miri asked. Did she sound convincing?

His nose twitched. "I see height runs in the family." He tried to come closer, but a dozen dirt-smeared soldiers marched at them. She and Sasha were forced to step back, to make room. The officer also moved, in the opposite direction. Between them the men pushed a platform on wheels. It was a gun mount, meant for a cannon. The metal squealed as it turned. Miri yanked Sasha. He understood without her saying a word.

They turned and sprinted through the throngs of men as fast as they could, toward the exit. The officer yelled after them, but he was still blocked by the cannon. Miri's dress caught on a crate and ripped. She didn't slow down. Fear had her moving faster than she'd ever moved. Any one of the soldiers they passed could have grabbed them, but they didn't. And as scared as she was, she knew what to do: keep running.

She and Sasha burst through the arched exit, into sparkling sun-shine. Out of breath, Miri tried to think even as she hurried down the stairs. Which way? She knew a dozen routes back to her neighborhood but she couldn't remember where to start. Besides, she no longer had a home to run to. "Through the park." She pointed ahead. There were crowds. Some soldiers with women on their arms. They could blend in.

Along the gravel path among the trees, Miri tried to look casual, tried to slow her pace, and Sasha followed. She kept her eyes down and saw only boots. Some with holes on the sides, in the toes. Others polished and gleaming. Starlings twittered. "Slower," she mumbled, trying to make it look as if she and Sasha were no different from the couples around them. She kept her hand tucked into the crook of his elbow, keenly aware that he cradled his bad arm.

"Can you get us to Karmėlava without a train?" Sasha asked under his breath.

"The town east of here?"

"Yes. Can we walk there?"

"It will take a day, maybe more."

"Good. There's a coal depot in Karmėlava. We can board a train there. One transfer, in Daugavpils. Then Kiev." He sounded like Babushka planning an escape. But how did he know the trains so well?

"This way," Miri said, and pulled Sasha across a street. The cobblestones were slick with pollen. "Do you think they followed us this far?" Miri asked.

"I don't know. Can we duck into an alley?"

"Soon." Miri continued to keep her gaze away from the men in uniform who walked past. Only a few weeks earlier there had been half as many soldiers in the streets. How quickly the czar reinforced his forts. If only they could get to America. Sixty paces, she estimated, to the first turn. Please, she thought. Please let us make it. Sasha's rucksack banged against his thigh. At the apothecary they turned. They passed a store thick with the smell of cologne, where a woman in elegant silks stood in the window, fingering ribbons hanging on rolls from the ceiling. Then they came to a roundabout anchored by a bronze statue of the czar. A pigeon sat on his outstretched finger. Miri felt dozens of eyes following them as they walked, but knew the paranoia was in her mind. The people of Kovno, even the soldiers, were too scared to look up. They slipped into an alley. In the shadows, Miri turned around to see if there were any soldiers in their wake. When she saw they were alone, she gasped great mouthfuls of air. She didn't even realize she'd been holding her breath. She was covered in sweat. A wagon rolled past the edge of the alley. The tram clacked. Every noise set her further on edge. "You can take off that coat now," she said.

"No." Sasha was behind her, pacing. Five steps and he turned, retraced where he'd been. "No soldier would stop an officer. We still need it."

"But it's summer. You're drawing attention."

"Doesn't matter. This coat, it's what got your grandmother onto her train. What will get us onto ours." He reached up and took off his visor, wiped sweat from his forehead.

"Listen to me," Miri said. "At the station, when that officer stopped us, you pushed me away. Never do that again."

"Why not? I was protecting you."

"If we travel together, we stand together."

"I wasn't sure what you'd do."

"And I knew what to expect from you? At the river, you broke a man's jaw. If you'd tried the same at the station, we both would've been shot. And wasn't I the one who got us out of that mess?" Her voice was too loud. Someone above opened a window. They walked another block in silence. Finally, Sasha looked at her.

"You're right," he said. "I'm sorry. We have to trust each other."

VI

The trail to Karmėlava started in Slobodka. To get there, Miri kept herself and Sasha hidden in the alleys behind the great houses, where it smelled like soap and fresh strawberries. They wound down from cobblestones to dirt, where perfume gave way to grease and then to sewage as they crossed over to the other side of the Neris, to the slums. Here the houses were low, spattered in mud and backed up along the edge of the forest. Black coats and white shirts were pinned on laundry lines strung across alleys, or over chicken coops. Listless men and women sat on chairs outside their doors and watched them hurry past.

At a dusty square, they stopped at a well to drink. The water was green and tasted like moss. Miri spit it out, her instinct being to wait and drink cleaner water at home. Too late, she remembered she'd never live on Vilnius Street again. They'd left dresses and coats on hooks, pots in the sink. Miri didn't know if it was easier or harder to leave everything behind like that. How long until someone broke a window and crept inside? It didn't matter. She preferred to remember the house the way they'd left it. Otherwise, Miri had to think about the truth—that they were all on the run. That Baba was older. She could fall ill and not make it through the winter. Or that Miri, Vanya, and Yuri could be caught in the wrong place at the wrong time, leaving Baba with Klara to wait. And wait.

Sasha lowered the bucket and offered her more. This time she drank. While she did, a woman with wide hips and a crooked nose came out from her house and walked past. Strings from her skirts hung limp at her ankles. For all Miri knew, the woman could have been Miri's age or twenty years older. "That could have been me," she said.

Sasha studied her face. "You think you would have settled for this life?"

"No," she admitted. But even if she'd fought, would she have made it out?

Somewhere a hen screeched. "How did your family move up?" Sasha asked.

"My zede's cousin was lucky. He was allowed to go to school."

"How?"

"I don't know. They found money for the bribe."

"Then it wasn't luck. They fought."

"Maybe. Zede's cousin learned to read. He taught my grand-father. They figured out how to keep a ledger and earned enough for their children to go to school. My grandmother says there's no physical difference between us and the gentiles—only the ability to read separates us."

"She's right," Sasha said. "But the czar will never let us all rise up. The German Jews, they're the lucky ones."

"What about American Jews?"

"That I don't know."

Another woman came out onto her stoop. Miri and Sasha were becoming a spectacle. The greatcoat was drawing curiosity. Or fear. No one in that slum would feel any warmth toward the czar's man. "We should keep moving," Miri said. She took Sasha to a trail that started on a flat expanse of marsh swarming with insects. Their feet squelched in mud. The squalor gave way to packed trails and hills overcrowded with trees.

Near sunset they found a waterfall tumbling from spiked cliffs, and a stream. Miri's heart caught on a memory of Babushka from those summer lessons in Birshtan. She had told Miri and Vanya to beware their instinct to seek cover near running water—it drowns your own noise but also makes it difficult to hear your enemy approach. Were there only hours between Miri and Babushka now?

"It will come in waves," Sasha said.

"What?"

"The memories. The sadness. It's what you're feeling, no?"

"It hasn't even been long. It doesn't make sense to miss her already."

"It makes perfect sense." Sasha leaned down to drink.

Miri splashed water on her face. With her eyes closed, it was easier to feel at peace. Still, she couldn't let her guard down. No officer wanted to risk the ridicule of letting a Jew escape, and surely the officer from the station had guessed they were Jews. Who else runs? She walked a wide perimeter to make sure the spot was as isolated as it seemed. All she saw were trees and sky. No footprints or remnants of fires. "Should be safe to camp here."

"Good," Sasha said. He pulled a thread and a hook from his pocket and reached for a stick. "A fishing pole," he said. "This stream is teeming."

"We'll have to eat it raw. We can't risk a fire." She stood and wiped her hands on her skirts. "Why do you carry hooks?"

"We always need to be able to feed ourselves, don't we? Make yourself a line. Here." He held out another hook and more thread.

"I can't fish," Miri said.

"All your baba taught you about survival and you can't fish?"

"You'll fish for us both. That's what she taught me."

"From any other woman I would have anticipated that, but not from you."

She grinned.

VII

Vanya was aware of Dima switching places with Stanislavovich, then Yuri, but he didn't volunteer to take a turn. Nor did he bother watching the countryside because the view wasn't important. All that mattered was his work. He sat with his legs bent and drawn close on top of a pile of crates, concentrating on his theory, on a way to incorporate acceleration and gravity into Einstein's principles. He was closer than ever. But what was he missing? Vanya went back through his notebook.

He'd been concentrating on Ricci at the expense of Riemann. Riemann's work started with the assumption of intrinsic curvature. Maybe that was a better approach. Vanya tried manipulating the tensor. But he still wasn't getting anywhere. Could he ask Clay to help? Would half-drawn equations be enough to convince the American to fold Vanya into his expedition? One minute, Vanya convinced himself it was. The next he knew it wasn't. And that wasn't good enough. He couldn't risk rejection—that would mean losing the only means he had of taking his family to America, and by now they had no choice but to go. He and Yuri were deserters. War was brewing. Vanya had to find a solution before he found Clay, or they'd all die.

By dinner, Yuri insisted Vanya eat. Dima had bartered for dried fish and black bread at the last coal depot. "It's better with vodka," Dima said, and handed Vanya a bottle. Stanislavovich was at his perch at the window. He didn't speak much and when he did he yelled, Vanya learned, because he couldn't hear. His ears had been damaged when a steam engine caught fire. It was why his skin was mottled and his smile hung crooked, and it meant Vanya, Yuri, and Dima were free to speak openly as long as they kept their voices low.

"You spend too much time on your numbers and not enough on real life," Dima said. "We could use help." Yuri elbowed Dima, as if they'd already discussed this, but said nothing.

"Numbers are real life," Vanya replied.

"No. The Germans are real. Do you know about their U-boats?"

"Horrible."

"And you, Doctor, what do you think of this war?"

"It means we should leave Russia as soon as possible."

"Then why wait? Why go to Brovary instead of fleeing for the border? What's the power of this eclipse?"

"My brother is in a race. He refuses to leave until he claims victory."

"We *can't* leave until I claim victory," Vanya said, looking up.

"You'll run in the dark, during this eclipse?" Dima asked.

Vanya shook his head. "It's a scientific race. Einstein himself issued the challenge."

"Who is Einstein?" Dima asked.

"A scientist. Philosopher. The most brilliant man ever. I think. He has an idea. He's laid it all out in theory. Now the only way to prove it is through math and a photograph."

"Which you're working on?" Dima interrupted. "That's what you do all day? Math?" Vanya nodded. "And this photograph will come from the American?"

"Exactly. I need it to show light bending around the sun. To check my equations. I'll show you what I mean." There was a cloth covering a few of the crates. Vanya grabbed it and asked Yuri and Dima to each hold the corners, in a tight square. He took a loaf of bread they were saving for breakfast and placed it in the middle of the cloth. A divot formed around the bread. "Gravity," Vanya said, pointing to the depression. Then he pulled an apple from his haversack and held it up. "Imagine the bread is the sun. See how it has curved the fabric around it. Now this apple. It's a planet. Without the bread, the apple would roll straight across the cloth. No?"

"Of course." Dima nodded.

"With the bread there, in the middle, when I roll the apple across, it veers toward the bread. Why? The bread has bent the fabric just as the sun bends space. The apple follows the contours of the cloth just as light follows the contours of space." He paused to make sure the sailor was following. "My math, what I'm trying to figure out, is by how much."

Vanya could feel Dima thinking. His eyes were narrow. He stared at the divot from the bread. "Equations and a photograph?" Dima asked. "You're after two things. Not one?"

"Yes." Vanya smiled.

"And this American, you think if you find him, he'll give you a photograph?"

Vanya looked at Yuri and said, "Yes. I think I'll convince him to give it to me."

"A race. For science." Now Dima smiled so wide his gold tooth flickered. Wind ripped through the slats in the train. It stirred the smell of tobacco and discarded fish bones from dinner.

"Yes. Whoever publishes photos and an equation to predict the curvature first, wins. It could be Einstein. Or me. Or someone else." Vanya smiled again. "I know Einstein wants to win, but above it all, he wants the world to embrace relativity."

"You know this Einstein, then?"

"A little. We've corresponded."

"You barely know the man you're fighting?" Dima shook his head. "Vanya, you speak of new science and math, but what about the truth in the past? In nature itself?"

"What truth?" Vanya asked.

"You've heard of the *Titanic*?"

"The boat that sank two years ago."

"Yes. It was doomed from the beginning. *Titanic* was a foolish name," Dima said. "Titans were deities. They named the ship after gods because they thought it would protect them. But the White Star's crown jewel couldn't stand up to nature. To an ice field. The captain ignored every sign, every hint the ocean gave. One thousand five hundred twenty-two people swallowed by the sea."

"What signs?" Vanya asked.

Dima fumbled in his pocket. There was the flick of a match, and then a flame lit his dark eyes. His face was lined with wrinkles different from any Vanya had noticed before. The smell of his tobacco was different, too. Thicker. "Sea serpents," Dima said. "Sea serpents were the signs. Captain Rostron, from the *Carpathia*, said there were serpents everywhere that night."

"Sea serpents aren't real," Yuri countered.

"Aye, they are. Have you ever been to sea? Two nights after the *Titanic* went down there was an eclipse. Did you know that?"

"The papers never mentioned an eclipse," Vanya said.

"Papers miss a lot, my friend. It's the sailors who talk about it. Who know what's real. And Captain Rostron. After he loaded the survivors on board and twisted back through the frozen sea, his ship fell in a band of night—smack in the middle of day. An eclipse. A final warning to men, an order not to believe that our power is equal to the Titans or to any other god."

VIII

Miri woke when the sun cracked through the trees. Sasha must have sensed she was awake. He looked at her and smiled. His face dripped with water, and the edges of his hair were wet from washing in the stream. He looked younger out here, happier. Could Vanya and Yuri be feeling the same? Was it possible they'd already found Russell Clay and were arranging their camp? She hoped so because one alternative was terrifying—that Ilya, and Kir, had caught them.

"Are you hungry?" Sasha asked. He held out a chunk of cheese wrapped in one of Babushka's kitchen towels. The smell of blueberry preserves floated off the fabric. Miri held it up to her nose and caught the undertones of nutmeg and handed it back to him. She couldn't stomach any food. Not then. Instead she pulled on her boots. Already her legs were tired and she had a blister on her heel. It would bleed but there was nothing she could do for it. They had to keep going. It might be hard, but it was nothing compared to what Baba endured after the pogroms. She had to just keep pushing forward.

Miri handed Sasha Grekov's coat and walked into the woods, came back with a branch in each hand, one with pine needles, the other with birch leaves. She bent down to scramble the soil where they'd slept. "How is it you know how to hide but not fish?" Sasha pressed again. When Miri didn't respond, he said, "My grandfather used to say: 'Better to overestimate your enemy than die from vanity.'"

"Are you calling me the enemy?" Miri asked.

"No. I'm saying you're smart to cover our tracks."

When Miri and Sasha finally hiked down from the hills and onto the flats leading to Karmėlava, they were surrounded by golden wheat and emerald trees. They avoided the houses that started to dot the fields. The roofs were thatched with a mixture of shingles and straw. Each had a brick chimney stuck on the side as if it were an afterthought. The town was small compared to Kovno, but its significance outstripped its size. It was a junction where the rails split, carving north or south, or staying west to east. "The Polyakovs built this junction. You've heard of them, the Jewish Polyakovs?" Sasha asked when they stopped to rest. They could just make out the gleam of the tracks they'd follow to the depot.

"No," Miri said.

"They were brothers. They started as tax farmers, paying for merchants who couldn't pay themselves. If the merchants couldn't repay, well, the brothers extracted payment. They were brutal."

"Why are you telling me this?" Miri wiped sweat from her face.

"Because you should know them. Beware of them." He paused. "One of the brothers moved into construction."

"It's illegal for Jews to own construction companies."

"True. Polyakov brought in a partner. A Russian named Tolstov. He signed where only Russians could sign. Got paid where only Russians could get paid while Polyakov did the dirty work. He paid laborers next to nothing while Tolstov sipped champagne. When the workers came to Polyakov and complained they didn't earn enough to feed their families, *he* turned them away. His own people. Then came the railroad.

"Building tracks is a dirty business. The czar wanted train lines crossing Russia. To build them, Polyakov was given permission to march onto any farm and take the land for the railroad. If the farmer protested, he was shot. If he gave in, he was homeless. And the destitute farmers blamed Polyakov—not the czar, or Tolstov. They blamed the Jew."

"Polyakov forced you from your home?" Miri asked.

"No. Not quite." Sasha stopped midsentence and pointed to the edge of the trail. A dog stood ten paces away. Miri hadn't heard him coming. He was black and bone thin with missing teeth. He growled and Miri's skin bristled. "He's sick," she whispered, eyeing the foam on his mouth. "If we stay calm, he might go away."

"Or he might attack." Sasha reached for a rock the size of his fist, and the dog's growl grew deeper. "Run when I throw—"

Sasha didn't get to finish. The dog leapt at them. Jaws wide. White foam spraying. As quickly as the dog sprang into the air, Sasha brought his arm back and shot it forward with enough force that his shirt thrummed. He hit the dog square between the eyes. The mutt landed hard on his side and scrambled back up. Sasha bent down and grabbed another rock. And another, pummeling the dog even as he yelped and ran away.

"You didn't have to do that," Miri said.

Sasha wiped sweat from his chin but said nothing.

IX

Stanislavovich stopped the train for the night in the center of a wide-open field because they couldn't travel at night when they couldn't see the tracks. As the engine cooled, the pound of pistons was replaced by the hum of cicadas. The smell of coal was overcome by the scent of soil. Vanya couldn't sleep, but he closed his eyes. He'd written and rewritten the Riemann tensor. The Ricci tensor. Manipulated them in dozens of ways. All of his results were convoluted, forced, and awkward. Vanya couldn't help but feel America, and safety, slipping away. "God damn it," he muttered. Without equations, how would he introduce himself to Russell Clay? How would he prove he was worthy? He was wearing rags. The letter from Eliot was stained now, too, and crinkled. By the look of it, it could have been a fake and there wasn't time for Clay to write to Eliot, to check his references as he should. "Think," he whispered to himself. "Think."

That was when he heard it. A footfall outside the train. Leaves cracked differently under a man's two feet than they did under four paws. Dima had warned that the train might be a target. That villagers were hungry now that the able-bodied men were being shipped to war. They must have thought the train had food. Vanya's hands clenched to fists. Another footfall. Another man. How many?

Vanya wanted to run. Miri had always been the fighter when they were kids, not him. But the train was his only way to Brovary. He couldn't give it up. He shook Yuri awake. Yuri jumped up and grabbed his knife in one smooth motion. Vanya held a finger to his lips to signal for quiet and pointed outside. Yuri's eyes went wide, and he nodded to show he understood.

By the time Vanya turned to rouse the others, Dima was already awake. Then Stanislavovich. Vanya tried to use two fingers to signal there were two men near the train, but his hands were shaking. His ears buzzed and he couldn't hear whatever Dima was whispering. Stanislavovich grabbed one of the swords and hoisted it to his shoulder.

The Talmud teaches that if someone comes to kill you, you must rise up and kill them first. That was one lesson Vanya remembered well from the rabbi in Kovno. *Kill.* Could he? Vanya reached for a crate and pried one of the boards loose to use as a weapon. At the same time, Dima grabbed an empty vodka bottle by the neck. Yuri huddled in the corner with the second sword in one hand, his knife in the other, but otherwise didn't move. Was he even more terrified than Vanya?

"Get a hold of yourself," Vanya whispered to him. Before he could say more, a hand bigger than any Vanya had ever seen reached in through the window and seized Stanislavovich by the throat. The hand stank of fetid flesh as if from a corpse. The skin was smeared dark. Blood or dirt. It slammed the engineer's head against the side slats. The wood cracked. In the same instant, Dima broke the glass bottle and sank the jagged teeth into the wrist with so much force Vanya was sure he hit bone. The howl that ensued was desperate. Stanislavovich fell and while Vanya expected the engineer to slump to the ground, instead he bounded out of the train brandishing the sword over his head. Growling and hissing.

"Light it," a voice outside called, its accent thick and different from any Vanya had heard before. "Light it. Light it."

A flame. A flash. A torch was tossed into the train and with it Vanya saw Yuri still cowering. His body appeared shrunken as if he'd inhaled himself into a ball. Dima stamped out the flames.

He had the fire extinguished in seconds, but in the interval, Vanya realized the blaze was never the point. The torch had been soaked in something horrid that made Vanya's eyes feel as if they were being pricked by a thousand needles and his throat raked with an ax. They had no choice but to run outside and that was the point.

He and Dima hurried down the steps, clutching their weapons. Someone grabbed Vanya, dragged him over sticks and rocks that sliced his shirt and skin. Vanya grabbed the wrist, expecting muscular flesh but instead discovered thin bones. Nothing but a boy. Vanya wrenched free.

"Kill them if you have to," a voice bellowed. Someone older. "Take the food." Vanya swung for the man's nose. He ducked, and Vanya missed. Before he could strike again, Stanislavovich roared from behind and brought the sword down on the man. Blood fell like rain on Vanya's face. The man toppled. In the gap that opened once he was down, Vanya saw Dima fighting another man. He didn't have the bottle anymore. He was using his fists. The sound of flesh on flesh made Vanya want to retch.

"Yuri," Vanya yelled. "Help us." Coward.

Another man approached Vanya. He was the same height. Twice as broad, but while there was a heft to his bones, his eyes were hollow. The man was hungry, which meant he'd tire quickly. Vanya would win just by running. And the man was after whatever was in the train, not Vanya. So Vanya scurried into the forest, kneeled behind a tree, and just as he'd expected, the man didn't follow. Instead he went back to the train.

Now the roar of blood in Vanya's ears was gone, replaced by an awareness he'd never felt. He was sure he could hear every leaf tear and ant crawl. Vanya knew he should run back to help, but he froze. And just for a second, a split second, he wondered if it would be easier if he didn't make it back. He didn't have his equations to finish relativity. Couldn't seem to get it right. What if he hid in the woods—let the others think he was lost? Then they could give up this madness, the danger they were all taking on for him. Just as quickly as the thought came, he banished it. He couldn't do that. Not to Miri and Baba. He touched the pouch sewn into his belt, the one with his grandmother's rubies, and he thought about the eclipse, Russell Clay. No, he couldn't let fear get to him. He stood. Then he heard a mechanical sputter. And smelled coal. Someone had started the engine. Without another thought, Vanya took off as fast as he could toward the train.

"Wait," he yelled, so out of breath it came out as a whisper. The engine was roaring by then. In silhouette he saw Dima shoveling coal.

"Vanya," Yuri yelled across the field. The wheels strained to start. Vanya tripped. Something cut his knee but he ignored it. Scrambled back up. Ran past a man on the ground.

"Wait," he yelled again. Louder this time. The train was gaining speed.

Yuri was perched on Stanislavovich's ledge. "Run," he yelled. "Vanya, run."

Vanya was sore, but his legs flew. He had to make that train. For Miri. For Baba. Yuri held out his hand and Vanya grabbed for it— once, twice, their fingers slipped apart from the sweat and grime— until finally, Yuri grabbed Vanya by the arm and heaved him inside. Vanya slid into the crates across from the roaring coal pit and gasped for air. "I'm safe. Safe," he muttered. But he had to get a hold of himself. He concentrated on his breathing, on calming down. He was only safe for now. Slowly, his heart rate fell and he began to realize how much his ribs hurt, that his hands and knees were scraped raw. "Yuri," Vanya said. He coughed to clear his throat. The act brought pain and relief. "Brother, why didn't you move earlier? Why didn't you fight?"

"I can't say. I froze." Yuri took a deep breath. "I remembered something."

"What?"

"Don't waste your time," Dima snarled from the other end of the car.

They fell into a dark silence and the engine worked to pull them around a curve that seemed to bend for hours. The trees over the train were tight and branches snapped as they made their way through, the sound sudden and loud like gunshots. "That won't be the end of it," Dima said when the train finally straightened. "They must have been deserters. Starving men. If we stop again at night, we'll be attacked again. Next time we might not be so lucky. Should we turn around?"

"No. We don't stop," Vanya said. "Not unless we have to. Not at night."

"This eclipse, it can't be worth this kind of danger," Dima said.

"It is." It had to be.

"Why? What holds you? A captain knows when it's time to abandon his ship to save his men. You know how dangerous it is to ride at night when we can't see the rails are clear?"

"You know there was a time when it was accepted the world was flat?" Vanya asked.

"Yes. Sailors were afraid they'd sail off the earth," Dima said.

"The Greeks were the first to posit it was round. They came up with equations to back their claims but somehow, they were lost. There are always doubters. People need to see, to touch, to believe. They needed a man to prove the earth was round by circumnavigating the globe." Vanya paused. "You've heard of Ferdinand Magellan. It wasn't until Magellan sailed around the world that the theory was accepted. That people believed the world was round again. Then, everything changed. Trade. Exploration. Math. The globe expanded exponentially."

Dima laughed. "You think you're Magellan?"

"I think my equations, paired with photographs from this eclipse, will make others believe, will inspire others to go out and explore even further."

Dima ran a hand over his cheek. Not the rough swipe he usually made, but a soft pass showing he, too, was sore. "This could be the death of us all." And then, "Tell me more about America. What excites you about that country?"

Vanya told Dima about his relatives in Philadelphia, that they felt safe for the first time in their lives in that city. "Yes, there's crime. Violence. But not like what we have in Russia. There's no Okhrana. They elect their president. It's the land of the free," Vanya said, smiling. He went into detail about the vast farms and the crowded cities, about the paupers who rose up out of nothing. "You don't have to be born into wealth or greatness there to achieve it—or to achieve anything."

"At least they want you to believe that," Dima replied. Vanya could tell Dima was trying to look nonplussed but that in truth his eyes were wide and his words came quickly—he was just as excited as Vanya by the idea of going to America, to Philadelphia. Still, Dima shook his head. "Your science is truly this important?"

"Without a doubt," Vanya said. And then he added, "If not now, when? If not me, who? This theory of relativity, it will change the world." Dima didn't reply. The rails carried them even deeper into the woods, where they were enveloped in a night as dark as dark can be.

X

"You don't think you look suspicious with that coat on in this weather?" Miri asked Sasha as they walked into the center of the town.

"The soldiers at the platform must believe I'm Grekov."

"Why would there be soldiers stationed out here in the first place? If anyone's there, they'll be civilians and they won't know about medals or rank."

"No, they'll be soldiers. The czar has men posted at every depot and station. He needs his trains to run his supplies for war."

"And if these soldiers know the real Grekov?"

"They won't. These men will be the lowest of the low. They'll have no idea."

When they found the depot, it was a half-built skeleton. Bins of coal sat out in the open, covered by a tarp. The wooden frame of the building stood flat and low. It smelled like pine tar. A wagon loaded with lumber sat in front, and a short soldier basked in the sun and smoked while his horse chewed on a square of hay. "Pavel!" a man yelled from around the other side of the building.

Pavel took a puff on his cigarette and quashed it. Then he pulled out a board from the pile in the wagon and hoisted it to his shoulder, began walking away from them toward his companion.

"Halt, soldier!" Sasha called. He and Miri were close but Pavel didn't seem to hear. Sasha spoke louder. "Halt! We need to be on the next train to Daugavpils. When's it due?"

"Save your breath. It won't stop here," Pavel said, not bothering to turn his head. In a heartbeat, Sasha was behind Pavel, shoving the board to the ground with enough force that Pavel yelped and turned around with his fists up, ready to fight. Sasha flung him into the dirt before Pavel even had a chance to take a swing. He landed like a heap of rags in the dust. A vein in Sasha's neck throbbed, the only sign he'd exerted himself. A cow nearby swished its tail, unfazed.

"I'm so sorry. Sir, I'm so sorry," Pavel said. He threw his hands over his head as if expecting another blow. "I didn't realize you were an officer."

"Call me Captain."

"C-Captain." Pavel's chest heaved. "Th-that train to Daugavpils is due in an hour but it only passes through."

"*You* will make that train stop for us," Sasha said.

"Pavel?" the man called from around the corner again. "I need that wood."

"Yes, but it isn't supposed to stop," Pavel continued.

"I don't care what it's supposed to do. You have your orders," Sasha said.

The soldier who'd been calling for Pavel stepped out from the side of the building. He had blond hair and skin rough like burlap. He gasped and saluted. "Captain," he said. "Captain."

"I need the next train to Daugavpils stopped," Sasha said. "I'll board with my cousin."

"Stopped?" the man repeated.

"Are you two the only ones assigned to this construction project?"

"Yes, Captain. The last station burned. We're rebuilding."

"Fine. Go. Get us food, drink. And then stop the train. Go!" Sasha yelled. Pavel and the other soldier scrambled, tripped over one another trying to fill their new orders.

"Just like that?" Miri whispered. Sasha smiled. He gestured toward a log in a shady patch of grass where they could wait, and Miri took a seat.

The soldiers came back with apples, cheese, and milk. Pavel, out of breath, presented a pile of cigarettes. They were smudged black with dirt from his fingers, and the tobacco was rolled too quickly so it bulged out of either end. Sasha thanked them, and without another word they were off, scurrying down the tracks to set the signals to stop the train. Sasha reached for a bucket Pavel had brought with fresh water. He offered a ladle to Miri. It was sweet and still cold. Sasha drank after her and then smoked one cigarette after another. Pacing. He moved as if barely aware of what he was doing, his mind working through a problem. When he looked at her, Miri smiled. "What?" he asked.

"You remind me of Vanya. He's always pacing, calculating. What are you thinking?"

"What will we do in Kiev? How will we find them?" A child skipped past. He didn't notice them hidden in the shade. "He'll stand out. If we ask in the right places, someone will know the American. We can look for your brother by looking for the American."

"Yes, but where will we ask? We can't go to the university. We'd draw attention. And we can't afford that," Miri said. "What about a school? A prominent teacher? Jewish teachers?"

"It could work," Sasha agreed. "Tell me, why do you flinch when I say the city's name?"

"Do I?" She hadn't realized.

"Kiev means something to you?"

"My parents went there once. My mother told me all about it. The beauty. The music. The city is famous for its musicians. Or at least that's what she said." And then, "Tell me about your family. You've barely said anything about them." She reached into the basket Pavel had brought and broke off a chunk of bread. She handed half to Sasha. He took it and sat next to her.

"It was five years ago. The last time I saw them," he said. "And by then, we were ruined. We had to leave Saint Petersburg years earlier, run for our lives."

"Why?"

Sasha shook his head. His voice started shaking. "We ran into the countryside. It was so cold we almost froze, but a farmer took us in. He hid us for a long time before a starving neighbor reported us for the reward." Sasha looked back at the half-built station. "When the police came, they took me first. They threw me into a wagon, said I was joining the army."

"And your parents?"

"The farmer, he still writes to me. He sends letters to a pub in Peter. I pick them up when I'm there. Did I tell you my father was the one who taught him to read and write? With me?"

"You didn't."

Sasha closed his eyes. A tear leaked down through his stubble. "They were killed after I was dragged away. The farmer watched the police shoot them, and then he was forced to bury them. He said he thought he was digging his own grave. But they spared him. For some reason, they spared him."

"I'm sorry," Miri said. She pushed tears off her own cheeks. She knew Sasha was waiting for her to say something, but she didn't have any words. When her parents died, people said they were watching over her or that their deaths were part of God's plan. She didn't believe any of them. And the pain she felt, the loss, was indescribable. There were no words. No way to help. "Try not to think about it," she said. "It hurts too much to dwell on something you can't change."

"At least you have your baba," he said.

"Sasha." Miri started to reach for his hand but pulled back before she touched him. "Is that why you stayed with us? Baba, she has a way. She makes everyone feel like she's theirs."

"Yes, she does, but it's not why I stayed." He wiped his eyes. "Your baba's right about America. There, at least people die of old age. Or so I understand. It'll be a better life."

"She'd like to hear that."

"I'll tell her then." He leaned toward Miri. "When we make it back to her."

XI

One hour of waiting turned into four. Every passing minute made Miri more tense. Whenever a horse brayed, Miri shivered. Any sound could mean another soldier was coming, a soldier who might know the real Grekov, and out here, there was no crowd to hide them. Even if they could get away, without the rails they'd never make it to Kiev by the eclipse.

When the train finally came, it was a mass of steel twice the size of the one Babushka had boarded for Saint Petersburg. The wheels lurched as if the weight was more than they could bear. Miri straightened her skirts, trying to hide the rip from the station in Kovno. In the distance, Pavel flapped signals, ordering the train to halt.

"It's going too fast, it won't stop," Miri said.

"There's still time." Sasha took Miri's hand and tucked it in his arm. The horse in front of the station whinnied, and a gust of air sent dust shooting across the tracks.

"It has to stop, please," Miri whispered. She narrowed her eyes as if squinting could help her will the train to slow down. There was too much dust to know if it was working. Then the brakes screeched. Miri exhaled. Pavel dropped the signal and they waited, watched as the wheels came to a halt. An engineer stepped down from the first car. He was black with soot, and the fetid smell of coal that hung around him turned Miri's stomach. "What's happened?" he asked. "Have the Germans taken the tracks?"

"I'm Captain Grekov." Sasha stepped forward. "I ordered the train to stop so that I might board with my cousin."

"Have the Germans ambushed the line?" the engineer asked again.

"Of course not! I told you, I ordered the train to stop so I could board."

"Why here?"

"Are you questioning my orders?"

"No, sir. It's just, just... Third car, there's one bank of seats left. You can sit there."

Sasha helped Miri up the three stairs. His fingers trembled even as they held her tight. Relief? Jitters? She stepped inside with him right behind her and blinked. From the outside, it looked like the train they'd entered was an ordinary first-class dining car. The windows were covered with lace demi-curtains. Through the glass Miri had seen a glittering chandelier. But now that she was inside, the facade shattered. The banquettes had been torn out. The carpet was ripped. The pink silk on the walls was shredded. Wooden splinters dangled where tables had been secured. And in their place, large, roughhewn crates were stacked, row after row, each sealed with the czar's crest.

"Ammunition," Sasha whispered.

"Bullets?"

"Shells."

"Greetings!" a bald man called to them from behind the crates. Miri jumped. She hadn't seen him past the explosives. He was at the one remaining table. It looked elegant, with salt and pepper shakers nestled by the window in a silver holder as if set for lunch. The man was an officer in uniform. His eyes were dark with circles so deep and purple they looked like scars. The whiskers that made his mustache reminded Miri of a seal. The train shuddered and Sasha reached an arm around her waist to steady her. This man seemed to make Sasha as nervous as Miri.

"Why the hell did you stop my train?" the officer said with a smile. Teasing.

"So we could board," Sasha said, and seemed to try to match the officer's smile. Miri looked back at the door. It was open and the train didn't have much speed. They could still jump.

"I'm feeling tired, cousin," she said to Sasha, trying to pull him back toward the exit, but Sasha wouldn't move, wouldn't let go of her waist. He was telling her he wanted to stay.

"Then sit!" the man said. "Welcome to my train. Grekov, eh?" The man laughed for too long. "I'm Colonel Zubov. Welcome, welcome to my train."

"Your train?" Sasha asked.

"Well, in a way. I'm escorting these shells to their destination. It's my official duty to the czar," Zubov said. "So, I feel I can take the liberty of calling it my train." He pointed to the seat across from him at the banquette. "Join me."

Sasha steered Miri forward. "I'm not feeling well," she said, still leaning back.

"Trust me," Sasha whispered. It was what Miri asked him to do after the first time they ran back in Kovno. She slid onto the leather bench, next to the window. Sasha took his place at her side, all while Zubov kept his dark eyes on them. Close now, Miri saw his nails were jagged, likely from biting. And his breath smelled like rotten cabbage. She tried not to think about the odor, tried to concentrate on being Grekov's cousin.

Zubov reached into his jacket and produced a flask, took a swig and offered it to Sasha. "Are you truly the infamous fool, the *durak*, Grekov? Or did you steal his greatcoat?"

"Stealing a coat like this would make me even a bigger fool, no?" Sasha laughed. To Miri it sounded fake, but Zubov didn't seem to notice. He broke into a wider grin that bared gray teeth.

"How true! Who but Grekov would dare to wear that coat!" Zubov clasped a hand over Sasha's. "Your reputation precedes you, Captain, but I'd never heard about your humor. A shame. Tell me, where are your Jews?"

"Karmėlava. Camping in a field."

"You were permitted to leave them?"

"Only for a few days, to escort my cousin."

"Cousin?" He paused. "I've never seen a woman so tall and so striking." The train bumped. A crate behind them crashed. "Not to worry. Plenty of crates have toppled," Zubov said with a wink for Miri. "They're made to withstand travel. And if we have a dud, well, we'll be dead before we feel any pain. Tell me, where are you escorting this *cousin* to?"

"Daugavpils."

"You did say cousin, right?" Zubov took another sip from his flask. "This vodka must be going to my head. I could have sworn I saw you put your arm around her waist. I've never seen *cousins* touch with such intimacy. At least not in public." He winked again. "Behind closed doors, well, cousins don't always act like cousins, do we?"

"Colonel, you look tired," Sasha said.

"I am. The czar has us working day and night. The Germans are coming. They're after our women, our children. It's terrible, really. Not a full night's sleep in weeks."

"Then sleep now," Sasha said. "You're among friends."

"If only I could. Seems my body's learned to stay awake." Zubov handed Sasha the flask again. "Why not take off your coat, *Captain*? It is warm, too warm for all that wool, no?"

"I'm comfortable," Sasha said. The train accelerated. The trees outside blurred.

"I, for one, will rest," Miri said. She laid her head against the window and forced her eyes closed, hoping that would end the conversation because there was no way off now. The train was moving too fast for them to jump. And while she feigned sleep, Zubov attacked his nails. The sound of him tearing at them put her on edge as much as the shells rattling at their backs.

XII

"Cousin," Sasha whispered. How long had she kept her eyes closed? The train still rattled. The shells behind them were creaking, bumping, louder now than they'd been when they boarded. How much time had passed? "We're close," Sasha said. Miri pulled her head up. She rubbed her cramped shoulder.

"Are we?" she asked.

"Fifteen minutes or so," Zubov answered. He sat with his feet up on his side of the seat. He had his empty vodka flask in hand, upside down. "Tell us, how was your beauty rest, *cousin?*"

"Fair," Miri said.

"You know I've been watching you. You look nothing like your cousin."

"Do all cousins look alike?" Miri asked.

"No, of course not. Tell me, how are you related?"

"Our mothers are sisters," Sasha answered.

The rails under them groaned. They were switching tracks. Miri tried to keep her face composed. Zubov flung his feet to the floor and burst out laughing. Miri couldn't help but think it sounded too jolly, couldn't figure out why he was making this show.

Zubov leaned toward them. The smell of rotting cabbage coming from him was stronger now. "Tell me, why do you wear that greatcoat buttoned to your chin in this heat? I see you sweating, Grekov."

"The temperature is fine," Sasha replied.

"Grekov?"

"Yes?"

"I need to stretch my legs," Miri said. She tried to urge Sasha out of the banquette. He wasn't moving. Couldn't he see Zubov was drunk, that his questions were dangerous? They needed to get out of there. She pushed, harder. Finally, Sasha moved and at that same moment Zubov's hand shot across the table. He grabbed Miri's arm so hard she cried out.

"Let go," Sasha said. His hand was at his waist, at his knife, Miri knew.

A moment passed in thick, awful silence. Miri could sense Sasha running a finger over his blade, considering, planning. Then: "Sorry, so sorry," Zubov said, loosening his grip but still holding her. He stroked the inside of her wrist now. It took all Miri had to keep her face steady. "It's the vodka. I should have asked nicely. Please, sit with me for another minute." They shouldn't. Miri knew it. Every cell in her body was telling her to run, to jump, even from the train at full speed. They needed to get away.

Zubov pointed outside. The trees gave way to leaning shacks that dotted the side of the road. The roofs had holes. The walls were thin and pocked so she could see clear through. A father with long *peyes* sat with his son in a cracked wagon. "Pathetic Jewish scum," Zubov said.

Sasha must have seen Miri was about to reply. He cut in quickly, "My cousin is only a woman. Let's not burden her with politics."

"I say we throw them to the dogs in Palestine," Zubov said. "Let them boil alive in the desert, fight to the death against the Turks. Do you think I'm wrong?"

"No, of course not," Sasha said.

"I was asking your cousin. What do you think, *cousin*, should we send the Jewish dogs to the desert, kick them out of Russia?"

"Yes," she said, hoping she sounded convincing. "Make them all leave."

"I don't believe you mean that for a moment. But perhaps there are too many of them to send to the desert. It would be expensive. Instead, we should kill them here. Be gone with them. They're nothing but a burden, an embarrassment to Russia."

Miri thought she caught herself before her face showed her disgust for Zubov, but she hadn't. She knew it because she could see his smile growing, his awful mustache pointing higher. Sasha must have seen the reaction, too. Like lightning, he stood and pulled her up with him. "Come, cousin, stretch your legs."

"Tell me, why do you like these Jews?" Zubov asked.

"It's the children," Sasha said. She was pushing him now, moving them toward the door, more certain than ever that jumping was safer than confronting Zubov or the risk of arriving with him at the train station, where he'd have men to help trap them. "She has a soft spot for children," Sasha called over his shoulder. The train shot into a tunnel. The force of air rattled the car. A shell clanged against its case, and in the dark, Miri felt a sticky hand close around her throat. Zubov. It happened so fast she couldn't react, couldn't reach her dagger. She felt his thick fingers, his barbed nails cutting her skin. She clawed at him, but he was cutting off her airway, and the more she struggled, the harder he slammed her against the side of the train. She didn't feel anything but raw fear. And she couldn't manage to call to Sasha for help.

She tried to fight. She didn't have enough air and already she felt heavy. She thought about kicking or scratching, or did she do it? Either way, she realized he was holding her with only one hand. His other hand held a blade under her ribs, placed with the accuracy of a surgeon at the exact angle to kill. "You're Jews!" he yelled. "Move and I'll kill her."

The train heaved out of the tunnel. In the light, Miri saw Sasha standing behind Zubov. He had an arm around Zubov's neck, another on his head, poised to snap the bones. He was breathing hard, and the look on his face was something Miri had never seen in him before. There was no doubt he'd kill Zubov, that he knew exactly what to do with his bare hands.

"Let her go," Sasha said. His voice sounded far away. Too far away.

"Remove your arms or I'll kill her, we both die." Zubov loosened his grip and ran his tongue over the nibs of his teeth. Miri was able to take a small breath, but just as she did, Zubov's grip tightened again. "Is that what you want? Me to kill this *cousin*, this fresh apple?"

"I said, let her go," Sasha said.

"And I told you to get off me or I'll kill her. Do you want to see if I'm bluffing?"

Sasha shifted his grip on Zubov and seemed to just stop himself from killing him. In response, Zubov dug the knife in deeper. Miri yelped. It came more from fear than from pain. In truth, she was numb. And the train, it seemed, was darker.

"What'll you do, *Grekov*? We'll be at the station soon. I'll have reinforcements. Don't for a minute think I believe you're the real Grekov—that man is dead. And I'm betting you killed him. One of his Jewish dogs went missing the night he died. Was that you?" He took a breath. "Either way, release me, or your *cousin* dies." Sasha said something. Maybe. Miri needed air. Zubov continued, "I've never had a Jewess." He pushed the blade deeper. Miri's dress ripped.

The train bumped. Zubov stumbled, and suddenly, she could breathe. But Sasha no longer held Zubov. "Good. Good you let go," Zubov said, but he kept the knife on Miri. He dropped his other hand from her neck, down to her breast. She shook. Revulsion. But she could breathe. She had air and couldn't fill her lungs fast enough.

"My Jewish apple." Zubov licked his lips.

The train wheels screeched. The brakes clamped down hard, and all three of them lost their balance. Zubov sliced her forearm. She saw the cut before the blood even started to flow, as if detached, watching a patient bleed rather than herself. Just before she hit the floor, Sasha had her. Miri's only thought was that he had her. The next thing she knew they tumbled out of the train and were rolling on gravel. It was sharp and cold. Sasha was on top of her, under her. It hurt but she was alive. They were alive and off the train.

When they stopped rolling, she landed on his chest. The train barreled away. Zubov hung from the side. "You're dead. You dirty Jew. I'll find you. You and your whore. You're hiding something. I know it," he yelled.

"You're hurt," Sasha said. He bent to examine the spot where her dress was ripped, the blood on her arm.

"I'm fine," she said. She'd recover. She sat up slowly.

"If Grekov's really dead, there's no question he'll look for us. Me having this coat, it's all the evidence he'll need to convict me."

"I know," Miri said.

Sasha draped his coat over her, kept his arms around her. "You're shivering," he said. The wool was warm with body heat and thick with Sasha's smell.

"Shock," she said. "We need to keep moving." She took a deep breath and handed the coat back.

XIII

Fourteen, thirteen days until the eclipse. Vanya was hurtling toward Brovary, but instead of feeling lighter he only felt heavier. He'd made no progress on his work to complete relativity and was dangerously close to arriving with nothing to offer the American to prove his worth. How would he convince Clay to part with a precious photograph without equations? Even all the rubies in the world wouldn't be enough to motivate a man who'd funded his own expedition.

No. He couldn't let that happen. He couldn't show up without them. He had to solve it. How? Einstein, Vanya knew, took to physical activity when he was stumped, and so Vanya began sawing branches and tightening bolts, refusing to rest even when Yuri urged him to go back to his notebooks. His hands were soon covered in blisters and his back ached, but he didn't slow down; he only worked harder.

At night, Dima helped Vanya rehearse his introduction in English, but kept saying his accent was too thick. "Put your tongue to the top of your mouth, toward your teeth. That's how to make the right sound," Dima said again and again.

"Sorry." Vanya shook his head. He wasn't paying close enough attention. "If only…"

"You've been saying that for days," Yuri said.

The train shot through a tunnel dug under a mountain. The initial jolt of air being displaced by steel was jarring, but it melted as they reached equilibrium. The four sat in darkness, surrounded by the amplified roar of the engine. There was no way for

Stanislavovich to see the tracks, to know if there was a boulder in front of them. Even if he could, they were going too fast to stop. The mountain walls were so near, Vanya felt their dampness closing in, drops of water on his skin.

"Coal. Last depot on this route," Stanislavovich yelled when they punched through the other side. An alley of trees soared over them, their trunks so thick Vanya couldn't see beyond the first line. Stanislavovich pulled the brake and the wheels slowed. Vanya closed his eyes. If only Mercury's precession were quadratic, simple. But then there would be no mystery.

Dima hopped down first. The depot was like others in remote areas, a gray box of a building stranded in a field with a single road leading one way uphill and the other into a thicket. Two men in uniform stood on the platform under a pewter sky smudged by exhaust. Usually the engineers at these depots looked bored, but that morning they were animated. Their steps were quick. Both ran to meet them. One held a telegram. "I need to speak to Stanislavovich," the man said. He was short with cheeks covered in angry, red blotches. Why was he expecting them? How did he know the engineer's name? "I'm Yasha," he added.

"We'll go for water while you handle this," Dima said to Stanislavovich. "Vanya, take your things." Without a pause Dima took hold of Vanya's arm and led him off the train. Yuri trailed behind. Quickly. Quickly, they walked toward a water pump. Someone had tracked them all the way out here. Who?

"I don't like it," Vanya whispered as they hurried. His notebook dug against his hip.

"Me, either," Yuri said.

"Try to look relaxed," Dima said. "It could be nothing."

But it wasn't nothing. Vanya could see that now from the way Yasha shook the telegram and pointed to them as he spoke to Stanislavovich. "Could Kir reach this far?" Vanya asked Yuri quietly.

"It seems impossible, but it has to be him," Yuri said. "Who else would care where we are? Or bother?"

"We're deserters," Vanya said.

"We're two Jews. Not worth this much effort. Not to anyone but Kir."

They'd made it to the pump by now. Dima levered the handle, and a cool stream of water fell into a bucket slick with age. Dima went through the motions of washing his face, but he missed his cheeks because he kept his eyes on Yasha and Stanislavovich. "It's nothing good. That's for sure," Dima said. "The telegram. It's some kind of order or directive."

"We're being arrested?" Vanya asked.

Yuri looked up. Vanya saw on his face he had a new idea. "Dima, did you kill the other engineers, the ones who were supposed to be on the train with Stanislavovich? Is that how you got us our place?"

"Don't be ridiculous. I paid. Tobacco and gold."

"Where would you get money like that?" Yuri asked.

"None of your business. Shhhh." Dima stopped abruptly. Held up a hand to signal that Yuri and Vanya should be silent, that he wanted to try to hear something. All three men stared across the field. Yasha was shaking his head. Stanislavovich was putting up a good fight but seemed to be losing.

"Orders are orders," Yasha said. And then something else. Water dripped, clunked against the pail. Vanya caught the words *arrest* and *Okhrana.*

Dima jumped to his feet. "You're sure your work is valuable enough to risk all this?" he breathed to Vanya.

"More than ever," Vanya said. Besides, by then, did he have a choice?

"We'll pay you more," Yuri said. "If you get us out of here. We'll pay double."

"Yes you will," Dima said. Without hesitating, he walked straight into the woods, away from the train. "Hurry," he said, but he didn't have to. Yuri and Vanya were right behind him. Twenty steps. Thirty and they heard a whistle. It was the kind Vanya knew from Kovno, one the police used to call for help. An alarm. Yasha and the others were chasing them. They picked up to a run, charged through mud and rocks. Yuri fell and was up. Around a boulder they doubled back into a cave. Vanya didn't know how Dima spotted it, but he was grateful. The jagged rocks were damp and spiked with the smell of lichen and salt. The only sound was their breathing. Vanya couldn't see Yuri, but he felt him shaking.

Yasha and his men came up on them in another heartbeat, only they were standing above, looking out over the lip of the cave. Vanya sensed they were so close that if he stepped forward and reached up, he could grab Yasha by the ankles. In the next instant, Yuri put his hand over Vanya's mouth. Was he breathing too hard? Too loud? Vanya closed his eyes and tried to calm himself, imagined the cave was a rocket, that they could fly away to safety. That Yasha would never catch them. He pictured himself shooting forward. Acceleration. Relativity. Gravity. They were connected, but how? Upward acceleration was different from falling. Oh, how Vanya hated not having answers.

"They're gone," Dima said. He leapt out of the cave. "Brovary should be this way."

"Should be?" Yuri said.

"I'm following the direction of the train tracks. It should be right. Right enough."

Soon all three men were running. All accelerating. They came to the top of a hill and slid in cold mud down the back side. In the distance, Vanya heard the police whistle. It was far behind them. Still, they continued running for what felt like hours. Finally, they stopped to rest at a seeping pond covered in clover. Frogs croaked all around. Vanya rubbed his legs. Yuri stood across from him. Under smears of mud, the lines around his mouth were exaggerated so he looked twenty years older. Dima, on the other hand, looked younger. His eyes blazed and his skin glowed. He reached into his bag and pulled out a bottle of vodka, took a long swig. "Knew we might need this," he said. "Always keep some with me."

"Those orders were from the Okhrana," Yuri said to Dima. "How did they find us?"

"Does it matter?"

"No," Vanya said. There was a long list of people that could have been after them. "It doesn't matter who. Or why. We just need to keep going."

"But Dima doesn't seem surprised that we've been hunted down."

"Who cares? He's running, too. In just as much trouble."

"Of course I'm not surprised. I've known this was a dangerous errand since the day we met," Dima said. "You're deserters. And you told me Vanya's work is important. Like anything in Russia, that means powerful men will try to steal it. I expected we'd be hunted."

"Powerful men?" Yuri asked. He narrowed his eyes. "Why would you say that?"

"Because it's obvious a powerful man wants my work."

"Obvious to you."

"Yes. Obvious this has Kir Romanovitch written all over it," Vanya said.

"Kir Romanovitch?" Dima asked.

"You know him?"

"I've heard the name. Perhaps you even mentioned him."

"We didn't," Yuri said.

"Either way, Yuri's right. It would be difficult even for a powerful man to track you from Kovno all the way out here." Dima held his hands out, motioned to the woods. "How could he do it?"

"The telegram," Yuri said to Vanya. "I knew it was a bad idea."

"No. I sent it to the baker's house. Even if Kir got his hands on it, he'd never understand it."

"Telegram?" Dima asked. "What are you talking about?"

"I sent a telegram to my family. Telling them we're headed to Kiev."

"Why would you do something so stupid?" Dima asked.

"I had to let my family know we were going. We promised to be back by the fall. But with war and snow, I wasn't sure we could make it. Not as deserters. And I wanted to make sure we had enough time, that I wouldn't rush. If I hadn't warned them, they would have thought we were dead. Besides, I sent it in code."

"You think you can outsmart the Okhrana? Or a great man like Kir Romanovitch?" Dima was on his feet, coming closer. "Stupid. Stupid. And you didn't think to tell me?"

"Why are you so upset? What's it matter to you?"

"You've put us in more danger than you know. This Kir, he has ways to persuade your sister to talk. If you told her where we're going, mark my words, Kir knows."

"No," Vanya said. "He would never hurt her." Would he?

"So smart and so dumb. You've made the hunt easy." Dima paused. "Friends, you're Jews?"

"We've been baptized," Yuri said too quickly.

"I don't believe you. And I don't care. I've known since the first night we met. I heard Vanya speak in Yiddish." Was that possible? Had Vanya made that mistake?

"You seem to hear us say many things we don't remember," Yuri replied, and walked over to Dima, with one hand on the knife at his waist. The tension between them crackled like the dead leaves under them.

"Enough!" Vanya said, jumping between them.

"That night our train was attacked. Why didn't you help us fight, Doctor?" Dima asked.

"I don't know how to fight."

"That's a lie. You said you're from Zhytomyr. Every Jewish boy in Zhytomyr is trained to hurt a man. To kill." Vanya blinked. Why had he never thought of that, of Baba's endless stories about the famous, brutal Jewish fighters from Zhytomyr? Dima continued, "From that first fight with Kolya on the docks, it's been obvious. You knew where the punch was going to land. You can stand your own. What are you hiding?"

"I could ask the same of you."

"You're imagining things," Dima said.

"Am I?"

"Come on," Vanya said to them. "Stop this. We need to keep going."

But Yuri didn't move. Neither did Dima. "Just tell us your proposal," Yuri said. "This whole time, you've had more up your sleeve. What is it you really want?"

Vanya wasn't sure whether Dima would lunge at Yuri or not. But then, suddenly, the sailor held up his hands in surrender. "I want you to teach me to read."

"To read?" Vanya said. He stepped back. "That's all you want?"

"Please, brother. Don't believe him. There must be more."

"There's not. My father, my father's father. They lived and died slaves to men who thought they were better, who had power because they could read. I don't want to die a slave."

"Stop lying," Yuri said so loud the birdsong stopped. "You called it a *business* proposition."

"It is. To be on top, to make a real business, I need to read."

"You know as well as anyone that education is power," Vanya said to Yuri. He had seen Baba's clients embarrassed by their illiteracy. It made sense that a sea captain like Dima would also be embarrassed, would want to read. "Maybe that is all he wants. Can you write or read anything, Dima?"

"Hand me a piece of paper." Vanya hesitated only because Yuri was still poised to fight.

"Brother, what do we have to lose?" he asked and watched Yuri consider what he'd said. Then slowly, slowly, Yuri stepped back, retreated to a log where he took a seat but didn't take his eyes off the sailor. Vanya pulled out a crumpled sheet from his bag, and Dima smoothed it out on his leg. He held Vanya's pencil like a child, balled in his fist, but his strokes were fast. He didn't hesitate and soon, Yuri's likeness jumped off the page.

"I was a kitchen boy in an artist's house, long ago, before I could grow this beard." Dima smiled but there was a sadness to it Vanya hadn't expected. And he kept drawing, adding sharp lines to define the edges, faded strokes to render shadows. He captured the fatigue in Yuri's eyes, even the darkness that Vanya had always sensed but somehow had never pinpointed the way Dima did now. Yuri looked as stunned as Vanya felt as the portrait's focus improved, and the more Dima added the more Yuri's shoulders dropped, his jaw loosened. And the more relieved Vanya felt because he took it to mean Yuri was easing back into having Dima on their side. They were stronger with a guide like him. "Yes, I'll teach you to read," Vanya said, finally.

Dima held out his hand and they shook on it. "Thank you. You're a good man, Vanya. Come. We need to find that American." Dima folded the drawing and handed it to Yuri.

The three set out again and Dima turned to Yuri with a grin as they walked. "Doctor, tell me more about your fiancée. Her thighs, they're firm? Dimpled?"

Yuri shoved Dima and the terrain pitched uphill in the direction Vanya hoped would lead to Brovary.

XIV

After hiking all day, Yuri and Vanya sprawled in the shade on a hill overlooking a town. The doctor and the scientist weren't used to living outside, but they were holding up well enough. At least they didn't complain. Dima had known sailors who would have done worse. "What's wrong?" Yuri asked Vanya. And Dima realized that Vanya was suffering from something worse than fatigue. His face was contorted. Purple. He was crying. Sobbing.

"I'm failing you. Miri. Baba..." Vanya gasped for air. Dima had never seen a man crumple like that, not without a fight. Perhaps the stress had been too much for him. Yuri had Vanya bend, put his head between his knees.

"Get a hold of yourself," Yuri said. "You don't mean it..." Dima had no doubt Yuri would talk sense into Vanya. The doctor was wily that way. Dima didn't know what he'd lived through, but it couldn't have been good—and survivors like that, well, they understood better than anyone how to get back on their feet. As the professor sobbed, Dima checked the woods behind them to make sure they were safe. That was when he saw them—telegraph wires.

"Thanks to God," he whispered. They were strung up on haphazard poles. Dima had been looking to send a telegram since he'd heard Vanya sent one to his sister and grandmother. The fool. Dima had to clean up after his mistake, needed to contact Ilya to take care of things. He looked back. Yuri was still calming Vanya down. It was Dima's chance to get away without raising suspicion. "Rest here. I'm going into town for food," Dima called. "And to make sure we're going the right way." He hurried down the hill before Yuri could object.

Dima ran, trailing the wires. Still couldn't believe Vanya had told his sister he was heading to Kiev. For such a brilliant man, he was an idiot. Dima never planned on telling Ilya their destination. It was how he'd made sure they weren't followed. And how he'd make sure he got paid. After all, this was about getting paid. And now Dima had two things to sell: math and photographs. Which meant he'd be able to ask for more.

But Dima had been just as dumb as Vanya, telling Ilya they were after an American. Putting both pieces of information together, knowing Vanya was after an American near Kiev would make them easy to find. If Dima was going to get paid, he'd have to take careful hold of the situation.

He paused. If a man like Kir was going to such lengths, maybe Vanya *was* an explorer like Magellan. It was possible. Dima stepped in a pile of manure and cursed. Served him right for being so sloppy. He cleaned his boot as best he could and kept going.

From the look of the awful town, there shouldn't have been any wires there at all. The houses were shacks. The farms were decrepit. But the czar needed to keep contact with his empire. Dima looked back, but Yuri wasn't following. He turned down a small street, where the wires ran into a barn. He just had to hold Ilya off until the eclipse was over, then he could wash his hands of this mess. A pity he was starting to like those two more than he should, Vanya and Yuri. He couldn't save them. Dima had worked with people like Kir before. He'd take what he wanted and kill them for their silence. Nothing Dima could do about it.

He opened the barn door and stepped inside. There were so many cracks in the walls that the space was well lit. The animals were cleared out, but given the smell and dirt, they might as well have been there. Inside a stall, two tables held a stack of machines plugged into the wires that fell from the ceiling. The soldier behind the desk was young and pale. His face was too soft, his nails too round. No doubt the boy came from a father with connections.

"No civilians," the soldier barked.

"I have a message for an important man."

"Don't we all?" The soldier laughed. "Why aren't you in the army? You're not crippled."

Dima came closer. "Kir Romanovitch of Kovno." The soldier's eyes went narrow. Dima continued, "I'm his man and I have a message for him. If you don't send it, his anger falls on you. Are you ready to risk that?" He handed the soldier an address Ilya had given him.

If you come before Aug 22 I'll burn equations STOP Cost is triple STOP Will have photos and math STOP You want both STOP

Dima watched the soldier tap out his message. "Are we near Brovary?" he asked when he was done.

"Yes. A day's walk. Maybe two. That way." He gestured toward the road.

"Good. Then I need food." The soldier was green enough that he didn't even ask for vodka in return.

XV

Just past sunrise, Miri and Sasha hid in a rank alley near train tracks headed to Kiev. Miri sat on a barrel. The skin where Zubov had cut her was sore, and she wore a shawl they'd stolen from a laundry line to cover the tear. We're alive, she thought to herself. At least we're alive.

"Do you know when the train's due?" Miri asked.

"I'm afraid there are no more schedules. Only orders. Whims."

"And you honestly think we should risk another train?"

"It's far. There's no other way. And Zubov won't be on this train, the Medved, headed to Kiev."

"He could have doubled back. Come for us."

"He can't leave the czar's cargo. He'd be shot. We have time before he can get word to the Okhrana."

"How will we board?"

"It's uphill here. And there's a curve. The train should slow enough for us to jump on."

Sasha rubbed the spot near his shoulder where he'd been stabbed. "Are you in pain?" Miri asked. "It was a hard fall, on that injury."

"It's nothing."

Three hours ticked by. A train passed. Not the Medved. An hour later, a smaller train composed of three cars passed. Still not theirs. "It will come," Sasha said.

"And if it's not running?"

"It's a central line. The czar would never cancel it."

"What if we jump into another car filled with shells? Guarded by another Zubov? Or even a supply car? That would be guarded, too."

"We have to risk it. If you want to find your brother before this eclipse, it's the only way."

Miri looked out on the tracks, saw a rat skitter under one of the ties. A man dropped a newspaper near the head of the alley. Sasha ran out to grab it and brought it back. They read huddled together in a shaft of light. Every article was a lie. The czar was mighty. His army was invincible. All lies. Then Miri spotted a small piece on what the paper called a Jewish uprising—a town where the Jews fought forced conscription. "Like Zhytomyr," Sasha said, nodding as she pointed to the article. "Good for them."

Zhytomyr. Yuri's home. He had finally told her about it one morning a year after she'd found him in the basement playing the piano. She'd come into the hospital early to check on a patient who'd been fighting a fever. She thought she was the first doctor to arrive, but the light was on in Yuri's office. She knocked. He didn't answer. When she eased the door open, Yuri stood at the window looking out on the men below in the brickyard. He wasn't wearing his doctor's coat or a jacket, only his shirtsleeves with several buttons undone. Aside from the time at the piano, she'd never seen him so rumpled.

When he turned to greet her, she noticed the candles on the windowsill in front of him. "Yahrzeits," he said. "It is the anniversary of my aunt and uncle's death."

"How many years has it been since they passed?"

"Four. I don't have a minyan, but I still want to say the prayers. Will you join me?" Men and women never prayed together, but nor were women known to be surgeons. She stood next to him. "*Yis'gadal v'yis'kadash...*" The men below yelled at a furious pace, but inside Yuri's office all was still save for their prayer and the flames twisting in the draft from the windows.

Yuri was curled forward. Sadness was all over him. More than anything, Miri wanted to comfort him, to put an arm around him as she would with a patient, but Yuri was her superior. Still, no one should feel such loss alone. She took his hand. Without hesitating, he threaded his fingers through hers, and as much as it took her by surprise she didn't pull back.

"I've never told anyone what happened," he said. "But..." He stopped. "Sharing will keep them with me. Isn't that what you tell your patients, their families?"

"You've heard me?"

"Of course." He kept his eyes down, perhaps on the ink stain still on the floor from the day she interviewed. "My mother sent me to live with my uncle when I was ten years old." He shook his head. "No, I should begin by saying I never wanted to be a doctor. Not like you. No, that's not where I should start, either." And then: "My father always had a bottle of vodka. He sold everything for a drink. Everything but my mother and me. And it made my mother miserable. She cried all the time. She pulled me aside at the end of the summer. When I was ten. Did I say that? I was ten years old?"

"It doesn't matter." It didn't.

"Anyway, one day my mother tucked a clean pair of socks and a shirt under her arm. They were my best but still gray with holes. 'You're leaving,' she said. 'You need to earn your own way. There's nothing here for you.' Her sister agreed to help. Her husband, my uncle, was a wealthy man compared to us. He lived in Zhytomyr, worked for a bank. They had a large house, not as grand as your babushka's, but to me it seemed like a castle. They had no children. Mama walked me there. I don't remember her goodbye because I was so angry. I didn't want to leave. Now I wish I could remember the way she held me, the color of her skirts. But I can't."

"I'm sorry," Miri said. Why couldn't she remember her own mother's embrace? Her skirts? "Your mother's dead?"

"No. But I don't want to see her again. Not after the way she left me."

"How can you say that?" Miri leaned back. "She had no choice." No mother could push a child away willingly. Miri had seen enough at the hospital, and with Baba's clients, to know. "But—"

"I can't forgive her. I won't. We always have choices, and she chose to let me go."

"What if you're wrong? What if she chose to let you live?"

He shook his head. "I don't want to talk about my mother. I want to talk about my aunt and uncle." Yuri shifted his weight. His shoe creaked. "My uncle told me I needed a profession. Science made sense. For Jews, it works in our favor that so few Russians want to be doctors." He paused. "I've never met anyone as committed to patients as you. How do you do it?"

"It's not something I think about."

"It wouldn't be." He blinked. "I'm still avoiding what I really wanted to tell you. My uncle, he had a beautiful piano in his library. He didn't have many books, only a handful, and they were all displayed on a shelf above his desk next to the piano. The walls were bare save for the two paintings he could afford. The candles dripped and burned my skin." He closed his eyes as if living every detail. "I'd never heard the piano before my aunt played for me. Once I heard her, I begged for lessons. My uncle told me it was a waste, it wasn't a path to a profession.

"I'm not even sure how my aunt learned to play, but she agreed to teach me. I suspect I fell for the piano just as you fell for medicine. Music came as naturally to me as breathing. It gave me joy. Sadness. Beauty. Yes, above all. Beauty."

"And medicine?"

"I applied for my uncle. The better my marks, the less he cared that I spent my free time at the piano. I dreamed of running away to join an orchestra. But all the great musicians live outside the Pale. To get to them, I needed to be *useful*. I stayed on course to become a surgeon, assuming it would help me escape. My life wasn't so bad. I sound spoiled. I know that. I had food, a roof over my head. And I became a surgeon." Yuri looked up now, straight into Miri. The hallway outside his office was no longer quiet. Nurses and doctors hurried back and forth, and Yuri, who was always punctual, lingered, surely knowing it was making him late. "The Jewish youth groups. What do you know about them?"

"I know that in Zhytomyr, they taught the Jews to fight."

"You admire that?"

"I do. Did you join one?"

"After I arrived at my aunt and uncle's house. Years before the pogrom. They approached me. 'Fight with your brothers,' they said at school, at synagogue. They waited in front of the house, at the market, always pushing, pushing. I gave in. I took their oath. The other boys, they couldn't wait to fight. But I didn't want to be there."

"You were scared. I understand that."

"I wasn't scared in the way you think. I feared what would happen if I didn't join." He leaned so far forward he was balanced on the balls of his feet. There, on the edge, she couldn't see his face, only his profile.

"You were there, for the uprising?" Miri asked.

"I wasn't there when it happened. But I could have been. In Zhytomyr, we expected a pogrom. After Kishinev, everyone understood it was only a matter of time. Some newspapers even predicted dates. Passover, Easter, or May Day. Anyway, I knew the pogrom was coming and I didn't want to watch."

"Of course not. You wanted to fight."

"No. Please, you make me out to be better than I am. I never wanted to fight. They tried to teach us to kill, to maim. All I wanted was to play the piano. I hated myself for that. All those people who died—and I survived. I lived because I wasn't even there."

"Is that what's bothering you? The guilt?"

"No."

"You want revenge?"

"No." He dropped his head to his chest. His fists were clenched now, and he was trembling. "I don't harbor grand notions that I would have been a hero. Revenge? What would revenge be? That night. I was playing the piano. I'd sneaked out to Kiev. A rabbi there invited me to play. He ran a small medical clinic in his basement for the poor, found me because he wanted me to work there. But then he heard I played the piano—and I played for him. He took me for the music, not medicine. But that's not the point. I heard about the massacre on my way home. My uncle's house was destroyed. I found him with my aunt, dead in the ashes. It was why I came here, to this side of Russia, to get away. If only I'd told my aunt and uncle the truth, they might still be alive."

"How?"

"They would have come to Kiev to hear me play."

"You don't know that."

"I do." Yuri stared at the floor. "The rabbi starting the orchestra, he could have paid me. He had a patron who was willing to support musicians. That salary could have given me a way to live by the piano. My family, they didn't care as long as I had an income." He took a deep breath. "They would have been happy for me. If I'd told them I had a salary and a concert, they would have come." Miri wasn't convinced but that didn't matter. What was important was that Yuri seemed to believe what he said. "Mirele, I'm telling you because..."

"You want to find them now? Your parents? You're leaving Kovno?"

"Leaving? No." He wiped his cheek. "This isn't about my parents. That night, at the concert, it was as if I were in a dream. When I close my eyes, I can still hear the man in the front row with the bad cough. I can still smell the lilacs the women were wearing in their hair. The lights didn't work properly, they stayed lit the entire time so I saw the audience. Men in suits, women in gowns. My fingers were as light as they'd ever been. The audience gave me a standing ovation while my aunt and uncle were slaughtered." He swayed, losing his balance. Miri steadied him, staying so close her skirts touched his knee.

After that day, they were closer. They began taking walks through the city together. Their conversations revolved around medicine and patients, Dr. Tessler, Russia's most prominent physician, his research and publications. And Yuri started coming for dinner, starting growing into her family.

Now Miri ran her finger over the headline in the newspaper Sasha had found. "Yuri's from Zhytomyr," she said. "He wanted us to be married already."

"And you?"

"I wanted to wait. Maybe I shouldn't have. What did it matter?" All those reasons that had held her back: wanting to be a surgeon, having to care for her brother and grandmother—and not even being sure she wanted to be a mother at all—they all seemed pointless as she and Sasha huddled in the alley waiting for the train.

Eventually, the sun ground across the sky, and the stars blinked to life. Near midnight, finally, there was a train. The rumble of the tracks started well before the engine appeared. Miri hoped she'd be able to make out some mark that designated the train as the Medved, but she couldn't see anything other than a dark object lumbering toward them. "That's it," Sasha said. He took her hand and they started running to catch it.

The train's wheels thundered when they were close, closer. What had looked like a slow pace now seemed too fast. "Ready?" Sasha yelled over the roar of the pounding steel. At least he was right about it slowing down. Even she noticed the speed decreasing as it approached the curve. Miri went as fast as she could. She ran even faster when she saw the elegant gold letters: MEDVED.

"Sixth car. Isn't locked," Sasha managed. Miri counted, grabbed onto a bar welded to the side, and heaved herself up. The pain in her arm where Zubov cut her seared, but she didn't let go. Sasha gave her a shove to help. She pushed the door with all her strength. He was right; it wasn't even latched. She tumbled inside, terrified, looking for crates of shells. For a guard like Zubov. But Miri rolled over something that bulged, soft. And then another padded lump. Sasha landed next to her. They bumped deeper into the train and came to a stop on a large sack that was damp and cushioned. The car smelled like burlap and paper. Miri stared up at the ceiling, tried to catch her breath. "We made it," she gasped. "We made it."

"Yes," Sasha said.

She sat up and looked around, searching for people. For clues. All she saw were dozens of sacks like the one she sat on now. Grain? No, the bags were striped. "Mail," Miri said.

"Never thought I'd be so happy to see piles of letters," Sasha said as he patted one of the sacks. A heap of dust billowed out and they both laughed. It was all they could manage. It hadn't even occurred to Miri that they could be so lucky. Mail depots were located in large train stations, at the end of the line. So long as Miri and Sasha were quiet, no one would set foot in that train car for the rest of their journey.

XVI

Vanya, Yuri, and Dima slept in the woods and rose at sunset to continue their hike toward Brovary. The terrain was flat but studded with fallen trees and unplowed fields, which made walking difficult, so Vanya was left alone with the muddle in his head. He stewed over Yuri's admonishment that he needed to get a hold of himself. Vanya had always thought he was the one in control. He had stayed strong when Mama and Papa died. He had fought to get Miri into school and himself into the university. And he had stood against Kir. Why was he failing now?

Yuri had suggested Vanya try thinking about relativity from another angle. That was how Yuri approached symptoms when he didn't have answers. And so as they walked, instead of imagining himself in a rocket as he considered acceleration and gravity, Vanya pictured an elevator so he could ride in both directions—up and down. There was something about that. He could feel it, but couldn't quite explain why. "Damn it," he yelled, but just as he did so, Dima clamped him hard on the shoulder and shoved him to the ground.

"Down. Get down," Dima hissed. All three crouched behind a bush. On the road running parallel to the path, a line of military trucks bumped past, rising and falling in ruts, passing under an awning of leaves that formed a green tunnel. Their engines choked and left the stink of burnt oil in their wake. The front of the line was loaded with cannons. The back was filled with soldiers in uniform, boys who didn't look old enough to grow a single whisker. Behind them came a man pushing a cart. A peasant. Then a priest holding a golden cross.

"What is it?" Yuri asked.

"A mobilization," Dima whispered. "It means the war has started. Officially."

"My God," Yuri whispered back. The priest was followed by two others holding a banner depicting Jesus. As they walked, they prayed. Peasants followed, forming a long line, a procession marching to Kiev to become soldiers. The men had families walking with them: wives, sons, and daughters. Some held crying babies. From now on, those women would have to drive a plow on their own. If they couldn't, their families would starve.

Vanya stopped one of the last men to pass. "Which way to Brovary?"

The man pointed. "Two hours' walk," he said.

"Two hours?" Vanya couldn't keep the excitement from his voice. He could barely believe it. He'd crossed Russia. Hiking and hiding. Fighting and running. And they'd found it. Brovary. They'd found it.

The man narrowed his eyes. "Why aren't you with us?"

"Let's go," Yuri said under his breath with his hand on Vanya's elbow.

"Haven't you been conscripted?" The man raised his voice. "*Deserters?*"

"Now," Dima said, and the three men hurried back into the brush. Green plants slapped at Vanya's knees. His boots bit at his blisters. Luckily, no one bothered to chase them.

"The timing, for the war," Dima said once they slowed back down to a walk. "It's bad for us. It'll increase tensions."

"When is the timing of war ever good?" Yuri asked.

"True. But now is worse than ever for us. Being here in the countryside, with an eclipse and a war." Dima shook his head. "The peasants will be terrified, and you never know what terror does to people. Remember what Kolya said? He called an eclipse the devil's work."

* * *

Just before sunset, the rise of a stately slate roof came into view. Under it sat a grand house, the only grand house they'd seen, made of stone slabs stacked like bricks that gave the architecture heft, an appearance that was more imposing than something so drab should have. There was no question they'd found Brovary; this was where an American would stay.

The men paused on the edge of the field, breathing hard. "He'll take me," Vanya said. "I'll make him."

"That's right," Yuri said. "Show him the letter first. From Harvard. Like we discussed."

"Then my work. It should be enough." It had to be; even incomplete, he had something.

Closer, there was a driveway framed by a swath of land recently cleared. Tree stumps poked out from grass and mud like sores, and a pile of trunks lay at the edge of the woods, likely waiting to be cut into kindling. Only an old oak was left standing at the intersection where the drive met the road. To Vanya, this was more evidence he'd found Clay. The American would need space like this, for his equipment. For his telescopes and tents.

"Why do you keep looking over your shoulder?" Yuri asked Dima.

"You think we made it this far without being careful?"

Vanya hurried closer to the house, as excited as he was terrified, and made out two columns framing the entryway and dozens of windows set deep into the walls. On the top floor, arched glass opened to a terrace spanning the third story. Before Vanya tried the front door, he heard someone around the back of the house. He followed the voice. When he spotted a man standing on an immense veranda, he broke into a run. The man wore a suit that was too short, too tight, to be Russian. He was round from his knees to his neck and topped with a few white strands of hair he brushed back as if trying to hide the fact that he was bald. He had to be Clay.

XVII

When Vanya rushed onto the terrace, Clay had his arms raised in anger. His face was red from yelling at two men dressed in rags whom Vanya hadn't noticed before. One was missing an ear, another had a peg leg. These were castoffs the czar wouldn't take. From the look on their faces they didn't understand a thing the man was saying. Of course not. It was English!

Did Vanya fall to his knees? Or did he trip? Either way, he kneeled. Tears leaked from his eyes. He wiped them away and cleared his throat. "Excuse me," Vanya said. He meant the words to be in English, but he couldn't think of a single syllable in that language. All that came was Russian. "I want to join you. For a photograph."

When Clay saw Vanya, he stopped seemingly midsentence. His face was square and his thick glasses shrank his blue eyes so they appeared twice as small as they should. The skin on his nose and cheeks was littered with broken blood vessels and pores that looked like gaping holes, as if he'd been pricked dozens of times. "Cam-e-ra," Russell yelled. "Cam-e-ra."

"Camera!" Dima said, finally catching up to them. Clay must have understood Dima knew English because he babbled something to the sailor that Vanya couldn't comprehend. While the two went back and forth, Vanya dug in his pocket for the letter from Eliot. He was sure he'd put it in his pants, but both pockets were empty. He checked his bag. His jacket. All empty. "No," Vanya said. He checked, again. Nothing. "No. No." He'd come all this way. Risked his life. His sister's. His grandmother's. "Maybe it's in my note-books," he said. But it wasn't. It was gone. So was Clay's article. How had he lost them? All he had to offer as proof of his qualifications was his notebook. He held it out, frantically, showing the page with Einstein's original equations. Clay batted him away.

Yuri was at Vanya's side now, pulling him back. And when he looked up, he realized the American had walked away and was talk-ing to Dima privately—but their voices were loud. And it was clear Clay was not happy. Vanya was sure he could help, that his work would soothe the American. He took a deep breath and stepped toward them, but Yuri caught him. "Let the sailor handle this." And then: "Don't you dare show the rubies. Otherwise he'll steal them. Or Dima will."

"I hadn't even thought of that." Vanya shook his head. "But the gems, they might help," Vanya said. "Or my math."

"No. None of that will help unless he believes who you are. Look, Dima's getting somewhere."

Vanya opened his mouth to object, but he saw Yuri was right. By the way Clay kept nodding, it was clear that whatever Dima was saying was working. The sailor even smiled, the familiar grin where his gold tooth glinted, and then came his laugh. The sound was a slow roll that didn't sound forced. Finally, Dima held out his hand to shake Clay's. Just as Vanya thought Clay would come over to shake Vanya's hand, greet him as a fellow scientist, Clay turned and made his way toward the main house. That was when Vanya noticed all the wooden crates piled on the grass behind them. Clay's equip-ment. Rows and rows of boxes.

"What happened?" Vanya scuttled across the veranda to Dima.

"We wait," Dima said.

"For what?"

Clay emerged from the house with an elderly woman in tow. She wore a dark, ruffled dress with a string of buttons from toe to neck.

"Hello!" the woman called in Russian. Her hair was white, her skin whiter.

"Go," Dima said to Vanya. He pointed to where the two farmers had been standing when they'd arrived. They were both gone now. "Wait over there."

Vanya didn't want to step away, but Yuri pulled him to his place. The old woman called to Dima as she walked, "You speak Russian and English? Did the colonel send you? I've been waiting for a translator for weeks."

Dima took off his hat and bowed. "I am Dmitry Velikoff. Yes, I can translate."

"Excellent."

"We're scientists." Vanya stepped forward.

The woman eyed Vanya. "Scientists?" For a moment Vanya wasn't sure what she'd do. By the look on her face, he thought she might scream. But then she laughed. "Very funny." And she turned to Dima so her back was to Vanya and Yuri. "Please. Tell the American I will be in Paris until the war ends. I've let the dacha to him for the year. I won't accept less and he's agreed. I think. Can you ask him to confirm?" Dima conferred with Clay, who nodded.

"Did everything arrive? His telescopes?" Vanya asked. "His cameras?"

"Stop interrupting," Yuri hissed and pulled Vanya further away while Dima continued translating. The woman gave instructions for the house. Clay asked questions. When it appeared they'd reached a conclusion, Clay took off his spectacles. Without the glasses, his blue eyes expanded to a normal size, and Vanya realized that while there was a girth to the American, he didn't have Romanovitch's brawn, nor did he command attention in the same way, and Vanya was relieved by it. Clay extended his hand to the woman, and the deal was done. She hurried back into the house, called for a driver to bring her carriage.

Dima turned to Vanya and Yuri. "The American has taken me on as his translator and you, you will replace the workers that were here when we arrived. He needs men to build tents and tables."

"He didn't bring his own men?" Yuri asked.

"They were all arrested in Riga. Clay didn't understand why. He only had enough gold to buy his own way here, I suppose. Either way, he's alone and he needs help."

"But you inserted yourself before us?" Vanya asked. "I'm the reason we're here."

"Your American didn't believe you're a scientist for a second. Trust me, I tried. At least I found a way for us to stay."

"We should thank you, I suppose? Pay you more," Yuri scoffed. "We didn't come all this way to build tents."

"As I see it, you have no choice," Dima said. "Do you think you can do better?"

"Did the czar even give Clay permission to be here? Or will he be captured, taken as spoils of war along with all that equipment?" Yuri gestured to the crates.

"He said all his papers are in order. The soldiers will leave him be."

"You really told him I'm a scientist?" Vanya asked.

"Enough!" Dima said. "I did my best. If you want him to think more of you, you'll have to convince him yourself."

XVIII

No. No," Sasha yelled. He kicked and a bag of mail slid. Letters ran like tears down the pile. He thrashed. Miri slipped on envelopes as she crawled closer.

"Sasha!" She shook him. "Sasha. Wake up."

"What? What happened?" he asked. He jumped to his feet so fast that, for a second, Miri thought he was still asleep.

"You were having another nightmare."

"Another?" He eased down to the floor, cracked the train door open, and leaned forward, gulping for air. The sun was just starting to tip up from the trees, and in the faint light, the train cut through a prairie blurred by mist.

"What are they about, your nightmares?"

"It's not simple."

"Tell me anyway." She sat, waiting. She'd had patients who worked through terror like Sasha, and she'd wait for as long as it took him to start. Around them, the smell of damp paper mixed with pine and the wheels beating against the rails kept a steady, slow rhythm. The train crawled forward.

"My nightmares are about the Polyakovs. And the farmers who saved us. In my dreams, I keep going back to the farmers. I see the czar's men slaughtering them."

"But they're alive," Miri said. She reached for his hand.

"For now. Only for now." Sasha looked outside. He told Miri about his mother and father, about the brothers and sisters who'd died in their cribs, or from fevers. And he told her more about the farmers who'd taken his family in. They taught Sasha what they knew, to smell soil, to taste it, to know if it needed manure. "They became family," Sasha said. "One day, the farmer took me out to his barn. 'Have you ever punched someone?' he asked. The barn wasn't large. Maybe the size of your baba's sitting room. It had wagon wheels hanging on the walls along with ropes and traps. Bear traps, rabbit traps. Of course I'd never hit anyone, never taken a punch. The farmer, he said it was time for me to learn." Sasha dropped his chin to his chest. Miri could feel him thinking, remembering. "There was dust everywhere. It made me sneeze, because he had me fill burlap sacks with hay, stuff it in as tight as I could. Then he showed me how to hold my fists so I wouldn't break my thumbs. How to watch a man's feet to know where he'll strike. The farmer hung the sacks from the rafters. I practiced on them for weeks. Then he had me practice on him. He hit me. Hard. It was how I learned."

"How did he know to fight so well?"

"Survival. He earned extra kopecks by fighting."

"That's what you said. The first night, in our cellar. You said the scar on your chest, it came from fighting, a good way to earn extra kopecks."

"You remember?" He paused. "The farmer trained me to fight like him. Once a month, men from nearby villages came together. They paid the fighters and gambled. The farmer whispered, the first time he took me, 'Don't touch the vodka. Staying sober takes you halfway to the win.' It was bloody but the farmer was the best. He introduced me as his nephew, and since he was their champion, no one questioned him. I lost in the beginning. But I got better. I started winning. I gave the farmer every kopeck I earned."

"Did he train his sons, too?"

"They didn't have children. It wasn't God's plan for them, they said."

"And your own parents, did they know?"

"No. They forbade it." He looked at Miri. "Those farmers. I miss them like parents."

"We can find them. We can visit them. I mean, you can."

"No." He stopped. "The villagers know I'm a Jew. If I show my face, they'll turn me in, and this time they won't throw me to the army, will they? The farmer and his wife, they won't be spared again, either. When I send letters, I write pretending to be his brother."

Miri took a breath. "America could be a fresh start for you, too."

Sasha shrugged. "I've thought of that but fate's complicated."

"You believe in fate, then?"

"Sometimes."

XIX

Seven days until the eclipse, that's what Vanya said. Finally, Dima had a chance to get away and find the telegraph office. He didn't even know if his last message had made it through—there was no way for Ilya to reply. Faster, faster he made his way along the pitted road. Already it was near midnight, but he'd sleep later. He was good at functioning without rest. Even though he'd been worked to the bone, worse than when he was a deckhand. Night and day the American, and Vanya, called on him to translate. To build. He'd hammered together tents and tables to hold the piles the American had carted across the ocean. Dima had never seen so much equipment. He couldn't imagine the expense, where the money came from—and for what? Photographs? Did he need all that for photographs?

Vanya said all that really mattered was the camera and the glass that would capture the photograph. They'd found the camera right away. Assembled it. But they hadn't found the glass—the plates. They dug in every crate. The camera, the plates, and the math. It was all Vanya talked about. Enough already. At least they seemed to be getting along better. Vanya and Yuri. All their bickering had died down. And that American, he seemed like a dolt. He never listened to a word Dima said when he tried to explain Vanya was a scientist. And Dima needed that American to know it so he could help Vanya. But every time Dima brought it up, Clay seemed to think he was joking.

He treated Dima, Vanya, and Yuri like dirt. Had them sleep in the loft above the barn. Never even bothered with their names. Lumped them together with Vadim and Stepan, the two who'd been there the day they arrived and, thanks to God, had come back. They turned out to be brothers. Strong as oxen even with one missing a leg and the other an ear. Good men. They helped Dima keep the pace fast. He liked them for that, had taken to drinking with them at night, late, after everyone else went to sleep. He also liked the red string they wore as bracelets, the charms around their necks, because they reminded Dima of his people. They believed in the power of talismans and magic. Vadim and Stepan had told Dima where he could find the telegraph.

And now that he was on the way there, he couldn't get to it fast enough. That American, he'd started asking why everyone was in the army but them. "Doesn't the czar need sailors?" Clay had said just that morning. Dima had brushed it off but couldn't afford questions like that.

Finally, Dima came to a rambling strip of houses and banged on the green door Stepan had described. Through a hole in the house's mud and mortar, Dima spotted a man lying on a cot, snoring, in the light of the hearth's embers. Dima banged the door again. This time harder.

"Go away," the man grumbled.

"I'll make it worth your while," Dima called back. "I'll pay double."

Dima saw the man stumble out of bed; a lamp flickered and the door flew open. The operator standing in front of Dima had a white beard so long it covered his chest. He wore a ragged shirt and no shoes. Dima saw he was missing two toes. The sailor held out his hand, and the man took the kopecks, waved Dima inside.

The house was a single room as small as a ship's cabin. Wires fell from one corner in the ceiling and were connected to the machine sitting on the desk. There was a notebook next to it, along with a typewriter with half the keys missing.

"What d'ya need to send?" the man asked. He pulled out a pair of spectacles. "It's about that American? That good-for-nothing lout?"

"Why do you ask that?"

"'Cause you're new here in Brovary. Why else would you be here?"

"Fair enough. Why did you call him a lout?"

"Took all my vodka when he came one day to send a message."

"Without paying?"

"Oh, he paid. Half its worth. Had those burls Vadim and Stepan with him as enforcers."

Dima dictated his telegram:

Price has gone up STOP Quadrupled STOP Meet in Brovary on the 22 STOP Keep soldiers away STOP If you come early you get nothing

Dima knew it was risky to let the telegraph operator know so much, or anything at all, but he needed to make sure Ilya, and Kir, stayed away. He left three bottles of vodka to buy the operator's silence. Now he just needed Vanya to finish up with those equations. Tie all those loose ends together. If he couldn't, if Ilya or Kir showed up and Dima had nothing but photographs, Dima would need Vadim and Stepan to help him get away.

"W e have to work faster," Vanya yelled as they dug. The men were expanding the dacha's root cellar, converting it into a darkroom. "Six days. That's all we have." Six days, fourteen hours, and twelve minutes left to set up for the eclipse, to find those photographic plates. Vanya had to get the equations somehow, and while he couldn't force the answers to come any faster, he did have influence over the photographs—he could push the others to help him find those plates. He was convinced they were there. Clay wouldn't come to Brovary without them.

Every time Vanya tried to ask Clay about them, with Dima translating, Clay brushed the question aside. "What do peasants know about my work?" Vanya thought about using the rubies to buy new plates, but he wasn't sure where to look for them, or if they could be sent in time. What would happen if, after the eclipse, Vanya left Brovary without equations *and* without a photograph? Surely, Eliot would refuse him. Then he'd have no way of getting his family out. They could try to slip through the border, but that was dangerous. They could try to buy papers, but during war that would be impossible. No. He couldn't let any of that happen. He had to find the glass plates.

And so he worked harder. Kept unpacking and searching. And running through equations. Sometimes he talked about an idea with Yuri. He didn't think Yuri understood it all, but he knew enough to ask good questions, and that was just as important. It kept Vanya going as they installed a telescope, built tents to cover the camera and supplies in case it rained, and unloaded a photometer and an interferometer. All the while, as they worked, Clay sat under an umbrella on the veranda with a bottle of vodka and gave orders. Once he'd tried to help but complained the effort hurt his back, Dima explained, and he hadn't lifted a finger since. It didn't make sense to Vanya. Weren't Americans cowboys?

Vanya and the others worked themselves up into such a frenzied pace that a man from the village they'd hired to fell trees tumbled from a ladder. Yuri diagnosed a fracture in the lower arm. He set the bone and lashed it to a plank of wood. Clay looked on, astonished. He hadn't believed Yuri was a real surgeon. So many in Russia claimed to have a degree but didn't. Clay asked Dima questions about Yuri's qualifications, and once he was convinced of Yuri's credentials, he invited Yuri to dinner. "There's something personal I need to discuss," he explained through Dima.

"I'll only come if I can bring Vanya," Yuri said.

"Fine. All three of you can come. Dima, tell Cook to make dinner for four."

They were summoned to the dacha's formal dining room at eight. Vanya had never seen much of the inside of the house before, and it was clear from the size of the table, and the number of empty chairs, that the owner was accustomed to hosting over two dozen people at a time. With just the four of them the room felt empty. There were squares and rectangles stained into the silk covering the walls where paintings used to hang. Clay explained they'd all been shipped to Paris for the duration of the war. The chandelier and sconces that normally would have dripped with a hundred candles were empty. Only a paraffin lamp burned, sending shadows into empty break-fronts that, like everything else, were empty.

The American spent the meal telling them about his observatory in America. He'd had most of the great scientists of the day come and lecture at his university. His guests, Clay said with Dima translating, coauthored papers with him. Vanya tried to ask Clay specific questions about Harvard first, and Einstein later, but Clay laughed. "Harvard? Ha! The famous university, so famous even Russian peasants have heard of it!"

"Yes, aren't you familiar with Professor Eliot's work? And shouldn't he know yours?" Vanya tried to ask, but Clay ignored the question, consumed plate after plate of food. The more he ate, the pinker his nose became, the more pronounced the broken blood vessels around his face grew. Never once did Clay ask a question.

And this response, Clay's refusal to admit he didn't know Eliot, gave Vanya an idea. The best idea he'd had since they left Kovno. He just needed to think it through. He spent the rest of the meal in silence. Thinking. And thinking. As Cook brought more and more food.

Once the last dish was empty, the American turned to Yuri and, through Dima, said, "I know you've been wondering why I asked you here. I have awful diarrhea. I need your doctor's opinion. Is it an ulcer?"

"Not likely. Not given the way you've been eating," Yuri said. Vanya saw Dima stifling laughter. "But diarrhea can be dangerous. I've seen you swimming down at the pond behind the estate. Do you drink the water?"

"Of course. Fresh water," Clay declared. "It keeps me healthy."

"No, no," Yuri said. "Don't drink that water. Still water is never safe."

"But the animals drink from there."

"They shouldn't. Come. Take off your shirt and I'll examine you." Yuri stood up from the table and pulled a stethoscope from his pocket. Vanya didn't even know he'd brought one on their journey. The American followed Yuri's lead, stood and disrobed there in the middle of the room. Yuri went through the motions of listening, tapping, and taking notes. Vanya had come to know Yuri, and he understood by the way Yuri looked at the American sideways, rarely straight on, that he didn't like him.

As Yuri worked, Vanya continued thinking. He'd come to Brovary convinced he'd persuade Clay to give him a photograph of the eclipse: that at best, his math would prove he was on the verge of one of the greatest revelations in history and so, of course, Clay would support him and gladly hand it over; at worst, he'd have to pay for what he needed with Baba's rubies. But ideas only moved people when they cared to understand their power, and already Vanya knew Clay didn't care much for math—only fame. And money only worked when people were hungry and Clay wasn't hungry, either. With all this equipment, with the entire expedition, it was clear that he had everything money could buy. Vanya could never persuade him with rubies. No, he'd need something else. And he'd need to be careful about it. He couldn't let Clay steal from him. Not like Kir.

"Do you have a diagnosis?" Clay asked, maneuvering back into his shirt.

"Other than your weight, you're in perfect health. Stop drinking the bad water. Only boiled water with honey," Yuri said, tucking his stethoscope back into his pocket. "And now I have a request for you."

"Yes," Clay said absentmindedly, still working on the buttons pulling tight at his chest.

"Just as you now believe I'm a doctor, you must believe me when I say Vanya Abramov is a scientist. He's the best in all of Russia. He's a correspondent of the great Albert Einstein, and has been offered a position at Harvard, in the United States."

"Ha," sputtered Clay. "If that were true, then what's he doing here? Dressed like that?"

"Sometimes circumstances, appearances, are out of our control," Yuri said. "But he's here for the same reason as you. To see the eclipse. To understand relativity."

"Truly?" the American asked, staring in disbelief at Dima as he translated. Clay put his glasses back on so his blue eyes shrank back down to beads, and he leaned close to Vanya. "Harvard?"

"Yes," Yuri said. "Hear him out."

Clay agreed and ushered them into the sitting room, where he said they'd be more comfortable. As they walked across the hall, Vanya pulled Yuri aside. "Thank you, brother."

Yuri smiled. "Go."

They had to peel dust cloths off the furniture. The only light came from the fire in the hearth so the space was crowded with shadows. Empty bookshelves lined the walls like bars. The hulking desk only added to the strangeness of the space because it was clear no one worked there. Clay fell into the largest chair, with a bottle of vodka. Vanya, Yuri, and Dima sat around him.

"Tell me, Vanya. What is it you want me to know?" Clay said.

Vanya cleared his throat. Where to start? He'd have to be careful. Very careful. When he'd practiced for this conversation in his head, he thought he'd talk about clocks, synchronization, and acceleration, and his gut told him now that none of that seemed right. Clay was a man concerned with his own greatness. Flattery was the key. Vanya leaned forward. "I know you come from a university of much prestige, Professor. It would be an honor for me if you would consider us working together. With all your vast experience, I'm sure there is a great deal you can teach me. I have ideas, many ideas but I need someone with experience, someone like you, to help me complete what I cannot finish on my own." He paused. "I want us to be coauthors." Just as Einstein worked with others, Vanya would, too. Especially if that was the only way.

"But you've been dragged in from the fields! Harvard," Clay laughed and shook his head.

"Professor," Yuri warned. "You promised to listen."

"Fine. Prove me wrong. Show me what you have. Convince me

there's something for us to publish together." Vanya pulled out his notebook. His hands shook and he was terrified now, not because he thought Clay would refuse him—but because he thought there was a chance Clay might understand him. That Clay might look at his equations and realize he had not yet achieved what he needed to achieve to make him great—that Clay might refuse to work with him. What if Vanya had risked all of this, their lives, their future, for nothing? Vanya felt every muscle and sinew in his body tense as he handed his work over.

Clay flipped through the pages of Vanya's notebook too quickly for him to take any of it in, then motioned for Dima to join them, to translate, and for Vanya to begin explaining his equations. Vanya started line by line. But Clay waved his arms and said, "Slow down." Vanya pared it back to smaller expressions. The more he reviewed, the more certain he was that he was correct, and he found himself speeding up again. When that happened, Clay reminded him, "Slower." And then: "Tell me one more time."

Hours ticked by. "Maybe some symbols don't translate?" Vanya asked.

"They do," Dima said. "But the ideas, they are very complicated. I can't follow them. Vanya, tell me, how many people at your university understood? Is it something the American should truly know?"

"No," Yuri answered. Vanya had been concentrating so hard he hadn't even noticed Yuri was still there. "His sister says there aren't more than a handful of people in the whole world who can check Vanya's work."

"Clay could be one of them," Vanya said. He had to be, because Vanya realized that the more he explained, the more he needed Clay to tell him he was right, or wrong. Even though it terrified him. "Keep going," Vanya said. Line after line.

When he came to the section of his proof that fell apart, Clay scratched his head. "You have ideas?" Vanya asked. "Acceleration? Gravity?"

Clay leaned back. "I'll be damned," he said after a long pause. "You weren't lying."

"Does that mean he can help with the equations?" Vanya asked.

"No. He has no idea what these equations mean," Dima said. "Can't you see that?"

"But he understands what I'm trying to do? Why I need a photograph of the eclipse?"

"That he understands well," Dima said. "He wants to support you, to publish with you, but he can't help with this math. Only the photograph."

"Then he has them, the glass plates. Where are they?" Vanya stopped. He was out of breath suddenly. "Tell him. For us to be coauthors, I need them. If he doesn't show them to us now, tell him I'm leaving. I'm taking my work and we're going."

"You're certain you want to draw that line?" Yuri asked.

"Why are we here, risking our lives, if he doesn't even have them?"

Dima translated and Clay took a swig of vodka. Then he smiled and looked Vanya in the eye for the first time. "A partnership," Clay said, nodding. "With you Russians, there's always something. But I like it. I need a partner." He stood up and stretched. His bones cracked. He headed for the kitchen. "Follow me." Vanya fell in line with Dima and Yuri behind him. Clay took them into the pantry off the kitchen. One wall was lined with shelves of preserves. Clay moved three jars filled with peaches, then reached to the back. Vanya heard a click. The wall moved because it wasn't a wall. It was a door.

Dima translated, "Clay says the owner told him to keep his valuables here. That if he needed to run, they'd be safe. He paid her extra for it."

"They let you know all that?" Yuri asked.

Dima smiled. "No. Somehow they worked it out before we arrived. He just told me about it."

The room wasn't more than four wooden walls and a dirt floor. The American pointed to a pile of crates. "Move the books, the ones in front," he said. "Open the one in the back. The largest one."

"We don't have time for games," Yuri said. But Vanya moved the crates of books and heaved the largest one up on top of the others, then pried off the lid. Whatever was in there was well packed, wrapped with layers and layers of horsehair stuffing.

"Careful," Clay said. He waited for the last strands to fall away and then announced, "It's the photographic plates! I brought them with me, of course. The most valuable cargo I had—along with the camera. You were right to suspect as much, that I wouldn't leave them to steerage with the rest. Nothing here would fit my American camera. Even the slightest bulge could ruin an image." Vanya stood, looked at the other crates. "No," Clay said, anticipating his question. "They really are books. You can put them on the shelf behind the desk when we're done. That one crate of plates—that's it. All that's left. I came with one hundred, but the rest, they shattered. On the boat, in the wagons."

"Eleven?" Vanya said. "I only count eleven."

"Eighty-nine lost," Yuri said.

Vanya shook his head. Already he felt his hands go damp. His voice trembled when he spoke. "How long does it take to capture an image with your camera?"

"Thirty seconds. Maybe less," Clay answered.

"Eight photos," Vanya said. "That's all we'll have time for. Leaving three for practice." It wasn't enough. They'd need to adjust the camera. Test it. Calibrate it. Surely, Vanya would need more. Even an experienced photographer would.

"Just one photo," Yuri said. He put his hand on Vanya's shoulder. "That's all we need."

Clay spoke again. "Of course, my photographer never did make it. You'll have to handle the camera on your own." He held up his hand to demonstrate. There wasn't a steady bone in the American's body. He'd never be able to take the photograph. "I was waiting to catch someone like you. Just wish I'd known sooner you were already here."

"What do you mean?"

"I mean, I knew my equipment would attract a coauthor, someone who could solve the math. Or, I hoped as much. That if I offered the photograph, the other half of the proof would come to me. And it has. But honestly I thought it would come from somewhere in America or England. Or Germany. I wasn't expecting a Russian peasant." Vanya was facing the American now. And Clay was still smiling. His tiny eyes pinched so tight there was no color to them. And he held his arms crossed over his chest so he appeared inflated. He continued with Dima translating, "This is the way the world works." Clay walked back to the kitchen, to his vodka. "Everyone has a place. You, you're brilliant. I see that now. But you're not capable of raising funds, organizing an expedition. That's my department." He refilled his glass. "In America. We have great universities, like Harvard. The name, Harvard. It belonged to a man who provided funds. Yes, there is brilliance on that campus, but it is always hand in hand with someone who is willing to back it. If your math stands, and our photograph is clear, we'll call it all the Clay Abramov theory of general relativity. Yes. This is perfect!" He clapped a hand on Vanya's shoulder and held his hand out to shake Vanya's.

"No," Vanya said. "Dima. Tell him. The theory is mine. The Abramov theory of relativity. When I publish, he'll be listed as someone who helped." Vanya waited but Dima didn't say a word in English. Instead, he pulled Vanya to the side.

"Friend, think what you're saying." Dima's voice was so quiet it was hard to hear. "Even in the Garden of Eden, the snake offered the apple, but Eve, she accepted it because she wanted knowledge. And I'd be the first to say she made the right decision."

"Most would call that sin."

"I call it progress. And I have a feeling you do, too. What other choice do you have? Think. Should I tell him yes?"

"Tell him we'll buy the photograph," Yuri said.

"That American isn't moved by money."

"I know," Vanya said. But it didn't seem right that Clay would claim so much and offer so little. But was it so little? Clay's equipment was the only way Vanya could secure his family's ticket to America. There was only one answer. And by Clay's smile, Vanya thought Clay knew it, too. Vanya had come too far to give up. He couldn't tell Miri and Baba he'd lost their way because he was too proud to add another man's name next to his.

"Vanya!" Dima said. "If you don't accept, you have nothing. You told me this is bigger than you. It's about understanding the universe, not vanity."

A log under the stove in the kitchen behind them popped, the last ashes from dinner burning out. Vanya blinked. He crumpled his hands into fists. "Tell him I accept."

XXI

Dima woke early the next morning and was surprised to find that Vanya and Yuri weren't next to him in the barn. For a split second he'd wondered if they'd run, that Clay had scared them off, but no. He didn't think they had it in them. At least Vanya didn't. Not when he was so close to the eclipse. He'd agreed to that American's terms and he'd stick to it. Besides, the American had a point. The man with the bigger wallet always wins a piece of every prize. If Vanya didn't know that yet, then it was time he did. But where were they? Did Vanya work all night with Clay? When it came to math, he didn't need a translator as urgently as he did with other matters; it was why he'd left them. Dima made his way along the mottled path to the kitchen to look for them.

Cook was boiling and frying. She nodded him through to the sitting room where Vanya was spread out on a divan. Yuri was on the other. Both were asleep. Thanks to God. Not that he was worried. Still, it was a small relief. Vanya had his notebook on his chest. Dima took it gently, tucked it up under his arm, intending to copy it. Even if Vanya never solved his math, well, Dima needed something to give Ilya. Whatever Vanya scratched in there had to be worth a high price, and if this American didn't understand it, there was a good chance, Dima figured, Kir Romanovitch wouldn't, either. Dima could tell Kir it had what he wanted and run before Kir figured out otherwise—if at all. Just as Dima turned toward the door, Clay caught him, stepped in front of him. "Take your hands off that. We can't afford to have you messing things up."

"What do you mean?" Dima asked, keeping his voice quiet.

"I mean there's no reason for you to touch that notebook."

"You understood his work?" Dima asked.

"That he's working on relativity, like Einstein? Yes. Now hand it to me."

"Why should I?" The better question, Dima thought, was why was Clay suspicious?

"Because I might be able to help him finish. Complete relativity."

"I don't believe that for a second."

"Don't be a fool," Clay said. Dima ignored him and pushed past. "I received a telegram," Clay called after him when both men hit the veranda. The strength in his voice, a tone Dima had never heard, stopped him. "From a man named *Kir Romanovitch*."

"I've never heard of him," Dima replied, trying to look unruffled. But in the way Clay said *Kir*, he made it clear he knew the name had meaning regardless of what Dima said. Why was the American in contact with Kir? He'd seemed genuine enough the night before. What had Dima missed?

"Don't you want to know what he had to say?" Clay continued.

Dima turned on the American with a fury he couldn't hold back. He grabbed the pathetic scientist by the neck and put his thumb over the nub right where he could control the man's breathing. "What did you tell him?" Dima seethed.

"That Vanya isn't here."

"Why would you lie?"

"I wouldn't be loyal to a Russian—not one I've never met or never heard of." Clay gasped as Dima eased his grip. "I want relativity, too."

"Liar."

Dima pressed harder on his throat and Clay's face turned a deeper shade of red. "I want. The credit," he whispered.

Few lied when pressed like that, especially blubbering men like Clay. Dima released him as quickly as he'd grabbed him, then turned and kept walking back toward the barn, tried to keep his pace slow and even. Dima didn't believe the American would be so loyal to Vanya in front of Kir, but at least he'd showed his cards and now Dima knew Kir and his men could be there anytime. Dima had been walking a plank and hadn't even known it. Did he still have a safe way out?

Dima looked up, turned the corner to the barn, and saw Vadim and Stepan. As quickly as he could, Dima tried to smile. "Greetings, brothers," he said, hoping he sounded relaxed. They were lounging in the grass, eating breakfast. The crickets were loud. Mosquitos buzzed. Dima swatted one and missed. At sea they had sharks; he'd take their razor teeth over the insects' thousands of pinpricks any day. At least with a shark he could see what he needed to kill it.

"There's our sailor," Vadim said. "Joining us? Cook brought bread."

"Better company than those snobs," Dima said, gesturing toward the house. He reached into his pocket for his vodka and took a long swig.

"I don't know how you stand it with those idiots all day," Vadim said.

"They pay me," Dima laughed, and took another swig.

"Vodka so early?" Vadim winked and held out his hand, asking for a swig of his own. Dima passed the dented flask, and Stepan handed Dima a hunk of bread and an apple. Dima opened his jaw and cleaved off a full quarter of the fruit in one bite. Then he went into the barn where he could settle into a corner unseen. He pulled out Vanya's notebook, and an identical blank notebook Vanya had given him to practice his letters. Even incomplete the notebook would earn him a fortune, so long as he copied all of it. Carefully. Correctly. But he'd have to get a hold of himself. And that Ilya, he better stay away or Dima's whole plan would be ruined. "Damn American," Dima said, still shaking.

XXII

Russia passed by Miri and Sasha slowly, slowly, as a stretch of forests and farms until the evening they stopped at a coal depot on a ridge overlooking a river. The lead engineer and his men jumped down and started shoveling. Miri huddled behind mailbags, next to Sasha, tried to imagine she was smaller than she was, that she could fold over and into one of the cracks in the floor in case they opened the mail car. It wasn't likely. But still. Outside, the men grew louder, bawdier. They were drinking. She was hungry, but all they had left was a bit of cheese from Pavel and a few berries they'd scavenged from the edge of the woods a few nights earlier when they'd eluded the guard and snuck out to forage for food and water.

Miri heard a stranger approaching. Whoever was coming had a slow gait and a lame foot. "You're here for the night?" the stranger called. He sounded young. One of the engineers replied but his words were muffled. "Good, then join us for a dance," the stranger said. Miri had been terrified the stranger would ask for his mail. "Come, for the price of one bottle of vodka per man, you can dance with us in the village. And trust that you and your train will be safe."

"We only have half a bottle left," an engineer called.

"Then you can't come!" The stranger dragged his foot across the gravel. A retreat.

"Okay, okay." The engineer laughed. There was a cheer from the other men. Bottles clinked. Footsteps hurried, following the stranger back to his village. They walked past the mail car so close that Miri saw the whites of their eyes through slats in the wooden walls.

Miri and Sasha didn't dare to move for nearly an hour. Not until wisps of moonlight slid through the cracks around them. Outside, wolves howled. In the distance, they heard an accordion. "Kalinka" was the tune. It was an old Russian folk dance, one of Babushka's favorites, played mostly at festivals or on special occasions. The music alternated between fast and slow, exhilaration and something else—uncertainty. Sasha jumped up to his feet. He smiled. "Miriam, you love to dance. I see you swaying." He bent at the waist and held out a hand. "Please, may I have one dance?"

"And if they hear us?"

"They're gone."

"One man stayed behind. There's always one man behind."

"If he's here, he's too drunk to know anything."

He was right. The man would be drunk. And Miri did love to dance. She'd danced with women at weddings, and with Babushka and Vanya. And she'd sneaked out onto a balcony, at a wedding of one of Baba's clients, to dance with Yuri once. He was slow and he'd stepped on her feet but still it was thrilling. "It's just one dance," Sasha tried. "Please. Yuri wouldn't mind."

"How did you know I was thinking of him?"

"Aren't you?" He grinned. "Just one dance?"

Miri looked at the piles of mail. Hundreds, perhaps thousands, of notes filled with dreams and fears. So many of them would never reach their intended recipients. Most would be dead before their mail was even delivered. Was it right to dance now, during war? She was being ridiculous, looking for an excuse when she didn't need one. It was only one dance. She took Sasha's hand. She remembered the night in the cellar when her hand was on his skin, at his hip, as she helped him to the hearth. "Okay?" Sasha asked.

"Fine." It was nothing she couldn't tell her grandmother about. They stood, facing one another, and then he leapt down to a crouch, shot one heel out and then the other, kicking his legs as he made a circle in their nook between the burlap sacks, in time to the music. Miri laughed.

He took her hand and in one smooth motion twirled her around so she landed with her back against his chest, their arms entwined. They fit together so easily it surprised her. He eased them around in a circle in time with the rhythm. "You dance wonderfully," he said. Never had she heard such a perfect accordion.

The music gained speed, and they unfurled their arms and linked hands, kicking their toes and heels. Even with the mail around them, there was space for them to dance apart, and yet neither of them let go of the other. Heels up, heels up. Not once did Sasha step on her toes. When the tune came back to its slower section, Sasha dropped his hands to her waist. They should have separated, sashayed side by side, but they stayed still. The accordion launched again into a speedier tempo and Sasha came closer. He brought his cheek up flush with hers. She expected her skin to chafe under his whiskers but he was soft. His breath was on her neck. The salty tang of his sweat mixed with the pine that still clung to him. He moved slowly and quickly at the same time.

She closed her eyes. When their lips touched, he was so gentle Miri almost thought she'd imagined the kiss. She lingered, slid her hand along the length of his jaw, to his neck. He tasted like the cheese they'd eaten for dinner. Sasha pulled her so close she could feel his every curve and yet she couldn't touch or taste enough of him. And she sensed he felt the same. She forgot where she was, forgot the train, the mail. All she was, was under his touch.

Suddenly, something outside the train crashed, and both Miri and Sasha stopped. They were out of breath. Her lips felt swollen and delicious, still touching Sasha's. But she was frozen, not moving, only listening, afraid to move in case the shift in weight made a board under them moan. The music outside was gone. A familiar voice, the head engineer, swore and groaned only steps away from the mail car. Miri would have stepped back but Sasha held her too tight to let her move. And he was right. They couldn't risk a stumble or sound that might give them away. All the men had returned. They were drunk, falling and slipping. In that pause, while she should have been thinking of a way out of the mail car in case they were found, she thought about Yuri.

She shouldn't have been there with Sasha. Not like that. She unwrapped her fingers from his neck. She shouldn't have kissed him. Shouldn't have been feeling anything like what she was feeling. Yuri was risking his life for her, to help Vanya. Kir was likely guarding Baba or at least after her—and her brother. She, Vanya, and their grandmother were spread across the country. How could she be doing this, betraying them all at once?

"I'm sorry." As she spoke, her lips brushed Sasha's and he only held her tighter. And if she was being honest, truly honest, she didn't want to move.

A man outside stumbled. He couldn't have been more than one car away. Another threw up. It felt as though it took years for all five men to clamber back inside the engine car. Then the train jerked forward. The wheels rolled through one revolution, two. Miri backed into a stack of mail. "We shouldn't have," she said. Her voice was so quiet. "I'm marrying Yuri."

"He could be dead."

"That's not fair."

"Was it the same when he kissed you?" Miri was grateful for the dark, that he couldn't see her face. After a long silence, Sasha finally said, "I won't kiss you again. But I won't stop you if you try."

XXIII

Two days before the eclipse, while Vanya, Yuri, and Dima were eating breakfast at a table on the veranda, under an already hot sun, Dima noticed Cook's arm. She was a round woman with hair so thin there were bald patches around her ears. She'd served them dozens of times, but this morning her sleeve was pulled up. She placed a pot of tea on the uneven table, and just before she turned to go back to the kitchen, Dima reached for her hand. "That mark, there, on your wrist." He pointed to the underside where she had a large, red, circular birthmark. "What is it?"

"A witch's mark," Cook said with a wink. "At least saying as much makes people think twice. Are you a believer?"

"In dark magic?" Dima smiled. "My mother taught me. I respect it."

"As do I," Cook said. "And Stepan and Vadim, they do, too. They left today. Your American will notice soon enough."

"Aye, I know. They warned me," Dima said.

"Left? Why?" Vanya asked.

"They learned all this work was for an eclipse."

"Well what did they think it was for?" Vanya asked.

"The stars. They thought you were observing stars," Dima answered. "Now they know it's an eclipse, they're terrified. They think you're here to make the eclipse."

"That's impossible," Vanya said. "How could we make an eclipse?"

"They're farmers, Vanya," Yuri said. "They've never seen technology like this."

"Is it true, then?" Cook asked Dima, pointing to Vanya. "Is he bringing an eclipse?"

"Of course not," Vanya answered. "I can't control the sun and the moon. We're here to observe the eclipse when it comes. When the universe brings it."

"An eclipse is dark, there's nothing to see," Cook said. "You're bringing evil and when it comes, I'll hide." She spit over her shoulder and hurried back to the kitchen.

The three men sat in silence. "What are you thinking, brother?" Yuri asked.

"Someday, she'll understand. They'll all understand there's nothing to fear about science."

"Maybe," Yuri said.

"Did you finish the duplicates?" Vanya asked. Dima had been working on mockups, wooden photographic plates that fit Clay's camera, but without glass, so they could practice.

Dima sighed. "I left them next to the camera."

"Thank you. Yuri, let's practice." Yuri nodded and they walked out together, toward the camera. Yuri, Vanya decided, was the one most likely to keep calm, to have a surgeon's precision in his movements under pressure. He would take the photographs. Vanya would act as his assistant. As they started learning the steps, Dima and Clay did the same, started practicing. They were in charge of measuring the Zeus cluster's intensity and spectra during the eclipse.

XXIV

August 21. The day of the eclipse. Miri opened her eyes at dawn when thunder hammered her awake. Sasha was across from her, against the wall, nestled between mailbags. His hair was rumpled. He hadn't slept, and Miri found she had to resist the pull of him, the urge to be closer than she was. The train pounded toward Kiev, the wheels sounding louder than they'd been. "Once we find Vanya, I'll be off," Sasha said.

"You said you'd wait to leave, until I was back with Babushka."

"I'll use the coat to secure your papers and then put you on a train to Peter with your brother and your fiancé. By then you won't need me." She was surprised to hear how cold his voice sounded. "I don't want to see you with Yuri."

Miri looked down and bit her lip, felt her cheeks turn red. Of course he didn't. Nor did she want Yuri to see her with him. Sasha must have known that, too.

They ate most of their remaining food for breakfast under icy drops of rain that wound their way through cracks in the ceiling. Wild plains gave way to organized fields of red wheat. The sweet smell of fall gave way to rot. A field that may have been barley lay as jellied decay. A woman stood with a shovel in her hand. Her hip bones jutted out like hangers. A girl no older than ten struggled to drive a plow.

"Didn't the czar know to leave at least enough people to work the farms?" Miri asked.

The train rumbled over a switch that directed them east. "The czar doesn't care how many people starve. His belly will always be full." Sasha kept his eyes on the dying fields. "There will be a coal depot soon. We should jump there. It's risky to pull into the station in Kiev. There'll be too many soldiers, and we're only a day's walk or so to the city from here."

"A day's walk?" Miri asked. That meant she had no chance of finding Vanya before the eclipse. And even though she had known it wasn't likely she could locate him in time, she had still been holding out hope. "Are you sure?"

"Fairly certain."

"I wanted to watch it with Vanya."

"I know. I'm sorry."

"But there is a chance. We have hours. We could get lucky." Even as she said it she knew it would never happen. She took a breath. Slow and even. "And all these clouds, they could clear. There's a chance Vanya could see it. Really see it. The eclipse won't happen until closer to noon." She thought about her brother coming down to breakfast with his shirt unbuttoned, his tie askew, announcing the timing of the eclipse down to fractions of a second—based on the clocks Einstein had set in Bern. But for Miri now, there was no precision. Time was a guess. Even if they had a watch, what would they use to set it? Or check it? And wasn't that Vanya's point all along? Time is unreliable.

She felt the tug of the brake and they jumped into a field. The landing was soft but Sasha groaned. He pulled his jacket down, unbuttoned his shirt to check on his wound. He seemed certain the edges had torn open, but Miri knew it was healed on the surface. The deeper tissue, the cause of the pain, would take longer.

XXV

Approximately three hours before the eclipse, in Brovary, Vanya stood on the great lawn, assessing the skies. "Damn the clouds," he said, looking up at the gray that seemed to never end. But it could clear. There was time, if Dima's chronometer was correct. The sailor said he'd used a good clock to set it—what did that mean? If only Clay had something better.

While Vanya waited and watched, the skies opened with a drenching rain. Vanya started pacing the lawn. In minutes, his shoes and clothing were soaked through. "Please," he said to the heavens. He'd come too far to be stamped out by rain. Or even by Clay. He was resigned to sharing his work, to thinking of it as the Clay Abramov theory of general relativity as a means to an end, the final price for a ticket to America. For Baba. For Miri. For Yuri. He just needed to catch the photograph. And solve the math. He'd been so sure he would have it by now. And he was close, he knew it. He could tell Eliot he had the equations knowing he'd have them before setting foot in America. Was that right?

"Brother, come inside," Yuri said.

"No. I have to watch. I'm so close."

"Please. The temperature is dropping. Miri would want you inside."

"I need to be ready if it clears."

"You will be."

Every time he finished three circuits across the grass, Vanya rechecked the calibrations on the equipment. By what he estimated to be eleven a.m., the downpour was so hard he couldn't see the trees across the way. Dima stood by his side. "Your notebook," Dima said. "I'm going to hide it for you."

"Why?"

"I just think it's better to be safe."

"Don't bother."

Dima leaned close and whispered, "I made a cutout in the wall, behind Clay's books. That's where I'll hide it."

"A smuggler's hole?"

"Exactly." Dima winked.

XXVI

By midmorning, Miri and Sasha stood in a dry spot under a tree, looking up at a blanket of clouds, trying to figure out in which direction they should travel. They had no map. No one to ask. Just the train tracks leading to Kiev. And it was too overcast to see even a dim outline of the city.

"Maybe if I run I can make it. Find him." Miri started toward the road. By the third step, she slipped in the mud. By the fifth step, Sasha had her. "Let me go," she said.

"I can't let you risk it."

"He needs me."

"He needs you alive. All this rain. It means floods. And even if it was clear, how could you possibly find him now? In time?" Sasha helped her back to the tree, to where they were sheltered, and they sat huddled on an oversize root. As much as she hated to admit it, she knew he was right. Wet now, she felt the temperature dropping. Sasha wrapped Grekov's coat around them both, and slowly she began to feel warm again.

"I know it sounds ridiculous, but every time I pictured this day, I was with my brother."

"I'm so sorry."

"We know where they are today, at least roughly, because of the eclipse. But what if they have to run? How will we find them afterward?"

"I'm not sure. But we will. They can't leave right away, can they?"

"No. They'll need to help the American pack, develop the plates."

"Then all is not lost." Was Sasha right?

She sat staring at the sky, waiting for it to clear. Every minute ticked past feeling like ten. The first shadow should have already started to come into view. It would take nearly an hour and a half for the sun and the moon to collide, and if the day were clear, they would have seen it happen in slow motion. But with the rain, they couldn't even sense darkness growing. "Please clear," she said. "Please." She imagined Vanya poised over a telescope. His hands shaking. Dripping in rain. Yuri would be at Vanya's side. Steady. Reliable. Yuri.

XXVII

When the chronometer read 12:16 p.m., the rain stopped in Brovary but the clouds were thick. Vanya stood in the middle of the front yard with his arms held up and out to the sky, begging for it to clear, but he didn't have much hope. He couldn't see a speck of blue and it terrified him. All he'd done. All he risked. He was being beaten by clouds. And he wasn't the only one scared. The farmers and townspeople, he understood from Cook, were all terrified, too. Hiding from the eclipse and the evil it would bring.

"There's still a chance," Dima said, pacing with Vanya now. "Still time."

"This weather can't clear quickly."

"I've seen it happen."

A folktale centered on an eclipse and its darkness ran through Vanya's head. His favorite. The myth of Prince Vseslav. Many Russians knew it and recited it in different forms, but Vanya loved the original. He never met anyone else who did. The old language was clunky, hard to understand. He'd dug it out of a library and read it for Miri and Baba at the hearth in Birshtan so many times he'd memorized it. Miri loved it, like she loved all stories. Vseslav was a prince born during an eclipse with a caul over his head—the mark of evil. By day the prince grew to become a fearsome warrior who never lost in battle. By night he turned into a werewolf, torturing and killing without remorse. It was said he was reborn on the eve of every eclipse.

"Might it not become us, brothers, to begin in the diction of yore the stern tale of the campaign of Igor, Igor son of Svyatoslav. Let this song begin according to the true tales of our time." Vanya called out the twelfth-century epic across the lawn in a voice as loud as he could muster. A bird, in the distance, took flight.

"Your eclipse will come. We'll see it," Dima said.

"How can you be so sure?" The chronometer read twelve twenty. They had eleven minutes left.

XXVIII

Near noon, Miri still stared at the dark sky. What was happening in Kiev? She was far enough away that the weather could be different; it had to be. She imagined a small slice of sunshine for her brother. Had he even found the American?

"There's always hope," Sasha said. She was so caught in thoughts of the eclipse and her brother she hadn't realized Sasha had stayed so close, kept Grekov's jacket around them both.

XXIX

The chronometer read 12:55 p.m. Twenty-four minutes after the eclipse slipped across the sky—hidden somewhere behind the clouds. Vanya had been staring at the face of the clock for the past quarter of an hour as if it would help him turn back time. He couldn't believe it. He had outrun the Okhrana, escaped the czar's army only to be defeated by a rainstorm. He clutched his stomach, doubled over from the pain. "No. No." He fell to his knees, rolled to his side, and closed his eyes. It was over.

He couldn't say how long he lay there. Whether he was shivering or still as death.

"Vanya!" Yuri had him by the shoulders. Shook him. Clay was behind him, a shadow. "Open your eyes. Look. Look!" The clouds had shifted from a thick blanket to gray wisps, like lines on a graph. The sun was out but there was something wrong with it. Its light was weaker—and it was fading. "It's coming," Yuri yelled. "The chronometer. It was wrong."

As quickly as Vanya had fallen, he was up, staring at the sky. "The eclipse," he shouted, already running toward the camera as fast as he could. "We didn't miss it." Then even louder, "We didn't miss it." How light he felt, suddenly, how quickly everything had changed, just as Dima said it might. "Get ready!" he yelled.

"Vanya. Brother. You need to slow down," Yuri said.

"Should we practice one more time?"

"No," Yuri said, and Vanya knew he was right. They'd rehearsed so many times they could perform without thinking. And there might not be time anyway. It was hard to tell. They needed to be patient. And Vanya tried. The clouds continued to move, so slowly he wasn't sure they'd be entirely clear in time. But they might.

Every second had the weight of hours. Chickens clucked. A cow mooed. No, several cows were making noise. Cook said all the animals would be inside where the villagers thought they'd be safe. Why did it sound as if they were outside? Then the wind kicked up. The barn door clanged on its frame.

"Closer," Yuri said when the sun was almost covered. "The clouds are almost gone."

"Still not good enough," Vanya said. But it might be, soon.

"War," Dima said, stepping under the canopy next to Vanya. "The wind. It blows now because war is coming. The eclipse and this wind mean a war to end all wars is due."

"Enough of the superstition. I thought you don't believe in that nonsense," Yuri said.

"A sailor never stops believing in the Fates or the Furies."

And as they stood there, second by second, the wisps of cirrus pulled away from the remnants of the sun like curtains. Vanya could barely believe it. Yuri was right. They still had a chance. A small window. The cows were louder now. Through Clay's equipment, Vanya saw the moon slide so far that only the smallest sliver of sun remained. "It's coming," Vanya yelled.

Like a miracle, a belly of blue sky opened. Babushka would say God had come down on their side. "It's happening!" Clay shouted. "Man your battle stations!" Dima took off as fast as Vanya had ever seen him move, toward the canopy where he and Clay would work.

The last shadows fell over the fruit trees in the orchard. Light came through the leaves in the quarter-moon shape of the eclipse.

Then a black veil slid over to the house and covered the dacha.

The animals that had been so loud just seconds earlier stilled.

Day turned to night.

Vanya was startled by a crash. It took him a moment to realize he'd dropped a photographic plate. The glass had shattered. "Vanya!" Yuri yelled. "Wake up, brother." He'd already taken two photographs. They'd used three to practice. Only five remained. Vanya scrambled to the table and grabbed a new plate. Yuri made room. Vanya slid the glass into the camera, and Yuri clicked the trigger. He reached for another.

The darkness descended into a deeper shade so dark it was purple. Click. Blackness. Click. Stars. The Zeus cluster. Vanya reached for another. Click.

Clay called out something in English. The words were jumbled but the meaning was clear—they were witnessing a miracle. Vanya worked with a precision he'd never experienced. No movement or time was wasted.

And just as quickly as night had come, it began to fade. The stars disappeared. A sliver of sun eked out around the moon. Light poured down on the lawn. "Another. Another," Vanya yelled. He rammed a plate into the camera, his last, and snapped the trigger for Yuri.

The sun began to reemerge as if it had never left.

"Vanya," Yuri said. His hand was on his shoulder. "We're done."

"There must be more. There's always more."

"No. It's over," Yuri said.

"Vanya," Clay yelled, running toward them. His glasses were crooked. Dima was at his side. "Have you ever seen anything more glorious?"

"The photographs?" Dima asked. "How many did you take?"

"Seven," Vanya said. "Some might be blurred."

"Six." Yuri pulled the last plate from Vanya's hands. "One was taken in the light. One shattered."

Clay took one of the plates off the table. "Six," Clay said. "Incredible." He took a step toward the darkroom. Vanya jumped up to take one of his own, to help develop the plates, but Yuri's hand came down on his shoulder like a metal vise.

"Brother," Yuri said. "You need to sit. Catch your breath."

"I can't."

"You must."

"He's right." Dima pressed Vanya into a chair so Yuri could examine him. "You're covered in sweat. Your eyes won't focus." Yuri held a hand to Vanya's forehead. "Look at how your hands shake."

"I'm excited." Vanya tried to break free. "Let go. I have to get to the darkroom."

"It's not fever," Dima said to Yuri. "He's crazed. I've seen it before."

"Ridiculous! I've never felt better."

"You need to rest," Yuri said.

"I'll do it. I'll develop them," Dima said, reaching for the plates.

"No. I'll go." He tried to stand. Dima shoved him back into the chair.

Vanya knew the folklore. Staring straight at the source of darkness could unhinge even the strongest of the strong. But that was only a myth. No, he wasn't crazed. He was thrilled. He was on the verge of history. "I have to develop those plates." He jerked away and jumped to his feet. The barn door slammed in the distance. Vanya grabbed one plate and set off toward the darkroom. "I must know if I have proof. Yuri, guard the rest," he said over his shoulder.

"There are parts in this world that not even science can explain," Dima called after him.

XXX

It's late," Sasha said as they watched clouds beginning to shift, the storm finished. "The eclipse must be over."

"But we didn't see anything. Just a dark afternoon," Miri said. Her face was wet from the rain, maybe from tears, too. And she felt the darkness Vanya had taught her to push away creeping back over her, this time heavier than it had been in years. "All of this, and for what? Vanya saw nothing."

"We don't know that," Sasha said gently. "Until we do, there is hope."

"Hope?" The word sounded hollow. "We don't have much time to find them. Before they run."

"Maybe, maybe not. You said they have to pack and prepare. That your brother would never leave the American alone."

"That's true." Miri nodded. There might be hope at least in that, that she could still find him in Kiev, but not in much else.

XXXI

Slowly, slowly, Vanya walked toward the darkroom. Six. All he had were six photographs. Six chances.

They'd used albumen, egg whites, to increase the quality of the images. Up close, the coating smelled both sweet and sour. He tried not to hold on too tight, to cause any damage. He opened the door to the darkroom, pulled the curtain aside, and stepped in. It took a moment to adjust to the lack of light. His eyes teared at the tang of chemicals. Clay was already bent over a series of trays.

Vanya carried the glass plate he cradled over to the table and submerged it in the first tray, the one Clay had already used. He sloshed the solution over the glass. Back and forth. He tried to be patient, but it wasn't working. "Come on," he mumbled to himself. Then Dima crashed through the door. Vanya jumped, splashing chemicals.

"There's a villager outside," Dima said in Russian, then in English, Vanya presumed.

Clay and Dima began arguing over something. Dima turned to Vanya to explain. "He thinks the villager is here to deal with the animals, because they made so much noise. But he's missing my point." Dima's voice was serious the way it had been the time they'd come up against the soldiers in the alley in Riga. "It's Vadim. He says his cows fell over dead because the moon swallowed the sun. You need to speak to him. Now. He's very angry. And scared."

"We can't talk now," Clay called.

"Tell him it's just an old superstition, animals dying during an eclipse. It couldn't have happened because of it," Vanya said.

"But it did. Call it superstition or belief, but it happened. His cows are dead. I saw them," Dima said. "Vadim says it was magic that forced the darkness. Your magic." The skin on Vanya's arms prickled. The solution in his tray continued to slosh. "The whole barn is dead."

"Every cow?" Vanya asked.

"Every one."

"Tell him to come back later," Clay ordered. "Go!" Dima closed the door behind him with so much force, dust fell from the ceiling. Vanya leaned over the trays to protect them. He and Clay examined the liquid developer to make sure no contaminants had fallen into the medium. Vanya swished the tray faster. Clay worked with him, in unison. They brought their trays up and flattened them.

Vanya transferred the plate to the next bath. Then there was a thud at the door. Vanya jumped and liquid splashed over the sides of one of the trays. Clay said something. Vanya understood he wanted him to ignore the door; his voice was high, excited as he pointed to the glass. Had the photo come through? Vanya tripped, trying to get a better look, and just missed disturbing the table. In the tray Clay held, the black splotch of moon was clear. So too were the sun's limbs, stretching out from behind. But where the sun's rays should have been straight, they blurred. There were no clear lines. Vanya couldn't make out the Zeus cluster. "No good," Vanya said. Clay shrugged as if to say Vanya could be wrong. He continued moving the tray up and down.

There was a voice outside the darkroom. Someone yelled. It was a woman. She sounded hysterical but Vanya couldn't make out her words. "Damn it. No, it's still out of focus," Vanya said, pointing to the image in Clay's hand. Only five more chances.

The door cracked behind them. Wood splintered. Someone crashed into the darkroom. Vanya threw himself over the plate he was developing to protect it from the light. His face was wet. His skin burned from chemicals. "Where is the American devil," a man yelled.

"Get out," Vanya screamed. He was still bent over the table. Someone grabbed Vanya's arms and twisted him up. Pain shot through his shoulder. "No," Vanya yelled. "They're glass."

Vadim had Clay. He dragged the American toward the stairs. Even with only one good leg he was stronger. "Let go," Vanya yelled, and tried to yank himself free. He had to save the negatives. Had there already been too much light? Were the ones in process already destroyed? "Please, close the door. At least close the door." The man who had Vanya by the arm shoved him, hard, into the wall. Vanya crumpled to the ground while Vadim dragged Clay away.

The door swung partway shut. The hinges were broken. Vanya ran to the table. Both negatives had shattered. "Damn it," Vanya yelled. He clawed his way up the stairs. There were still four more plates. Four more chances. Vanya hoped Yuri had protected them.

Outside there was a crowd of villagers. Old men and young women, even children, held swords and rakes. They were loud. Vanya ran for the table where he'd left the plates with Yuri but the table was empty. The plates were gone. Where? No shattered glass. No toppled chairs. "Yuri," Vanya yelled. "Yuri, where are you?"

Suddenly, Stepan appeared at his side. He swung his fist into Vanya's stomach. Vanya gasped. Convulsed. Pain. All he felt was pain as his gut caught fire and he fell, crashing against a chair. He clawed at the ground.

XXXII

Miri and Sasha followed the road toward Kiev. Mud oozed under their boots. It stuck to their heels and gave every step the weight of three. Late in the afternoon, it was clear they wouldn't make it to Kiev by nightfall and so they huddled under the thickest tree they could find, ate the last of their berries, and saved the end of the cheese for the next day. At sunrise, they continued their hike, and again, by nightfall, it was clear they still wouldn't make it to Kiev. This time they were so cold, so wet, they looked for a farm where they might take shelter in a barn for the evening. The first one they found had a straw roof tinged green with mold. An orchard rimmed the fields. Every branch was plucked naked, not a single piece of fruit left. A black-and-white dog came at them, baring its teeth. Sasha gripped his knife.

"You stealing my pears?" a woman asked. She stepped out from behind one of the trees. She held a scythe, pointed it at them, the blade clean as if it had just come off the whetstone. The dog sat at her side, his teeth still exposed.

"There are no pears to steal," Miri said.

"You were looking to steal." She raised the blade. Sasha stepped in front of Miri.

"No!" he said. "We're traveling to Kiev."

"If you did steal my pears, I'd kill you both." A child peeked out from behind her skirt. Her face was withered and her hair hung like greasy string.

"We're not thieves. We're looking for my brother. And an American."

"An *American*." The woman barked out a laugh. "That's the best I've heard in a while. What do you really want? Soldier, you here for my pig?"

"No!" Miri said. "We didn't even know you have a pig."

"That's what they said when they came for my mule, my husband, and my boys. Your husband, he's wounded?" She pointed to Sasha's neck, to his open shirt.

"Yes," Miri said. Husband. Miri shook off the heaviness of that word as she reached for the rucksack around Sasha's good shoulder. She moved in slow motion, not wanting to startle the woman, and found the last corner of cheese they'd saved. Miri held it out toward the girl.

"For the child," Miri said. "Please."

The woman hesitated, only for a moment. She leapt forward and grabbed the cheese without touching Miri. Then she retreated, equally as fast, but now she leaned the blade against her shoulder and unwrapped the food. She brought it up to her nose, inhaled like she hadn't smelled anything so good in a long, long time. "Fresh," she said with approval. She handed the full piece to her daughter without even a nibble for herself. "You can sleep in my barn."

Miri exhaled. She realized her hands hurt. They'd been balled into fists so tight her joints were frozen. The skin of her palms was scored. "Thank you," Miri said.

She and Sasha started walking toward the barn. No Americans. That was clear. And for the first time she wondered if she'd misunderstood. Surely if there was one even close by, the woman would have heard. What if Miri had misunderstood "Levi's Monster"? What if it didn't mean they'd gone to Kiev?

XXXIII

Vanya felt nothing but pain and terror like he'd never imagined. He knew he was on the ground but he couldn't get up. He must have lost consciousness. A crowd of villagers, the army's rejects, huddled around him in a tight circle with clenched fists. It was loud. Someone heaved him up to his feet. He faced Vadim and Stepan. "Your American killed our cows," Vadim said. His eyes were narrow and fierce. He pointed to Clay, who was on the other side of the circle, leaning against a wagon. Blood from Clay's mouth pooled on his shirt. His spectacles were gone and one eye was swollen shut. It looked as though he'd lost a few teeth. Had Yuri and Dima escaped?

"The American unleashed the eclipse," a woman in the crowd yelled. She was the villager who sold them butter.

Vanya looked around. "Yuri," he yelled. "Yuri!" Stepan punched Vanya in the gut again, hard. Lights exploded behind his eyes. He slumped to the ground. He heard a woman yelling; she seemed far away. When he could breathe again, he focused on the woman still yelling.

"My child is blind," she screamed. "It was the devil that did it."

"The devil in the form of the eclipse."

"It's the American and his split tongue." Each accusation was louder than the last.

"Blood requires blood," yelled Vadim. "My cows died, all at once. They broke out of the barn. While I was hiding I heard them splashing in the pond. The sun came back and they were…"

Did Vanya get his photographs? Where were his glass plates? His head throbbed. With every breath he felt as if he was being stabbed. They'd broken his rib. He lumbered up to his feet. The enormous effort was excruciating, but he was better off standing; it seemed to relieve the pressure on his chest. "The eclipse didn't kill your cows," Vanya gasped.

"Shut your mouth. Traitor." Vadim was so fierce it was clear he wouldn't hesitate to strike—to kill. "Your American, he brought the devil to Brovary. Admit it. *Admit it.*"

"How could a man control the moon?"

"Not a man. Lucifer."

Stepan heaved Clay up into a wagon. Clay screamed something. Stepan cracked a whip on his mule, and the old animal heaved. The wagon wheels lurched but slid into a rut. Stuck. Vanya began clawing his way to the wagon. The mud and stones scratched his hands but he had to find a way to stop this.

"Vadim. Listen to me!" Vanya shouted as loud as he could manage. Vadim looked back at Vanya, his face lined with fury. "It was not the eclipse. You heard splashing." Vanya gasped for air. "It must have been algae."

"What's he saying?" The crowd pressed in, angry and loud.

"Algae. A poison. Can grow in ponds," Vanya said, again. "Vadim, please. Let the American go." Did Vadim hesitate or did Vanya imagine that?

Either way his eyes went dark. "Traitor," he said. "Why defend the devil?" Stepan climbed down to push the wagon. He angled his shoulder under the back to give it a shove.

Clay lay in the back of the wagon, whimpering. He rolled his head to the side and his one eye, the one not puckered and already black, caught Vanya's gaze. He held him there, for a moment. Then Clay tilted his chin toward Vanya, took a deep, deep breath, and yelled one unmistakable word: "Jew."

Stepan and Vadim stopped. Vanya froze, feeling the label and its meaning trickle through the crowd. It cut as deep as ever. Their anger would boil now. They weren't going to kill a man—they were going to kill a Jew. Of course a Jew had slaughtered their cows.

"A Jew?" Vadim turned to Vanya.

The crowd began jeering and hissing. Stepan said something. Then came Dima's voice. "Don't listen to the American devil," he called as he pushed his way through the crowd. Dima! But where was Yuri? The crowd paused. Just then a flash of lightning split the sky.

"A sign, a terrible omen," someone screamed, and at that, the crowd surged. Vanya had never seen so much hate. They dragged him down into the mud with enough force he was sure they'd crush him. There were too many blows to count or distinguish. The pain was so excruciating he couldn't see, couldn't breathe. No mob would ever spare a Jew. Surely, Clay had known. All Vanya could think about was death. And he prayed it would come faster.

XXXIV

The crowd was out of control. Dima had seen it before, on ships, on land. Crowds were powerful. Lout. It was what the telegrapher had called Clay, and the word was perfect. Clay's betrayal was despicable. Pathetic. Was that what Kir's telegram had told Clay, that his scientist was a Jew? Whatever else Vanya might be, he was a good man. He didn't deserve to die like this. Dima spit on the ground, wiped his mouth with his hand. There was no question this crowd would kill Vanya, and if they went that far, they wouldn't stop. Blood wants blood. Dima, Yuri, and Clay all worked with Vanya—they were all in danger. Dima knew he should run. But he couldn't do it. That man, that Jew, had gotten under his skin.

Cook had screamed over all that noise, calling the lightning a terrible omen. Of course, Dima thought. Her birthmark was a witch's mark, and that's what Dima needed, a witch. He'd seen her flee toward the house. He took off after her, slammed through the barricaded kitchen door. She was cowering under the table. Her face was wet with tears, her thin hair a mess. The worse she looked the better, anyway. He dragged her toward the door, grabbed two pans behind him. He was in too much of a rush to be gentle. She must have fought but she was easy enough to handle. "Please, no," she said through hard sobs. "Not outside."

"You saw the lightning?" Dima asked.

"Yes." Her tears were harder now and she'd dropped to her knees.

He grabbed her wrist at the birthmark. "You're a witch? And the villagers know?"

"Yes, yes!"

"You can stop this madness." Dima jerked her back up to her feet. He hated being rough with her. "Come with me or I'll slit your throat. Understand?" She shook like a rag doll, and he realized it was because he was doing it, shaking her.

"What's happening?" It was Yuri. At the door. His eyes were wild, his clothes torn.

"I'm saving Vanya. What are you doing?"

"Also saving Vanya. Hiding his work."

Yuri was gone, in the blink of an eye. Dima didn't have time to wonder—he could hear the mob roaring. He hauled Cook outside, fought through, kicked and shoved, and scrambled up onto the wagon where he expected to find Clay, but Clay was gone. The wooden rails tore into his skin but there was no time to feel it. From above, it was an awful scene. More than one had blood soaking their hands, Vanya's blood. Cowards, Dima thought. Anyone can kill in a crowd.

The sailor banged the pots together. The noise sent his ears ringing and his hands numb, but it did the trick. The villagers turned to face him. Finally, Dima could see Vanya, a bloody heap in the mud. Was he too late? Where was the American?

"You all know this witch?" Dima yelled, pointing to Cook.

"What's it to you?" a woman replied.

"Let her go," Stepan said. "We've got a Jew."

"Friend, I asked if you know this witch?" Dima said. "You saw the omen? Lightning?" He took a deep breath. "It wasn't the filthy Jew who brought the eclipse, who killed the cows. It was the Germans. Their leader, they call him kaiser," Dima yelled. He knew his words were dangerous, but every villager had given a son, a father, a brother called to fight. "This war did it. The Germans cursed Russia. You felt the wind earlier, another sign? And now the cows, the lightning. They're all omens. Signs that we're cursed. The war that'll kill us all." Dima spit over his shoulder three times to show he was warding off evil. "Tell them or I'll kill you," he growled to Cook, pushing her forward. "Tell them what I say is true. The signs are warning us that the Germans' war will kill us all."

She nodded. "He's right." Then she turned and yelled, "The kaiser brought the plague. His war'll kill us all." She paused. "The kaiser cursed us, not the Jew."

"Even if it was the German, the Jew's his tool," Stepan shouted back. "Friend, you've been taken under the Jewish spell."

"No. I know what I say," Dima replied. "Cook can stop more from coming."

"More?" someone in the crowd asked.

"He's lying," another said.

"Yes. More. More cows. Pigs. Chickens." Dima paused. "Children. They'll all die. The cows, they were only the first."

"Can't be," a man yelled.

"Are you willing to risk it?" Dima asked. He held his breath. His own hands were trembling now. Surely they'd come for him next if he couldn't persuade them. He never believed, himself, not since he was a boy and the spells had failed to save his mother in childbirth, but he respected the old ways, knew how to navigate them. "Cook is going down to the pond where we found the cows. They were drinking the poison, but she can cure it. Cook can write her magic on the water and cure it." He could see his words working their way through the villagers. They were whispering, nodding. He kept pushing. "Let's follow Cook to the pond. Take her to the water. If I'm wrong, what do we lose? But if I'm right, we're all in danger." He paused. "What do we have to lose?"

"Nothing," Stepan said. "We lose nothing."

"Why should we trust him?" a villager called. "That man's a stranger to us."

"Not to us," Stepan said. "I can vouch for him."

"He's right," Vadim agreed finally. Dima was shocked and

relieved. He watched them tie Vanya to the wagon. The scientist looked awful, but he recoiled when they grabbed him—it meant he was alive. Alive! He'd hurt for a long time, but Dima had seen sailors survive worse injuries than those.

"To the pond," Dima yelled as loud as he could.

Cook led the procession down to the water. Vanya wasn't safe, not yet, but Dima just had to keep Cook writing on the surface of the pond for as long as he could. The longer they were away, the cooler the crowd would be when they returned—and that might, *might*, give Vanya a chance to survive.

XXXV

Before the sun had tucked away for the night, Miri and Sasha washed up at the farmer's well. The water was cold. She watched it turn the skin above Sasha's stubble pink. "She could be wrong," Sasha said. "There could be an American near here, she might not know."

"Do you think I read the telegram correctly? 'Levi's Monster'?" Miri asked.

"I trust your instincts."

Miri sighed. "Wherever he is, if he's safe, my brother could have his proof by now."

They climbed up to the loft and found the hay on the floor was loose, not baled as it should have been, as it would have been if the woman had had more help. They dropped to their knees and began to clear space to sleep. When their nook was finished, it was narrow and there wasn't room to make it larger. They stayed on their knees, facing each other.

"I can sleep downstairs," Sasha said finally.

"This will be fine." Miri lay down on her back as far to the side as she could. Sasha followed. There was a finger width of space between their shoulders. She felt him tapping his hands but didn't dare turn to look. Their faces would be too close.

The lap of rain started on the thatch. The smell of turned mud and fresh moss grew stronger. And while they weren't touching, it was all she could think about, the feel of him, the taste of him. "When we find Yuri, I'll leave," Sasha said.

"Right." She was surprised at how unconvincing her voice sounded. Sasha must have noticed it, too. He rolled over to face her. His weight, shifting, shook the loft. He propped an elbow up and leaned his head on his hand. He looked at her with eyes so dark she could barely make them out. "Is that what you want, Miriam?" He reached to touch her face, perhaps to tuck her curls behind her ear, but before he touched her, he pulled away. He rolled back, folded his arms over his chest. "You don't know what you want, do you?"

She lay there for a while. Hoping he'd fall asleep, knowing he wouldn't, while rain spilled through cracks in the roof. She wanted to say something, but everything that came to mind wasn't right.

It was Sasha who broke the silence. "You never told me why you became a doctor."

"It's a long story." One she'd never told because no one ever asked. Even Yuri had just assumed her talent drew her to it, never asked if there was more. Miri closed her eyes. There was no question where to start, but she wasn't sure she should.

"Please," Sasha said. "Tell me."

"Remember the night we spent in the hills, fishing? You were surprised I didn't know how to fish?" Her voice was quiet, almost covered by the rain. "Helping women give birth, it's what brought me to surgery. The births, they haunt me. Even when the mother lives, death comes so close, just at the moment when another life is starting. It's powerful and terrible. I—I can't describe it." Miri despised the fact that birth and death were so closely linked. It was something no other surgeon at the hospital, not even Yuri, understood. He was confident in his abilities, certain he could save any mother, save Miri and their own children. But she'd seen him lose women in childbirth. Even the healthiest and strongest could go in a heartbeat. She continued. "For those first few seconds when a mother holds her child, when they're still connected by the cord, they call it elation, they believe the worst is over. But it's not. That's when death is closest. Time stops for them, for me." Like an eclipse, she thought. "And as soon as it starts again, everything rushes back. The pain. The joy. That's when they die. Or most women do. When they bleed to death. But none of that answers your question. Why don't I fish?" She tried to smile. "Our dacha. The house is deep in a pine forest. Near a sulfur spring. When I was twelve, my babushka came back from the market, and she told me she was going to teach me to fish. She told me to follow her to the spring. I thought Baba was going the wrong way, since there were no fish in the baths. 'Patience,' she said.

"The path was steep. Hot. The higher we climbed, the stronger the smell of fouled eggs, the sulfur. Near the top, I heard a woman scream. Instinct had me jump forward to help, but Baba grabbed my arm. Baba's stronger than she looks."

"I don't doubt that." Miri could hear the smile in Sasha's voice.

"She pulled me close. 'At the market, I heard a wealthy man vacationing from Kovno sent for a doctor to help his wife through childbirth,' Baba said. I'd never heard that urgency in her voice before. 'While he waits for the doctor, he's taken his wife to these baths to ease her pains. I warned him there wasn't a doctor or midwife within a day of Birshtan, but he didn't believe me. Miri, you must help. You've delivered a baby,' she said.

"A month earlier, I was there when my cousin, Natalya, Klara's granddaughter, went into labor. It was late. The doctor came, but it was only him. He needed help. And my cousin's screams were unbearable. I would have done anything to help her."

"Of course you would," Sasha said.

"But why would you say 'of course'? I was a child. What could I know?" Miri paused and looked at Sasha. Here, in the barn, under the leaking roof, she felt close to him in a way she didn't expect, a way that kept her talking. "The cord connecting the baby, it was caught around his neck. Because of my height, I looked older than I was. The doctor looked at my hands. They were smaller than his. He asked if I was brave enough to save the baby. Could anyone say no?"

"Many people would say no."

"I don't believe that. Would you refuse?"

"I'd never be asked in the first place."

"I guess that's right," she said. "The doctor guided me, walked me through each step. I slid my hand inside my cousin. I cried— it wasn't sadness. Or fear, but something else. I felt the baby, my cousin's pulse. And Natalya, she was so exhausted she barely had the strength to push again. I had to save them both. And I did."

"That was when you knew you wanted to be a doctor?"

"No. I'd never met a woman who was a doctor. But I thought I'd be a midwife. It's why Babushka pushed me to help."

"In Birshtan?"

"Yes. In Birshtan, my grandmother insisted I could do it again. 'I saw you taking in every detail,' she said. I went to the woman at the spring. She was squatting next to the pool. Her husband's face was like ashes. The pools are good if you're ill, but something told me not if you're in labor. There's blood, and fluid. The woman needed to be cool, not soaking in salt. I told the husband to spread a blanket over in the clearing. 'Are you a doctor?' he asked. Babushka told him I was the closest thing he'd find to a doctor, and for the first time in my life, I was thankful for my height, for looking older than I was.

"When I looked between this woman's legs, I could already see the crown of the baby's head. I told the woman it wouldn't be long, and I tried to examine her just as the doctor had. I wasn't skilled enough yet to know from sight as I do now, but my hands were steady. I thought the infant was in the position I'd seen with Natalya, and so I told the woman to push with all her might. She clenched my wrist and screamed. Sasha, when the baby came, she was pink and screaming. Perfect.

"When the husband asked how much to pay me, Baba stepped

in. 'No money can pay for this happiness, but we will accept a kind favor in return.' Anything, the man insisted. 'We love to eat fresh fish. Does your cook or kitchen boy fish in the morning?' Every day, the man said. 'Is there a chance he could catch one or two extra fish for us?' But that's nothing, the husband objected. Baba insisted the fish were worth more than the man knew."

"And so the husband agreed to deliver fish to your door every morning?" Sasha asked.

"Yes. Every morning. At least for the rest of that summer. Baba explained, 'We will always need to eat, and this is how we survive, how we fish. Knowledge is the most important currency, and you, Mirele, you were born to be a doctor.' On the way home, though, I asked her, 'Isn't love the most important currency?'"

"And?"

"'Love,' Baba said. 'Love is what makes you want to survive in the first place.'"

XXXVI

Vanya cried out. He opened his eyes. He was wet. The sun was dim. The eclipse? No, the sun must have been setting. Someone had thrown water on him. Every part of his body screamed with pain. He didn't know what was broken and what was still intact. He was shivering from terror more than from cold. He was in a cellar, or a prison. No, a barn. It smelled like manure and rot. Animals. Dirty animals.

"Baba," he moaned. If only she could help him now. If only Miri were there to fix him.

In the dark, he made out Stepan standing in front of him. Vanya tried to ask Stepan to hurry, to free him before his captors came back, but it came out sounding like a groan, and any relief he'd felt thinking Stepan was a friend evaporated into fear as Vanya realized he was splayed over a roughhewn table, stomach down, while a man leaned on his back to keep him in place. Vadim. Vanya felt his peg leg jutting into the back of his knee.

Stepan and Vadim were the men torturing him.

Stepan leaned down and took hold of Vanya's hand. Blood already poured from his thumb into a puddle on the straw below him. His fingernail was gone. His vision was going dark again at the edges. He'd never felt his heart beat so fast, the air so thin.

"Swear not to send another eclipse," Vadim said.

"I swear," Vanya cried. Still death wasn't coming fast enough.

Elul

The sixth month in the Hebrew calendar, Elul, is marked as a time of repentance that leads up to the holy days of Rosh Hashanah and Yom Kippur. *Elul* comes from the Aramaic, meaning *to search*.

The Talmud tells that the Hebrew word *Elul* can be understood as an acronym for the verse "I am my beloved and my beloved is mine," words from the Song of Songs.

I

On Rosh Chodesh Elul, Miri woke before sunrise and said a quiet *l'chaim*, imagining her brother toasting with her. Her heart ached at the thought that they hadn't been together for the eclipse, and now all she could do was hope he'd succeeded. She and Sasha set out before the farmer and her daughter were out of bed and soon it was clear they were finally close to Kiev. They approached the city by taking the road along a river, huddling in ditches when they saw soldiers. When the way was clear, they trudged through mud that sucked on their soles and clung to Miri's skirts and Sasha's uniform. He still insisted on carrying the greatcoat no matter how much Miri fought him over it.

Away from the forest, the river was dark. It smelled of waste and moved so slowly that sticks oozed past like slugs. Wherever her brother and Yuri were, Miri had to find them—soon. She and Sasha would search in Podil among the factory workers, the poorest of the poor: tradesmen, fishermen, and Jews. This was the safest place to ask for an American, not because he'd be there but because someone might know something and no one in Podil would dare go to the Russian police, not even to turn them in.

It was after noon when Miri spotted Kiev's smokestacks. Hulking marble buildings glittered as if they'd been kissed in gold, crowned with red and green tiled roofs. A church's five spires reached up toward the sky like a lady's fingers bedazzled with jewels. Miri had always imagined coming to this city would be magical, that she'd feel the spell her mother wove around it, but as they got closer, she felt only fear underscored by the smell of burnt sweets from the factories owned by Russia's sugar beet barons. Miri and Sasha took the road that turned toward the outlying slum. Soon their feet crunched over fish carcasses, potato peels, and rocks. They wound through throngs of bone-thin children dressed in rags. The head teacher at the first school they stopped at knew nothing about an American. It was the same at the next. And the next.

"Someone must have heard about Russell Clay. Read something in a newspaper," Sasha said. The only good news was this meant that Kir, or the Okhrana, might have just as much trouble finding Vanya as they did.

They stood outside a yeshiva. The walls were black with mold and shivered in the wind. "I have another idea," Sasha said. He stopped a crippled boy missing a foot. "Where's the hospital?" he asked.

"Two turns to the right," the boy said.

"The Jewish hospital of Podil. Of course," Miri said. The hospital was the only one in Russia more famous than Kovno's and just as modern. Russia's most renowned Jewish physician worked there, Dr. Tessler. Yuri devoured every article he published and talked about him endlessly. "I should have thought of it. If Yuri's nearby, he will be there with Tessler. He won't sit idle while Vanya is busy." She paused. "But you weren't thinking about Yuri, were you. You think they've been injured?"

"I think we need a way in that won't be suspicious."

"We could fake an illness. You could have stomach pains, appendicitis. Then you'd see a surgeon, maybe even Yuri."

"Stomach pains won't be enough," he said. "It needs to be convincing." He added something else, but Miri didn't hear. There, in the middle of the hustle and crowds, she went still. Yuri could be there. In two turns to the right.

"Sasha," she said. "Yuri will know what happened between us."

"There's nothing to know."

"There's everything to know. That's what makes him a great doctor. He can look at patients and see everything."

"See what?" Sasha asked. "A kiss?" A mule barreled down the street, trailing an empty wagon. A team of men ran after the animal, cursing. Sasha and Miri stepped out of the way just in time. "You could tell him the truth," Sasha said, and she looked away. "Or do you want me to leave?"

Her lips moved but there was no sound. She was promised to Yuri and she loved him. That kiss had been the beginning and the end between her and Sasha. When she didn't answer, Sasha tucked her arm into his, and together they slid into an alley so narrow they had to thread around one another to fit. He reached for his collar and popped one button out of its hole and then another until his wounded shoulder was exposed. He wiped a tear from Miri's cheek, and she held his palm there, on her face. Then he was quick. Before she understood what he was doing, the knife gleamed and he plunged it into his shoulder where the skin had started to heal. Miri cried out. He covered her mouth with his good arm. "If we must go to the hospital, this is our way in. I need a surgeon. Don't you understand? There's no question now." Blood oozed out over his skin and spread too fast. He'd gone deeper than necessary.

Miri grabbed his hand and began to run.

II

The Jewish hospital loomed three stories tall with an arched ribbon of marble roped over the entrance. Juxtaposed to the slums, the gray building looked grand. A cobbled walkway led to the paupers' entrance, and Miri couldn't drag Sasha to the door fast enough. She had his uninjured arm around her shoulders. He leaned on her, harder, with every step. He was bleeding dangerously. What had he done? Miri burst through the iron door. The smell of blood and sweat—of hospital—curled over her. "I need help," she said. Her voice echoed. The waiting room was cavernous. A woman in a white nurse's uniform and head scarf came up on the other side of Sasha and put her hand around his waist to help. She looked exhausted and ancient. "I need a suture kit," Miri said. "He's losing too much blood. And a cot. Do you have a cot? If you don't, the floor is fine."

"Yes, child, I can help. Please, stay calm," the woman said. Her Yiddish was warm with the same accent as Babushka's. She stood on her tiptoes, peeled the top of Sasha's shirt back so the cut was exposed. The edges looked raw. Blood tangled down his tunic to his chest. "If I ask how this happened, will you tell me the truth?"

"We don't have time for this," Miri said. "You're a nurse? Or a surgeon?"

"I can find you help, but you must stay calm."

"Calm? He can't wait. Look at the blood," Miri said. "I'm a doctor, a surgeon. I can take care of him. I just need supplies."

"You're a surgeon?"

"Yes." It was the first time she'd said it in a long time, and the words took her by surprise as much as they did the nurse in front of her. She realized she'd never told Sasha, either, but he was too far gone to react.

"Even if that's true, I can't let you walk into my hospital and work without references."

"I'll pay," Miri said. "I can even stitch him here, in the waiting room. I just need supplies." The nurse hesitated. "Please?"

"Where did you study?"

"I told you, we don't have time for questions. My patient needs help. Now." To Miri it seemed that the nurse thought through their case for an hour, but it was more likely a matter of seconds. "Please," Miri said. "Please."

"He's more than a patient, child, isn't he?" the nurse asked. Finally, she nodded. "I'll take you to a cot."

"Thank you."

A dozen faces blurred past as Miri and the nurse dragged Sasha through a side door and into a long, narrow men's ward. Like Kovno's paupers' clinic, beds were packed head to foot, row after row, with barely enough room to stand between them. But unlike Kovno, all the sheets were crisp and white, and the room was flooded with natural sunshine. And instead of clay dust layering every corner, this hospital was tinged with the smell of sugar. The nurse pointed to a cot at the end of the room. "A surgeon will come."

"I told you, I'm a surgeon. I only need room to work. And supplies." The nurse was suspicious, and Miri could see she was sharp. She bent down to look at Sasha.

"Sir," the nurse said. "Sir, do you trust this woman?"

"Yes," Sasha mumbled.

"Do you want her to stitch your wound? You understand she says she's a surgeon?"

Sasha's eyes were rolling in his head, but he managed to speak. "Yes."

The nurse stood. "I'll fetch bandages and supplies."

"Thank you," Miri said.

"And I'll watch you. Closely."

"That's fine. Just hurry."

The nurse scurried between beds. Miri eased Sasha out of his tunic and took a closer look at the wound. The edges were thick but clean. His knife had been sharp. She grabbed a bandage from a stack on a shelf near her and applied pressure. "You shouldn't have done this." Was she crying?

"You. Can fix me," Sasha said. It looked as if he was trying to smile. She held the wound tighter. "You are better. Than him."

"Than Yuri?" She shook her head. "Shhh. You need to keep your strength." She felt his forehead and cheeks, looking for fever, but he was cool. It was too early for infection anyway. He needed blood. Would they be able to offer a transfusion? It was a new technique, but this was Tessler's hospital. The nurse returned with a tray that included gut for stitching, a needle, and a syringe. "Boiled water, and bandages. And I need soap. Doesn't Dr. Tessler require clean hands for his doctors?"

The nurse paused. "You know Dr. Tessler?"

"Every surgeon worth his salt has read about Dr. Tessler."

The nurse handed Miri a syringe half-filled with morphine. "Our supplies are low, but this should do." Miri flicked the glass tube, pumped out an air bubble, and inserted the needle in Sasha's arm. He mumbled. His head lolled to the side.

The nurse brought a bowl of steaming water and soap. As Miri scrubbed her hands and dunked a pile of cloths in the water to wash the wound, Sasha mumbled something.

"What's that?" the nurse asked. She stood behind Miri, watching over her shoulder.

"Nothing. The morphine," Miri said.

"Husband. The farmer said husband," Sasha managed.

"Husband, you say?" Miri heard the nurse's tone relax into a smile. "I suspected as much. You're newlyweds, then?"

"Newlyweds?" Miri was speechless. She dug into the wound to spill carbolic onto the slashed flesh. He moaned. "I'm sorry, Sasha," Miri whispered to him. She wiped away more blood. Podil was filthy and she didn't want to risk infection. The man in the bed opposite Sasha sat up. One of his eyes was covered with a bandage. She hadn't seen him when they came in. He'd been buried under his sheet but now he was exposed, watching. Was he Okhrana? There was no way to know. Even the nurse could be an informant.

"Back to your own business," the nurse said to the man. She moved to the other side to block his view. There she stood between the sun and Sasha, in silhouette, and Miri saw this nurse was small and perhaps not as old as she seemed when they'd first met. Miri threaded the needle and then pulled the two sides of the gash together.

The nurse leaned close so her forehead almost touched Miri's. "No respectable Russian woman walks into a hospital holding a man so close who isn't her husband."

Miri finished the next stitch. "Do you have the ability to transfuse him?" she asked.

"I'm right, aren't I?"

"The transfusion, can we perform a transfusion?" Miri asked again.

"Answer me, child. You're married? Even in times of war we have standards."

"Of course." Miri had no choice. The nurse was telling her that if she said no, they'd have to leave.

The nurse nodded, satisfied, then said, "He hasn't lost enough blood to warrant a transfusion."

"Look at him. He's pale. He's mumbling."

"Morphine. Your relationship is clouding your judgment. He'll be fine. We don't want to waste care." Miri finished a knot, snipped the end. Three stitches. Then ten more. The blood slowed to a trickle, and she began to wind a bandage around the wound.

"Here, let me wrap that so you can rest. You look exhausted." The nurse reached for the snake of bandage, and Miri realized she was grateful for the help. She let the nurse finish while she sat to the side and held Sasha's hand. "Your stitches are impressive. Precise," the nurse said as she worked. "I can see you're well schooled." She tucked off the end. Miri slid a finger under the dressing to test the tension and then covered Sasha with a blanket. His cheeks were tinged just a touch pink now, and he'd fallen asleep. Miri stood. She realized her back was sore. She stretched, reached up for the ceiling, and for the first time since they'd lain together in the hayloft, she let her shoulders drop.

"Come. We need to talk," the nurse said.

III

"I said let him go." Vanya's eyes were too swollen to see, but he recognized the voice.

"Yuri!" Vanya tried to yell, but the pain from his broken ribs was so intense he lost focus. Still the terror kept him conscious. He was hanging by his wrists, on a rope strung over a rafter in the barn. His blood was everywhere. He could smell it. Taste it. And he was cold, colder than he'd ever been. Was it morning? Night? The pain of losing his fingernails was nothing compared to the screaming he now felt in his shoulders and wrists. "Help," Vanya managed.

"Listen to him," another voice said. Dima. "The doctor's killed for less."

"Your doctor has never hurt a fly," Vadim or Stepan said, laughing.

The laughter was cut short. There was a scuffle. Wood cracked. The thump of a body hitting the floor. A bloodcurdling scream. "That's my warning," Yuri said. He was out of breath. "You come after us and I'll take the other eye, too."

Vanya felt them cut the ropes. Dima slung him over his shoulder. Pain, everywhere, was so intense the world went black.

IV

"Come, we'll talk and your husband will rest," the nurse said. The word hit Miri hard every time. But what else could she have said in that moment? When the news spread to Yuri, if he was in the hospital, she'd explain. And he'd understand. He knew her heart.

"I can't leave him," Miri said. She realized she'd locked her fingers through Sasha's, sitting there at his bedside. With her other hand, she ran a finger over his cheek, over the spot where he had a dimple when he smiled. Then she brushed her hair back from her face. She'd wound it into a loose braid the way Babushka used to do Miri's hair, the way Miri liked to wear it before she'd started at the hospital and Yuri had warned her to keep it in a tight bun.

"Please, you also need to rest."

The nurse pried her loose and led Miri back down through the ward. They passed a man who cried in his sleep. Another hid under his sheet and shook so hard the bed rattled. These were the familiar sounds of a hospital, and Miri felt herself begin to relax, despite everything. This was a world she knew. At the end of the hall, they went down a narrow passage and into a small kitchen where the smell of sugar was stronger. The room was filled with shadows from the late day sun. Through the window, she made out a lonesome tree backed by a field of cockeyed houses. Miri sat at a table that took up most of the room while the nurse set out teacups and dried apricots. The china was swirled with flowers, like Babushka's from Odessa.

The nurse got to work lighting the stove. She balanced a teapot on the burner. "A newly married Jewish surgeon?" Now with the nurse's suspicions seemingly gone, Miri saw her eyes were brown and warm. Unlike most, she had all her teeth. Despite being well groomed, however, she looked as if she could sleep for days.

"You're from Odessa?" Miri asked.

The nurse smiled. "The Odessa accent is distinct."

"My grandmother was there as a child."

"What's her name? Perhaps I knew her."

"I doubt it," Miri said. She sat up straighter, remembered to keep her guard up. The hospital might feel like home, but the czar had eyes everywhere. Ironic to think that thoughts of Odessa might lull her to safety.

"Then your name," the nurse said. "What's your name?"

"Miri. Miriam Pe-trov." She tripped over the last two syllables not because she thought it might give them away; Sasha Petrov was a common enough name that it wouldn't raise suspicion. Likely there was at least one other already in the hospital. No, she tripped over the syllables because she was taking the name. His name.

"Dr. Petrov. I'm nurse Anya Tessler." She bowed her head.

"Tessler?"

"My husband."

"My God," Miri muttered. "Can I see him?"

"No, child." She leaned closer and put a hand over Miri's. "He's with the czar, called up as a personal physician. He was escorted on a private train, given a retinue of guards. They never let him out of sight." The pot rumbled. Steam shot through the spout. Anya filled their cups and added a dollop of jam to each, just as Babushka would have done.

"He allows you to work? Even though you're married?" Miri asked.

"There are husbands who understand the world is changing. Your *husband* must be of the same mind." Anya took a long, slow sip of her tea. There was no mistaking her emphasis on the word. "Now, tell me. You're filthy. Your Sasha has a knife wound. You came here with nothing. And yet you're a skilled surgeon. I can see as plain as anyone there's trouble behind you. Where are you headed?"

"Here," Miri said. The answer was the simplest of all. "We were headed here."

"And after your husband recovers?"

Miri stared down at her tea. "If you need me to pay, I'll find money." She stood up and walked to the window. Below, a horse pulled a gilded hansom cab up under the hospital's porte cochere, the entrance reserved for the rich.

"Was the marriage forbidden?"

"No," Miri said. "That's not it."

"Where's your ring?"

"I don't have one. I couldn't..."

"It's okay. I understand." She paused. "I have a proposal. It's unorthodox but in times of war, conventions can cloud our way. Can you work for me?" Anya asked.

"What do you mean?"

"The czar has my husband. He's claimed our other surgeons for his army. We're short. I need help or the hospital will be shut down. And I saw your work. You've been trained."

"There are no other surgeons in this hospital?" Yuri wasn't here?

"Only one. Dr. Orlen. A sweet man. And a skilled surgeon. Too old even for the czar. I know I'm lucky to have him here, but he's not enough. If you stay and work, I won't charge you for your husband's care. And I'll provide room and board. But I can't afford a salary."

Miri paced the length of the room. Yuri wasn't there. Sasha was wounded and they had no money, no food. They needed safety, to stay away from the Okhrana and even Zubov now. And she needed a base she could use to look for Vanya and Yuri. "I can't promise to stay for long," she said. She needed to find Vanya quickly, before he started the long journey to Peter. "Maybe only a week."

"I'll take what you can give."

"And I'll only work during the day. I'll need my nights free." Yes, that could work. She could search at night. It would be better that way, easier to hide. Especially for Sasha, who would surely help as soon as he could and would want to keep his face hidden.

"As I said, I'll take what you can give. I have one room to spare." When Miri avoided Anya's gaze, she continued. "I see you're hiding something. I won't ask more, not now. I need your help. Perhaps you need mine more than you're willing to admit. At least we've come to an arrangement."

"Without my credentials or records?"

"I know not to ask. You wouldn't be here, not like this, if you had them. I will choose to trust you, so long as you prove yourself. You're not the only woman who's desperate in Russia."

Miri nodded her thanks. And in truth she felt grateful. Then Anya took Miri up to the third floor to show her to her room. It was tucked into the back, down a slim hallway. It was small with one narrow cot. A hearth was set into the corner. A tangle of wood lay next to it. The window looked out on the paupers' entrance. Beyond that, a line of wagons, piled high with beets, wobbled over the cobblestones on their way to the factory gates. Anya handed Miri a skeleton key. "When your husband is better, in a night or two, you can bring him up here with you." She smiled.

"And what will Sasha do, once he's healed? Before he returns to his unit, I mean." Because of course Anya would expect him to be serving the czar. He'd come wearing a uniform; he was otherwise strong. "While he's still recovering. Surely he can't sit in this room all day."

Anya hesitated. "I meant to ask earlier. Sasha Petrov. Is his family from Kiev?"

"No. No, certainly not."

"Petrov? I'm sure I know the name."

"Perhaps you're confusing his family with another."

"Either way, is he a surgeon like you?"

"No. But he can read and write."

"Then he'll work at the front of the hospital. He can take names, organize the ledger and records until he's well enough to return. Do you think that would suit him?"

Miri nodded. "Thank you."

"Good. Then we're settled." Anya made her way to the door. "I'll let you rest."

"Wait," Miri said. "Was the sun out yesterday? Around lunch?"

"The sun?" Anya looked confused. "Oh, you're referring to the eclipse. Are you superstitious?" Miri shook her head. "I assumed not. It was gray and rainy all day. It did get darker, but only for ten minutes or so. I was helping a patient and needed to call for lights, but with all those clouds there wasn't much of a difference. In any case, don't let the eclipse, or the weather, trouble you. Rest."

Miri closed the door behind Anya and leaned against the frame. Poor, poor Vanya. Everything he had risked to reach this eclipse— for nothing. His life's work wasted. And yet, she felt sure they'd find another way out of Russia, as long as she could get to him before Kir. As long as Sasha could recover before Zubov hunted them down. Oh, what a mess they were all in.

V

When Vanya woke up, he couldn't see. His eyes were swollen shut. Every piece of his body was in so much pain it hurt to breathe, to think. But, he realized, he was alive. He smelled onions frying. And he heard voices. Yuri and Dima were talking. They'd survived.

"Clay took everything?" Yuri asked. The last time Vanya had seen Clay, the coward was covered in blood, too beaten to move.

"Everything," Dima replied. "American bastard. How did he find the plates?"

"I have no idea. I hid them well. I thought." There was a pause. "That's right. We have no way of knowing if we got the photograph Vanya needed." Another pause. "All those chemicals spilled."

"Vanya's notebook, too?"

There was something else Vanya couldn't hear. Then Dima said, "Yes. He's left us all to die." His notebook? Gone?

"We shouldn't stay here. It's too dangerous," Yuri said. "What if Clay comes back?"

"For what? He thinks Vanya's dead. All the villagers do. I told them he died after we brought him home. That should buy us time." And then: "Yuri, we can't leave. Look at him. He truly will die if we move him."

Vanya's notebook. Gone. All that work. He wasn't done, but he was closer than ever. How much could he remember without any notes? And the plates gone, too? Vanya tried to speak, but pain swept him back into unconsciousness.

VI

Miri climbed out of bed at sunrise. She realized she'd been dreaming about her brother and the proof he was after. Anya had said there was a period of darkness over Kiev, but that the rain never let up. Was there any hope he had his photograph? Had he solved the equations? Either way, how would she find him now in this vast, confusing city? Where was Vanya hiding?

Sasha smiled when he saw her coming. He was sitting on the edge of his cot looking tired, but well. He'd shaved his beard. And changed into a shirt and pants that were too small, but adequate. In the sun, his eyes were light like caramel, and the color was back in his cheeks. There was no denying he was handsome, no pretending the nurses didn't pay more attention to him than they should even as they saw Miri coming.

Miri unraveled his bandage. His stitches had held. The scab was already growing strong, and there were no signs of infection. As she rolled a new bandage around his shoulder, he asked, "Why do they call you Dr. Petrov?"

Miri kept her eyes on the bandage. "You don't remember?" He shook his head, and she paused. "The nurse who took us in, Anya, made it clear that we can stay so long as I work, and only because we're man and wife." She leaned down to whisper, "I've warned her we might only stay a week."

"Never thought I'd marry for a week," he said, and smiled. He seemed much less distressed by the idea than she was. "Does that mean Yuri isn't here?"

"It seems not. But we're safe. I'll work as a surgeon. You'll work the desk. We'll search at night."

"Kir might find us. Or Zubov. He knows we were headed this way."

"Exactly why we need to look for them quickly."

"Where will we sleep, *wife?*"

"Upstairs. We have a room. And we can eat in the kitchen."

"Food? We have a private room together, and food is what concerns you?" He smiled.

"Don't be crude. I'll sleep on the floor. Come," she said.

He hesitated. "No. I'll take the floor."

"Either way, you need to get up and walk so you can heal. Yuri believes exercise helps every patient, no matter what the ailment."

"Did you ever care for a patient without him looking over your shoulder?"

"Not until he left with Vanya." She slipped an arm under Sasha, around his waist, not worrying about her hand on his bare skin now. They paced to the end of the ward.

"I've heard wagons rolling past all morning. Military?" Sasha asked.

"No. Beet deliveries." They turned back. "There's a factory next door."

"Will I see you again today?"

"Midday, I'll find you if I have time," she said, and helped him into bed.

Miri met Anya in the lobby and followed her on a tour of the hospital. It was divided into distinct sections. The third floor was a converted attic where sleeping quarters were carved into the rafters. The second floor was for patrons and paying patients. Separated by a marble lobby, the men's and women's wards were gilded and frescoed, lit by chandeliers. The women read books and sewed. The men smoked cigarettes. Without the men wearing uniforms,

Miri couldn't tell who was an officer, but Anya confided there were several. Since the hospital was known as the best in Kiev, even non-Jews came, and so Miri kept her head tucked low and didn't say a word. Any one of them could have been someone who would recognize Sasha—or even Miri.

The first floor was for those who couldn't afford to pay. The men's and women's wings were gray and loud. Cots were shoehorned into every corner. Patients played cards and groaned and gambled. Children slept under their mothers' beds. It felt like Kovno's free clinic. As they walked through, Miri checked every male patient's face for her brother and fiancé, just in case.

Then came the operating theater. This room was the common denominator among the floors, where all bodies were treated equal. Miri was in awe of the bravery it took to care for the rich and the poor in the same theater, a radical design only a doctor as renowned as Tessler could achieve. And she knew he'd received a great deal of criticism for it. She wanted to know why he continued to fight for this arrangement, but she'd have to ask later.

Anya took her to the hospital's surgeon. He was preparing to amputate a leg below the knee. "Dr. Orlen, I'd like you to meet our newest addition, Dr. Petrov."

Dr. Orlen looked up. His face was covered with an operating mask so only his eyes were exposed. They were blue and looked young despite a thin film growing over them. "Dr. Petrov." He raised his eyebrows. "I've never worked with a female doctor."

"Surgeon," Miri said.

"She'll take charge of the women's ward," Anya said.

"Fine. Fine. Just keep her away from my patients. A woman. Surgeon. I told Tessler to stay away from that." He frowned as he positioned the saw blade on the patient's skin. "Tell me, Doctor. Once I open this man's leg, which artery do I need to find as quickly as possible?"

"The peroneal artery," Miri said without hesitating, even as her own pulse quickened, thinking of Anatoly.

Orlen nodded curtly and went back to his patient.

At the laundry in the basement, Anya helped Miri find a new dress. She held out a nurse's apron, but Miri shook her head and reached for a surgeon's coat. "The patients won't accept you dressed like that."

"They will, in time." It was something Babushka had said more often than Miri could count. Anya nodded and helped her with the coat. As they walked back up to the paupers' wing, Anya told Miri about their care standards, but Miri didn't listen. She couldn't. The absurdity of her situation descended on her in a rush. What would Baba say about her being called Dr. Petrov? Even if she or Sasha slept on the floor, they were still sharing a room. What would Baba believe? And Yuri? And her brother—where was he?

"Dr. Petrov!" Anya said. "Come along."

In the women's ward, already there was a line of patients along the wall. There was no time to keep thinking about herself. Five women were on beds, at the end stages of labor, crying and sweat streaked. Injured, teary-eyed children clutched their mothers. Women cradled broken arms or legs or fiddled with bandages.

"The doctor will get to you as soon as she can," Anya said. She kissed the head of a child no more than six years old who lay in a narrow cot. The child's arm was a bandaged stump.

"Are there any other doctors in Podil that come to consult with Dr. Orlen?" Miri asked.

"No. No one comes to the Jewish hospital." She dropped her voice to a quiet whisper. "Tell me, why are you asking about other doctors?"

"You have so many patients." Miri wasn't sure if she hesitated. "You need help."

"Which is why you've joined us. Is your father a doctor? Is that the problem, that he might look for you here?"

"No."

"He disapproves of Sasha?"

"No. It's nothing like that. I'm curious. That's all."

"No one's *curious* during war." And then: "Our love was also forbidden, Lev's and mine." Anya stopped. "It was years ago. Our parents came around. Yours will, too. Don't fret, child. I understand. I do."

Miri spent the rest of the morning with her new patients. She started with the women giving birth, checked to make sure there were no complications, and then left them to the nurses. Then she turned to the children. One tiny infant lay listless in his mother's arms. The woman had a scarf around her hair. Her hands were wrapped in rags she used as gloves. A taller, older woman next to her wrested the child from his mother and handed him to Miri. She unwound the layers of blankets around him, and his bare skin, when she found it, was too white, not pink as a newborn's should be. "He won't suckle," the older woman explained. "He's been silent since the moment he was born."

"My sister is blind to the truth," the mother said. "He's been cursed. Born during the eclipse. That's his problem."

"The eclipse?" Vanya's favorite poem was about Prince Vseslav, the great warrior born during an eclipse. She hadn't realized even these people had been aware it was coming.

"Yes. I can see it. Even you were scared."

"No. The eclipse is about science."

"No!" the mother replied. "The worst pains came when the sky went dark. Even in the rain, I saw it coming. The devil. He came and toyed with my baby's tongue. He's hexed. Hexed by the unnatural dark."

"Natasya, silence," her sister said. "This nurse can fix the boy. Can't you?"

"I'm a surgeon," Miri said.

The mother spit. "You have magic greater than the devil?"

"It wasn't magic," Miri said patiently. "And it wasn't the devil." She went back to the child, who was thin and angular. His belly was stiff.

"He won't eat unless we spoon the milk in," the sister continued. "Even then most of it dribbles down his chin." A laboring woman screamed. A nurse scurried with a bowl of steaming water. "Can you help him?" He was so pale that Miri could trace his every vein.

"The child is starving," Miri said.

"She's a witch," the mother cried. "Magda, look at her! If she cures my child, she's a witch, not a doctor."

"It's science, that's all," Miri said. She rested a hand on the baby's forehead to feel his temperature. She closed her eyes to concentrate.

"An incantation!" the mother crooned, but Miri ignored her. She and Yuri had seen a child like this once before, an infant who couldn't suck. Yuri had examined his mouth. Miri tried to ease a finger between the boy's lips, but his jaw was locked tight. "I need wine, or vodka," Miri said. The aunt and the mother looked at one another. "Not for me, for the child."

Magda reached under her skirt, which Miri realized wasn't actually a skirt at all. It was layers and layers of scarves folded on a diagonal and pinned at her waist. She was a street peddler, and the scarves were her wares. Out from under a flowered square, she produced a flask.

"Sweet child. Will you open up, please, so I can take a look?" Miri tried to keep her voice light. When he didn't respond, she sang the same message, and the child cooed. To the mother, Miri said, "Please, sing to him." The woman's cheeks were soaked with tears as she obeyed. The moment the baby opened his mouth, Miri squeezed a few drops of vodka onto his tongue. He squinted and squirmed at the taste. A good sign. A few more drops and he'd relaxed enough to allow Miri to feel his gums.

The mother hummed, and the child's eyes began to close. Miri reached inside his mouth. His gums were hard and hot, as they should be. But his tongue should have pushed her away. She tried to slide her finger under it but she couldn't. Ankyloglossia. Of course: the baby was tongue-tied. A short, tight band of tissues tethered his tongue to the bottom of his mouth. "He can't suck, or eat, or cry, because he can't move his tongue."

"Devil's work," the mother said. "I must have said something. Oh, lord."

"Natasya, quiet! Can you fix it?" Magda asked.

Miri spooned the child up into her arms and bounced him. "I can help, but I'll have to make a small cut under his tongue."

"Or else, what?" For the first time, Magda seemed to doubt Miri.

"He'll die," Miri said. She didn't like delivering the news, but she needed to be honest. "He's starving."

The mother dropped her head onto her sister's chest. Her tears ran fast and hard. Magda rubbed her back. "It's science, sister. Science. Not the devil."

"It won't hurt him much," Miri said. "Please?"

"No child should suffer for my sins," Natasya said, and nodded to Miri slowly.

Miri reached for the smallest scalpel. When Yuri cut the child's tongue, he had been fast. It was one clean motion, but the mouth had been too small for Miri to watch. Miri tried to use her own tongue to feel inside her mouth, to judge the distance she would need to cut, but it was impossible to guess.

She eased the baby's mouth open. Using her tweezers to hold his tongue, she quickly, in a fluid swipe, severed the band of flesh. There were only a few drops of blood. After a momentary shock, he broke into a healthy, full-bodied cry, and Natasya knew it. She smiled wide, as did her sister and Miri. Miri handed the baby to his mother. "Feed him," she urged. "Please, now. Feed him." Magda led Natasya to a rocking chair in the corner and unlaced her dress for her. Natasya pulled out her breast and pushed the child up in her arms. The child jumped at the nipple and suckled.

"Well done," Anya said. Miri hadn't noticed she was watching.

As Miri moved along to her next patient, a nurse hurried toward her. She was short with a chin that jutted so far forward her lower lip looked oversize. "Dr. Petrov," she said, panting. "Dr. Orlen requests your help. A man's come in. He's missing an eye. It's as bad as I've ever seen. Someone plucked out his eye."

VII

lucked out his eye. The words were so specific. The action so horrific. It was a defensive move, one that Miri remembered Baba explaining the Jews had used in Zhytomyr. Miri hurried across the hall. By the door in the men's section, a man was stretched out on a cot. His hands, his body, were so caked in mud it was difficult to see where his clothing ended and his skin began.

"He's missing an ear, but that's an older injury," Dr. Orlen said to Miri when he saw her. "He was left at our door. Not Jewish, can't pay. It happens more than we like." A nurse was wiping the patient's face, scrubbing grime away so they could see where the eye had been. "Petrov. Tell me, can you stand the sight of pus?"

"I'm a surgeon. Of course."

"So you say. Help me drain it so we can get a better look."

Miri washed her hands and picked up a clamp to hold back the eyelid while Orlen worked. The patient flinched when she pulled his skin, and so she knew he was better off than he appeared. Feeling pain meant life, Yuri said. "No. Stop the doctor," the patient mumbled. It wasn't so uncommon for patients to be afraid of physicians.

"We need to give him something for the pain, to keep him asleep," Orlen called. The nurse scrambled to the tray next to her.

"The doctor and his devil," the patient mumbled. "My eye, my eye!"

"What are you trying to say?" Miri asked. She leaned so close she could smell the rot on him, coming from the gash. She caught

Orlen's gaze and shook her head. There was likely no way to save this man. Orlen nodded to say he agreed. All they could do was clean the wound and see if his body would heal itself. Orlen kept working.

"The American devil," the patient mumbled. "My cows. The eclipse."

"It's the morphine," the nurse said, shaking her head.

But Miri leaned closer. "An American? Where? Where were you? You saw the eclipse?"

"Dr. Petrov, pay attention," Dr. Orlen said.

"Tell me. Where?" Miri said to the patient again. Louder this time but he didn't answer. She let go of his eyelid, came around to face him. She moved so quickly, Dr. Orlen stepped back in surprise and she grabbed the patient's shoulders. "Who was with you? Tell me. Where?"

"Get her out of here," Orlen boomed, regaining control.

"Where?" Miri asked.

"Out!"

"Shhh." Anya took hold of Miri, dragged her to the door. "Shhhh, child," Anya said. "War rattles us all."

"I'm not rattled." She ripped her arm away from Anya. If anything, Miri felt sharper than ever. That man who'd lost his eye, he'd been with an American and a doctor, and he'd seen the eclipse. She was certain of it. No peasant would think to talk about an American otherwise. It couldn't be a coincidence. "I—I . . ." She needed to get back to him, but Anya stood at the door, barring her. "I—I need to see Sasha." Her words sounded gruff because she was as angry as she was scared. If this man lost an eye, what had happened to Vanya? Or Yuri? Miri shook Anya off and hurried to the men's ward, to Sasha's cot. She couldn't get to him fast enough.

"There's a man," she said before she'd even reached his bedside. Then she realized she was being reckless, speaking too freely. But the man who'd been next to Sasha was gone. His bed empty, his sheets still dirty.

Sasha pulled Miri close. "Slow down. What happened?"

She took a deep breath. Whispering, she told him about Orlen's patient, what he'd said. "It can't be coincidence." She paused. "I think he was saying the American took his eye."

But Sasha shook his head. "You were with Orlen, operating together, and he made you leave?" She nodded. "You said too much." Yes. She'd panicked. And she hated that, but she couldn't change what she'd done.

"Sasha, what matters is the American. That man saw an American and the eclipse."

"Maybe you're shaping his words to hear what you want to hear."

"No. How many Americans do you think there are here now? For the eclipse, with a doctor? He must have been with Clay and Yuri— and Vanya. They found Clay." Sasha opened his mouth to say something, but her words were coming so fast she wouldn't let him speak. Not yet. "I have to talk to him before he dies. The infection is far along."

"It's possible, but..." He held her tighter, must have felt her ready to run back to the one-eyed man. "Who lines Dr. Orlen's pockets? Who lies in the next bed over? You must be more careful." Baba would have said the same. "And if you're right, at least we know they likely made it to Kiev. They're alive."

"Then you agree, you think I need to speak to him as soon as possible?"

"I think you can't be so conspicuous. What we should do is watch that one-eyed man, wait for someone to come for him and question his visitor."

"What if he dies?"

"Someone will come either way, dead or alive. Someone loved him enough to bring him here. They'll come back."

She took a deep breath, and tears started before she even realized she was crying. "Vanya." He wouldn't be able to defend himself, not if someone came at him with a fury like the one-eyed man must have faced. "Sasha, what if my brother is hurt?"

"We're close." Sasha sat up in bed and wrapped his arms around her, whispering into her hair. "We'll find them."

VIII

Y ou're just in time," Dima said. "I was about to give up on you."
He stood at the charred tree in front of the dacha, the one
struck by lightning after the eclipse. Ilya stood across from him, his
boots deep in mud. His pitted skin. His brown eyes. All of him looked
darker than before, like he was scared to be there, worse than a green
sailor facing his first storm.

"Give me the equations and the photos," Ilya said. His voice shook.

"It was good you stayed away."

"I had no choice."

Dima could see the purse hanging under Ilya's shirt. The idiot,
had he learned nothing? Dima pulled out his knife and pointed to
the bulge. "It's all there? All the money?"

"Every kopeck."

"Where's Kir?"

"In Kovno."

"His men?"

"With him in Kovno. I'm alone. Just as you requested."

"Then why are you so nervous?"

Ilya looked over his shoulder, then back at Dima. "I heard there
was a fight here. And I see your bruises. Your knuckles."

"It's over."

"I heard talk. Vanya, he was beaten? How bad?"

"He's dead." Ilya blinked. Swallowed. His face went ashen. Dima
continued, "The villagers thought the eclipse was a curse. They
killed him. Said the Jew had brought it on them."

"Professor Abramov's dead?" The man looked as if he could barely stand. Was it possible he really cared for Vanya?

"Dead as dead can be."

"Vanya's sister." Ilya turned to the side and wiped his eyes. "I received a report that she's missing. She left with a cousin, a neighbor said. A man. An injured soldier. Someone no one had ever seen before. They escaped with her grandmother while one of the guards at their house was asleep. Kir thought they were all heading to Saint Petersburg, but only the grandmother arrived."

"You think she's dead, too, the sister?"

"What else can I think? Their neighbors, bakers, another family I helped, were killed for conspiring against the czar. Now Vanya's dead. And Miriam's missing. What else can it be—she's dead, too."

"Get a hold of yourself. It's only a couple of Jews." Dima forced a smile. "I'm proposing a new deal. Yesterday, you saw the rain? The clouds? There are no photographs. They couldn't take any in that weather."

Ilya sniffled and straightened his shoulders. "No photographs?"

"None."

"But Kir..."

"Will understand. No one has them. It was impossible."

"But you have the equations?"

"Of course I have those. But you heard about the American who ran away?" Dima watched Ilya nod as he continued talking. "He was a coward. Tried to steal Vanya's notebook. I stopped him. Gave him a fake copy."

"Then hand over the real one. I'll pay what we agreed to in the alley in Riga."

"No, you'll hand me all of it. Every kopeck in your purse."

"I can't. Kir would kill me for that, for paying so much without the photographs."

"And he'll kill you if you come back empty-handed. I'm sure you'll find a way to explain. For all I've gone through, as I see it, you're getting a bargain."

"No."

"Suit yourself. Go back to Kir empty-handed or pay me and get what you need."

It wasn't until Dima had his money and Ilya had the notebook, had made his way back down the road, and dropped out of sight, that Dima saw Yuri. The doctor wasn't even trying to hide. He was standing in plain sight, ten paces away, fury in his eyes. "How long have you been there?" Dima asked.

"Long enough," Yuri replied. "How long have you been working for Ilya? Or should I say Kir? It's Kir pulling the strings, isn't it?"

"I've been protecting you from Kir."

"That's not what I asked." Dima didn't like the sound of Yuri's voice. And he'd seen the doctor take an eye, pop it clear out of a man's head with his bare hands. No, Yuri wasn't someone he should underestimate, not someone he'd dare lie to.

"I met Ilya the day I met you and Vanya. While you two were in one of your hotels." The doctor could have him in one lunge. He stepped back. "I have a plan."

"A plan to make yourself richer?"

"No. A plan for Vanya." He could see Yuri didn't trust him, not one bit. Dima couldn't blame him for it. "If you don't believe me, you can go after Ilya. Take the notebook back. But you'll see it's a fake."

"A fake? Like the one you said Clay took? Who made all these fakes?"

"I did."

"Stop with all the lies." The doctor's voice was as cold as it had been when he took the eye, and Dima watched him curling his hands into fists. The sailor took another step back. "You're a traitor. I want you to leave. Now."

"Can't you see I'm helping?" Dima stumbled in a puddle. "Will you listen to my plan?"

"Go!" Yuri spit on the ground at Dima's boots. Dima startled— and ran.

IX

An hour after she'd been dragged away from the patient with one eye, Miri found Anya and Dr. Orlen huddled together in the small kitchen, drinking tea. Miri thought she should apologize but what she needed most was to prevent any further conversation about what had happened. Before she could say a word, Anya smiled. "No need to say anything. These are difficult times for everyone," she said. "Go back to your patients. We'll forget it happened. But don't try to see that man again."

Miri wasn't willing to risk objecting. She'd sneak in later instead. And so she returned to the paupers' ward and concentrated on the women in front of her. Pushing aside her worries for her own safety, and Sasha's, and her fears for Yuri, Vanya, and even the one-eyed man, she plunged herself into her work. By the time she was done, it was late. A lamplighter perched on his ladder was polishing glass before he struck the flames. And it was quiet. Orlen had gone home. Anya was nowhere to be seen.

Miri hurried to the men's ward hoping the man was awake and not being watched by a nurse, or that Sasha had seen someone, anyone, come for him. But when she walked in, the cot by the door where he was supposed to be was empty. "Where is he?"

"Shhhh. He's dead," Sasha said. He sat in a chair nearby, watching.

"Dead?" She shook her head. "Did you see anything?"

"No one came. He died. They took him away. He didn't wake up to say anything more."

"How can you be sure?"

"I watched him all day—for you. And the walls here are thin. I can hear the nurse at the desk. No one's asked about a one-eyed man." He stopped. "Miriam, you're exhausted. There's nothing to do now. We should both get some sleep. We'll look for information in the morning. Maybe someone will come tomorrow."

"The trail could be cold by then. I can't wait." She stopped and shook her head. "And I don't know if you'll be well enough to help tomorrow."

"Anya already told me she expected me out of that cot in the morning."

"You won't be ready." She gestured toward his stitched shoulder, but even as she did, she knew she was only stalling because as soon as he was well enough, they'd share the room upstairs. And yes, she'd slept next to him before, but this would be different. Even if one of them took the floor, they would be sharing *their* room. *Their* locked door. She'd have to tell Yuri. Unless she could find them before then.

"Go to sleep," she said.

She walked him back to his cot and then hurried as fast as she could toward the foyer. No, there was no way she'd wait for morning. Sasha was right. Someone loved that one-eyed man enough to bring him into the hospital. And they weren't likely to disappear before knowing what happened to him.

She slipped outside. A bald beggar asked her for a kopeck. She gave him her last one. "Where can I find a poor family waiting for a patient?"

"Public house down there. Barkeep's soft. Offers food if you'll clean for him."

Miri hurried. She knew it was dangerous to go alone, but she was used to rougher crowds. They were her patients. And she had her dagger. She hoped to walk in unnoticed, to ask the barkeep if he'd met anyone who'd left a one-eyed patient at the hospital.

She opened the door slowly. A man accosted her even before she could get her bearings. "What's a lady like you doing here?" He stood two heads shorter than Miri and stank of vomit.

"I'm from the hospital." She tried to push past. He wouldn't move. "Get out of my way."

"Think I need an examination, do you?" He smiled, revealing a black hole of a mouth. Miri felt everyone in the room watching her. She was a fool, she realized now, to think she could come to a place like this on her own. The only other women present were prostitutes. The toothless man grabbed her wrist.

"Let go." She tried to pull away.

"Leave her be," another man yelled. He elbowed his way through the crowd. He wore a dark apron and a clean shirt. He must have been the barkeep. "Back to your vodka," he yelled at the man who'd stopped Miri. When he didn't listen, the barkeep raised a wooden baton, and then the toothless man scurried to a table. "Are you lost?"

"No. A man came to the hospital. He couldn't have walked in on his own. I'm looking for the family that brought him."

"Lots of men who can't walk get dropped at that hospital."

"This one was missing an eye. Do you know anything?"

"Depends. Can you pay?" He held out his hand.

"Later," she said. "When I have proof your information is good."

The barkeep laughed. "You don't have a kopeck," he said, shaking his head. "Lvov!" A boy scrambled out from the crowd, holding a tray. "See she makes it safe back to the hospital."

X

Yuri held a spoon to Vanya's mouth. "Please, brother, drink." It was hot soup. Vanya's tongue burned, but that pain was less than he felt in the rest of his limbs. He drank.

If he'd heard correctly, then Clay had stolen his notebook. But that didn't matter. Not much. He hadn't solved anything. What did matter were the photographic plates—but Clay had those, too, Yuri said. He had to because they were missing, and by the way he ran off, Vanya knew Yuri was right. The American would never honor his promise, would never give Vanya credit for anything. Vanya should have known not to trust that man. Hadn't he learned from Kir? Oh, he was a fool. Baba taught him to always have a backup plan in place, an escape route ready. How soon until he was strong enough to leave, to go after Clay? He let his eyes close again.

"Stay with me," Yuri said. Vanya wanted to tell him it hurt too much, that he was tired, but he couldn't. "I know there's pain. Even when patients can't talk, they can listen. Should I tell you a story about Miri?" Yuri sniffled. "Yes, I think it's a good time to talk about her." He didn't wait for a response. "I'll tell you about the first time I saw your sister. The instant I laid eyes on Miri, I knew I had to marry her. She came for an interview. The other doctors refused to see her. But I'd worked with a female surgeon in Zhytomyr. She was a fierce and brilliant woman, more capable than many of the men. And from your sister's written exams, it was clear she was more than qualified.

"Within minutes of her arrival I had spilled the ink on my desk.

You always tease me for being formal, but I was too scared to tell her the mistake was mine, not hers. I froze at the sight of her. Never had a woman affect me like that. Never. I should have apologized, but there wasn't a single clear thought in my head. And her eyes, those gorgeous green eyes, went wide with fear. That such a small accident could be the end of her career is ridiculous, but I knew it was what she was thinking. For a man it would mean nothing, but for a woman—she was right." Yuri dropped his chin to his chest.

"I'd already decided I'd take her as my student. I'd teach her everything she needed to know. I wanted her to be mine. To be my wife. Have you ever met a woman who made you feel that way? I sound like a madman, but I'm being honest."

No, Vanya thought. He'd never felt that kind of passion. Not for a woman, not for anything but his work. His notebook—was it really gone?

"I told her I'd only moved to Kovno a few years earlier. And I wanted to tell her more. That I was a coward. An awful, terrible coward." Yuri paused. "It must be hard to believe that I wanted to say so much in that first instant. Me, a man who keeps to himself. But with Miri, it was different. It's always been different."

Vanya didn't see the tears on Yuri's face, but he heard him crying. He heard the scrape of a handkerchief against stubble. He wanted to hold out his hand, tell Yuri it would be okay, but he couldn't move. Yuri continued, "I never told her the whole story. As much as I wanted her to know everything, I couldn't. I tried, but I didn't have the courage.

"It was the way she looked at me. She looks through all of us, Vanya, doesn't she? Past the pretenses and lies. And she understands. She listens. Her willingness to listen, it filled a hole. I didn't know how deep and jagged it was until she came. I love her more than anything." She's lucky to have you, Vanya wanted to say. Yuri's voice began to fade.

XI

"Come back to me," Yuri said. He patted Vanya's face with a wet towel. "Come back. Has Miri told you about my parents?"

All Vanya could manage was a blink.

"My mother sent me to live with my uncle when I was ten years old," Yuri said. "In Zhytomyr." He told Vanya about his uncle pushing him to earn his way, his aunt teaching him piano. About the youth group. He told Vanya he'd been trained to fight. Yuri walked over to the window. His creaking shoe was as loud as ever, telling Vanya exactly where he was. "I didn't want to be a doctor. Not like your sister. I wish I shared her devotion to medicine." He paused. "All I've ever wanted was to be a pianist. And I had it, for a split second. Then it was gone.

"If I'd invited my family to my concert, they would have come and then they wouldn't have been in Zhytomyr when the pogrom started. When I told Miri all of this, she tried to twist my story, to make me into someone I wasn't. A brave man. A hero. A fighter. I'm none of that."

Yuri fell into a terrible silence. The scratch of the house creaking in the wind was between them, the sound of old, bloated boards adjusting to the weather outside that was turning toward winter. "I've already broken. I couldn't protect you. I took a man's eye, and I left Miri just like I left my family—alone. And now, well, there's no reason to hold it back anymore, is there?" Yuri asked. "You were right about me. From the beginning, you thought I was hiding something awful. I could see it in the way you looked at me. You never liked me. Well, now you'll see who I am. Who I really am.

"When I heard the Russians, our neighbors, had killed my aunt and uncle, I lost my mind. Vanya, I tell you. I saw madness in you, too, at the eclipse. Madness just like what I'd felt that night. I was blind with rage. My aunt and my uncle, they were my true parents, and they never deserved any of it. And that madness, it was lust for revenge. I told Miri when I returned to Zhytomyr I found my uncle's house destroyed. I said I'd found my aunt and uncle dead in the ashes, but it's not true." He dropped his head into his hands and took a deep breath.

"The truth is when I got back to Zhytomyr, the pogrom was over. There was glass everywhere. Blood running through cobblestones like rain. I threw up. There were piles of books burning in the street. I even saw a lump of Torahs smoldering. The velvet covers held their shape while the parchment under them was dust. But my uncle's house. It stood untouched. Worse, the windows blazed with light. For a split second, I thought, somehow, my aunt and uncle had survived, were waiting for me. But of course they weren't. Behind the glass in the dining room, there were Russians in uniforms. Dancing. They'd shoved the table to the side. They'd slashed the paintings on the walls, the two my uncle was so proud of. And his books were all in the fireplace, burning. One of those disgusting men was sitting at my aunt's piano, playing.

"My uncle and my aunt, their bodies lay in a heap inside the front gate. They were naked. Their eyes were wide open. I knew they were dead, but still I thought they had been looking for me. Waiting for me. Remember, I was touched by madness. I heard my aunt speak to me. 'Revenge,' she said.

"I covered them with a tarp and hid behind a tree in the yard. I watched the men inside drink all my uncle's vodka and wine. Kosher wine. It was cold, but I was sweating. I waited.

"Later, much later, all but three of the Russians stumbled out into the courtyard, then down the street. If they hadn't been so drunk, they would have seen me or noticed the tarp. The men who remained went upstairs." Yuri stopped to blow his nose. "I slipped inside, went up to the second floor. It was strange, on the top landing the house looked untouched. The rug was pristine. Snoring came from behind closed doors. I banged into the table at the top of the stairs where my aunt kept a pitcher of water. I caught it before it fell. Not that it would have mattered. The Russians were too drunk to hear me.

"I slit their throats. Vanya, brother, I laughed as I did it. I used an antique knife my uncle had hanging on the wall. I think it was used in a war, a battle to defend the czar. Ironic, no? I laughed. While I killed them in their sleep. And I watched them bleed out on my aunt's white sheets.

"I'd always imagined revenge made the victor feel a spectacular triumph, but I didn't feel anything. That made the madness worse. I stripped the men. I tossed them into the courtyard where they'd left my family. I took an ax to the piano and destroyed it. A splinter caught me, here on my lip. It ripped the skin." He paused. "I was the one who set fire to the house, and I was sure someone would have seen me do it, but they were all drunk. Reveling in spoils. I knew it was risky, but I couldn't just leave my aunt and uncle there under a tarp. I lay them in a wagon and took them to the Jewish cemetery. I buried them before dawn and was on the first train. That's the truth. The real truth I could never tell Miri." Yuri started pacing. Vanya wished his head wasn't still so muddled. Never had he imagined anything so brutal, so awful. Had he heard correctly?

"At the train station, I wasn't angry. I was racked with guilt. Not guilt that I'd killed, or guilt that I hadn't been there." He took a deep breath. "Guilt that I couldn't tell anyone. The youth groups, the stand they took, everyone talks about it. It makes the fight real.

But my fight, if I told, I'd be caught and killed. If I didn't tell, if there was no one to celebrate that I'd extracted some small piece of Russian flesh—did it matter that I did it? There. That's the truth of who I am. Why I'm guilty, so guilty." He fell into the chair at the window. "I'm guilty because I want to brag about it and I can't. So many times when I try to sleep, when I close my eyes, I see them, my aunt and uncle.

"I boarded the train thinking I'd slip out of Russia somehow, head to Paris to find an orchestra. It was the only plan I could conceive. I was supposed to transfer in Kovno when a child, a boy, fell onto the tracks. Another man pulled him up to safety. My train was due in ten minutes, but I could see even from across the platform that his femur had snapped. If he didn't get help quickly, he'd lose the whole leg. The child was a Jew. No one came forward to help. There had to be another surgeon in the midst, but not one stepped forward, Vanya.

"By now you know, I'm not sentimental. I'm not soft, brother. But a child shouldn't lose a leg for no reason. The world's hard enough with two strong feet under you. I set his leg. I accompanied him to the hospital. And I stayed."

Yuri leaned against the bed. "I've never told a soul what happened that night, until now." He stopped. Fingered the scar over his lip. "Your sister's more kind than I deserve. I can't say I'm perfect, but with Miri, I'm better." He reached for the bowl of soup. "It's cold now. Maybe it won't burn and you'll eat some. Please eat, brother," Yuri said. "Eat so we can find Miri."

XII

Early in the morning, as Miri walked downstairs, she tried to think of a way to earn money to pay the barkeep. He knew something. She was sure. And time was passing quickly. She needed to act—to do something before she missed her brother. But what? Without this job, she and Sasha had nothing. No food. No safety. Perhaps she could trade medical care? Either way, she wasn't ready to see Sasha because she knew Anya would want her to say he was recovered enough to leave his cot. To join her upstairs.

By the time she made it to the women's ward, the line of patients waiting was twice as long as it had been the day before. Already, it seemed, word had spread that a lady surgeon had taken up residence. Miri heard them whispering as she walked past. "It's true," one murmured. "Some things only a woman understands," another said, nodding. Miri had seen the same surprise and wonder in Kovno. People who needed help were coming now when before they wouldn't. And she was proud of that, of herself.

A nurse brought her a list of patients compiled by Sasha. Anya already had them both hard at work. Miri settled in, tending to women with care, comforted by a confidence that Yuri would be making the same diagnosis in each case. She delivered baby after baby, set a broken arm, stitched a half dozen children, and more. At supper, still avoiding Sasha, she made her way to the kitchen to fetch soup. The laundry was next to the kitchen. The cook and the laundress used the same hearth for their boiling cauldrons. The space was humid. It smelled of soap and the floor was slick. "You the new surgeon?" a woman asked. Cook. "Nurse Anya says she's brought on a lady surgeon. That you?"

"Yes," Miri said. She slipped, reached for the corner of a table for balance.

"I met your husband already. He got you dinner." She snorted. "Never seen a husband fetch food for his wife unless he's in trouble. What'd he do?"

"What did he do?" Miri repeated. Why was he even out of bed, fetching dinner?

"You don't need to act innocent with me," she laughed. Her face was round, a perfect circle, and her cheeks were bloated. "You a real doctor?"

"Miriam," Sasha said. He appeared at the door. His shoulders took the width of the frame. His cheeks were flushed. He held two steaming bowls. "I thought we'd eat upstairs."

"Why are you up?" Miri asked.

"Anya doesn't want me taking a cot I don't need. Not when I have one..." He cleared his throat. "With you."

"Tomorrow, then," Cook said. She winked. "I'll see you tomorrow. Make that a thorough apology," she called, and shooed them out of the kitchen.

"Apology for what?" Sasha asked.

"Nothing." Miri kept climbing the stairs. She heard Sasha bobble, turned to see he'd tripped, spilled some of the stew. "I told you I'll sleep on the floor," he said, recovering. Miri looked around, made sure no one heard. They were stopped on the landing between the first and second floors. With Miri standing on a riser above, they were eye to eye. Sasha continued, "Anya told me you went to a pub, alone, last night. Looking for the man's family. Miriam, you know how dangerous that was?" She did now. "And people report to Anya. You can't be reckless."

"I had to. The trail could have gone cold. Time is rushing by too fast."

"Were you hurt? Is that why you've been avoiding me all day?"

"I haven't been avoiding you. I've been busy. And of course I wasn't hurt."

"I'll go with you. Next time, if you go. Promise me, please, that you'll take me?"

"I shouldn't need your permission."

"It has nothing to do with permission." He stopped as a nurse scurried past. When she was out of earshot, he continued. "Just please, don't go alone."

"I didn't find anything," she said. "The barkeep wouldn't say a word unless I paid. Where could I get the money?"

"We'll find a way. But I wouldn't trust him. Barkeeps are known for saying what you want to hear, for a price. Better to make our own inquiries elsewhere." They heard a noise on the stairs below. "Let's talk more in private."

They walked single file in the hallway on the third floor, bent under the slanted roof. She heard the fabric of his pants swish, the sling around his arm crinkle. Miri fumbled in her skirt for the key while Sasha leaned against the gray wall. Under the scent of barley soup, she smelled him, the faint wisps of pine and sweat. She dropped the key and picked it up. Once they stood inside the room, the space felt smaller than Miri remembered. Sasha's height, his shoulders, all of him seemed to occupy more space than he should. She couldn't move without touching him.

"Let's have our soup on the floor," she said. A flare bellowed out of the sugar yard's chimney. In the sudden bright light, she saw Sasha was as nervous as she was. She squeezed down into the tiny space in front of the bed. Sasha angled himself in next to her. He seemed to be folded over twice just to fit. "Better than sleeping in the woods," she said. "Or in a barn."

"I liked that barn." He grinned. Miri spooned her soup but didn't eat. Nor did Sasha.

"How's your shoulder?"

"Much better. Look." He meant to raise his arm over his head, to show he'd been healing, but instead he knocked his soup into her lap. He fumbled to get a towel from the bedside table. He tried to mop her skirts, but he must have realized he was too close. His hand stopped and he pulled back. They sat in silence until he surprised her by smiling. "Tell me, wife. Tell me more about you. Shouldn't I know you better than anyone?" She looked down at the spoon in her hand. What was there to say? Hadn't he already seen so much of her? When she didn't reply, he went on. "Fine. Then I'll tell you something about me. I love tomatoes. And honey."

"Tell me something important."

"Food's not important?"

"Have you been in love?" Miri asked.

"I've kissed women."

"How many?"

"More than I should."

"And?"

"There's nothing else to say."

"Do you drink too much?"

"You know I don't. But I wanted to ask you the questions."

"You know everything that's important. Tell me more."

"I'm a thief. I stole from a baker. We hadn't eaten in two days."

"That's not stealing."

"It is. And as a soldier I've killed men."

"That's not killing."

"Why do you insist on changing the truth? I'm not ashamed. I'd do those things again. For my family. To survive."

"I'm not trying to change anything. It's just…" Miri looked at him. "The labels, 'thief' and 'killer,' they don't apply. It's the words you use that I object to, not the actions."

"But where do you draw a line and why? It kept me alive. I survived."

"That's what you want in life, to survive?"

"No. I want more. I want to close my eyes and not be scared of what I might find when I open them. And I want a wife to share it with. If there's a chance I could find that in America, then I'd go. Does Yuri want to go to America now?"

"I haven't asked."

"Why not?"

"I told him that was where I was going, and he said he'd come."

"I see." Sasha's voice was deep the way it had been the night they'd kissed. And Miri thought that maybe he was thinking the same, remembering their time on the train. "We should get some rest," he said.

"Yes," Miri agreed. "We need to look elsewhere tomorrow for my brother."

Sasha made his pallet on the floor just as he promised he would. She slid under the sheets, alone, and didn't close her eyes.

XIII

The first frost hit Brovary like an unexpected bullet—hard and too soon. Vanya knew it was a bad sign. The winter to come would be brutal. "Yuri, we can't stay here," Vanya said. He pulled back the sheets and edged himself to the side of the bed, prepared to stand on his own for the first time since the eclipse. "We can't wait out the winter. We don't have enough food. Or wood. And the villagers, they'll see me soon enough. And they'll come for me."

"Where will we go? You're not well enough to travel."

"I have to be. We'll start the journey to Saint Petersburg."

"In your condition, we can't."

Vanya slipped off the side of the mattress, eased his feet onto the worn floorboards. Now standing, for the first time, he took a closer look at the room around him. Bare walls. A dresser. A hearth and a single chair facing the only window. Webs of ice on the glass were melting in the sun, pooling on the sill. Vanya walked toward the chair. It was only five paces, but to Vanya it felt farther. He slid into the cushions, winded. "Was it algae that killed the cows?"

"Yes. Purple algae. A deadly strain," Yuri said. "I have to tell you something."

Vanya tried to wave him off. "I know. I heard you. Clay's gone. He took my notebook and the plates."

Yuri shook his head. "Dima, he betrayed us, too. He's gone. Ach. Why does it still have to come down to that—to being Jewish?" He pushed his hair back, his nails scraping his scalp. "I'll kill them both if I ever find them."

"No," Vanya said. "Not again."

"You remember what I told you?" Vanya nodded and Yuri looked surprised, but he nodded back. "They're both louts. Clay and Dima."

"No. Not Dima. He's different." He'd become a friend, hadn't he?

"You're wrong. He sold your notebooks to Ilya. He's been in contact with him this whole time. Working for Kir."

"What?" Vanya said. He leaned to the edge of the chair. The sudden movement caused pain that sent him back into the beaten cushions, left him breathless again.

"Yes, Ilya." Yuri waited while the news sank in. "I wouldn't have believed it, either, if I hadn't seen it myself. Dima sold your notebook. When I confronted him he said it was a fake, that the one Clay stole was a fake, too, but that's impossible. Isn't it? I don't know. All I know for certain is that Dima sold your notebook to Ilya."

"But—but then who's watching Miri and Baba?"

"Did you hear me? Kir has your notebooks."

"There are no answers in there," Vanya said, his voice quiet now. Of course it hurt to lose the work, but it wasn't what mattered. "If Ilya left Baba and Miri…where are they now, my sister and grandmother? Did he say?"

Yuri hesitated. Vanya could tell he was struggling to find words. "We need to focus. Make new plans," Yuri said finally. "We'll run out of food soon. And we can't just sit here. Waiting. I have an idea. You remember the rabbi, the one I told you about, the one who invited me to join his orchestra?" Vanya nodded. "He lives in Podil, or he did. A day's ride from here. If you're well enough to go that far, he might take us in. In exchange I can work in his clinic while you recover, if he still has one. Did Miri tell you that's how I met him? He wanted me to work as a doctor, but he took me for the music. If he'll still have me, I can earn money so we can eat and travel."

"Can you go back to him? After what you told me? What would you say?"

"I have no idea what I'll say, but it's time. Isn't it?" Yuri balled a fist into his opposite palm. "Ever since I heard that manager in the hotel in Riga say Brovary, since I knew we were headed here, I've thought about the rabbi. When I left, after the concert, I told him I'd be back. He must think I was murdered." Yuri looked out the window. "Every day we've spent at this dacha, I've thought about finding him."

"Yuri, you can't just start where you left off."

"I know." He turned back to Vanya. "But I can't stop thinking we're here in Brovary, where so many paths cross at once, for a reason. You can't travel yet. I'll go and look for him on my own. And while I'm there, I can check on the trains. See if I can find a way for us to Peter." Vanya wasn't convinced it was a good idea, but he understood what is was to feel compelled, to have a path you must follow. And he knew Yuri was right, he couldn't travel that far—not yet. Yuri continued, "I'll leave food for you. And kindling. If I can work, I will, so I can bring back more food. Give me four days. If I'm not back by then, you should run."

"What about Miri and my grandmother? Didn't Ilya say anything?"

"Nothing," Yuri said but Vanya knew from the look on Yuri's face it was a lie.

XIV

Miri left the room before Sasha woke. She tiptoed around him and went downstairs to see patients. At noon, Miri went to the front desk to look for Sasha at his new post, but he wasn't there. A nurse was filling in for him, explained that Sasha wasn't feeling well. Had Miri missed an infection? She went to the men's ward but he wasn't there in a cot. Nor was he in the kitchen. "I haven't seen him," Cook said. She was bent over a pot. "Not a good apology, was it? Does he usually run when he's mad?" Miri's face dropped. It hadn't occurred to her that he'd run. Cook laughed, "Not *leave*, I just mean walk around." Miri thanked her and turned to go, but Cook called after her. "I like that you're wearing your braid down today. It suits you."

All afternoon, as Miri listened to wheezing chests and examined swollen limbs, registered fevers and rashes, she wondered about Sasha. "Have you seen him?" she asked Anya near the end of the day.

"He said he had a personal matter." Anya smiled. "Child, don't look so worried. Cook said you had a disagreement, but that man loves you as much as any man can love a woman. We can all see that." Miri tried to protest, but Anya folded Miri's stethoscope for her and tucked it into her pocket. "Go and rest. You can eat with your husband when he returns."

Miri made her way up the staircase. *He loves you as much as any man can love a woman.* When Miri opened the door to their room, he was there, untying his shoes. "You're back," she said. She put her hand on his forehead, his cheek, examining him as if he were ill, as if that would explain his absence. He was warm. He smelled different. Was that a growing bruise on his chin? "Where have you been?"

He took her hand. "Did you think I'd left?"

"No."

"I can see you did. I wouldn't." He held her hand tighter. "I went to look for Vanya. I went back to that public house you found. And I fought, earned some kopecks."

"Sasha, no! I don't want you fighting. And what about your shoulder?"

"It was nothing. All the good men are gone. Part of the bet was I fought with only one arm against another man with only one arm."

"You have stitches."

"It doesn't matter. I won. That's what's important. I paid the bastard barkeep. He didn't know anything."

"But he said…"

"I know. I don't think he expected me, didn't think there would be consequences for lying to a woman—he must have thought you were alone. But I talked to him for a while and he's going to send us a midwife who might have seen Yuri. Or heard of him if he's been working in these parts. Lvov will bring her here soon."

"Lvov," Miri repeated. It gave her an idea. "Can we send him to the university for us? To ask about an American?"

"Of course. Why hadn't I thought of it! He's a child. He won't draw attention or suspicion."

"Do you think we can trust him?"

"I don't know. But he's not getting any of our money unless we're satisfied with what he finds."

XV

The midwife knew nothing, but she gave them the name of a man who worked as a mystic. "He'll tell your future," she said. "And he knows when new faces come to Podil." But it turned out he knew nothing about Vanya, Yuri, or an American. Soon, Lvov discovered the university had been closed because of the war—another dead end.

How long would Vanya and Yuri stay in Kiev? Miri's impatience grew. She paced their room in the dark while she and Sasha tried to come up with a plan. Her brother wouldn't risk sending another telegram, which meant he wouldn't expect her and Baba to be at Klara's until spring. "Start with our assumptions," Miri said. "I assumed they'd run soon after the eclipse, but it's possible Vanya and Yuri will find a safe place to hide in Kiev, like us. Vanya can't change his plans. He doesn't know where we are, or even that I've left Baba."

Sasha nodded. "It does seem likely they'd hide here for a while."

"Yes, he could still be hard at work with the American."

"Or perhaps they've already left. We can't be sure."

"If they've left, we'll never find them. Are they on a train somehow? If they are, to where? The best thing we can do is keep looking here for a little longer, in case they stayed."

Sasha nodded his agreement and rolled out the blanket. He sank into his bed on the floor. Miri slid under the sheets on her cot. She heard Sasha turn, pictured him pulling the covers the way she'd seen him settle in on the train, in the woods. She thought about the hayloft.

"Are you okay, Miriam?" Sasha asked. "Why can't you sleep?"

"Vanya." And you. You're both keeping me awake, she thought. And Yuri.

"Tomorrow we'll visit the rabbi the mystic told us about. He might know something."

But he didn't. Nor did the half dozen other leads they tracked down after him. It seemed no one knew anything. Still, every night they went out, looking. Spending more and more time together, talking and sharing.

"You tell me about Birshtan often," Sasha said one night on their way back from questioning another midwife.

"I guess I miss it more than I thought. Vanya and I used to race to the lake. He always took the route in the grass. I ran the other way, up to a rock ledge overlooking the water. I dove off, while Vanya walked in." She smiled, imagining she was back standing over the lake.

"I wish I could go to Birshtan with you," Sasha said.

"Me, too, but we can't return to our childhoods. Just like you'll never go back to the farmers who took you in. Tell me more about them."

Sasha told her about learning to use all the different traps the farmer had hanging in his barn and then about learning how to make and set his own. He explained that the farmer's wife taught him to pray like a proper Russian, in a church, in case he needed to prove his faith. He talked about railroads, train engines, tracks— all the lines in Russia. "Why do you love the trains so much?" Miri asked.

"They're the future," he said. Perhaps if she were in Kovno the friendship wouldn't have been proper, but this was war. Besides, there was nothing she did with Sasha that she couldn't share with Yuri. And she felt a newfound freedom in these circumstances. She performed appendectomies and amputations and whatever else was necessary, filled with a new confidence that made her an even better surgeon. Yet all the while, she watched the doors, scanning every new face for Vanya, conscious that Yuri faded with each patient she cured on her own.

Sasha grew into his own role as guard and administrator. He kept order, tossed out drunks until they were sober and men who came after their women until their tempers subsided, watched for Vanya and Yuri and even the American. Miri had described her brother so many times she was sure Sasha would know him. And as Miri's reputation grew, word spread that she was searching, and patients started coming to her with leads, but still she and Sasha found nothing.

XVI

Waiting for Yuri to return made the dacha feel like a prison to Vanya. The house that had been brimming with energy so recently, before the eclipse, was now empty. Vanya started wandering around upstairs and found dust covers over chairs and beds and furniture. Candles were gone from candelabras. Most closets were empty. There weren't even footsteps in the dust accumulating on the floors. Making it all worse was the terrible silence. Since all the trees in the front and side of the house had been cleared to make room for Clay's equipment, there wasn't even a leaf rattling or a bird chirping.

Could Vanya find Miri and Baba on his own, if Yuri didn't come back? What about Clay? What would he do with the photographs? And Dima, how could Vanya have been fooled by the sailor? For that betrayal, Vanya felt shame. And sadness. He'd been so certain Dima had become a friend. Was he really so wrong? One night, Vanya thought he was well enough to go downstairs and check. It took him nearly an hour, a rest on every tread, but he made it. He found the first floor to be just as deserted as the second. An enormous white sheet covered the table and chairs in the dining room. Vanya made his way into the sitting room. He was surprised to find Clay's texts were all still there on the bookshelves above the shrouded desk. The American ran and left everything, Vanya realized. With a rare burst of energy, thinking about Dima, he tore at them, toppled the tomes onto the floor and clawed at the back wall. There was the cutout, the smuggler's hole the sailor had described. Plaster dust crumbled around Vanya's fingertips and easily slipped to the side.

His notebook. It was just where Dima told him he'd left it. Along with a letter. The paper was still crisp. The handwriting wasn't elegant but it was clear.

Vanya,

I gave Clay a fake notebook when he ran. You've found your original, as promised—safe and sound. If you need money, sell Clay's equipment. There are other things to say, but not here.

Your devoted friend,
Dmitry

XVII

It was night. The Sabbath had just ended, and Miri and Sasha were walking up the stairs when a man barged through the hospital's front door. His face was black with soot and his clothing was singed. The smell around him wasn't burnt sugar, it was death. "A fire. A terrible fire." He tried to yell but his voice was hoarse. Sasha carried him to the men's ward. "Synagogue." The man gasped. "Okhrana."

By the time the man settled onto a cot, another burn victim trickled in. Then another. A wide stream began to bleed through the door, men and women flayed black and coughing. Dr. Orlen appeared just as Miri finished cutting a man's shirt from his back. He shooed Miri away, toward the women. "It's just as bad there, worse because of the children," he said as he straightened his pince-nez.

Even before Miri entered the ward, she heard the babies and women crying, the clatter of feet running and surgical tools being set on trays. Just inside, she stopped short. She'd never seen anything like the scene in front of her, not even when the mill collapsed in Kovno. And the smell. Charred flesh. Never had Miri lost control in front of a patient, but here she couldn't help herself. She vomited straight into the washbasin. Anya rubbed her back. "I know, child, but you're all they have."

Miri wiped her mouth, moved to a woman charred in every crease, who still clutched her child. Not a flame had touched the infant and yet she screamed as if she already knew she'd lost her mother. Miri eased the baby away, unwrapping her from the mother finger by finger. Then she scoured the woman's body for flesh she could save. It didn't take long to see there was no point. Miri forced herself to smile, to keep her face as calm as she could. "Rest," Miri said, knowing if the woman closed her eyes she wouldn't wake.

"Cold water," Miri whispered to the nurses. "It's all we can do. Wet her lips."

"And the others?"

"Cut off their clothing and wash the burns, only the light ones. If the skin's black, or blistered, leave it. Give them morphine. Anything we have." Which Miri knew wasn't much.

A young girl would lose her leg. A mother's face would be scarred, but she wouldn't lose her sight. Miri washed and stitched a gash on a child's arm. But those were the lucky ones. In truth, the most she could do for too many was offer comfort.

"Doctor," Anya said. It was hours later, when the women had received the most treatment Miri could give. The sun was just poking back up through the other side of Podil. "Did you hear what happened?" Anya asked. Her hair, usually neat, fell from under her scarf. Her apron was stained and crooked.

"A fire," Miri said. Her voice sounded exhausted. "The Okhrana. A synagogue."

"But did you hear more?" There was something in Anya's voice that made Miri freeze. "The synagogue caught fire when the flames spread. The Okhrana set a medical clinic, a free clinic they accused of harboring deserters."

"Who was the doctor?" Miri asked. "Whose clinic?"

"Dr. Listoken. I don't know him. Someone mentioned he's from Kovno. Dr. Orlen is..." Miri didn't hear the rest. She ran. She didn't even realize she was screaming until Sasha stopped her at the entrance to the men's ward. He held her so tight her ribs ached.

"Let me go," she said, kicking and squirming. Listoken could have been a fake name. Surely, Yuri wouldn't use Rozen, not as a deserter.

"It's not them," Sasha said. He held her tighter.

"How do you know?"

"Miriam, you must stop yelling." A nurse stood across the hall, staring. A group of men, huddled over prayer books, were watching. She didn't care.

"I have to see him. Dr. Listoken. I have to see him." She willed herself to be still. She blinked. "I can be calm. I can be calm," she repeated. Sasha eased his hold and walked with her.

The men's ward was as shocking as the women's. Blackened bodies moaned. The smell of burnt flesh made Miri's stomach turn, but this time she held it down. Dr. Orlen was in the back corner. Miri wanted to move quickly, but there were too many patients packed on the floors to manage any speed. The man on the cot next to Dr. Orlen moaned. Dr. Listoken. "Oh, God, oh, God," she said. Her throat went tight, she tried to breathe. She doubled over. "It's not him." The man on the cot, Dr. Listoken, was old and bald. Surely not even from Kovno, or she would have known him. But what if one of these other patients was Vanya or Yuri? Or what if they'd burned beyond recognition? Someone said Kovno for a reason.

She started jostling through the patients. From man to man. She checked every face, and when the face was too badly burned, she checked the hands for ink stains. Not Vanya. Not Vanya. No, none of these men were Vanya or Yuri.

Finally, Miri wrapped her hand around Sasha's and they walked up to their room. She sat on the bed, on his lap, sobbing.

XVIII

Sasha unlaced Miri's boots. He was so gentle she didn't feel him slip them off. He helped her out of her doctor's coat. The white had turned gray, matted in red, and he unwound her braid so all her curls hung loose over her shoulders. She'd cried for as long as she could, and now the sun streaked bright through the window. The bustle from the market kept the room from being silent. "Do you want water?" Sasha asked.

"It wasn't them," Miri said. How many times had she repeated herself?

"You should sleep, Miriam." He reached for the blanket and she grabbed his arm.

"I need to say it."

"What?" Sasha asked.

A woman outside yelled after a child. "I—I realized I didn't want to find Yuri."

"Of course not. That poor doctor downstairs will be dead within hours."

"No." She held him tighter. "It's awful to think it. Now. When there's such horror downstairs. But I can't help it." Sasha sat there, on his knees in front of her. The stubble around his lips blazed red in the sun, and she could feel him trying to figure out what she meant. "I didn't want to find him. Not yet. And I feel so guilty." She took a deep breath. "Yuri, I know he loves me. And I'll marry him. But I didn't want to find him." She put a hand on Sasha's cheek, over his scar, and then she leaned in to kiss him. His tongue was sweet the way she'd remembered, now tinged with the sugar that seeped through the cracks in the hospital. Sasha seemed unsure, but Miri pressed closer and he stopped holding back. This kiss was different from the kiss on the train. Here they had privacy, a locked door. They were slow and deliberate, but with a need that kept her out of breath. The tragedy had them both starving for life.

Sasha trailed his lips down the side of her neck, to her chest, along the seam where her dress ended and the curve of her breast began. Miri fumbled with his belt. He helped and then stayed still while she eased his shirt up. When he stood there, bare, she ran her hand over his abdomen, over the ridges and along the pale scar she'd seen the very first night in the cellar. She kissed the wound she'd stitched so carefully.

He unlaced her skirts and ran his tongue over her knees as he rolled her stockings down, one leg at a time. And he left a soft, lingering kiss on the scar where Zubov's knife had nicked her arm. He guided her, and what she imagined would seem awkward felt natural, with Sasha. When he pushed inside her, she cried out as much from the shock of pain as from the unexpected sensation of him. While she'd imagined this moment, she'd never anticipated what it felt like to hold him there, in that way. "Should I stop?" he asked.

"No."

Miri woke first, after noon. She tried to untangle herself from Sasha, but when she moved he held her tighter, pulled her closer and smiled, revealing that dimple she adored. In the new morning light, she noticed a scar just below his eye that she hadn't seen before. It was so faint, barely even there. She ran a finger over it lightly, and he smiled again. "I need to check on my patients," she whispered.

Sasha kissed her ear and she smelled him, his delicious smell that had drawn her in even that first day they met. She opened her mouth to say something, and he kissed her raw lips. Feeling him was exquisite. He ran a finger down the length of her spine.

"Doctor!" There was a rap on the door. Anya. "Doctor, we need you back in the ward."

Miri grabbed for her stockings, her skirts, and her surgeon's coat as Anya clopped back down the hall. Another second and Miri would have stayed with Sasha, in bed. His skin, his taste. She wanted it all. But how could she do that with so many burned and dying downstairs? And Yuri. How could she do this to Yuri?

"Please, don't regret what happened," Sasha said.

"So many people are suffering. And look at what we did."

"We were honest with one another."

"I'm engaged."

"You said you don't want to find Yuri."

"A promise is a promise."

"You're Dr. Petrov. Why shouldn't a man and wife sleep together? Love each other?"

"We've never stood under the chuppah." She pulled her skirt up over her shirtwaist.

"Miriam, if that's what you want, I'll find us a rabbi today."

She sat down on the edge of the bed, gripping the stethoscope. Sasha wrapped his arms around her. Next to them, staring up from the white sheets, was the bloodstain that marked the end of her virginity.

"We need to change the sheets." She untucked them quickly. Sasha was on his feet, naked, in front of her. She kept her eyes down and realized he made no move to cover himself or to help. If anything, she could feel him holding himself back, keeping himself from reaching for her. And if he had reached for her, was she so sure she would resist? Why not find a rabbi in Podil? Didn't Baba tell her that paths change?

Baba. What Miri had done was reckless. Shameful. Baba might

approve of her marrying Sasha but not of her giving herself to him before they were married. And Yuri? He was protecting Vanya for her. Risking his life for her. Miri ran down the stairs, terrified one of the nurses would see the sheets she carried and know what Miri and Sasha had done.

XIX

Miri found her patients were not much improved, but at least some were sleeping. She walked cot to cot, checking bandages and stitches. Yet with every step she thought of Sasha, felt the soreness he'd left behind and how she loved that. Hated loving that. Shivered when she imagined him touching her. But it couldn't happen again. Never.

Later, Miri escaped to the kitchen and made herself a cup of red raspberry leaf tea with evening primrose oil, a concoction that prevented pregnancy. Just a precaution. Baba had told her years ago that women in their family had always struggled to conceive. Miri was fourteen the first time she'd seen her baba prescribe the tea. Babushka had just made a match between two families. At the announcement, the bride began to cry. The families assumed it was happiness, but Babushka pulled the girl, whose name was Oksana, into the kitchen. Babushka put a kettle on the stove and waited for it to whistle before she spoke. She stroked Oksana's hand. "You're with child?" Baba asked.

Oksana nodded and her tears came harder. "It wasn't my fault. My brother..."

"Your brother?" Miri asked, horrified.

"His friend. I flirted. I shouldn't have. He came into my room while I was sleeping."

"When?" Babushka asked.

"Last month. I begged but he wouldn't stop. It happened so fast."

"Drink, child. Drink," Babushka said. She set the fresh brewed tea in front of Oksana. The liquid was dark and putrid, but Oksana drank as if it were as sweet as wine. "Come to me every night so no one will see. You'll drink until you bleed."

"My fiancé?"

"You don't know him well enough to tell him, not now." Babushka leaned closer. The scarf around her head fell back, and a white curl bounced forward. She kissed Oksana's forehead. "When you lie with your husband, cut yourself, a small nick he won't see, but the blood will be enough. I know Timor's mother well. She'll never question you."

Only two days later, Oksana's courses came. She'd sent fresh meat to the house for the Sabbath every Friday since. Once Miri was a doctor, she'd prescribed that same concoction dozens of times. The sooner they were taken, the more effective they proved to be.

As Miri reached to brew herself another cup, Sasha appeared in the doorway. There was just enough room for him to stand tall without scraping the ceiling. "Miriam," he whispered. Her cheeks blazed. "Your patients, how are they?"

"Not well." He brought his palm to her cheek. His touch was soft and hot, the way it had been in their room.

"I'm sorry for that." She knew he meant it. He leaned to kiss her but she pulled back.

"I don't know what to do," she said. "What we did was wrong."

"I know you don't believe that." He traced her collarbone. "It's what we both want and you said it yourself. Life can end suddenly."

Anya came bustling into the kitchen from the opposite door. "Miri!" she called. When she saw them, Sasha's hand still lingering on Miri's collarbone, she chuckled. "Newlyweds, newlyweds." She pretended to brush dirt from her skirt to give Sasha time to pull away. "There's a man here from the newspaper. The Yiddish paper. He's heard about the lady surgeon and he'd like your photograph for a piece they're printing about the fire."

"A photograph?" Miri said.

"You're a novelty, it seems." Anya hesitated. "The photograph should be the two of you together. I don't want people thinking you're alone here in Podil."

"No photos," Sasha said.

Anya turned to him. "Please. This is important."

"Why?" Miri interrupted.

"We are open only because we have donors, and they need to see what we do. How important we are to the community." She looked at Miri. "These are hard times for this hospital."

"I understand that," Sasha said. "But I can't agree to it."

"We are running out of money. We have been since so many men were called to war. You saw last night. There is no morphine even for those who need it most."

"Can't the newspaper publish a story about Miriam without a photograph?"

"An image on the front page will be much more effective. Please don't be stubborn. It could mean life or death for people in this hospital. Such a simple thing for you and your wife."

"It's fine." Miri leaned in to whisper to Sasha, "In the Yiddish paper no one will see it." She could see by the way he frowned that he still wasn't happy.

"After all I've done for you two," Anya said. "You must do this for me." She looked over at Cook to make sure she wasn't listening. "I know that you're running from something. If you don't want your names attached, we can arrange that. Sasha, wear your uniform, pull the visor down so no one can recognize you. But this photo, this famous lady surgeon, will help my hospital more than you know. There have been rumors that without my husband, we've fallen." She blinked and pulled Miri close. "You owe me this."

"We'll do it," Miri said, and took Sasha's hand. Perhaps if she couldn't find Vanya, he could find her—through the newspaper. "We'll pose for your photograph. But no names."

XX

Yuri returned. He rode down the drive in a mule-drawn wagon with an energy to him Vanya had never seen. At the barn, he jumped down and ran toward the dacha. Vanya wanted to meet him at the door but only made it halfway down the stairs before Yuri came barreling inside. "You found the rabbi?" Vanya asked.

"Yes," Yuri said, out of breath. The moon was high. Its light cast shadows so the stairwell around them looked haunted by ghosts. "He still has his orchestra."

"He wants you to play?"

"Yes. His pianist was conscripted."

"But we're trying to leave, to get back to Baba. What about the train?"

"Brother, you couldn't even make it down the stairs. I can play while you recover. I know it won't be long, but even a few weeks..." He paused. "Once you're ready, we'll leave."

Vanya nodded. "And the medical clinic? Were you able to work there, too?"

"Yes. It's why I stayed so long. So many still come to him when they're sick. And he's lost his surgeon, too. He's asked me to stay and help there as well." Yuri stopped. "It's dangerous, though. Another clinic was burned to the ground yesterday by the Okhrana. Accused of helping deserters. The rabbi thinks he's safe, at least for a while, safe enough for me to work there while you recover."

"I understand. But now that you've started all this, will you truly be able to leave?"

"Yes, for Miri. When you're well enough to travel, I'll be ready to leave for Miri."

Tishrei

The seventh month in the Hebrew calendar is Tishrei. The name is Babylonian, meaning *beginning*. It is during this month that Adam and Eve were created. It is also the month during which Jews ask for forgiveness for their sins.

I

On the first of Tishrei, Rosh Hashanah, the streets in Podil were quiet. The market closed. Anya brought apples and honey to the hospital, along with a round challah they shared for lunch. Miri had told Anya she'd stay for only a little while, but she'd been out searching for an American, for her brother and Yuri every night, and wasn't ready to leave yet because she'd still found nothing. If only she could warn Baba that it was taking her longer than expected, that winter was bearing down quickly. "Miri, what is it?" Anya said.

"You know I'm looking for my brother." Miri had long since given up trying to keep that secret. With her patients offering tips, bringing midwives and anyone else who might know something to the hospital, her search was known to everyone around her—especially Anya. "I was supposed to see him today. That was our plan. To meet on Rosh Hashanah."

Anya leaned down and kissed Miri's forehead. "You may stay as long as you need while you search. *G'mar chatima tova.*"

"Thank you," Miri said. But she was as relieved as she was anxious. She wanted to keep looking for Vanya, but what about Baba?

At dusk, Miri and Sasha went out for a walk. They wandered the maze of alleys surrounding the hospital, passing a half dozen small synagogues. The murmur of men praying leaked through the walls, sounded like home. When the blast came from the ram's horn, Miri took Sasha's arm. "You don't think my brother went to Peter, do you? That he's there, with Babushka already?"

"No."

"Did I misunderstand the telegram? Maybe he never even came to Kiev."

"No, he was here. The one-eyed man said as much." Sasha ran a finger along the scar between her thumb and pointer finger. "Miriam, we should go to Petrograd now. I know it's on your mind, too. Snow will come soon and if we don't leave, we'll have no choice but to wait it out. Food is running low already. And your grandmother can't be alone for the winter."

"She has Klara." Miri looked away. Klara was only a few years younger than Baba, and their jewels wouldn't buy much if the whole city was starving. "I can't leave without Vanya. Please. Just one more week."

A group of children burst past. Their voices were light; their laughter was loud. Sasha turned to Miri. "My grandfather had a powerful friend, Avram Noskov. He lives in Kiev. Do you want me to ask him for help?"

"How do you know you can trust him?"

"I don't, but I'm willing to risk it. Or we can go to Peter, spend the winter with your grandmother, and come back in the summer if the war is over."

"If we leave, we'll never come back."

She felt Sasha hesitate. Finally, he said, "Would that be so bad?"

II

On Rosh Hashanah, in Brovary, Vanya was alone. Yuri was back in Podil, at his clinic. Vanya walked through the deserted apple orchard hidden behind the dacha where none of the villagers could see him. He hobbled, he moaned, but he pushed because he needed his strength. Ignoring the pain, he collected the three apples he could find and returned to the kitchen. He scrounged for honey, said the blessings to himself, but they were hollow. Out of breath, in pain, all he could think was that he'd failed. He'd failed his grandmother and his sister. He'd been so close, but too weak to solve his equations, and he'd had his hands on the photographs and he'd lost them. He'd always been able to puzzle together every other problem, but in this, the most important of his life, he had failed. The Jewish New Year is a time to reflect on the past and to look forward to the future. To what future?

Yuri came back early, before his second four-day tour with the rabbi was done. "Is something wrong?" Vanya asked, hurrying to meet him. This time he was fast enough that he made it to the driveway before Yuri had even stowed the rasping wagon and mule in the barn. Yuri jumped down and stomped over the freezing ground toward Vanya, his steps so loud their smack covered the creak of his shoe. "Why are you angry?" Vanya asked. "What happened?" Yuri shoved a newspaper in Vanya's direction. The date showed it was recent, but it looked older, as if it had been read hundreds of times. There was a picture of Miri above the fold. "She's here!" Vanya cried.

"She's married," Yuri said. He paced ahead, turned, and came back to Vanya. "Married." Vanya looked again. The caption read: *The great lady surgeon of Podil and her husband.* There was a soldier next to her. He wasn't facing the camera. He was facing Miri, leaning into her.

"Photographs can be staged. The Okhrana prints lies all the time."

"Not in Yiddish."

"Of course in Yiddish. Brother, you're missing the point. She must have come for us."

Yuri kicked a stone. "Remember I saw Ilya with Dima? There was something I didn't tell you." He stood tall and looked Vanya in the eye. "Ilya told me he'd received news, that Miri left Kovno with a man, an injured soldier your grandmother called their cousin.

But neighbors said they didn't recognize him, had never met that *cousin*. Ilya thought it meant she had disappeared with him." He stopped. "What if she did? What if she married him before she even left Kovno?"

"What?" Vanya reached for the garden wall to steady himself. "Why didn't you tell me?"

"You're recovering."

"It's not for you to decide what I can handle. Not when it comes to my family." He was shaking with anger but had to control it. He took a deep breath. "We can't trust Ilya or anything he says. He betrayed us. Nor can you believe that paper. Miri will explain it all. If she's here, it's for you. For both of us." Vanya reached for Yuri's arm, but Yuri jerked away. "Brother, this isn't like you. Not the Yuri I've come to know. You should be happy she's so close."

"She came for you. Can't you see how he looks at her? He's in love with her."

"You can't tell that from a photograph."

"I can because I know the look. I know what that man's thinking. I feel the same way."

Vanya shook his head. "Focus on what matters. Miri's in Podil. It's tremendous. She must have agreed to the picture because she figured we'd see it. She's looking for us." Yuri was already walking toward the house. "Why?" Vanya yelled after him. "Why would she come across Russia? Did it occur to you something could be wrong?"

Yuri waved an arm over his head to dismiss Vanya, and Vanya looked back at the newspaper. "What are you doing, Mirele?" he whispered.

IV

The first snowflakes are here too early, Miri thought as she stood in the basement kitchen and watched them swirl through the small rectangular windows. From her perspective half underground, all she could see were feet and ankles. The flurries curled under boots and felt shoes, along the edges of frayed skirts. Podil wasn't ready for winter. With so many men gone to war, the women hadn't finished with the harvest. Hunger would be as brutal as the cold to come. Sasha stood next to Miri, while Cook kneaded dough across from them. She slapped and pounded the loaves and pressed them into pans. "Have some broth, while we can," Sasha said, handing her a steaming bowl. "Didn't your babushka teach you about the importance of food?"

Miri smiled and took the bowl but couldn't stomach a bite. The tang of acid from the cabbage and beets turned her stomach. "I can't eat," she said.

"You haven't been eating well for days now," Sasha said. "Are you ill?" Cook huffed across the room and closed the oven door. Smoke curled from the edges of the tray in her hand. "Some bread, then?"

"Oh, Lord," Cook said suddenly. There was fear in her voice. "Hurry, have a look." She waved frantically toward the windows on the other side of the basement. A swarm of boots ran past. Soldiers. They were coming to the hospital, to the front door.

One shouted orders. "A woman pretending to be a surgeon," he said in a voice like a bark. "Find her and the bastard with her."

"We know that voice, don't we?" Miri asked Sasha. His hand was on her hip as they peered out. He'd tightened his grip.

"Zubov." Sasha took her hand and tried to run up the stairs, but Cook stepped in front of them. "They'll be at the back and front entrances by now." Her eyes were pinched tight. A smear of flour was across her cheek. She pointed toward the storage room. "Follow me." Cook hurried. Her skirts billowed behind her. "You have to hide."

"I thought he'd forgotten us," Miri said.

"Men like him don't forget," Sasha said. "We humiliated him."

"It has to be more than that. No one else knows what happened on the train."

"Stop making noise," Cook said. "Come and hide. Now. While you can."

The storage area was six stairs down, deeper underground than the kitchen. That small difference kept the room insulated, warmer in winter and cooler in summer—and dark. Normally it was filled three sacks high with potatoes, grains, and flour. Now it held only one layer. "Hurry," Cook said.

"If they're here for us, you're risking your life," Miri said.

"Haven't you done the same for us?" Cook started moving sacks of flour to make room for them as she spoke. "The way you stayed at the hospital. We all knew you were in trouble. Would have been smarter for you to keep running, but you stayed to help."

Sasha had four sacks in his arms. "Pile these on us," he said to Cook. Then he and Miri crouched together in the deepest, darkest corner. Miri sat between Sasha's legs, her back to his stomach, and he pulled her so close she felt his heart beating, his breath in her ear. Miri thought about her own basement, about hiding with Babushka amid the screams and smashing glass. How long ago that night seemed. She pulled Sasha's arms tighter around her. She wanted to tell him he'd been right. They should have left. Yuri and Vanya could have gone back to Peter. Maybe they'd never even found their American. Or maybe they were dead. But Baba wasn't. And Baba needed her. Who knew what would happen to Miri and Sasha now?

Covered, she listened to footfalls above. Boots marching. Doors banged shut, creaked open. The soldiers were searching every corner and weren't being gentle. Someone clomped down to the kitchen. Miri's heart was beating so hard her ears buzzed. She wanted to shrink into the floor, and she knew Sasha was thinking the same because his arms went even tighter around her.

"The woman, the doctor in the photograph, she's gone," Anya said.

"I told you, no one's in my kitchen," Cook yelled at the same time. Feet scuffled. Cook grunted as if someone had pushed her.

"You're lying. You're all lying," Zubov said. "I saw them in the newspaper. They're here. I know it. And they're not who they say they are. I've done my research. I know his real name."

Miri didn't mean to make a sound, but she must have. Sasha slipped a hand to her mouth.

"Aha! I hear them," Zubov cried.

"Nothing, I heard nothing," Anya said. "Please. Leave us in peace."

"They're rats. Jewish rats. All of you." Zubov kept talking but Miri couldn't hear. Pots and pans clanged. Miri wanted to reach for her dagger, but she knew better than to move.

"No," Anya said, her voice no longer steady. She was next to the storage room.

"I said shred every bag," Zubov roared.

"Please, it's all we have!"

"They're in there, aren't they?" Zubov yelled. Miri could smell the rotten cabbage from him. Or was that just a memory? Nothing was clear except she knew he was going to find them. And kill them. There was the rush of a blade, the sound of a puncturing bag. Grain sluiced out on the floor. "Please, it's all we have," Anya pleaded, again.

"I said search. Every. Sack," Zubov yelled. Miri didn't know how many men he had. She heard more tearing, fabric slitting, grain spilling. The men were so close she could hear them grunt and sniffle. They were going through the row just in front of Miri and Sasha now.

"Up here!" Cook screamed from another room. She sounded hysterical. "They ran that way!" The soldiers stopped shredding sacks. Then there were heavy steps on the stairs. "Out there," Cook yelled. "By the laundry." She was leading the men to the back of the hospital. But had they left guards behind? Zubov could have forced Cook to yell like that to draw them out. Even so, she felt Sasha take a deep breath. His shoulders collapsed forward. And she was aware now that they were both shaking. Suddenly, someone heaved the bag of flour off of Miri. It was Anya. "Use the coal chute. It leads to the alley."

As Miri crawled out, her legs weak, Anya pulled her close and kissed her. Miri whispered a thank-you. Sasha was at the far end of the kitchen, already inspecting the chute. The bins were mostly empty. They had been since they'd arrived. Miri could hear Zubov yelling from the courtyard. Anya grabbed Miri's hand as she moved to follow Sasha. "There's one more thing," Anya said. She spoke quickly. "A boy came yesterday asking for the lady surgeon..." She stopped. "I'm sorry. I should have told you. But I wanted you to stay."

"Who?"

"I'm sorry."

"Tell me."

"The boy, he gave me this." Anya held out a slim silver cigarette case. Vanya's cigarette case. The equations, the etching, Miri would know it anywhere. "He said your brother saw your photo in the paper. He can't come because he's been injured." And then: "It could be a trap."

"Where? Where is my brother?"

"Brovary. Dacha Lavroskavo."

Where's Brovary? How far? Miri couldn't picture the map or calculate the distance, but it was too late to ask any more questions. They needed to run. Anya helped Miri hoist herself up and through the chute. She rolled out onto the cobblestones, covered in soot. She and Sasha disappeared into the maze of the slums.

V

Miri and Sasha didn't stop running until they were both so out of breath they needed to stop. They slumped against wooden walls in an alley near a market. Behind them vendors called out prices. Chickens clucked. Sasha's face was black with coal dust, striped by sweat.

"You heard Anya?" Miri asked, still catching her breath. Sasha nodded. "How will we find Dacha Lavroskavo?"

"Zubov will be looking for us. Everywhere." Sasha was also gasping for air. "We can't go. We need to find a hole, a basement, and hide. Find your brother later."

"No. We have to get to Brovary. Now. Vanya's injured."

"What if Anya's right? If it's a trap? Maybe they told Vanya the same to lure us all there at the same time."

"It's our only lead so far. I can't ignore it."

"It's what you want?" he asked. He came closer and pushed a curl away from her face. She knew he wasn't asking about Vanya, but Yuri.

"I have no choice," she said. "You know that."

They washed off as best they could in a rain bucket and waited an hour, and then another, until they were sure Zubov and his men were gone. Then they sneaked out of the alley and sat on the steps of a burnt-out synagogue around the corner while they tried to come up with a plan. They went back and forth until a woman approached from the side. Neither Miri nor Sasha saw her coming. And her grip was so tight, her appearance so sudden, Miri cried

out. Sasha reached for his knife, but in that instant Miri recognized
her. "Magda," Miri said. She'd brought her sister and the baby with
ankyloglossia to the hospital. She still wore a skirt made of scarves
folded on a diagonal and pinned to her waist. She took Miri's hand
and kissed her palm.

"You saved my sister's boy. He's fat as a pig and just as pink. I can
never thank you enough." She grinned and then pointed to Sasha.
"This man gives you trouble?"

"No." Miri shook her head.

"But you look unhappy with him."

"Since when do men make us happy?"

Magda laughed. Miri, too, felt the tug of a smile. "You're lost,
then?" She winked. "In love? In life?"

"We're looking for a guide to help us to Brovary."

Magda nodded. "I can help," she said without asking any other
questions. She returned half an hour later with a boy of perhaps
eleven or twelve, who said he could show Miri and Sasha the way.
They followed him along the road out of Podil, sticking to darker
alleys and looking over their shoulders every few steps. Once the
alleys broke out to wider roads, they spotted soldiers and had to hike
along smaller trails to avoid them. Miri was as terrified as she was
elated. Yes, it could be a trap, but it could also be true. They could be
walking to Vanya. She hated thinking what shape she might find him
in. Had he been injured by the czar's men? Had Kir found him? And
each step closer to Vanya, of course, brought her to Yuri, too—away
from Sasha. She was caught in a vise. Miri stumbled, slipped in ruts
of frozen mud. She walked so close to the boy that she stepped on his
heels, bumped into him when he stopped.

By dusk, they started down a narrower dirt road, and Miri
spotted the rise of a slate roof. It was the only non-thatched construction they'd seen, and there was no mistaking it for anything but
the grand house of Dacha Lavroskavo. The roof gave way to sand-

colored stone and the full outline of an imposing manse set back from the road.

As they got closer, Miri saw tree stumps and swaths of pummeled mud. The lawn had been trampled, bushes destroyed. Only a singed, ancient oak still stood. A single window was illuminated on the ground floor. Inside, a man walked in front of the glass. His silhouette was thin but she recognized him. Yuri. She started to cry out his name, but the word was only half out of her mouth when she thought of Sasha next to her. She turned and put her hand on his cheek. He wrapped his arms around her and pulled her close. "I love you," he said. His head was bowed down so his chin was at her neck.

"I promised...to marry Yuri."

The front door cracked open. "Mirele!" Yuri shouted. He must have heard her. Silhouetted by light coming from the house, she saw Yuri walking toward her, but she could tell from his squint that he couldn't see her.

She looked at Sasha, slipped out of his arms, and started walking to her fiancé.

Yuri came at her fast and slow, young and old at the same time. In the puddle of light coming from the open door, he stopped just short of her. "Yuri," Miri said. Why was he hesitating? "Yuri. At last! Where's Vanya? What's happened?"

He reached for her, but before he touched her, he paused. "Are you married? Is it true?"

"Married?" She shook her head. "Of course not."

"I saw the photo. The soldier?"

"He kept me safe. I'm here to marry you. To find Vanya." At that, Yuri took her in his arms but didn't hold her close or tight. He searched her face. Could he see her guilt even in that poor light? After a moment his face softened. He reached up to touch her hair and finally kissed her cheek. Where he'd felt strong when they'd said goodbye in Kovno, now he seemed fragile. Yuri had left dressed in a new, spotless uniform. Here he stood tall in a suit that was too large, bedraggled in a way he would never have let himself be before. His bones jutted out from under a thin layer of skin. And where his hair had always been pale, now it was closer to white. Yet he smelled the same, like tobacco and, somehow, still like brick clay from the factory next to the hospital in Kovno. "Where's Vanya?" she asked again. "The messenger said he was injured."

"You're even more beautiful than I remembered, Miri. I missed you. I missed you so much." He looked at her again closely. "You're different. You're wearing your hair down."

"Were you injured?" she asked at the same time.

"It's only hunger. Like all Russians. But, Miri. Something's different in you. Not just your hair."

"Where's Vanya," she interrupted, and tried to peer over his shoulder.

He nodded finally and cocked his head toward the house behind him. "Vanya's inside." She didn't wait for him to say more. She ran. "It'll be a shock," Yuri called after her.

"Vanya," she yelled, following wisps of light coming from a hearth. She navigated down a hall, around a corner. "Vanya?" she yelled again.

There he was, slumped in an armchair with a blanket around him. She dropped to her knees and grabbed his legs, started to cry as she repeated his name again and again. His hand was on her head, smoothing her curls. His blanket wasn't soft and worn like Baba's. His eyes were hollow and he was skeletal, even thinner than Yuri. But he was here. Now. Here with her.

"I knew you'd come," he said.

Miri reached for her brother's hand, and that was when she noticed his nails, or the expanse of raw skin where fingernails should have been. Now they were gashes rimmed in scabs. She wiped her eyes. "What happened?"

"Who's the soldier?"

"Aleksandr Grigorevich Petrov," Sasha said. He stood in the doorway next to Yuri. Neither man looked happy. She knew them both well enough to know they'd met outside and already had words between them.

She turned back to her brother. "Sasha helped me find you. And the boy. Where is he?"

"I sent him home," Sasha said.

"Sasha?" Yuri asked. "Not Aleksandr?"

"She saved me. I owe her my life and so I swore to protect her while she looked for both of you," Sasha explained. How did his voice sound so clear, even now?

"You left Baba alone with Aunt Klara, in Peter?"

"How do you know?"

"Ilya." He frowned. "It's a long story. Why didn't she come with you?"

"It was too dangerous. At her age." Miri stopped. "She's waiting for us all."

"The paper said you were married," Yuri said.

"Miriam's traveled across Russia for both of you," Sasha said.

"Why didn't you wait in Saint Petersburg?" Vanya asked. "I don't understand."

"Your telegram." Miri held on tighter to her brother. "We couldn't wait for you until spring. With the war. And Kir, he had guards at the house. He's after you."

"I know."

"You know? Is he the one who did this?" Already she could see he'd been beaten badly. And she had so many questions. She was speaking quickly. All of them were.

"First I want to hear more about Kir," Vanya said.

"As soon as you left. He came for your equations. I don't think he knew anything about Clay. Or Kiev." She shook her head. "Brovary. He put our house under guard."

"And the borders will close soon," Sasha said. "You won't be able to escape Russia by spring. If you want to go, you must go now."

"How long have you been in Podil?" Yuri asked.

"We arrived right after the eclipse. Did you see it? Did you get your photographs?"

"I was a fool to think you could wait for me," Vanya said. "Did Kir hurt you?"

"No, Sasha—"

"What's done is done," Yuri said, cutting her off.

"Why are you angry?" Sasha asked him. "Your fiancée risked her life for you."

"It's just a shock," Vanya said. "Yuri, you're in shock, aren't you?"

Yuri didn't answer. He walked away, and as much as Miri wanted to go after him, even more she wanted to be with Vanya. "Tell me what happened," she said, stroking his arm down to his fingertips where his nails used to grow. "Dearest Vanya, what did they do to you?"

VI

Sasha and Yuri retired to upstairs bedrooms while Vanya and Miri unwrapped their stories in painful strips, under candlelight in the sitting room where they were surrounded by shrouded furniture and empty bookshelves. "I survived," Vanya said. It was deep in the night and they'd talked for hours, with Vanya taking breaks to rest twice. The fire burned low and they didn't have kindling to build it back up. Miri pulled another blanket over her brother. His bones jutted out like clothespins holding the wool on his frame. "Baba taught us well."

"You didn't just survive. And it's not over. You could still solve the equations."

"But without the photographs, Eliot won't help us."

"We can find Clay. We can track him down. If he has the plates, maybe one is clear enough to use."

"Mirele, please. Any good scientist knows when his experiment has run its course."

"But it's not an experiment. This eclipse is more than that. Isn't that what you said?" Miri dropped her head into her hands, and the room went quiet save for a log that collapsed in the grate. She'd told her brother everything—everything except what happened with Sasha in the mail car and on the night of the fire. But Vanya knew her better than anyone. He had to see she was holding back. "Tell me more about Sasha," he said. When she didn't answer immediately, he patted his pocket. "Do you have my cigarette case?"

Miri handed it to her brother, and he filled it with a supply he kept in a desk drawer, under a dust cover. Even with his sore fingers he was able to light two cigarettes, hand one to his sister. The tobacco, real tobacco, tasted like Vanya, delicious. "How did you get this?" she asked.

"Dima had his ways. He left plenty behind." Vanya frowned. "Don't tell me, Mirele. Whatever it is or was with Sasha, it's in the past. Yuri is a good man."

"You didn't used to think that." She smiled.

"What I've lived through with him. I understand now what you've always seen."

Miri felt the tobacco rush to her head, and she took a closer look at her brother. There was a dullness to him now, one she had never expected to find. He looked as if he was shrinking. She hated seeing him like that, deflated and beaten. And the house seemed so still, so quiet in the middle of war. "Yuri's lovesick for you. It's why he's angry," Vanya continued. "He's jealous and I can't blame him. This whole time, he's talked about you, his brilliant fiancée. And now the photo. He can't stand the way Sasha looks at you. I told him he was imagining things, but he wasn't, was he?"

Miri walked to the fire. "There was no marriage. It was to keep us safe, in Podil."

"Did you share your bed?"

"How can you ask that?"

"Because I'm your brother."

"I'll still marry Yuri."

Vanya paused. "Then tell him how much you love him. Make him believe it's true. You changed him, or filled him where he was empty, he said." Miri tried to imagine Yuri as happy as Vanya had said he'd been with the rabbi and his orchestra. She couldn't picture him humming. Would he find that in America? "I risked too many lives," Vanya continued, so quietly Miri almost missed it.

"I did the same. I even took a life."

"That drunk? It wasn't your fault, Mirele."

"Still, I feel the guilt."

"As do I. The guilt for dragging you here."

"Vanya, what you've done was for science. For progress. And for us. To take us to America. You were right to come."

"I'll never be sure, but Mirele, the eclipse, it was like nothing I'd ever seen or felt. Those moments in the dark, those perfect moments. And then it shattered. I shattered. I questioned myself. I questioned it all. After they beat me, I wondered, was something that powerful truly just science?"

"How can you even ask that?"

"Have I cursed us?"

"No. Those men, they had you at your worst, Vanya. There's no curse."

"Either way, the photographs won't do it justice." He flicked the end of his cigarette into the embers. "I survived because Yuri saved me. Mirele, he's a man like no other."

"He may be. And this Dima fellow, too. But you, you survived because of your own strength. Come, we should go to bed. You need your rest so we can run."

The sitting room, the house felt safe on the surface, but Miri knew that could shatter in an instant—the moment the villagers realized Vanya was alive, or Kir or Zubov came for them. Miri walked Vanya toward the stairs leading to the bedrooms, through a hallway skirting the back side of the house. The floorboards underfoot were bloated with a dampness that pervaded the dacha along with the smell of mildew she hadn't noticed while they'd sat at the fire. If it were up to Miri, she would have thrown open all the windows and let the walls breathe for a week to get rid of that stale air.

At the bottom of the grand staircase there were windows, and the moonlight was so bright Miri didn't need a candle to take in the faded grandeur. Scars along the walls showed outlines of a missing sideboard and the trace of a ceiling medallion. The stairs were slanted. The paper on the walls peeled at the edges. Vanya went up first, but one foot trailed the other. Halfway up, he tripped. Miri kept him from falling backward, but he landed hard on his shoulder and screamed. The sinews in his neck bulged, and he squeezed his eyes shut in pain. She leapt to help him, realizing even in the dark that his arm stuck out to the side at an unnatural angle. His shoulder was dislocated.

"Miriam, what happened?" Sasha called from the top of the stairs. Yuri was just steps behind him. Miri felt for a radial pulse and began angling the arm as Yuri pushed his way down the stairs toward them.

"Is he all right? What happened? Is it his rib?" Yuri's voice sounded too loud in Miri's ears.

"The pain," Vanya cried. His legs twitched on the stairs. "No more pain, please."

"Shhh, Vanya, just another minute," Miri said, bracing herself against the wall of the stairs. To Yuri and Sasha she said, "It's his shoulder."

"I've got him," Yuri said, reaching down to move Vanya.

"No," Miri said. "I've got him."

"But it's dark here. You need space and light. Dislocations can be complex."

"She knows," Sasha said. Did he bristle?

Miri concentrated on folding the elbow and straightening the bone in line with the socket. "This will be the worst," she warned.

"Ahhhh." Vanya let out a yelp, and the shoulder snapped into place.

VII

Miri settled Vanya into bed while Sasha set the fire. Yuri hovered over Miri as she tore sheets to make a sling, peppering her with observations about potential complications, signs to observe and treat. He was so close his watch bumped against her arm. It was how they always used to work, but now she felt crowded.

"We must let him sleep," she said. Vanya was already beginning to doze. "I'll stay to watch over him."

"I'll keep you company," Yuri said.

"No. I'll be fine."

"He could have a seizure."

"He didn't hit his head." Yuri looked like he'd object, but Miri stopped him by holding up her hand and said, "Thank you for taking such good care of him, Yuri. But tonight, we'll be fine. Please."

Sasha nodded and slipped out. Yuri followed. When the door clicked closed behind them, Miri drank the rest of the vodka she'd poured for Vanya and collapsed into the chair. Horsehair jutted out from worn velvet where the stitches had failed. Outside, snowflakes swirled. It wasn't a full storm, but it meant heavier snow and ice were coming. Sasha was right. If they were going to leave for Saint Petersburg, they needed to depart quickly. Which meant she needed to rest, but couldn't. As quietly as she could, she paced from the chair to the window. An hour passed and then another. A gentle knock on the door made her jump. She looked to Vanya. He didn't stir, and so she went to check to see who was there.

Sasha. He'd washed and shaved. He was trailed by the smell of soap and the scent of sugar. He wore a pressed shirt with creases along the arms, sleeves that were too short and a middle that was too large. Perhaps it came from Clay's closet, whatever he'd left behind. Miri pulled him to the window where spindled fingers of frost climbed up the glass. "Why aren't you sleeping?" she whispered.

"I could ask you the same." Their faces were so close she made out the tiny frayed edges of the scar under his eye, the one she'd noticed the morning after the fire. "Your fiancé is angry, but it will pass. He'll be good to you."

"He's still my teacher, isn't he?"

"Is that what you want?"

"He's not wrong. There's more for me to learn."

"There's always more to learn. But in Podil you were a surgeon in your own right." Sasha looked down. "If I'd been the one seeing you tonight for the first time in months, I would have recognized that you can work on your own. And I'd be holding you in my arms. Now. I wouldn't have let go."

"You'd be jealous."

"Of course. It's why I'd hold tight." He was so close all she could think about was kissing him, and she was sure he thought the same. She saw it in the way he stared at her lips, tilted his head. But he stayed where he was. "You've put all your hair up again. I haven't seen those tight braids since Kovno." She'd done it without thinking. He went on, "I'm leaving. At sunrise."

"No." Her voice was too loud. Vanya rolled over. Miri grabbed Sasha's arm. She felt his skin sink under her nails, but he didn't pull away. "Please, don't go."

Sasha took a deep breath. "I'm going back to Kiev, to my grandfather's friend, Avram Noskov. With Zubov onto me..."

"What do you mean?"

"Grekov's coat has lost its power, that's all. But Avram likely hasn't. I'll ask him to help find a way onto a train to Saint Petersburg. I'll secure passage for you, your brother, and Yuri. And then I'll go." Miri leaned against him so her waist was pressed to his, and he came closer so she could taste the sugar on him just by smelling him.

"Where will you go? How will I be sure you're safe?"

"I don't know. But I can take care of myself."

VIII

Back in the chair next to Vanya's bed, after Sasha left, Miri watched dawn break in streaks of gray that cut across the scratched wooden floor. She had just finished making a list of the supplies they'd need for the train when something in the hall shattered. She jerked up, checked her brother. He was still asleep. There was a crunch on the other side of the door. "Damn it," a man said. Yuri. Miri dropped her head back and stared at the ceiling, blue-gray rafters hewn from ancient oak.

It sounded like he had a broom now. There was the crack of something fragile being swept away. It seemed the shards gouged the floor as he worked. She put her hand on the doorknob, took a deep breath, and stepped out to the hall. "Yuri." She said his name quietly. He leaned against the striped, papered wall. A shattered vase was piled next to him. His hands gripped a broom, hands she could draw from memory.

"My mind was elsewhere," he mumbled. "You did well last night."

"Thank you."

"You didn't need my help, did you?"

"Of course I did."

He leaned the broom against the wall. It began to fall but he caught it and set it right. "Your brother is healing nicely. Since the eclipse. He takes baths with witch hazel, thyme, and rosemary, all good for the circulation. At least he thinks so."

"A patient's beliefs are crucial to a cure." One of Yuri's first lessons to her. A ghost of a smile flashed and fell across his face. She couldn't remember a single moment when she'd felt this uncomfortable in front of him. Nor could she recall seeing him so disheveled. His eyes were red, the lids thick and swollen. His belt was cinched so tight the mark on the leather where he used to buckle the clasp was exposed far to the side of his hip.

He knew, she thought. He had to know she'd shared her bed with Sasha. He could see it on her, just as he saw ailments in his patients. "I'm sorry for being angry. Last night," he said.

"I understand." And then: "I came to marry you."

"I believe you. In your heart, it's your plan. I just don't know what the future holds." He dropped his chin to his chest.

"Is it the rabbi in Podil? The orchestra? You want to stay?"

"Vanya told you."

"He said you come back to the dacha, humming. That you love it."

"It's true. But it's not the same. We can never go back." He cleared his throat. "Vanya will make a full recovery."

"Thank you. For Vanya, I mean." She bent to pluck a shard of vase off the carpet, a piece he'd missed. The porcelain cut her finger. Yuri reached to take a look, and she recoiled without meaning to. "I'm sorry," she said. Embarrassed. She'd never shrunk from his touch before.

"Is it the soldier? He was good to you?"

"Very good." She should have hesitated.

"He forced himself on you?"

"No. Of course not. He'd never do that." She had to steady herself and look him in the eye. "I pulled him out from the riverbank, after you and Vanya left. He said he owed me his life, that he'd help me find you. He risked the firing squad bringing me here."

"So did you."

"I had no choice. You know I'd do anything for Vanya." She

pulled a handkerchief from her pocket and wrapped it around her bleeding finger. "I'd do anything for both of you."

"He's Jewish, your soldier?"

"He's not my soldier."

"He has money? He's been wounded? How was he excused from the army?"

"It's not that simple."

"It never is."

"He'll leave soon," Miri said. "He can help us find a way onto a train to Peter. I didn't want to ask for his help, he's done so much, but now that I've seen Vanya, I understand we have no choice. He can't travel by sledge. Only by train." She was babbling to fill the stillness between them. Why wouldn't Yuri say something, or at least touch her? But it wasn't his habit to touch her. That was Sasha. Sasha who held her hand or draped an arm around her waist. Sasha who could never be close enough. "I'll go with Aleksandr, secure our passage on the train. If you can take Vanya to your clinic, we can meet there." She took a deep breath. "Yuri, Sasha will leave when we board the train."

"You're different, you know," Yuri said. "I told you that even before I'd realized. But now I understand. I've seen the change before."

"What do you mean?"

"Miri, I'm no idiot. I can see you're pregnant."

Pregnant.

The word hovered between them with a weight she'd never truly understood before. "No." She'd been careful. She'd taken primrose oil. Queen Anne's lace. She would know if she were pregnant. She was a surgeon. "I'm not." How many times had she told patients the only true protection was separate beds? And she understood anatomy, the timing of the cycle. It had only been five weeks since her last courses. Yes, she was late, but with the hunger, the travel, the stress, the delay wasn't unexpected. "I can't be."

"You're telling me you didn't know?" Yuri asked, his voice rising. "How many weeks? How long since you bled?"

She closed her eyes and tried to count again, but all she could think about was the smell of the bricks baked into Yuri's clothing. And his anger. His words coming now had an edge of violence, something she didn't recognize in him. "Think. How many weeks?" Five? No. Six? Her knees must have buckled. Yuri had his arm around her to hold her up, but he wasn't strong enough. She was halfway to the floor. He eased her down, next to the pile of broken porcelain. The hall seemed darker.

A horrid smell seared her nostrils. Smelling salts. She tried to wriggle away but couldn't. She put her hand on her stomach.

"Babushka said our women take years to get pregnant." How could she have been so stupid, so thoughtless? "I—I'm sorry." She couldn't lose Yuri. She'd promised him. And they had a plan. They'd find Babushka. They'd marry. They'd sail for America. What would her grandmother say? Or her own parents, if they were alive? How could she admit she'd given herself away before she was married?

"A million apologies won't alter what you've done," Yuri said. He turned now, away from her, so they both sat with their backs against the wall.

How long did they sit that way? An hour? A minute? Miri had no sense of time. Eventually, Yuri pulled his knees up and used the wall to push himself to his feet. "It's war. Much happens during war, much that shouldn't but does."

"It was only one night. I've come for you," Miri said.

"You've come for Vanya." He stood over her now. And where he'd always been soft, around his eyes, in the curves of his mouth, he was hard—sharp lines and angles. "Mirele, I'll ask you only once. Tell me. Do you love me? Or your soldier?"

"I love you both." It was true.

"But whom will you be with? Please. Tell me only once and I'll accept the child. I'll raise him as mine. Who do you choose?"

"How can I choose?"

"Then you know. You know and you're afraid to say."

"Why are you doing this?"

"If you love us both, it shouldn't matter whom you choose."

"Yuri, I can't decide like this."

"Then marry me. Marry me."

"But…"

"Exactly. You hesitate when it comes to me. But not when it comes to him. I saw it last night. The way you spoke to him. Even when you took something from him, his hand brushed yours and you smiled without even realizing what you'd done. Marry your soldier, Miri." He spit the words at her, then turned and paced across the hall. "I knew it when I saw the photograph in the newspaper," Yuri said. Suddenly, in one awful motion, he pulled his foot back. For a split second Miri cowered, convinced he'd kick her, but he pounded the shattered porcelain instead. Pieces skittered and exploded against the wall far away from where she sat.

Miri held her hands to her face. She was more ashamed than frightened. She was being honest when she said she loved them both. She didn't want to hurt Yuri. She never broke promises. If she could only go back, she'd take it all away. She'd never go to her room after the fire, never take the train with Sasha, never even go to the river. It was a string of smaller, poor decisions that brought her here. She couldn't let them alter her entire future. Not when she'd planned so meticulously, worked so hard and made larger, smarter decisions with Yuri. Her future had always been, and would always be, Yuri.

"Go, take your soldier with you," Yuri said. His watch swung wildly from the pocket in his vest. "Are you afraid he won't marry you once he knows? Have you chosen so poorly?" Yuri stepped back. Even his hair was disheveled now.

"What happened?" It was Sasha. He stepped off the top of the stairs. His boots crunched over shards. He dropped to his knees next to Miri and took her bleeding finger into his hand, covered it with his palm. "What did you do?" he asked Yuri. His voice was quiet but there was a fury behind it. A fury she'd heard before, with Zubov. "You hurt her?"

"No," Miri said.

"I thought you were leaving," Yuri replied, and pulled his vest down with a swift jerk.

"I forgot my cap. Miriam, why are you on the ground? Tell me. Why are you bleeding?"

Yuri walked toward Sasha with his fists raised, challenging him, but Sasha didn't stand to face him. He stayed down next to Miri with his arm around her. The silence in the hall was sharper than any blade.

Pregnant?

"I'll follow your plan. I'll take Vanya to Kiev while you and this *soldier* go to his friend. We'll meet at my clinic and then we're done. Done," Yuri said. He turned and disappeared down the hall. Sasha bundled Miri into his arms and stayed there with her, on the floor, while she cried.

IX

Sasha held Miri so close there was no air between them. She was pregnant. She'd ignored all the signs. Pregnant and unmarried. What would Babushka say? Vanya? How could she have been so thoughtless? Shame and guilt twisted together into a bolt that pinned her to the floor.

"How much did you hear?" she asked.

"I heard him say he won't marry you. Did you tell him you have feelings for me?"

How could she answer? She couldn't bear to walk away from Sasha any more than she could bear to break her promise to Yuri. And if she told Sasha she was pregnant, there was no question he'd marry her. But Baba said marriages made during war were never strong. They hadn't known each other long, not the way she'd known Yuri.

Yuri. She'd never thought about a future without him.

Pregnant. The longer the word sat with her, the heavier it felt. Its meaning sank below the layer of shame. How many women had she seen in her position, had she pitied? Her grandmother would look down on Miri in disgust. The surgeons in Kovno would, too. They'd believed she was only good for what any woman was born to do— to marry and have children. She should be begging Sasha to take her, but she couldn't bring herself to do it. No marriage should start in shame. Or was that an excuse? Baba had patched together many marriages that started this way, many that led to happy lives. And some that didn't. Yuri had said he would accept the child as his own. All she had to do was say it.

Pregnant. As the word fell even deeper, she faced another reason she hated it. She didn't want a child. Not now. Maybe not ever, but especially not now. She wasn't ready. They weren't safe. They had to escape. She had to find a way to Babushka, to America.

Pregnant. Deeper still, she closed her eyes and below it all reached an even more raw truth: She didn't want to die. Not giving birth. Not running from Zubov or Kir. She wanted to live—to make it to America with her brother and grandmother. She wanted to live. Could she run, could she make it if she were pregnant?

She was spinning in circles. What she needed was time, time to think and plan, but there was none. She should tell him. Sasha. She should tell Sasha she was pregnant, only the moment she did everything would change between them, and she didn't want that, either.

They needed to leave the dacha. That was the only thing that was clear. Sasha wiped a tear from her cheek. "Tell me what happened," he said.

Miri stumbled to her knees, to her feet. "I shouldn't be sitting with you like this."

"What happened to your hand? Why did Yuri walk away?"

Miri pictured Yuri at the hospital in Kovno, the smile on his face whenever she walked in. "Yuri saved Vanya for me," she said. She fumbled with the door to her brother's room. Her hand was slick and she couldn't turn the knob. She had to bundle her skirt around the brass to grip it tight enough to open it. Finally, she slid through, leaving Sasha on the other side.

X

Vanya sat in the chair by the window. He was playing with the horsehair breaking through the seams, with a notebook on his lap and a pencil in his sore, scarred hand. He had dressed himself. His curls were brushed and his arm was in the sling Miri had made. She leaned against the door and stared at him. "You're feeling better," she said.

He didn't move. Miri heard Sasha's footsteps in the hall, his retreat down the stairs. "I heard it all," Vanya said. What was in his voice? Anger? Disbelief? Miri wished the house could swallow her whole. Her brother leaned forward and pinched the bridge of his nose the way he did when he was working, struggling for an answer.

"I'm sorry."

"For what? For being pregnant? For breaking Yuri's heart?"

"For all of it."

"A baby with a soldier you barely know?"

"But I do know him."

A door somewhere in the house slammed. The glass in the window shook. "Will you tell Sasha about the child?"

"I don't know." The words came quickly because they were true.

"Why not? What you have done to Yuri is done. The soldier loves you, Miri. And you love him, much as I wish it weren't so. I can see it on both of you. Tell him before he leaves."

"Aren't you ashamed?" Yuri could walk away, but Vanya would have to bear the burden of this illegitimate child with her. It was their family, their future. The sound of someone crunching across the snow made its way into the room. Only a snow with frost on top was that loud. It meant the weather had changed. Raw cold was setting in. A horse whinnied.

"Yuri's hitching the wagon," Vanya said.

"To take you to the clinic."

"Yes, then to the train. If you won't marry him, shouldn't we let him go without us?"

"Maybe I can convince Yuri, change his mind?"

"That's not what you want, is it?" What she wanted was for the pregnancy to disappear. She'd drink more of the tea or find another way. "We all make mistakes. It's how we learn," Vanya said. His shoulders had fallen even further now. "We test a hypothesis. It doesn't always pass muster. I've made greater mistakes than you. Like coming here. I never should have dragged us all to Brovary. I'm not ashamed of you, sister. You're a strong woman. You've been through a lot. I of all people understand this world is changing. And I know Baba. She won't like it but she'll accept it. She sent you with Sasha. She must have trusted you two together for a reason.

"Yuri is a good man. You were right about him. But, Mirele, think how many times Baba has pulled new brides into the kitchen to fix their mistakes. If you don't want either man, we'll go to America and say the father, your husband, is dead. No one will know better. If anything, I'm the one who's ashamed. I risked all our lives, for what?"

"I made my own choices."

"Only after I made mine. That time you spent with Sasha is only a small part of the whole. Everything in our universe is made of pieces. There's no one point at which anything is truly distinct." Vanya put his arm over Miri's shoulder. His ribs spiked into her side. "Remember, I told you other men called Einstein a fool for this theory, and how he seemed to shrug them all off. How he had such conviction he persisted even after all that ridicule. What I'm trying to tell you is that Einstein persisted because Newton wasn't right. No laws are absolute. Life, the universe, they aren't written in stone. Yes, you were supposed to marry Yuri, but that doesn't mean you must."

She dropped her head on Vanya's good shoulder. They listened to the screech of a wheel outside. The wagon. Vanya hobbled across the room, toward the dresser. He was tiring quickly. He wrenched open a drawer. Then he reached in and slid out a sheet of wood—a false bottom, one of Babushka's tricks. He smacked a stack of rubles on top of the dresser.

"Yuri sold Clay's equipment to someone in Kiev. You'll need the money for bribes, for this friend of Sasha's, for the train. Use it all. Whatever it takes."

"What if you need it to buy off the American? To get the photographs?"

"Russell Clay." Vanya exhaled. "We'll never find him. Use the money. The only thing that's certain is that we need to get to America with Baba."

XI

Miri, Sasha, Vanya, and Yuri traveled to Podil in silence, dressed in old clothing they scrounged from closets around the dacha. Yuri drove the wagon. Vanya sat covered in piles of coarse blankets next to him, his notebook tucked into his belt. Miri and Sasha walked behind with hoods pulled low, looking out for Zubov's men. They tripped through snow in the high grounds and freezing puddles along the flats. Branches weighted by ice snapped around them. No peasants braved the slick conditions. Even soldiers stayed clear. Near the city limits, they split. Vanya and Yuri headed toward the clinic. Miri and Sasha continued on to Avram Noskov.

"What happened with Yuri?" Sasha asked as they wound through alleys, near the docks where the smell of rotting fish grew thick. Battered boats had been hauled up to the shore, away from encroaching ice. Fishing nets hung like ghosts.

"I can't. Not yet." She bit her lip to keep herself from crying. "You still haven't told me how you know where this man lives. Avram Noskov. Or why he'll help."

"I told you he was my grandfather's friend."

"Who is he that he has such power? How did your family know him?"

Sasha stopped next to a skiff covered tight with a tarp. "I tried telling you." He took a deep breath. "Remember, after our first night in the woods. I told you about the Polyakov brothers. That one broke away and started the railroads?"

"I remember. He forced your family from your home."

"No." Sasha dropped his head. "My mother was Ethel Sergeyevna Rabinovitch. Her father was Shmuel Polyakov." He looked at Miri without blinking, and his voice dropped to a whisper. "Polyakov was my grandfather."

"Your grandfather?" Miri stepped back.

Sasha continued, speaking quickly. "Yes. And Avram Noskov was another railroad baron. He controlled a different section of Russia. In a sense they were competitors, but because they were both Jews they were also allies. My grandfather helped Noskov stay alive. I don't know the details, only that before Zede died he told me to go to Noskov for anything I ever needed. That he owed our family a deep debt and he'd never turn me away." Miri leaned against the skiff. It shook under her weight, but held. "You understand now?" he asked.

"You're a Polyakov?" Sasha had talked about the Polyakov family with such disgust. Hatred. Or had it been shame? "You could have told me."

"I meant to. But look at how you're pulling away. Even now. I can't bear it."

"I'm...surprised, that's all. But I know you, Sasha. We are not our parents. Or our grandparents," Miri said. "You'd never do what he did."

"How can you be so sure? He was hungry. Terrified. And he saw an opportunity."

"You'd never starve your own people."

"It's not that simple. If it were *you* starving, if I could save you, I might."

"I wouldn't let you."

"What if we had a family? Children crying at night because their bellies were empty?"

"A family?" she gasped.

"Is that so repulsive to you?"

"I didn't mean it like that," Miri said. "It's just..." She reached for him. He moved to her immediately and held her as tight as he had the night of the fire.

"Tell me. Please. Whatever it is," Sasha said. "Tell me."

"Later. I promise. Later."

Sasha handed her Baba's handkerchief. He'd kept it clean, washed it every night, and she used it to wipe her eyes. Then he leaned down to kiss her there, where her skin was still damp.

"We're close," he said. "Are you ready?"

"Yes," she said. "I'm ready." But not a bone in her body felt prepared.

XII

Noskov's building was nestled above a quagmire of sewage. Miri and Sasha skidded as they made their way up a slope of pebbles toward the brick entrance. Up close, the foundation looked so weak it might tumble at the next storm. They trudged up rickety stairs inside. "Avram," Sasha called as he knocked. He put his ear to the door. "Avram, I hear you in there." A door downstairs slammed shut. Small feet, a child, scampered.

"Patience," Avram crooned. His voice was a rasp. They could hear him grunting as he moved and then the slide of metal rings on a curtain rod. "Patience for an old man," he said. The door swung open, and a wave of tobacco smoke hovered around Avram so he was too blurred to see clearly. He peered at them for a moment, saying nothing, and then he leaned out the door, scanned the hall, and ushered them in.

It was dark. Every window in the apartment was covered with thick drapes. Avram lit a candelabra, and Miri realized he was bigger than she expected. His chest jutted out and his stomach bulged. He smelled like rancid grease. "Did anyone see you coming?" Avram asked.

"Of course not," Sasha said. "But what do you care? You're not a hunted man."

"No." He shook his head. "But I made my deal with the devil. Never trust the devil. Or a woman." He pointed to Miri, then Sasha. "I know who you are. Aleksandr Grigorevich Petrov, né Polyakov. But who is she? Has she compromised us both?"

"No."

"Shh! Keep your voice quiet. These walls have ears." Avram led them down a hall and into a library. The walls were decrepit, like the rest of the building, but the floor was covered in an ornate carpet. Paintings hung on exposed beams. Piles of books sat on heavy shelves. "You're in trouble? It's this woman, she's done something? Speak already. Don't waste my time," Avram said in Yiddish.

Sasha walked to the window. He poked a finger into the drapes and pulled them back, just a touch. He seemed to survey the crumbling pebbles below. "We weren't followed." He dropped the curtain and turned to face Noskov. "We need train passage to Petrograd for three people."

"For four," Miri said.

"No, just for three," Sasha replied.

"You know it's dangerous," Avram said. "There's ice. War. You should wait for spring."

"We can't wait."

"Ah, I see. You have a problem, then. Problems can be opportunities." Avram limped to a cabinet with inlaid ivory. He set a bottle of vodka and three thimbles on the table and poured before settling into a chair. "To opportunities." Avram held his thimble up to toast. "To profitable opportunities."

"Profitable?" Miri asked.

Avram laughed and swept his arms around the room. "You see, I've sold all but my few pieces of furniture, some books. These are not easy times. And what I share with Aleksandr's family is not a debt but a horror. I will help and that is more than generous, but there is a cost. Tell me, Aleksandr, how much do you love this woman? How badly do you need her to escape?"

"We have money," Miri interrupted, thinking of the purse Vanya had given her.

"Whatever you have isn't enough, or you wouldn't be here," Avram said.

"How much?" Sasha asked.

"Even if I sold everything in this room, combined it with what's in that purse, it wouldn't give me the reward offered for a Polyakov."

Sasha and Miri both froze. Avram laughed. "He didn't mention that, I see. His grandfather tried skimming extra gold here and there. He was brilliant at running books. But all brilliance has its end. He got greedy. Or sloppy. Either way, the czar found out. It's why they came for them when this one was a boy." Avram leaned closer. "Your lover is worth a fortune. Or at least his head is."

Miri stood quickly. "We should leave."

"So I'm your price," Sasha said evenly, ignoring Miri. His eyes were locked on Avram.

"No!" Miri said. "I won't do it. I won't let you."

But Avram kept speaking. "Your ransom will be enough to put me on a boat and send me far, far from this wretched country. Enough even for me to purchase a house or an apartment in an American city." Avram steepled his fingers and thrummed them together. "You don't have to accept my help, but then you'll have to find your own way. The last train for civilians leaves tomorrow."

"What kind of man would offer that sort of bargain?" Miri asked.

"An honest man," Avram replied.

"I knew you'd do this," Sasha said, shaking his head. Avram narrowed his eyes. "I have something more valuable than the reward for my head. My father, he hid the deeds to his property. I can tell you where. I'll give them to you. Every last one."

Avram threw his head back and laughed even louder than he had before. "That was your plan? To walk in here and offer me worthless paper in exchange for a train ride?" His laughter grew. "Even if those deeds survived, who would honor them? Coming from a Jew?"

"They're signed by the czar," Sasha shot back.

"That means nothing. Paper is worthless, even signed paper, without the backing of the man himself. The czar signed those before he knew your grandfather betrayed him."

"You're lying," Sasha said.

"We'll see once the police start questioning you, and you tell me where the papers are anyway. I'll retrieve them and see if they have any value." Avram swirled more vodka. "In any case, if you want this woman safe on the train, you have my terms and you have tonight to decide. The train, the Rudov, leaves at eight a.m. If you are there, you will find a conductor, Erik, waiting at the shed behind the station. He will make sure your three friends board the train. As they board, Aleksandr, you will report to the police. It's my price. If you don't turn yourself in, Erik will find out and he will kill anyone he helped board the train. You will decide your own fates. Ticktock," Avram laughed. His mouth fell open so wide it looked like a gaping hole that would swallow them both.

XIII

Miri and Sasha started arguing the moment they made it past the pile of pebbles that held up Avram's building. "I won't let you turn yourself in," Miri said. "We can wait out the winter here. Find a train on our own in the spring."

"My fate is not your choice," Sasha said. "Baba needs you. Your brother needs you. You must get them to safety."

"I'd never forgive you."

"Miri. As a Polyakov, as a deserter, as someone who impersonated Grekov: I'm a dead man. Any day someone will catch me. And it looks like today was the day. Even if Yuri won't marry you, you have a long life ahead. This way, I will have done something good."

Miri was terrified and furious. They walked in silence, following Yuri's directions to the clinic, until they stood in front of a two-story brick building. Miri's shoulders relaxed, just a touch, when she realized it wouldn't burn, at least not completely, if the Okhrana came. A candle flickered in a window in the back.

Miri squeezed Sasha's hand. "I need to talk to Yuri."

"I'll wait here." He gestured to the shadows. "Not for long."

Trying not to look back at him, trying not to imagine him trapped in Avram's thick, greasy fingers, Miri crossed the street and opened the clinic door. It was heavy, its hinges screwed too tight into the bricks so it didn't swing easily. Inside, downstairs, she found Yuri working. He was down on one knee, examining a little girl who was so thin she was barely thicker than a shadow. He held his stethoscope to her chest. "Do you ever eat green vegetables?" Yuri asked. He shifted the stethoscope to her back.

"Mold?" She giggled.

"Beet leaves. Cabbage. Carrots."

"Carrots are orange."

"Then you eat them?" Yuri wasn't smiling. Miri remembered he was always serious like that with patients. Even children. "Tell your mother to come talk to me tomorrow."

"Mama is at the factory."

"Your papa?"

"War."

"Sarah, please tell the child what she needs to do to feel better." A woman wearing a nurse's apron stepped from the corner. She was petite with bright eyes and luscious braids wound into a bun. She didn't hesitate to bundle the child onto her lap. "Bubbeleh, you feel sick because you're hungry. And if you don't eat more vegetables, you will lose your teeth."

"Gentle," Yuri murmured. He stood over Sarah just as he'd stood over Miri.

"The rabbi serves cabbage soup every night. Can you come for meals? I'll give you extra greens," Sarah continued.

"Mama says we're not desperate."

"Please tell her I told you that cabbage soup is the cure you need. Now, run home. Before Baba Yaga finds you!"

The girl jumped off the chair and skipped past Miri, into the alley. "What's next, Doctor?" Sarah asked. Miri had posed the very same question when she'd started at the hospital. Yuri whispered something, and then Sarah disappeared up a back staircase Miri couldn't see. She only heard Sarah's light step moving up and up.

"Miri, I see your shadow," Yuri called. He kept his head down over a tray that held his stethoscope and other instruments. To an observer he would have looked like he was focused on organizing his tools, but to Miri his shoulders and back were stiff with nerves. "You didn't tell your soldier yet, did you?"

"No."

"Why not?"

"I want to marry you."

"I won't let you." He turned back to face her. "I need to apologize. I truly am sorry I was so angry at the dacha. I'm ashamed of the way I acted, but that doesn't change things." Miri could imagine herself back in Kovno, in his office. She even thought about the ink spilling between them, that first day they'd met. Perhaps Yuri was thinking the same because he lingered there, staring at her. "We've changed, Mirele. Both of us. We missed our chance. Or perhaps we never had a chance. Either way, we can't marry."

"Is it the nurse? Sarah?"

"Of course not."

"The orchestra, then? This clinic? You can't leave. I understand. I'll stay. With you."

"No."

"I love you."

"I know you do. And I love you, too. I won't say it doesn't hurt to see you and the soldier together, but I don't want..." He paused. "I can't spend the rest of my life thinking I took him away from you."

"You're not taking him away. It's my choice." The thought, again, of Sasha being tortured by the czar's men caught her.

"If you marry me, it's what you'll think. Maybe not now, but in time. Once the child's born, you'll see Sasha in him. You'll compare us. You couldn't help it. You'd wonder. I'd wonder. Surely, Babushka has shown you that marriages die for less?" He reached for her hand and held it but didn't wrap his fingers around hers. "Maybe you don't even notice yourself pulling back from me. But you are, even now. Listen, Miri. Every time you see the child, you'll think about this soldier. And he's a good man, Vanya says."

And a Polyakov, she thought. "You've discussed this with my brother?"

"Of course. I know you don't want to see me hurt. It's one of the things I love about you. It pains you to see others injured. But I'll heal."

"You're still a deserter. Aren't you worried about staying here in Podil? After what happened?"

"You've decided to stay, Doctor?" Sarah asked. She stood in the doorway holding a steaming cup that smelled like Yuri's favorite black tea with strawberry jam. She placed it on his desk and turned to Miri. "You must be the great lady surgeon."

Sarah's smile was warm, and Miri saw Sarah was younger than she'd realized, just barely a woman. Miri couldn't respond. The weight of Yuri's words, of everything that had happened in the last twenty-four hours, lay heavy on her. She reached for a chair and sat down, dropped her head into her hands. My God. She couldn't fathom what it had taken for Yuri to say what he'd said. And as much as she wanted to tell him he was wrong, was he? But what future could she and Sasha even have together?

"Miri?" Yuri shook her shoulder gently. "I'm trying to introduce you to Sarah. The rabbi's daughter. She's training to become a nurse. Did you hear she's already heard of you, regrets she didn't put it all together earlier and bring me to you before the fire? That all of Podil knows you've saved so many?"

"I'm sorry," Miri said.

"It's fine." Sarah smiled at her, misunderstanding. But Yuri nodded, and she saw he understood the apology was to him. "I see you have a lot on your mind," Sarah continued. "We're happy to have you. Your brother is upstairs, sleeping."

Just then, creaking hinges announced Sasha's entrance through the side door. He came up beside Miri, and Yuri was right, she reached for him before she even realized what she was doing. She tried to pull back, but Yuri had already seen; his jaw tightened. "Miriam, we should go before it's too late," Sasha said.

"Go where?" Sarah asked.

"We'll find something."

"Nonsense," Sarah said. "Stay here. My father and I welcome you. All of you." Sarah pointed to the back stairs. "We don't have much but you can sleep near the fire. Come."

"We can't. There's a man after us. We don't want to put you in danger," Miri said.

"There's a man after everyone who's done something worthwhile in Russia."

"It's only one night," Yuri said. "Stay. I have a room next door."

XIV

Together, Miri and Sasha followed Sarah upstairs to the apartment she shared with her father. It occupied the second story of the building. "Your brother's in there," Sarah said. She pointed through the kitchen, to a small sitting room where soot from the hearth had stained the walls. In the dim light, Miri tripped on a footstool. "I'll bring food," Sarah said.

Deeper in the apartment, the walls were lined with thick tomes, most in Hebrew. A single piece of art sat over the hearth. It was a faded map. The city of Jerusalem was marked with a Jewish star. The Okhrana would have shot the rabbi for owning any one of the books, let alone the map. But they would have also executed him for running a secret, unsanctioned clinic. Sarah's father must have paid a heavy price to remain unharmed, to hold on to such a sanctuary.

Vanya lay on a worn divan next to the hearth. He was covered in so many blankets Miri couldn't see the outline of his body. Watching him sleep so soundly there, she began to feel that this small space existed outside of Podil, and even Russia. It was soothing and calm where the rest of the city was chaos. She understood, a little, what drew Yuri to this life.

She pulled back the layers of blankets covering Vanya. His skin looked sallow. She squeezed his hand to make sure the blood flowed back. His thin shirt hung off of his gaunt collarbones. Somehow he looked older, sicker than he had only hours earlier, but even in sleep he clutched his notebook to his chest. He seemed to have healed on the outside, but she'd seen soldiers in Kovno who looked the same.

There were no problems to diagnose and yet still they faded. Miri kissed Vanya's soft curls and he opened his eyes. "You need to come back to me," she said.

Sarah brought warm broth with black bread. Miri was hungrier than she realized. When they were done eating, Sarah brought more blankets. All had holes that had been mended more than once, but they were soft, like Baba's blankets. Sasha lit the single log Sarah offered. It was damp and covered with moss that made the room smell like the forest. A drunk in the alley below the window crooned. A bottle skittered over cobblestones. "We'll leave first thing in the morning," Miri said.

"Stay as long as you need," Sarah said, and then disappeared down the hall.

Sasha insisted on taking the floor, on giving Miri the other divan, and Miri was too exhausted to object. She unlaced her boots and sat with a weariness she'd never felt before. She'd had hundreds of patients tell her that pregnancy made them tired beyond description, but until now hadn't fully understood. Still, once she lay down, she couldn't close her eyes. "Sasha, I won't let you do it. We'll find another way."

"Is Yuri going with you to Petrograd?"

"He says he won't. He thinks you should come in his place."

"What do you think? What do you want?"

I want you to be safe, she thought. But she couldn't speak. She closed her eyes and saw a parade of sobbing women who'd come to Baba to break engagements. All of them pleaded the same, claiming they loved someone else. At the time, Miri thought they were scared. Or selfish. Maybe both. Yet Baba did everything she could to stop the marriages. She had explained that the heart doesn't follow what it should—only what it wants. *It's the most honest organ in every body, Mirele. Any good doctor should know that.* But Miri had never agreed. Until now.

Sasha pressed, "Miriam, I can't follow you to America, not like this. You and your brother have to leave tomorrow on the Rudov and then..."

"Come. I want you to come with me."

"What?"

"Please, will you come with me to America?"

"You're sure?" His breathing was shallow. Nervous, she knew. And she felt the same. She slipped off the divan and onto the floor, next to him. He hesitated. She didn't. "I'm sure. I've never been more certain in my life," she said, and he opened his arms wide so she could lean into his chest where he held her tight. She fell asleep before another thought entered her head.

XV

"You must go. Now," Sarah said. She was on her knees, shaking Sasha and Miri awake. "There's a man downstairs. A colonel. Zubov." Miri jumped, her hand on her belly. It was a new instinct. Sasha was already on his feet. He heaved Vanya out of the couch, threw him over his shoulder before her brother even opened his eyes. "The back stairs," Sarah said.

There were voices arguing. Miri thought she heard Yuri in the mix. How did Zubov find them? She didn't have time to think or even lace up her boots. She ran. The apartment was a blur. Sarah hurried them down a flight of stairs. The whole house seemed to sway under their weight as they hurried. Sasha was three steps ahead, holding Vanya. They burst through a door, into an alley thick with shadows. The sun was just breaking.

Zubov. He stood in front of them. Grinning. Baring his gray teeth. "I knew you'd try to scuttle away again, Polyakov..." Before he'd finished, Sasha put Vanya down and threw a vicious punch that cracked Zubov's nose. Zubov reeled backward into the wall. He was scrambling quickly, back to his feet. Blood poured down his face.

There had to be more men. Zubov couldn't be alone. But there were only two ways out of the alley and both looked clear. Zubov was up on his feet now. He came for Sasha, and Sasha landed another punch, this one up under his ribs. Zubov flew against the same wall. A spray of dust billowed in a cloud from loose mortar. He looked dazed, but he came right back at Sasha, faster now. He was stronger and more agile than he looked.

Men outside the alley were yelling for the colonel, trying to find him. And yet for some reason they didn't come. Was Yuri keeping them away? Still, Miri knew they would find them soon. They were running out of time to escape. Miri looked for a board, any weapon she could use to hit Zubov. "Go!" Sasha yelled at her. In the instant he took to say it, Zubov landed a vicious jab to Sasha's ribs. Sasha stumbled. Zubov shoved him to the ground.

"I know exactly who you are. Jewish scum. Polyakov. It wasn't hard to figure it out. A Jew wearing Grekov's coat." Sasha clawed his way to his knees, and Zubov kicked his arms out from under him so he fell again. "I knew something was wrong when you refused to take it off. Then I heard Grekov was dead. Murdered. His star soldier missing. Only he never knew you were a Polyakov. That whole time he had you and didn't even know it. No one did. But I put it together."

"How?" Sasha asked, but didn't wait for an answer. He punched Zubov. That was when Miri saw it. A thick, solid wooden board. She ran at the colonel with it over her head. Sasha ducked and she brought it down hard on the back of Zubov's skull.

Zubov reeled. Miri kicked. The man howled as his leg bent backward, the joint extending beyond its range. With a quickness that surprised even Miri, Sasha jumped on Zubov and pulled his knife, plunged it into Zubov's chest. The colonel got both hands around the hilt but it was too late. She could see in Zubov's eyes that he knew it, too. Sasha must have pierced his heart. Sasha rolled off the colonel. He was out of breath and clearly in pain.

"We need to get out of here," Miri said, pulling Sasha to his feet, helping him gather Vanya in his arms.

"To the train," Sasha said. He was limping. "We have to get you to the train."

"You're coming. You said you're coming. We'll tell Erik you're Yuri," Miri said.

"It won't work."

"It will. We'll be gone when Avram realizes what's happened. Three places. He said he'd reserve three places. You, me, and Vanya."

"Avram's smarter than that," Sasha said. "And you heard him. His man will kill us if I don't turn myself in."

"Then we jump off the train early. We've done it before."

"It won't be that easy this time."

"Yuri," Vanya said quietly, interrupting.

Miri stopped. Her brother was right. They couldn't leave like this. Yuri, Sarah, and the rabbi would be blamed for Zubov's death. "They'll take revenge on the clinic, the synagogue. They'll kill Yuri for what we've done." But her heart beat so hard her head was spinning and she couldn't think straight.

She heard a clatter around the corner and braced for the sight of Zubov's men. Instead a Jew came sprinting into the alley. He had a wheelbarrow. "Quick. Quick," the man, a stranger, yelled. "Sarah said you'd need help. Thought you'd be injured." Without a pause he began heaving Zubov's dead body into the wheelbarrow. A single arm hung over the side. Miri noticed Zubov had bitten one nail so hard that blood dripped from the cuticle. "Didn't think he'd be dead. That's fine, though. Fine," the stranger babbled.

Miri stood to stop him. "I can't let you take the blame for this."

"Blame?" He laughed. "No one's taking any blame. I'm getting rid of him, dumping him. If they find him, they'll kill everyone on the block just for being alive. Just because we're Jewish. I'm doing it for Sarah. And for her father."

"But they'll know he's missing," Sasha said.

"This is Zubov, right? He has a reputation. No one in Podil, or Kiev, will care. Missing is fine. Dead, well, they'd have to deal with that." He shoved the arm in as they spoke, pulled a tarp out from under his arm, and used it to cover the body. "The rabbi and Sarah, they'll be fine," he said.

A police officer nearby blew a whistle. Miri heard boot steps running toward them. "Go," the man said. Miri, Sasha, and Vanya started running to the other end, away from the police. "Officers! Officers," the man yelled, holding the wheelbarrow in plain sight, pointing in the other direction. "I saw Zubov run that way after the Jews!"

Miri, Sasha, and Vanya hurried into the maze of Podil. As they ran, Vanya held something against his chest. His notebook. Still.

XVI

Miri and Sasha led Vanya through the muddy alleys of Podil, toward the wide boulevards of Kiev where they'd find the train yard and the man Avram had sent them to meet. They stayed in the shadows, watching carefully for Zubov's men, dodging in and out of alleys. The more they walked, the stronger Vanya seemed to be. To Miri, every woman they passed appeared to be pregnant or holding a child.

Miri and Vanya's footsteps were fast and loud. Sasha, on the other hand, even bruised, moved without making a sound. As they hurried, Miri whispered Sasha's family story to her brother, explained that Aleksandr was a Polyakov, that he'd used that to secure their train. When they crossed over from the slum into the city, they entered a world so different it was as if they'd crossed Russia itself. Where Podil was faded, Kiev sparkled. The streets were framed by electric lines, streetlamps and apartment buildings shining with new stone. The train station was a monument of marble and gold, framed by a brilliant domed roof. They ducked around to the back, where Miri was surprised to see the grandeur replaced by the same filth found in Podil.

There was a bustle on the platform at the station. A group of men in three-piece suits and women in travel cloaks appeared. Porters stacked their trunks. A child cried. These were the families hoping to ride the same train, the Rudov. Opposite the platform, down the tracks sat the shed Avram Noskov had described, the place where they'd meet his man.

Sasha turned to Miri and Vanya and held out his hands. Miri gasped. They were covered in blood. Zubov's blood. Had she been so scared she hadn't even noticed? "I need to wash up."

"Sasha, you should have told us."

"There wasn't time. I wanted to make sure we made it. And I kept them in my pockets. No one saw." Sasha shook his head. "There's a pump over there. Wait for me at the shed."

Miri knew there was no point in objecting. She and Vanya crept along the rails in the shadows toward the small structure. While Miri and Vanya huddled in the dark, a group of four soldiers ran past. They didn't appear to see Sasha. Still, Miri held her breath. Were they Zubov's men? There was no way to know. Were Yuri, Sarah, and the rabbi safe? The man with the wheelbarrow seemed certain they'd be fine. There was no reason to doubt him. Still, Miri wished she'd gotten to say goodbye to Yuri. The soldiers ran past, all the way to the platform and into the crowd.

"You love him more than you've ever loved Yuri, don't you, Mirele?" Vanya asked after the soldiers were far away. His voice was hoarse. He put a hand on his chest as if that could help him breathe. "I've been over and over it in my head. Why would my brilliant sister throw her future away for a stranger?" And then: "When I hurt my shoulder. You knew what to do. But Yuri hovered over you as if you were a child. Sasha understood you, though." Vanya coughed. "Yuri, I told you I've come to love him. I truly have. But he's a man who needs an apprentice. Not an equal. Listen to me, Mirele. You've found Sasha. Don't lose him."

"Why are you talking this way?"

"If Zubov's men come, or if the police come here to arrest Sasha. If Avram suspects our plan, I'll tell them that I am Aleksandr Polyakov. I will take his place."

"Vanya. No."

"My work is gone. I'll never find Clay. I can't fight Kir."

"No. You can finish this. You can solve the math. You are so close, you can't give up."

Sasha was coming back toward them now. The smell of coal mixed with steam from the trains was suffocating. "Please, if the police come, convince them I'm Aleksandr Polyakov. And tell Sasha about the child. He won't turn himself in if he knows."

"But I don't want the child."

"Tell him. Before the chance is gone. It might be the only thing that makes him break the promise to turn himself in. That could keep him safe."

"I won't let you sacrifice yourself."

"You must."

"Must what?" Sasha asked. His face was slick with sweat and water. His eyes were wide. His shirt cuffs were wet, too, and dripping, tinged pink with the stain of blood. "Tell him," Vanya said. He was right. Sasha would never go back on his word, not unless he had a reason so strong it would justify his actions. Vanya stepped off to the side as if trying to give them privacy. A train whistle blared. An engine heaved past so loud it hurt her ears. It was the Rudov pulling into the station.

Miri put a hand on Sasha's cheek. As much as she didn't want to say it, the fact was the child would come. And no matter where or when, she wanted Sasha to be there. If she told him, she had no doubt he'd want to be there, too.

"I'm pregnant," she said. Sasha didn't move. She'd never seen the look on his face that she saw now. Was it fear? Surprise? Had she made an awful mistake? Just as she regretted telling him, Sasha buried his face in her curls and kissed her neck, then her stomach. "Magnificent," he said. "Magnificent."

"You'll pose as Yuri. Promise me, you'll pose as Yuri and get on that train with us."

XVII

Friends!" a man called. He was short and slight with a mop of orange hair and eyes that darted from one of them to the other as if he were an animal looking for weakness. Miri stood taller and saw Sasha was careful to keep his hands, his stained wet cuffs, in his pockets. "Avram's friends? Of course, of course. I'm Erik." He wore a red and blue conductor's uniform with a whistle around his neck. For a second, Miri thought he was pulling his pants up but then she saw, in fact, he was reaching for a revolver. Miri gasped. "Noskov gave me instructions," Erik said. "The man named Petrov, he's with the police?" And then: "I'll find out if you're lying."

"Of course," Sasha said.

"Good. Then go." Erik shoved Vanya toward the train. Miri and Sasha followed. The platform was even more crowded now than when they'd arrived. It seemed it was no secret this was the last civilian train. Men elbowed and women bared their nails to press forward. Erik waved Miri, Sasha, and Vanya to the back. He pointed to a ladder welded to the steel and shoved Vanya toward it. Told him to climb. Miri wasn't sure he'd make it, but he did and they all followed.

Unlike the train that Miri and Sasha had taken with Zubov, the carpets here weren't torn, and all the seats were still bolted to the floor. Erik corralled them inside a private compartment meant for four. A light shivered above on a thin cord. The leather seats smelled like opulence, an awful juxtaposition to Podil, to war. "Stay quiet, I have to take tickets," Erik said before closing the door to their berth. The latch clicked. He turned the lock.

"No," Miri said. "He can't keep us in here like prisoners."

"Until he's checked with Noskov, he will. He's gone to make sure I turned myself in."

"You could be wrong. The train will leave any minute."

Sasha shook his head, took Miri's hand and kissed it. "Your brother knows?"

"That I'm pregnant?"

"Of course I know," Vanya said.

Voices and footsteps trudged along the corridor on the other side of the door "Marry me, Miriam?" Sasha asked. "Please, marry me?"

"You're coming, then? To America?" The train lurched.

"Is that a yes?" He kissed her hand again. "Say yes."

"Yes. Of course." He kissed her, but only quickly. "Wait for me," he said.

"Wait for you? Why?"

"They're here."

A whistle blared. The first time Miri mistook it for the train but it sounded again, and now it was clear it wasn't what she thought. A soldier ran toward their compartment. He was outside, with the whistle in his mouth. More whistles followed. Not two or three, but dozens of soldiers with whistles were in his wake. They were ordering the engineers to stop the train. "Polyakov!" one yelled, the tallest and thinnest.

"We have to run," Miri said. She knew she was screaming because her ears started to ring and her throat hurt. She tried to open the door. She pulled and pulled. "No. No," she said. It didn't budge. "The window." She pounded the glass, searched the compartment for something, anything, to break the glass. "Why are you sitting there? Both of you? Why are you sitting there? We need to run."

Both Vanya's and Sasha's faces were pale, drawn. More soldiers ran alongside the train.

"Get up and help," Miri screamed. She tried to pull Sasha to his feet but he wouldn't move. His stillness was terrifying.

"I told you, Avram is a smart man. He knew I'd never turn myself in."

"And you won't. Sasha, we need to get off this train. We still have a chance."

"It's too late."

Miri kicked the door. She dented the metal. She kicked, harder. "Let us out!" she yelled. Only later would she realize she'd broken a toe.

"Sister, it's no use." Vanya's voice was as still as Sasha's. "I'm Aleksandr. I told you, Mirele. I am Aleksandr Polyakov."

"No. I said no."

"We never had a chance," Sasha said at the same time.

"Stop this. Both of you. Help me get us out of here." Miri pounded the door harder. The bottom was kicked out by now, almost far enough for her to fit her arm through.

"If we run, they will shoot us all before we make it onto the tracks," Sasha said. "I'll turn myself in. Vanya, take your sister to America. I'll meet you there."

"Let them take me instead," Vanya objected.

"You wouldn't last ten minutes in interrogation."

"They'll hang you in a day. At least with me, it'll be fast."

Someone in the hallway was fumbling with keys. "Both of you, stop talking. When the door opens, we run," Miri said.

The key ground in the lock and the tumblers clicked. The moment the door slid open, Miri jumped to barrel through, but Sasha caught her. "Miriam, let me go," he said.

"No."

"I am Aleksandr Grigorevich Polyakov." Vanya stood. "You've

come for me." Sasha had his hand over Miri's mouth. She thrashed and kicked, tried to yell.

"I've never seen that pathetic man in my life," Noskov said. He stood in the hall outside their compartment. He poked his finger over the threshold and pointed to Sasha. "Take the other man. The one holding the woman. That is the Polyakov boy."

"Miriam, please. For me. For our child," Sasha whispered. She jerked to the side and he held her even tighter. The scar across his cheek was red again, as red as it had ever been. "Let me do this. They will kill us all if I don't."

A soldier bullied his way into the compartment. His hands appeared like claws. He grabbed Miri and tried to toss her to the side. Sasha jumped to fight, but the soldier brought the butt of his pistol down on his head. Blood streamed over Sasha's face. Miri screamed.

The soldier shoved Sasha out of the compartment. Voices shouted. Miri thought she heard Sasha say, "I'll find you," but then there was nothing but feet dragging. She tried to run after him but Vanya had her. How was he suddenly so strong?

"If you leave this compartment, they won't hesitate. They'll shoot," Vanya said.

"They'll kill him."

"And if you run to him now, you'll both be dead. And the child with you." He was right, but there had to be choices. There were always choices.

"I won't leave Kiev without Sasha." The train's wheels were already rolling. When had they started to pick up speed? There was a shout outside. Sasha kneeled in the train yard, on the gravel. A group of soldiers stood around him. One was smoking. Another was moving his mouth, saying something. An officer in a long greatcoat approached.

"No." She banged the glass. "No. No." The train was picking

up speed. The officer pulled his revolver out from his belt, but instead of aiming it, he used it to backhand Sasha across the face. She watched him crumple to the ground. Miri must have screamed. The train banked around a curve and Sasha was gone.

Cheshvan

The eighth month in the Hebrew calendar, Cheshvan, is the only month during which there are no holidays, celebrations, or special *mitzvot*. It is said that Noah's flood began during this month, and so it is known as a time of judgment and hardship that must be endured.

I

Cheshvan came without any vodka, without a toast between Miri and Vanya. One day slid into two as the train inched along icy tracks, traveling even more slowly than the mail train Miri had been on before. The sun skidded up from the horizon and tumbled back down, trailed by the moon. Miri sat across from her brother in a daze. She felt empty and broken. The engine thrummed while they heaved through the first true snowfall of the winter. Sasha had said he'd find her, but she knew he'd be dead soon if he wasn't already. The wind howled. Day fell again to night. "He could still be alive," Vanya said. "Sleep, sister. You must sleep. For you and for the baby." She closed her eyes without registering time. What did the hour matter, anyway?

She woke. Vanya brought broth he scrounged from the first-class dining car. She managed a piece of a carrot, a slice of potato. "I must go back for him," she said. Vanya shook his head and pulled a blanket over her shoulders. Soon, snow had turned the countryside white and barren. As brutal as it was beautiful. "I think we're going to have a son." Yes, it had to be a son.

II

Vanya shook his sister awake. She'd barely eaten. Barely spoken since they'd lost Sasha. He didn't know what to do, only that she wasn't well. He held her, when she let him, ignoring his own pain, whispering the old stories he used to tell when they were children after their parents died. But she only cried.

He walked with her up and down the train's corridor, trying to keep both of their strengths up. Erik had been replaced by a simple conductor, and that man kept the door to their berth unlocked and ignored them, didn't even offer to help, though he surely must have seen Vanya bending under Miri's weight. And while she slept, he stared out on the countryside and thought about relativity. He'd come so close. If only he could have solved the equations. But while he'd held his notebook, taken it everywhere with him since the eclipse, he had yet to work in it. But then he had a thought. Not about his equations, but about his sister. There might be another way to help her. He couldn't remember the last time he'd seen her with a book or a journal.

"Miriam," he said. "I need your help thinking through a problem. When Dima, Yuri, and I were hiding in the cave, after we stopped for coal, I imagined I was in a rocket, shooting upward—acceleration." He waited for Miri to focus on him, but she continued to stare at the window, seemingly at nothing. He continued, "What if I wasn't on a rocket, but rather in an elevator? Free fall, acceleration. They're related. I know it. But how?" The train barreled forward louder than ever, echoing on snow. Miri said nothing, but Vanya knew she liked to puzzle through pieces that stumped him. Her mind was as sharp as anyone's. Maybe if he could convince her to think it through with him, she'd come back. "Can you help?"

Miri kept her eyes toward the window, toward the snow. Why wouldn't she respond? Hours passed with them sitting in silence. Vanya was about to give up hope, but then Miri turned to him.

"You're thinking about it wrong," she said. The first words she'd spoken in days. "In an elevator. If you're going up, your feet are pressed to the floor. But if you're not moving, your feet are also pressed to the floor. The force only gets lighter when the elevator is in free fall. If you closed your eyes at any point, how would you know whether the elevator is stopped or moving upward?" She lapsed back into silence. Or maybe it was Vanya who went quiet because he was stunned.

Yes, yes, she was right. She had a point. An obvious—brilliant point. It had been there in front of him the whole time, but it took Miri to see it. In an elevator, you wouldn't feel any difference between gravity and acceleration. They are the same thing.

Gravity equals acceleration.

He pinched the skin on the bridge of his nose. And he thought. And thought it through. "Gravity and acceleration are the same," Vanya whispered later, much later, when it was dark, when the rest of the train was asleep. "My God, Mirele. You're right." It was simple. Elegant. There was no question in his mind it was correct. Up to then, he'd been trying to balance gravity and acceleration, but he didn't need to do that. Gravity not only bent space—it was equal to acceleration.

Would it solve his equations? He opened his notebook for the first time since the eclipse. "Mirele, you're brilliant," he said, and took out his pencil—and began to write.

III

Vanya worked for a day. Then another. He could feel in his bones he was close because he sensed the changes he was making to space itself as he calculated, the curves smoothing and the heights coming to a plateau. He sensed their depth and weight. Even their moment in time. When he made a mistake, he could see his error as plain as a child who'd drawn outside the lines. Through all of it, he felt as if he were putting something back where it belonged.

On the third night of work, he stopped. Miri dozed across from him, her head resting on the glass. "I've done it," he whispered, knowing she wouldn't respond even if she were awake. "Mirele, it's complete. I've solved relativity."

Still, he'd check one more time. He went back and compared the version of Mercury's path that he'd calculated to actual observations. It took hours. He checked and rechecked his work. Yes. "Yes!" he shouted.

It matched. Precisely. Absolutely. "Good God," Vanya said. "Finally. Finally."

"What?" Miri asked half-awake now. "What's wrong?"

Not one deviation between observation and calculation. He didn't have approximate numbers, like Einstein. Vanya had exact numbers. His field equations were elegant. Precise. Exactly as they should have been. "I have my math." Did he yell? Was he shaking? "I've done it!"

"You did?" Miri asked, rubbing her eyes.

"Yes. Yes!" Vanya's heart beat so hard he felt it in his throat. He scrambled to hold his notebook over his head, waved the pages high. He grabbed Miri's hands. She didn't get up, but she swung her arms with him in a small dance and smiled for him. "I have it. Finally, I have it. Because of you. You're brilliant. Gravity and acceleration. They are the same." Through the glass he saw the stars twinkled as bright and clear as ever. There wasn't a cloud in the sky. He felt weightless. He'd been told it was impossible. Other professors told him he was wasting his efforts. They said no one could challenge Newton. But they were wrong. All wrong. He, Vanya, had found the answer.

But was he too late? He had no photographs, no way to reach Eliot safely with his news. The Okhrana were after them. They'd lost Yuri, and Miri's soldier, too. They had no way of knowing if Baba was even safe.

He'd beaten Einstein, but for what?

He had solved his puzzle, but in his single-minded focus on the science he had dragged everyone he loved into danger. Without the other half, without the photographs, he had failed them all. He couldn't remember ever feeling more tired. He rolled into a ball on the seat and closed his eyes. Sleep must have come quickly.

IV

V anya," Miri said. It had been another day since he'd stopped speaking, stopped holding her hand. He hadn't moved from his seat since he'd finished his equations. At first she thought it was because he was tired, working without sleep for days. But now she saw there was something different about him. Something she wasn't yet ready to name.

Morning came and still Vanya didn't get up. His skin glistened with sweat, but their compartment was cool. His lips were thin, thinner than ever, and paler. "Vanya," Miri said. "Tell me about your equations." She put her hand on his forehead. His skin burned. His pulse was weak and thready. She threw the blanket off of him and inspected his clothing. Had he been cut? He showed signs of an infection, but where? She couldn't treat it if she couldn't find it.

She examined his hands, where his nails had been pried off. Nothing beyond fresh ink stains. Whatever ailed him was internal. "Vanya!" she yelled. She slapped his face. He moaned but didn't open his eyes. She dropped to her knees. "Vanya, come back to me. What's wrong?"

"Take it." He waved his notebook toward her.

"Vanya," she said, shaking him. "Don't leave me. Not now."

Day bled to night. She covered him in blankets. And she spoke to him, spinning tales about their future, about their reunion with Babushka. She talked about finding their family in America. They wouldn't go to Massachusetts—to Harvard. They'd go to Philadelphia. "Vanya, it will be beautiful. I can't wait to see their great bell.

Remember, they have a giant cracked bell? And our cousins. Our aunt and uncle."

"Sasha will find you." He kissed her hand. She stayed awake, deep into the night, talking to her brother. His pulse slowed. Their light burned away and Miri's eyes closed. When she awoke, their compartment was still. And cold. She didn't need to examine Vanya to know he was gone.

V

Miri sat with Vanya's body for half the day before a porter came and took what was left of her brother away. She had no choice but to let him go. She wanted to give him the burial Baba would want and that he deserved, but she couldn't watch him rot while they crawled to their grandmother.

She endured the rest of the train ride in silence, tracing the silver numbers and symbols on his cigarette case with her nail. The countryside passing by seemed to be in a state of mourning with her, smothered in snow that left no room to breathe or move. The silence was as agonizing as the screams she'd unleashed for Sasha only days earlier. Now she'd lost all the men in her life, and she didn't even know if Baba was still alive. All for what? For the eclipse? For a chance for easy passage to America? She looked down at his notebook, at the frayed edges. It was stained now, and bloated. All those nights ago, in Kovno, when they'd first discussed the eclipse, hadn't she known then that he was pushing too far? Like Icarus, he was bound to crash. Still, Vanya didn't listen. Why didn't she do more to stop him? But he wasn't blameless, she told herself. His ambition, his dreams, had blinded them all. Under the sadness, she realized, was a layer of anger she hadn't recognized before.

When the train arrived in Petrograd, soldiers began pulling apart the compartments and seats before she'd even stepped onto the platform. Miri walked out of the station in a daze. Stumbling down the streets toward Klara's, wagon and tram drivers yelled at her. She'd only been to Saint Petersburg once before, but there were more beggars than she remembered, and where facades used to sparkle, now they were caked with soot. Stores stood empty.

Aunt Klara's apartment building was grayer, too. She didn't wait and watch the apartment before she entered. Didn't even try to hide or send Baba a secret message through the butcher with a place for them to meet. What did she care if the Okhrana were watching? If they wanted her, they could have her. And if Baba and Klara had already run, well, she needed to know that, too.

But there was Babushka, waiting. It was almost impossible to believe that after everything, Baba was exactly where she was supposed to be. Miri stopped two paces in front of her grandmother's open arms. She'd crossed the country two times to get here. She'd lost and found her brother, and lost him again. She'd found Yuri and pushed him away. And, of course, she'd fallen into Sasha and he was gone now, too. While the rest of Miri's world crumbled, Baba was the only piece that still stood.

"Child, my poor child," Babushka said as she wrapped Miri in her arms.

"I'm so sorry," Miri sobbed. "I've lost them all."

VI

The first morning Miri woke up in Klara's apartment, when all her failures came rushing back to her, she opened the window and flung Vanya's notebook out into the snow. She'd thought about burning it but couldn't. "Let someone else use it for heat," she said, and slammed the glass back into place. Not long after that, Kir's men banged on the door. Miri didn't listen to whatever tale Baba spun to explain Miri's appearance, but she understood they'd be watching the flat, didn't believe Vanya was dead. Once they left, in the background, she heard Babushka and Klara discussing their situation. After everything Miri had done to prevent them from trying to break through the border in spring, there was no other way. If they tried now, they wouldn't make it. The ice and snow were too harsh to brave a sledge across the Neva, let alone Ladoga. Even if they could escape Russia, they had nowhere to go now, no way to America. And so they tucked into Saint Petersburg for the duration of the winter.

The city starved slowly, but the three women managed to endure. All the while, the child in Miri's womb kicked with a fury she hadn't expected. While other mothers may have rejoiced in that, all Miri felt was desolation. She wouldn't have eaten or even slept if Babushka hadn't forced her. Come spring, the money Vanya had given Miri was gone. Babushka sold the rest of her rubies, Vanya's silver cigarette case, and every other scrap of gold she and Klara could piece together to secure passage north and west for the three women. To stay warm, they burned every speck of furniture, anything that would light. They watched out the windows as their guards dwindled, lost to hunger or sacrificed for the front. She didn't know which. Soon there was only one left, the laziest of all—the easiest to evade.

As they boarded the first of several trains that would take them up and out of Russia, Baba handed Miri a dirty envelope, greasy and worn, but unopened.

"What is this?" Miri asked.

"The café owner stopped me on the street this morning and gave it to me."

"But who is it from?"

"Open it, child." Baba smiled. "There's only one way to know."

VII

Dear Miriam,

My name is Dmitry Velikoff. I am a friend of Vanya and Yuri. I hope they are well and not too angry with me still. I have not been able to find them, but, praise the gods, I have found you. Your grandmother's building is watched, so this letter must do.

I write to tell you I saved the notebook you threw from the window. Perhaps you thought a soldier was coming to search the house? The formulas are all safe.

Dima looked back at what he'd written. His script was pathetic. It looked as if a child formed his words, but he needed to tell Vanya's sister what happened so she could find him in America—so he could tell Vanya and Yuri what he'd done. But where to start? Dima was used to telling stories around a fire, not by hand. He wrote a line, crossed it out, and began again.

I write also to tell you that I'll do whatever I can to help your brother. He's a good man, even if he is not a sailor. The only man I've ever met who wanted to change the world with an idea—not a fight. I admire that. But when I left him, he wasn't strong. He'll need help.

Dima hated leaving. But he had no choice. Yuri would have killed him, and Dima couldn't blame him for it. Besides, he needed to find that American, Russell Clay, to get those plates before Kir murdered them all.

After Dima left Dacha Lavroskavo, after the fight with Yuri, he'd run first to Vadim. If the American had gotten away, he would have needed help. And sure enough, it didn't take much persuading to get Vadim to talk, not after he'd watched his brother lose his eye the way he did. Vadim said he escorted Clay to the hospital in Kiev, the best hospital—the Jewish hospital where he took his brother later. Then he took Clay to the train station. Put him on a train to Saint Petersburg.

Dima went straight to that very same station, and the army's poor luck was Dima's opportunity. With so many men at the front, they were desperate for engineers, and thanks to Stanislavovich teaching Dima all about trains, Dima found a position taking him to Saint Petersburg in no time.

If Clay was in Saint Petersburg, Dima figured he'd be at the university looking for help out of the country. Or Clay might have told Kir he'd meet him there—there was no way of knowing how much they'd been in touch. Either way, that's where he'd look. He just had to hope he'd get to Clay before Kir did.

After a day's search in the city, Dima found it, the university: an imposing building grand enough to rival anything in America, he figured. But no sign of Clay. The next morning, at first light, Dima went back with a cart of apples and tried to sell to every man who came and went, to get a look at their faces. He gave a free apple to the janitor leaving the building, in exchange for innocent information on the great Kir Romanovitch—was he at the university? Would he be visiting soon? The janitor had nothing to report.

For three weeks all Dima had to show for his apples were a few kopecks and a frozen ass. He was starting to think he'd somehow missed Clay. Or miscalculated. Then, finally, a man who looked like a pauper limped past the bronze statue in the checkerboard courtyard. The man dragged one leg. He clutched a valise—an expensive-looking valise. He didn't have a hat and his few white hairs were matted. His clothes torn. But even fallen as Clay was, Dima recognized him. No doubt about it.

Now that Clay was here, there was a good chance Kir would be close behind. Dima didn't know if he had a minute, an hour, or a day, but he didn't intend to waste any of it. Still, he'd need to be careful. He watched.

Instead of shuffling to the doors of the university, Clay veered slowly, weakly around the corner into the dark alley nearby. Dima looked over his shoulder and followed. He had his knife in his fist. Dima found Clay sagged against the bricks, relieving himself in a corner, the valise still tucked tight under his arm.

Dima crept up behind Clay and, in one swift motion, clamped a hand on the valise and wrapped his other arm around Clay's bloated throat. Clay tried to resist, but he was no match for the sailor. Yanking the valise free, Dima slammed Clay against the wall, heard his feet slap the bricks. Clay had lost several teeth and he smelled like shit, real shit. "Well, well," Dima said, dropping the American into a pile of sludge and snow. "The bastard's fallen to a pathetic husk."

"Please don't hurt me," Clay cried in English.

"Are the photographs in here?" Dima growled, holding up Clay's bag.

"You can't have them. I need them. I'm trading for my freedom."

"You think they'll keep you safe when Kir arrives?" Dima asked. The American's eyes widened and he pointed to the valise. "They're all in here?"

"I told you, you can't have them."

"You going to stop me? You're not in America. This is Russia. Kir'll kill you. And take them anyway. Don't you know that?"

"No, he'll give me papers. And passage. And we'll publish together."

Dima almost laughed. "Fool. He'll take everything he can, wring you out until you're dry, and then kill you so you can't talk."

"You're wrong."

"What will keep you alive? Your nice request? It's an agreement you have no power to enforce."

The lout broke down then. He must have realized what Dima said was the truth. He dropped his face to his hands and sobbed. "Don't hurt me," Clay said. "Please. Don't hurt me. Your friend's work is cursed."

Dima unclipped the buckle of the valise and there they were. The fake notebook. And four glass plates, covered and protected. All in perfect condition. None even developed. He was so surprised to find them there like that, intact, that he let out a shout that sent Clay skittering. In another instant, Dima was running down the alley, without even looking back.

Also, I found Russell Clay. He had the glass plates. They were undeveloped and intact. Well protected. I took them. He didn't resist.

Dima knew he'd put himself in danger by letting Clay see his face—and by taking the plates. Kir could track him if he had to—question everyone at the university, and that janitor might be made to talk. But that poor man knew nothing, really.

It would be safest for Dima to walk away—or run. Or maybe try to sell the plates to Kir himself. At the beginning of all this, Dima thought he'd make extra money by doing just that, but somewhere along the way his plans had changed. These plates didn't belong to Kir. They belonged to Vanya. And he had to get them back to him.

Dima ran as fast as his legs could carry him, straight to Vanya's aunt Klara. Vanya had given Dima the address when they'd started, asked Dima to send his sister word if anything happened. Dima hoped he'd find the professor, and the doctor, there now, but even from a block away Dima spotted the agents watching the building, and he knew he'd have no such luck. Had they been there since Vanya left Riga? Did that mean Kir suspected Vanya was alive? It was the only reason there would be men watching the building. A trap.

Dima couldn't stop or they'd suspect him of something, and something was good enough to get a man killed. He ran past, pretending he had a direction, praying Ilya wasn't among the men on guard.

Dima found a café a block from the apartment. He didn't care that it was run-down and dingy, even compared to Pyotrovich's in Riga. He just needed a place to sit, to watch. And he still had the money he'd earned as an engineer so he could pay, at least for now. The waiter wouldn't ask questions. Better to have your pocket lined than to know.

During the second week of watching, a woman showed up at Klara's house. There was no question she was Vanya's sister. They had the same height, the same curls. She walked slowly. And she was alone. She didn't look hurt, but she walked as if she'd been beaten. Where had she been? Had she run off with that mysterious soldier Ilya talked about, and was now coming home in shame? No, he thought. The weight she bore was defeat—not sin.

Dima wanted to run to her and help—she looked so much like Vanya—but the guards had noticed her, too. She didn't seem to care. It could have been her death sentence, walking into a trap like that with those guards, but luck must have smiled on that family, because the guards stayed back.

That first morning after she'd arrived, Dima saw her throw a notebook outside. It landed in the bushes. A soldier saw her do it, too, but he was dumb. Or drunk. Or both. He walked over to look for it but only glanced around. Found nothing. Dima found it later that night, wedged near the gutter. He couldn't understand what was in it, but he recognized Vanya's handwriting. And he'd copied enough of his older notebooks to know this work was new. Different. Did Vanya do it? Finish his equations at last? Either way, this meant his sister must have gotten to him somehow, before Kir did. That was one thing to be grateful for.

It took all of Dima's powers to keep himself away. More than anything he wanted to find out what had happened, what she knew about her brother and fiancé. But if he tried, the Okhrana would have him. He'd be as good as dead. By spring, food was growing harder to find. Dima paid three times what he'd paid the first day he sat at the café. And he'd seen two soldiers eyeing him just that morning. It was time to move on before someone made the connection.

Where would he go? America, of course. He'd find Vanya and his family there somehow, at the university called Harvard or in that city Vanya talked about—Philadelphia. Yes, Vanya said he had family there. Oh, how Dima dreamed of that beautiful, peaceful American life Vanya told him about where there was no Okhrana. No czar.

But Dima couldn't travel with the notebook or the glass plates. It was too risky. As luggage, they could be seized at the port in Saint Petersburg or in America. And if they were found and identified, the Okhrana might even take him just as he boarded a boat. He had to find a way to get them out of the country, and back to Vanya in America.

Miriam, when I was a boy, I worked for a great artist here in Peter. He is an honest friend to me still. One of his masterpieces is being shipped to Philadelphia, to their great art museum. The photographs your brother and fiancé took will travel with that artwork—along with Vanya's notebook— in the back of another painting. My plan is to make it to Philadelphia by then, and maybe I will find you all there. Perhaps we could meet at that museum and share our stories. Celebrate what your brother achieved.

Dima pulled out his purse. It was too light, but should be enough to pay the café owner to get the letter safely to Miriam or to her baba. Before sending it, he read back over his letter. What else was there to tell her? No reason to say he prayed every night for Vanya even though he was not a praying man. Or that he was sorry he didn't get to help her even though she looked like she needed it.

I am about to board a sledge north. My men found work for me on a boat bound for America. I wish for you a safe journey out of Russia. Be well. I hope to see your brilliant Vanya and my old friend Yuri again soon.
Your devoted friend,
Dmitry

VIII

Miri, Babushka, and Klara made it through the Russian border into Finland and across the sea to Sweden. It helped that Miri's belly was swollen with child. And that they'd stolen clothing from a convent. Baba and Klara posed as nuns. The guards took pity on them. They even offered advice on the best route forward. As hard as Miri had imagined it would be to cross the border, it turned out to be one of the easiest parts of their journey, of that impossible year of war. How could she have calculated so poorly? And yet even if she could go back in time, knowing the borders wouldn't be as tight as she'd expected, she wouldn't change a thing. If she went back, she'd make all the same decisions again—they had brought her to Sasha. And now that she carried his child, she'd protect him with everything she had and try to look forward.

In Gothenburg, Miri, Baba, and Klara boarded a ship headed west toward Philadelphia. Miri walked up the plank in silence, trying to shake the memories of her parents' departure so many years earlier, telling herself they would not share the same fate. She would make it to America. The boat heaved against the dock, braced against the waves.

They tumbled through storms and swells. What should have been a two-month journey slogged into three. As they neared America, Miri's birth pains began. Despite it being her first child, it took only an hour for Miri to feel the frequency of her contractions condense. The child would launch into the world with the same ferocity in which he was conceived. "Deep breaths," Babushka said. She held Miri's hand. They were in a cramped cabin with no one but Babushka and Klara to shoulder the weight of the event.

"I'm being ripped to pieces," Miri screamed. Her stomach muscles cinched so tight she couldn't breathe. The uncontrollable urge to push was all she knew. She was too hot. And too cold. She was thirsty but she couldn't drink.

And, God, this child was going to kill her. He was going to split her apart. Hundreds of women had told her the same, but this had to be different. None of them could have felt pain like this, could they?

She thought she smelled pine trees. Sasha.

"Stay awake!" Babushka said. She soaked Miri's face with a wet cloth. The vacant look she'd seen on so many new mothers' faces, she felt now. In her head she wanted to live, but her body was beyond exhausted.

A wave dashed the porthole. Miri imagined she could taste the brine in the spray of salt water. Babushka said something. She sounded far away, farther than Vanya or Sasha, who sometimes came to her in her dreams. Why had she been such a coward? Why had she let Vanya and Sasha go? Surely they could have run from the train without being shot. The guilt hurt as much as the child breaking through. The pain was coming, harder than before. She couldn't focus. She couldn't think but she had to. "Can you see the head?"

Before Baba could answer, Miri's womb gripped down with a force Miri had never fathomed. The wave of pain was white and devastating. Would she bleed to death?

"Miriam," Babushka shouted. The waves slamming the hull were so loud Miri could barely hear her grandmother. "The head, he's here."

"Can you see the cord? Is it around his neck?"

"No. No." Babushka smiled. "You're free."

The pain shuddered and waned. The worst had come. "A girl," Babushka said. "As strong and beautiful as her mother."

"A girl?" Miri reached for the child and brought her to her breast. "Sasha," she whispered. He had promised to find her, but he would not. "Sasha." Miri kissed her daughter's face. Her fingers. Her feet. For a moment she felt Sasha there, with her and the baby. Curled around them, crying. Her tears flowed down and splashed on the child, who grabbed at her with a will to live that Miri had almost forgotten.

"I'll name her for Sasha's mother. Ethel."

2000: Philadelphia, United States

Ethel Zane sat in a chair at the end of the exhibit, next to Lena. After she'd snatched the portrait of Einstein off the wall, she'd been asked to sit there, like a scolded American child told to think about her actions. Her mother, Miri, would have told her to be grateful, that in Russia she would not have been treated so gently. But she still resented the two museum guards standing on either side, making sure she didn't move. Worse, she was stiff and her dress was still damp from all that rain. "My mother faced far scarier situations," Ethel whispered, nodding toward the guards.

"I know." Lena smiled.

"And I was right. That curator should have had Vanya front and center—not Einstein."

"But look, he did his job. We were just impatient." Lena pointed to a photograph of Vanya leaning against a towering larch. It was a focal point, five times the size of Einstein's image. The photo had been taken in Birshtan, near the dacha where Mama and Uncle Vanya had been taught to fight. Vanya looked so young, so hopeful. The curator had found it somehow, just before the exhibit opened, hidden in a corner in the basement of the Hermitage, buried in boxes and boxes of Kir Romanovitch's archives. How they got there, no one knew, but on Ethel's advice the curator had been searching for those records, for anything from the czar's preeminent physicist, for months. And he'd left this as his final surprise for her.

"Who imagined that boy would change the world?" Ethel asked. "Einstein published equations in 1914, you know?"

"Of course I know. They were wrong. He corrected them himself."

"Several years later. Vanya corrected them first."

"Yes, Bubbie, but Einstein deserves something, no?"

Ethel shrugged. Every wall around them was an homage to her uncle's work and family. The stunning centerpiece hung across from the photo of the teenage Vanya. It was an enormous, colorized print of a photograph taken at the 1914 eclipse. Yellow streams of light flared around the edges of the moon, and off to one side were a series of distinct dots: the Zeus star cluster—Vanya's proof that light bends.

When Ethel was little, she'd fall asleep listening to her mother spin the tale of Uncle Vanya racing to capture the eclipse that devoured Russia. He'd deserted his unit, braved the firing squad all in his quest to understand the universe. And he'd done it. Except the war had gotten in the way. If things had been different, Abramov would be the name people knew. Einstein would be a footnote. Ethel devoted her life to finding Vanya's work, to showing the world that her mother and father were right about their family legend.

Papa. Sasha. He was the man in the military greatcoat, in the photograph with her mother at the beginning of the exhibit. Ethel saw that now. The picture of her parents was taken in Podil, published in a newspaper, back when they'd just met. They were so young, they looked nothing like she remembered.

Ethel closed her eyes and imagined her father. Just as she couldn't remember a day in her life without relativity hanging over her, so too would she be hard-pressed to remember a day without him. "I was head over heels for your mother from the moment we met," he used to say.

Ethel had been too young to remember the day he found them in Philadelphia, yet her mother had told the story so many times she could picture every detail. Papa materialized on their front stoop three years after he was separated from Mama in Russia. The officer who captured him did fire his gun, but the bullet only grazed Sasha's temple. Head wounds bleed profusely, even minor ones, and Sasha was left for dead. Once he came around, he crawled to the Jewish hospital. Anya nursed him. She hid him.

Once Sasha recovered, he walked across Russia and up through the northern border, careful to stay deep in the forest where no one could recognize him. He knew how to hunt and trap. And ski. Ethel couldn't imagine what he'd gone through and he never talked about it. Brutal, her mother used to say. One word that held it all.

He worked his way across the ocean as a deckhand. When he showed up at Mama's door, he was as thin and pale as a corpse. No one would have known him, but Mama, she recognized him in an instant by his eyes—the same eyes that she saw every time she looked at their daughter.

Mama told Sasha and Ethel all about the letter she'd received from Dima Velikoff, and the family spent years tracking the sailor down. Miri and Sasha had both passed away by the time Ethel finally found Dima—but he, too, was gone. By then Ethel's only living family member still excited about the chase was Lena. Lena was the one who pushed her grandmother to contact Dima's great-grandson, the only other Velikoff still alive. And it was that great-grandson, Danny, who told them Dima's story.

"Tell us everything," Ethel said to him the first time they met. They sat around a rickety coffee table on the side of a Russian market in northeastern Philadelphia. Next to them, at the deli counter, dozens of colored herring dishes were on platters arranged like a rainbow. Women buzzed, gossiping and ordering in Russian. "Did Dima ever tell you about a painting from Russia? He mentioned it in his letter. The missing notebooks and photographs were supposed to be with it somehow. But no one at the museum received the painting."

"A painting? No, he didn't mention anything, although he loved the museum. He spent hours there drawing." Danny shook his head, seemed to remember something. "I did find one in the attic when I cleaned out his house."

"Where? Where is it now?"

Danny took them to his apartment. He hadn't opened the wooden crate. It sat in the back of his closet, buried behind three suits and a row of starched shirts. "My great-grandfather must have forgotten about it. The dementia," he explained as he pulled it out.

The nails on the crate were rusted through. The heads snapped when they tried to pry them off. When they finally succeeded in peeling back the lid, the three of them, Ethel, Lena, and Danny, looked at the canvas together. Danny was the one to hear the glass rattle inside. And Ethel was the one to cut into the burlap and find Vanya's photos and journals. Most of the plates had shattered but one survived.

"Bubbie," Lena said. Ethel blinked. The exhibit was crowded now. Ethel hadn't noticed when it opened. She was too deep in her memories. "Bubbie, do you need some water?"

"No." Ethel smiled. "Do you think they'd mind if we look at the photos one more time?"

"So long as you promise not to take anything else off the walls." Lena threaded her fingers through Ethel's and walked her grandmother back into the exhibit. They started at the beginning, at the photo of Miri and Sasha together in Russia.

It had taken scientists and art historians a full year to authenticate Vanya's work and the photographs, to declare him the true winner of the race to prove relativity. And once Vanya was crowned, the museum begged for the chance to showcase the discovery. They offered a handsome price for the painting that held Vanya's work, and that helped Ethel to say yes. Once Ethel agreed, the curator worked magic. He dug up photos of Miri, Sasha, Yuri, Dima, Anya, and even Russell Clay, the American who had gone missing after the expedition for the 1914 eclipse. All of them were enlarged and framed, arranged in chronological order. The equations themselves were gilded behind bulletproof glass.

"Gorgeous," Ethel whispered as she stood, transfixed again by the photograph of the eclipse. The sun's arms seemed to reach out around the moon. She could feel the gravity of the photograph. "It's what I've always told you," Ethel said to Lena. "Life and the universe are not written in stone. Gravity bends direction. Always keep your mind open."

"Open to what?" Lena asked.

"Open to anything."

ACKNOWLEDGMENTS

The path to this book was a long one and I have many people to thank. Above all, I need to start with Adam, Ezra, Lily, Jonah—and Zishe. They inspire me every day with their unwavering belief that I can fix any problem and rewrite any scene. They are my first readers and my last. I can never thank them enough. Especially Adam for leading the charge.

Thank you, thank you to my parents, Sol and Edna. And to my second parents, Nancy and Jerry. To my siblings, who know exactly when I need someone to remind me that everything is going to work out somehow: Aaron, Adam, Jen, Joshua, Joshua, Nicole, Sarah, and Stacey.

I am grateful beyond measure to my mighty, mighty editor Millicent Bennett who has labored over every word with me and understood from the beginning that writing is love. And I can never thank the phenomenal Eve Attermann enough. She is my dream agent in every way, a woman who understands what I mean no matter how convoluted it may appear in a first draft or when I spill my guts on the phone. You two are a dream team. No writer could ever ask for more. Thank you.

Marjorie Gellhorn Sa'adah was the first to ask: If you love writing so much, why are you wasting time on anything else? I couldn't be more grateful for that, and for her teaching and mentorship. Thank you to Beverly Horowitz, who reminded me again and again to get inside a character's head—and to just keep writing. To Karun Grossman and Judah Grossman, who taught me to write a better fight scene. To Linda Kleinbaum and Steve Anderson, who made sure I got to the point faster. To Sylvia Horowitz, who braved even the roughest early drafts. To Hilary Ryder, who offered crucial medical advice; any mistakes that remain are my own. To Matthew Henken, who helped me through those first one hundred pages—on my one hundredth pass. To Rebecca Makkai, who pointed out exactly what worked and what needed to go. To Erin Harris, who did the same—helping me slash pages. To Clio Seraphim for her brilliant eye and early cheers. To Joanna Josephson, Elizabeth Posner-Navisky, and Ernest Sachs, who read my earlier books that weren't up to snuff but still pushed me to keep writing. To Joni Cole and her Writer's Center in White River Junction, who got me to start all over again. To Ryan Hickox, who helped me untangle Einstein and his field equations; all mistakes that remain are my own. And to Miriam Udel, whose expert knowledge helped me check several facts at the last hour. Again, all mistakes that remain are my own.

The incredible Michelle Hoover and her Novel Incubator are the best thing that ever happened to my writing. An enormous thank you to Michelle and to my NI5 classmates: Louise Berliner, Helen Bronk, Denis Carey, Janet Rich Edwards, Robert Fernandes, Jen Johnson, Ayaz Mahmud, Andrea Meyer, and Tracey Palmer. And especially to those of you who kept reading—and keep reading. Thank you to all of Michelle's alums, especially Susan Bernhard, Colwill Brown, Michele Ferrari, Kelly Ford, Louise Miller, Alison Murphy, Patricia Park, Julia Rold, Emily Ross, Elizabeth Shelburne, and Jennie Wood. All of you have gone above and beyond to help me at some point and I truly appreciate it. To Marc Foster for opening his family home for retreats and for talking engineering. And a huge thank you to Jenna Blum for introducing me to Grub Street in the first place.

Eve Bridburg, thank you for building the amazing Grub Street with Christopher Castellani and so many others I can't even name them all. To Chris in particular, your advice is always brilliant and appreciated more than you know. As I tell you all the time, you make my writing world a lot less lonely and you've inspired me to dive in headfirst. I can't thank you enough for that. Thank you to Sonya Larson and Hanna Katz for the Muse. To the Grub staff, teachers, supporters, donors, and incredible fundraisers who made my scholarship possible: Thank you. You changed my life.

A big, huge, giant thank-you to my exceptional team at Grand Central. Andy Dodds, your energy and enthusiasm are infectious and your talent is unmatched. I cannot thank you enough for all you've done to launch this book into the world. Other incredible team members that I'd like to thank include Ben Sevier, Karen Kosztolnyik, Beth deGuzman, Brian McLendon, Alana Spendley, Meriam Metoui, Anjuli Johnson, Angelina Krahn (who can spot a homophone from a mile away), Karen Torres (whose love of the book pushed me to believe it was all going to come together), Chris Murphy, Alison Lazarus, Ali Cutrone, and the rest of the incomparable sales team at GCP.

A huge thank-you to the WME team that always pulls me back together again. Haley Heidemann—you rock. Thank you to Matilda Forbes Watson and Alina Flint for careful reads and critiques early on. And thank you to the amazing duo on my international sales team, Svetlana Katz and Siobhan O'Neill.

As for the text itself, thank you to Vladimir Nabokov and Robert Mann for their artful English translations of the *Song of Igor's Campaign*. I used a sentence from each in the text. And thank you to George Bruce Halsted. I used his 1913 English translation of Poincaré's 1898 publication "The Measure of Time" in the epigraph. Thank you to Eric Kimmel for his version of *Gershon's Monster*, which reminded me of the tale I'd heard decades ago from Rabbi Cynthia Kravitz, who loved nothing more than sharing a good story. I may have acted like I wasn't listening but I was hanging on your every word. "Levi's Monster" in this book is based on the many versions of this old folktale.

While writing a book is a solitary endeavor, publishing is not. Dozens and dozens of people are involved in the magic that pulls a manuscript together, and while I'm hoping I've thanked everyone, I need to apologize to anyone I might have missed. Truly, I could not have polished this book and sent it out into the world without the army of helpers at WME and Grand Central, and my family and friends cheering along the way. You all matter more than you could ever know. Thank you.

READING GROUP GUIDE

DISCUSSSION
QUESTIONS

1. In the novel's opening scene, Ethel says to her granddaughter, Lena, "Life doesn't travel in a straight line. Knowing the end doesn't mean you can follow it back to the beginning." Where did this bit of wisdom come from? What is she trying to teach Lena? And what does this particular lesson mean to you?

2. *A Bend in the Stars* is organized by sections that are based around the Hebrew calendar. Why do you think the author made the choice to structure it this way? How does it change your experience of the story?

3. Baba's role as a successful and trusted matchmaker allows her an elevated position among the Jews of Kovno, yet it places her and her grandchildren in a liminal spot in Russian society, members neither of the working poor nor the more comfortable, respected higher classes. Is this "in-between" status good or bad, do you think, for the Abramovs? Can you think of examples of the ways in which they benefit or suffer from this unique spot in the social hierarchy? Are there any people or groups of people in our modern society who exist in this in-between space?

4. When Yuri originally agrees to take Miri on as his student and train her to be the first female surgeon in Kovno, he warns her that her choosing this career path will require them both to make sacrifices. Did you have to make any sacrifices to follow your professional dreams? What about your personal dreams? Do you think Miri would have gone ahead and followed her ambition if she'd known where it would lead?

5. At first glance, Dima and Vanya could not be more different: a gruff, violent, seaworn sailor looking only to save his hide and a timid, cerebral Jewish physicist with a head full of numbers and idealistic dreams. Yet, by the end of the book, they have both made immense sacrifices for the other. Do they have more in common than it originally appears? Why or why not?

6. Many of the novel's most pivotal scenes take place on trains. Why do you think Barenbaum made this choice? What importance do trains hold in the larger scheme of the book?

7. After Miri saves Sasha from the river and their trust begins to grow, she finds herself with an unexpected problem: she is caught in a love triangle between two good but different men, both of whom are determined to love her the best way they know how. Do you think she makes the right choice in the end? Would you have chosen differently?

8. On the day of the fateful eclipse, Vanya and his companions are starkly confronted by the dangerous superstitions that the villagers still hold about scientific events. Miri faces this in the medical community, too, when she tries to cure the tongue-tied

baby who has been "cursed." Can you think of any modern day equivalents to this fear and distrust?

9. Baba encourages Miri to make her way in the world: "The word 'Jew' is not stamped on your forehead." Does this idea of "passing," of allowing your cultural, racial, or religious identity to be obscured, remind you of other similar situations either in the past, or even today? Is it ever defensible, or indefensible, to try to "pass" for something you're not? Are there cases that can necessitate or excuse it?

10. The historical crimes of the vicious Polyakov brothers haunt the novel, but Miri and Sasha don't agree on whether they could happen again. With whom do you agree, and why?

11. Why do you think the book is titled *A Bend in the Stars*? Is it purely about the eclipse, or does it hold other meanings for you?

12. Are Vanya and Miri right to believe that ideas can change the world, or is Dima closer to the truth when he argues that greed and a lust for power are more powerful?

13. Early in the novel, Ethel says, "History needs a narrator. Perhaps this museum chose the wrong one." Do you agree? In your opinion, is there such a thing as a "right" or "wrong" narrator for history, and if so, how do you choose?

AUTHOR Q&A

Where did the idea for *A Bend in the Stars* come from?

In 2014 I was reading *Scientific American*'s monthly installment of "50, 100 & 150 Years Ago" and learned that in 1914 an eclipse fell over Russia that could have proved Einstein's theory of relativity but because of war and bad weather no scientists were able to mount an expedition and record the event. Even more, the brief noted it was a good thing because in 1914 Einstein's equations were incorrect and a photograph of the eclipse taken then would have likely discredited him. Before I even put the magazine down I knew it was a book idea: What if someone did make it to the eclipse and did manage to take a photograph? Could he have taken Einstein's place in history? I was already a bit obsessed with Russian history and knew it was one of the most fascinating and tumultuous times in the country's history. And I knew that Einstein wasn't working in a vacuum, that there were other scientists working to help him—and beat him. Could I bring that race to life?

Why did you have such an interest in Russia?

My father's family came to the United States from Russia. When they arrived in Philadelphia they stopped speaking Russian and Yiddish and refused to speak anything but English. It never bothered me until I was around ten years old and my parents plastered our house with old family photographs, many of them from Russia. Who were those people carefully dressed in black, staring at the camera? Why did they look so scared? When I asked my grandparents and aunts and uncles, none of them wanted to talk about it beyond mentioning names and what they did in the United States. When I pushed for information about Russia, their answer was always the same: *We left for a reason. Let's not talk about it.* And I hated that. Now that generation has passed away and I'm left knowing the end, but what I wanted more than anything was to follow it back to the beginning.

What could have been so awful that they'd drop everything they had to come to a country they'd never seen, to learn a language they'd never heard, and to look for work where none of their qualifications would matter? That question has haunted me for a long time. And it's one I ask often when I read about migrants today doing the same. Can you ever know if leaving is/was the right decision?

Are you a physicist?

No. But I love and respect science—and facts—and find myself frustrated by the common refrain "I don't do numbers." Why not? I studied philosophy in college because I loved the idea of faith in the human ability to understand and decipher knowledge. Just because a person feels more comfortable reading a book doesn't mean they are not capable of understanding an equation, the meaning of a line of scientific inquiry, or even relativity. Einstein himself wasn't a mathematician—he was a theoretical physicist. He started with ideas and worked with others to code those ideas into equations. His greatest strength, and I might argue his greatest legacy, are those thought experiments that bring complex ideas down to a size and shape that anyone can comprehend.

I wrote about relativity because this concept is powerful and yet understandable on so many levels that I want to encourage everyone to think about it. The universe bends. What does that mean? How does that affect space and time? And how does that change the way we understand our world?

Other than the eclipse, why did you focus on the year 1914?

The turn of the twentieth century is one of my favorite historical periods because I would argue it was the last time ideas were more powerful than fear, when a rash of optimism and faith in our ability to change the world led to inventions, art, and ideas that truly altered history. There was an energy and optimism that hasn't existed since.

But that kind of exuberance brings out the best and the worst in humans. In this case, it led to greed and culminated in World War I, a moment so horrendous most of what was invented or created in those years right before is often overlooked. Today many people talk about the internet as the single invention that has changed our lives, and it has, but I'd argue it's changed our lives by encouraging seclusion—enabling people to stare at a screen, alone, for hours on end, while the inventions in the early twentieth century encouraged inclusion. People could suddenly travel freely to meet and find other people, to work and collaborate. Telephones, radios, newspapers shared ideas widely. All of these booming networks brought us together. And I like that: the romantic notion that science should bring humanity together. I wish we had more of that today.

Are the characters real people from your family?

No. Save for Einstein, none of the characters are real people. Only Baba is based loosely on someone I knew—my great-aunt. Actually, when I first sat down to write this book I thought she would be the main character. I wrote about two hundred pages before I realized she wasn't the focus—that Miri and Vanya were the center of the story. From that new perspective the story gained more energy and a faster pace. I found that being tied to a real person was too heavy. It kept me worried about what was "right," whereas once I let go of that I could take Miri, her brother, and all the others on far more exciting adventures.

But I want to be clear. While the characters are all fictitious, the history and setting adhere to real life as much as possible. I wanted to drop Miri and Vanya into a world that actually existed because that world, to me, is fascinating, and as they say, "I can't make this stuff up." So in describing the details and settings, the math and science, I stayed as true to fact as I possibly could.

How much research did you do for *A Bend in the Stars*?

Tons and none. I love this time period and read dozens and dozens of books about czarist Russia, science and philosophy around the 1900s, and the life of Jews living in Russia long before I sat down to write. In addition, growing up around my grandparents and great-aunts gave me a sense of some of the nuances I wanted to add, like the split in the Jewish community between those who wanted to assimilate and those who didn't, and the constant fear of the czar's men.

But all of that only gave me a base, a general feeling I could incorporate into the novel. To truly write scenes, I need to see them in my head, and so the bulk of my research involved finding photographs. The best trove I found was in an old *National Geographic* that I purchased on eBay, published in 1914 right before the war started. The issue was devoted entirely to a survey of life in Russia and featured dozens of stunning photographs of Russians from all walks of life. Two things struck me in particular in this truly spectacular photo essay: 1. The faces of the citizens in the photos were so clear and so gorgeous I could imagine them as real people, living today. And that made the time period come alive. I could imagine what the teenager staring at me might have been thinking as she stood next to that boy, or the mother as she held her baby. 2. The vast size and diversity of the country. I was blown away by the largely uninhabited, untouched landscapes and just how separated groups of people across the empire were by those expanses. To me it was gorgeous and terrifying and something I wanted to be sure to capture in this book.

YOUR
BOOK
CLUB
RESOURCE

VISIT
GCPClubCar.com

to sign up for the **GCP Club Car** newsletter, featuring exclusive promotions, info on other **Club Car** titles, and more.

 @grandcentralpub

 @grandcentralpub

 @grandcentralpub